Acclaim from both sides of the Atlantic for THE PSALM KILLER

"This original thriller is so finely tuned it hums. . . . As fast-paced and involving a suspense story as any, with a superb shocker of an ending."
—*Rocky Mountain News*

"A thriller that more than fills its end of the bargain: Its grip tightens almost unbearably . . . but Petit never loses sight of the serious issues behind his story."
—*Time Out*

"Malignantly atmospheric . . . Petit's Belfast is a petri dish of perversion, mayhem, and moral depravity."
—*Kirkus Reviews*

"Petit's look at subversive tactics and unexpected alliances are on the bead, and few readers will forget his villain, the cruel, horrifying Candlestick."
—*Publishers Weekly*

By Chris Petit:

ROBINSON
THE PSALM KILLER*

Published by Ballantine Books

THE PSALM
KILLER

Chris Petit

FAWCETT GOLD MEDAL • NEW YORK

A Fawcett Gold Medal Book
Published by The Ballantine Publishing Group
Copyright © 1996 by Chris Petit

Owing to limitations of space, acknowledgments for permission to reprint previously published material may be found on pages 471–72.

http://www.randomhouse.com

Library of Congress Catalog Card Number: 97-97017

ISBN 0-449-00289-6

This edition published by arrangement with Alfred A. Knopf, Inc.

Manufactured in the United States of America

First Ballantine Books Edition: March 1998

10 9 8 7 6 5 4 3 2 1

Author's Note

Parts of this story are drawn from actual incidents, so certain guidelines, and the glossary, should assist in helping to understand Northern Ireland's recent troubled history. Because of the nature of the conflict, much of what has gone on there has necessarily been secret. But clandestine activity is by its very nature clouded with disinformation and lies, and nowhere more than in Northern Ireland. Take two steps in any direction and you are in the realms of fiction, in realms stranger than fiction. Deniability is an essential part of this world. Even when something is true—and shown to be true—it can and will be effectively denied. The unwary enter this quagmire at their peril.

I leave the reader to decide what is fact and what is fiction.

Prologue

CANDLESTICK lay in the boot of the car, as still as a dead man. He wondered how it would feel if this were his last drive. It was a favourite method of transporting captured Catholics—Taigs—bundling them into a boot and driving somewhere quiet to finish them off. But this was different.

He shifted position and looked at the illuminated dial of his watch. So far the ride had taken seven minutes. The woman was being careful, driving inside the speed limit. They stopped for lights, then were off again. The licence plate was clean and a woman alone at the wheel would attract no attention from the watching security forces. He calculated another seven minutes to reach the Ulster Defence Association's East Belfast headquarters in the Newtownards Road.

They had collected the car from a workshop under the arch of a railway viaduct in a district that he didn't know. The garage mechanic he knew, a fat cunt in dirty blue overalls, with the lardy pallor of the city's poor and a wispy moustache that was failing to grow. They exchanged barely a dozen words as he showed them the red Cortina, the keys in the ignition, and fetched the gun from a drawer, a .38 wrapped in an oily rag, with six rounds in a separate piece of cloth. It looked well cared for, its dark metal gleaming dully under the neon. Candlestick had specified a revolver rather than an automatic so there wouldn't be a problem with jamming.

The woman told the boy to make himself scarce. Before leaving he offered them cigarettes, which they refused, and as he opened the door into the alley bright sunlight spilled into the workshop, turning the dust hanging in the air to golden motes.

1

A car up on the ramp had its bonnet open. The Cortina was parked alongside.

Candlestick stood in the doorway of the cluttered office at the rear of the workshop, loading the gun, watching out of the corner of his eye as she sat on the edge of a greasy desk, after arranging an old newspaper so as not to spoil her skirt, and picked up the phone and dialled the Newtownards Road number.

They were in another of those dingy back spaces that most of his business seemed to end up in. This one was windowless. A train rumbled overhead as the woman asked for Tommy Herron and in turn was asked who she was.

"Tell the fat fuck it's Maggie."

She laughed and turned and pulled a wry face at him, slipping her pump free from her heel and jiggling the shoe impatiently, from nerves perhaps, though she seemed relaxed enough. His own mouth was dry. Her feet were slim, he saw. There were oil spills on the workshop floor. They reminded him of old newspaper pictures of dead gangsters.

"Tommy?"

He heard Herron asking if it was her.

"Who else?" she said tartly.

She arranged to pick him up and Herron said something he didn't catch and she laughed, smiling at him as she spoke.

"A white blouse, my red skirt and the French knickers. And I've had my legs lengthened."

He listened to her playing up the sex in her voice until Tommy at the other end gurgled in anticipation, and he wondered about her age—several years older than himself, thirty, probably, and experienced. She was buxom, with a good figure and bright lipstick, and there was nothing wrong with her legs. The grimy surroundings exaggerated her sensuality, which she flaunted at him.

He knew nothing about her except for a suspicion that she, like he, had secret masters. Whether they were the same as his he had no idea. Her intimacy with Herron was part of the larger game, he imagined, and he thought of the childish code name his had given him: Candlestick.

Herron was grumbling in the background when she cut him short. "Long enough for a frisky boy like yourself."

She led him by the nose until, as she was about to hang up,

Herron said something to make her frown. She recovered quickly, with a sarcastic laugh.

"Tommy Herron, if you want to fuck me in my lunchtime, bloody well pay for your own parking."

Herron wanted to take his own car when she collected him because it was illegally parked. He had a reputation for being obstinate over the most trivial matters. She ended the argument by telling him to get one of his flunkeys to move it.

"Pig-headed at best, our Tommy," she said after, amused at the idea of a big-shot like Herron worried about a traffic warden.

LYING in the darkness, he checked his watch again. Twelve minutes gone. The car swung left then right.

Herron got in as the car drew up. They had arranged to meet around the corner from the HQ and he must have been waiting. Herron had been increasingly wary of late and stuck close to his bodyguards. Seeing Maggie was the only time he travelled without an armed escort.

"Ah, Maggie, a sight for sore eyes," he said, closing the door.

From the boot he could hear Herron settle in his seat and lean across to kiss her, followed by the laugh of a man enjoying his clandestine assignment.

As Maggie drove off she said, "That's a good haircut you've got."

"Found a new feller. It means going over to the Crumlin Road but you can't have everything. He'll be a poof too, but like I said you can't have everything."

He sounded relaxed and amiable, easily flattered by her compliment. Tommy's hair was his crowning vanity, dark and lustrous like early Elvis Presley, a distraction from his bulk and lack of height.

It was pitch black in the boot and Candlestick wondered if the perpetual darkness that awaited Tommy Herron would be any blacker.

HERRON'S fate appeared to have been decided by his own Protestant paramilitary colleagues in West Belfast. Candlestick doubted if this was the whole picture. He had been approached by Herron's rivals in the UDA but he wondered if the security services weren't playing a part. When he had mentioned the plan to Captain Bunty during one of their regular meetings Bunty had shrugged and said it was news to him.

"I can't say I'm altogether surprised. Tommy's hobby is making enemies." Bunty spoke with a nasal drone, tinged with English North Country. "There's lots of people happy to chip in for the collection that pays to get rid of Tommy Herron."

Bunty finished his drink. They were in the Candlelight Inn, as usual, where there was no chance of being spotted. "Well. Fine. So be it."

By then a death in Belfast was easier to arrange than crossing the road.

Herron betrayed no signs of nerves as they drove south through the city. He was his usual garrulous self, grumbling about how he had been forced to give a boy a hiding because of his reluctance to collect protection money, and complimenting Maggie on her perfume.

"Smellin' as grand as ever, that's what I like about you." He noticed she was not wearing tights.

"Not much you miss, is there, Tommy?"

From the boot of the car Candlestick could hear their conversation quite clearly. He could even hear the click of the indicator as she prepared to turn. Their destination was a secluded lane the lovers had used before. Tommy whistled flatly through his teeth, a popular hit from the summer.

Petrol fumes made Candlestick nauseated, and his ankle itched but he dared not move as every sound seemed magnified.

They were lighting up cigarettes in front and one of them must have opened a window because the engine noise was louder. He pictured Herron staring idly at the passing landscape, squinting from the sunlight and smoke, thinking of the sex to come.

"Another grand day, but it's supposed to change tomorrow," he said.

They turned on to a dirt track and bumped down it for a while. When Maggie switched off the engine it was so quiet that the rustle of her skirt carried as she moved towards Tommy. He could hear the birdsong outside and the wind in the leaves, the noise of the engine settling on its mounting, and Tommy Herron's breathing as they kissed. He waited for his cue.

They were still kissing, by the sound of it.

"Ah, Tommy's getting awful stiff," said Herron and Candlestick had to overcome an impulse to giggle.

"Come on, fat Tommy, let's get in the back," she said.

"I amn't," he protested.

Candlestick gave the seat a sharp kick and it went down, like the mechanic had said it would. Brightness flooded his eyes and, as he blinked away the dark, the split second he had of them kissing was like a developing photograph. Herron broke and turned in time to see the gun swing up towards his face.

"Hold it there, Tommy," he said.

As it dawned on Herron that he knew the man manoeuvring himself out of the boot he gave a little yelp, a bewildered half-laugh, like a prank victim.

"What the fuck is yous doing back there?" he said when he managed to find the words.

"Candid camera," said Candlestick, sitting up. He held the gun two-handed.

"Well, blow me down," said Herron, recovering fast, a man who could joke his way out of any corner.

"We will, Tommy, we will," said Maggie.

Maggie watched his expression shift from comic surprise, to outrage, to fear, as it dawned on him that he had been set up.

"What a face, fat Tommy, a wonder to behold."

"You bitch! You sow's arse!" he roared, his voice cracked and vicious, then spat in her face.

"Don't move, Tommy!" Candlestick shouted. "Or there's brains on the windscreen."

"Still stiff, Tommy?" Maggie murmured, wiping his spittle away with her hand.

"Jesus," he said, looking from one to the other. "As cool as you fucking like. Am I allowed a smoke at least?"

Maggie considered. She lit one of her own and passed it across. Herron inhaled deeply. "Look at us," he said. "Are we daft or what? Here we are, we're supposed to be friends, so let's be reasonable. What say you to five hundred quid? I've it on me now, right here."

It was widely thought that Herron carried large amounts of cash in the event of having to disappear without warning. He gestured towards his inside jacket pocket, waiting for permission to show them.

"Uh, uh, Tommy," said Maggie with a shake of the head.

There was a look of animal cunning in his eyes as he crushed out the cigarette. "And there's more at home. What about five each and another two next week?"

"Time's all used up, Tommy," said Maggie. "You're not worth the five hundred, and we're taking that anyway."

Herron angrily continued to stab the dead cigarette into the ashtray. "Yous is dead in this town. You're top of the fucking list."

Maggie stared at him with beady sensuality.

"Anything happens here," he went on, "you're dead ducks, that should be as plain as paint. Do you think they don't know who I'm with?"

"Ah, quit blathering, Tommy."

"I tell you, the boys in the Romper Room've not had a Judy to play with before."

Maggie smiled sweetly. "All wind and bluster, Tommy."

His look of disgust used up most of his dwindling courage. "You're enjoying this, aren't you? Getting yourself all turned on."

Maggie smiled again, leaned forward and kissed him on the lips. "You bet, Tommy. Now give us your gun."

Tommy wiped his mouth with the back of his hand and held open his jacket while she took his pistol. He had taken to sporting one in a fancy shoulder holster, and even had a licence, fixed by a bent CID man.

"Now open your door, slowly." He did as she told. "Put your hands on the back of your head and we'll all get out."

Candlestick shadowed Herron with his gun, until they were standing in the open, then stuck the muzzle hard in his ear. Herron, already unmanned by the removal of his gun, looked even more beaten. What little colour he had left drained from his face as he stood unsteadily in the lane, trembling.

"Ah, fuck it, please, Maggie." There was a whine in his voice. "Anything you want, the both of yous. Am I to kneel to beg for mercy? Then I'm kneeling."

"Do you know what, Tommy? Afterwards I'll fuck the boy," she said. "All the while thinking of you, Tommy, only the best thoughts."

Candlestick wondered about this Maggie woman. A hard bitch and liking every minute of it. He wondered if she'd ask to pull the trigger and what he'd say then.

She went to the car and fetched a half-bottle of Haig, took a swig and told Tommy to drink the rest.

As Herron tried to take hold of the bottle, he lost control and went down in a heap. Candlestick followed the move with his gun, his finger tightening on the trigger.

Sensing him about to shoot, Maggie said, "Not yet."

She pushed Herron up into a sitting position, splaying his shaking legs to give him balance.

"Drink up, Tommy. Last orders," said Maggie.

Big tears rolled down Tommy's cheeks. "Ah, please. If not for me, for the kids. Please, Maggie. I've held you in my arms. Have mercy for the kids' sakes. Dessy and little Billy, not yet two, don't take his Da away from him."

He held the bottle to his mouth but his teeth were chattering so with the fear that most of the drink slopped down him. A stain spread over the front of his trousers and Candlestick saw that he was pissing himself. Maggie made Herron finish the bottle.

"Well, Tommy, at least you'll miss the hangover," was the last thing she said as she grabbed his jacket from behind, lifting it high over his head and down over his face, then pulling tight. Looking up at Candlestick she grunted, "Do it now," in the same voice she used for fucking, he thought.

Tommy made a strange gurgling noise then started to bellow and flap like a landed fish. She needed all her strength to hold him down. Candlestick found it hard to take his eyes off the sight of her calves and thighs tightening with exertion. It wasn't until she shouted at him to help that he kicked Herron's feet and booted him in the stomach until he was still enough for her to roll him over. She knelt, straddling his back, wrenching the hooded head back, offering it to Candlestick's gun.

He stood spellbound. He was too slow for her, he knew, but he could not respond. He had killed others without any hesitation. It was doing it in front of this woman, he decided.

"Quick, do it now!" she shouted.

He tried to shake himself free of his paralysis. Her guttural voice drove him on.

"Kill the fat cunt, stick the fuck!"

He saw the strain of desire in her face. He could feel it travelling like an infection into him.

"Come on, baby, do it."

She offered him Herron's head. He put the gun close to the back of the skull, steadied it with his free hand and pulled the trigger.

"Ah yes," he heard her murmur, just after.

As the report faded, and the birds flew away, the woods fell eerily quiet. The only noise was the last of Tommy's pumping body, feet thrashing on the dry mud. There was a powder burn around the bullet's entry hole in the jacket. The exit he couldn't see. The woman was transfixed by the final spasms of Tommy Herron, her lips parted.

She put Tommy's gun back in its holster. Neither spoke as they dragged Herron's posthumously farting body to the boot of the car and with a lot of grunting and sweating hauled him up and tipped him in.

He went to fix the seat. She told him to leave it.

"I want him to see."

He didn't understand.

"We've got to go," was all he could think to say.

She looked at him. "After what we came here for."

"We have to go," he repeated.

She went and sat behind the wheel. He got in front with her and waited, thinking about how he was sitting where Tommy Herron had just been. She made no move to drive away, but stayed there, transfixed, her hands driven deep between her thighs.

He was frightened by her intensity and nearly panicked when he saw that she wanted him to finish what they'd stopped Tommy from doing. But then he told himself that shooting Tommy Herron made him eligible for Tommy's things, including her.

He wanted to get in the back with her, Tommy or not, but she dictated their moves. She slid her legs from under the wheel and manoeuvred herself to his side, pushing her skirt up to straddle him.

He rucked the skirt up further, and felt his way between her legs with his hand. He'd never seen a woman so urgent and his awe of her made him uncomfortably hard. He worked a finger into her but she wasn't having it, so he tried removing her knickers instead.

"Leave them," she said hoarsely as she yanked open his flies. "I'd have fucked him first if he hadn't been such a pig."

The thought of eyeless Tommy watching, growing cold in the boot, and him having Tommy's fuck, made him feel like a god. He remembered Tommy's words to the woman while they were kissing, and repeated them.

"Tommy's getting awful stiff by now."

She gave a harsh bark of laughter and drove herself against him even harder, until he was unaware of any time or any thing other than the tight heat around his groin, her weight and her teeth and tongue. She grabbed the hair at the back of his neck as she started her climax, and he listened to her orgasm being wrenched from her in a series of grunting moans, and watched her face screw up with pleasure or pain, he couldn't tell. Christ, he thought, the whole thing was far more violent than the murder of Tommy Herron.

She lifted her head and searched his eyes, like he was the dead man not Tommy. Then she got off and sat back in the driver's seat and leaned down and took him in her mouth, but he stopped her, saying it didn't matter because he wouldn't come. She carried on for a while, then put his still stiff cock away, asking him if he was sure and he said yes, and as she drove off he could smell the sex on them.

"I owe you," was all she said.

Three and a half minutes, he saw from the clock on the dashboard. It had felt like a fuck in eternity.

Two days later Tommy Herron's body was found by a roadside in Drumbo, south of Belfast. The jacket was still pulled over his head, the gun in its holster, his arms neatly arranged across his chest. No one claimed the killing.

One

January 31, 1985, South Armagh

IT WAS always the same nightmare. Cross saw them lined up in rows, in stretches of city wasteland—those derelict spaces once described to him by a child as the blank bits where things had been before they'd got blown up. There was a box for every one killed since it began.

He could put a name to every box, those he'd known and the hundreds he hadn't, which he knew was impossible. Then without warning he was back in some police examination hall and across from him were men whose funerals he would attend. Tommy Farrell blown up in his car, with none of him left to put in his box, which they had to weigh with sandbags, and Robert McNulty shot by a sniper. Cross found himself stuttering painfully to conceal from McNulty's widow that there was nothing to recognize of her husband after the high-velocity bullet had done its job.

McNulty got muddled up with the dead paratrooper as the dream switched to invade his childhood. He saw himself aged seven standing in the hallway of his childhood home, transfixed by the hammering on the door, and when he opened it the paratrooper, shot in the head on the path outside, fell bleeding on to him.

After that, the army patrol held his family at gunpoint for the rest of the night, threatening torture and shooting, while Cross watched in guilty fascination as his mother fell apart in spite of the tranquillizers.

Knowing that this part of the nightmare was wrong only made it worse, even as it happened. There had been no war where he grew up.

* * *

CROSS heaved himself free of the dream, not sure where he was, thinking at first that the train was a continuation of it. He wondered how long he had slept and how much time they had lost. Trains rarely ran on time and his had been late leaving. They had been gone nearly two hours, he saw, which meant that they ought to be near the border. His spirits sank at the thought.

Outside, night was falling on winter fields and the threat of rain in a troubled sky made it feel like another day altogether from the mild, sunny afternoon he had enjoyed in Dublin. Cross thought about the wretched limbo that awaited his return.

The charge was ridiculous. When informed of the complaint by the acting Detective Chief Inspector, Cross had trouble recalling the woman. The DCI had made it plain that he believed the accusation was false, but in the present climate of inquiry the police had to be seen to be investigating itself properly.

The train braked to a halt. At first he thought it was Newry, but there were no lights. Catching sight of his reflection in the window, he wondered if he looked like a man capable of sexual assault.

He could only vaguely picture her, a rail-thin, pinched woman with a face he had trouble remembering, an air of doped hysteria and a look of collapsed determination. Cross thought she could have been anything between forty and sixty. She lived in one of the modern jerrybuilt towers that had aged as badly as its tenants, known as "stack-a-prole." He wondered sometimes if the bombers couldn't put their work to better civic use by blowing up something whose demolition none would mourn.

Her living room was dominated by the usual Catholic icons of the Virgin Mary and the flickering television set that stayed on regardless. It was a routine questioning, which he was only attending because he was concerned about the WPC's lack of experience. The smell was what he remembered most—the stale saturation of years of fried food, alcohol and an endless chain of nicotine.

According to her statement, the WPC had gone off to make a telephone call as there was no phone in the flat. Cross had forgotten about that until the DCI had reminded him. He probably should not have continued the interview alone, but this hardly seemed of consequence until the woman had lodged her complaint.

"Sexual assault," said the DCI, looking embarrassed and apologetic.

The train showed no signs of moving. A ripple of impatience ran through the carriage. It was fuller than Cross remembered, with people standing in the corridors. Eventually they moved forward a few hundred yards and stopped again.

"Bloody security alert," said a woman across the way and went back to reading her book.

It was curious, he thought, how everyone behaved as though everything were normal until they were told otherwise. A guard passed through the carriage, instructing everyone to evacuate the train, making sure that they took their belongings. "These things are sent to try us," he announced cheerfully, earning murderous looks.

Cross sighed, reluctant to leave the warm fug. Outside, through the opposite window, were lights and movement. He wondered again if he should get out of the force. The last post he had applied for—chief security officer at the Electricity Board—forty other officers had put in for, a fair indication of the state of morale in the force. He lacked the civilian contacts enjoyed by his Protestant colleagues, and stubbornly refused to make use of his father-in-law's influence.

From the top of the makeshift steps down from the carriage Cross saw a line of men in uniform standing inside the range of the train's lights, the dark green of the police and the camouflage of the army. Soldiers were herding the passengers into groups a short distance from each carriage. The scene was further lit by the headlights of armoured Land Rovers.

The faces in the crowd looked apprehensive and subdued, like the victims of a mass arrest. Cross too felt the vague guilt of the innocent in the face of authority (and he a policeman). The scene was strangely silent. No explanation was forthcoming. He reckoned a delay of two hours at least. It was chilly and wet underfoot, and mud sucked at his shoes. A raw and steady breeze blew across the fields. At least the rain was holding off, he thought, shrinking into his overcoat as the last of the heat of the train slipped from him. The mildness of Dublin seemed like an illusion.

Dublin had been a relief from Belfast and Cross was able temporarily to shake off the low cloud of apprehension that had hung over him since his suspension. The trip had been fixed by a colleague who knew of his frustration and had asked Cross to replace him at one of the informal meetings the RUC held with the Irish Gardai. The two forces met regularly, in spite of a reputation for poor co-operation.

McCarthy was the senior officer, about ten years older than Cross, a battered, friendly-looking man who seemed more like a rumpled teacher than a policeman. The junior man, Doyle, had struck Cross as quiet but keen.

It was the post-Christmas lull, when nothing much was going on. They noted the usual border movements and discussed an illegal arms shipment from the United States, which McCarthy's sources said would take place in the spring and arrive in the South before making its way North.

"These are pretty low-level scraps," said McCarthy. "Hardly worth the bother of dragging you down here."

"Not at all. I'm glad of the away day."

The meeting had finished early and McCarthy reminisced about when relations between the two forces had not been so amicable. He had been involved in the investigation into the Dublin car bombings of 1974, which had killed nearly thirty people in the evening rush hour.

"The ambulancemen in Talbot Street couldn't tell the living from the dead, and the gutters were running with blood. There was a young girl decapitated and another two had been thrown together by the explosion so you couldn't tell them apart. And we know who did it. Within a week we had their names, and we passed them on."

"And we did nothing?" asked Cross, who remembered the story, though not its details.

"Too bloody right, because the Brits told you to sit on your arses and suck your thumbs. After twenty-eight people had died."

"What were the Brits trying to hide?"

McCarthy spread his hands. "How far do you want to take it? We knew and you knew the Brits had a hand in the bombings. It was the Prods that did it, of course—it doesn't take a genius to work out that the IRA isn't going to bomb Dublin. It was a UVF gang out of Portadown, but everyone I spoke to says they didn't have the expertise for an operation that size, not without help. At least one of the UVF fellows had been in the army and one school of thought is that they were being run by the army. It's no big secret. Some of the newspapers said as much at the time, and we're still waiting for an answer from you fellows. Most of the ones that did it are dead now, but I hardly call that justice, certainly not for the relatives of the victims."

On the question of British motive, he said it was probably to do with the British and Irish governments signing an agreement over the North, which had angered the Protestants whose paramilitaries had close links with the security services. The message to Dublin was a clear one of hands off, and after the bombings the agreement fell apart.

"I'm told the politicians in Belfast were crowing. Do you know what one of them said?"

Cross shook his head.

" 'Slap it into you fellahs—you've deserved every bit of it,' is what he said. And you wonder we're still talking."

AFTERWARDS Cross had turned down the offer of a lift to the station. The younger officer, Doyle, insisted on accompanying him. Cross enjoyed the walk in the pale sunlight with its hint of spring, though he would have preferred it alone, to savour the rare occasion of being able to feel entirely safe. In Belfast part of him was always alert to the possibility of sudden danger, the peripheral moment of warning, the car drawing alongside or the hot blast of air that preceded the explosion.

Cross let himself be talked into a beer and they stopped off at a bar by the station. Doyle asked Cross about his English accent and he replied that he had transferred to the RUC because his wife was from Belfast and had wanted to go back.

"How long have you been there?"

"Twelve, thirteen years."

"Do you still feel an outsider?"

Cross smiled. "What else?"

THE STATIC of a loud hailer broke the silence. Its booming announcement told them that because of track damage buses would take them to another train.

"Abso-fucking-lutely typical," said the man behind Cross, slapping himself to keep warm. "No sign of any buses. How long can they reasonably keep us here?"

Cross shrugged.

"I'm serious."

It was hard to tell. The man's rabbity look gave an air of humour to everything he said. He offered Cross a cigarette, which he refused. The first drops of the rain arrived to add to the misery and Cross thought of announcing himself to one of the RUC, then decided against it, without being sure why, when he could use his rank to shelter in one of the vehicles. Maybe he identified with the huddled group of civilians more than with the sinister-looking phalanx lined up against them. Several soldiers, big-boned raw youths and surprisingly short ("Feckin' midgets," muttered the rabbity man), stood around looking impassive. Cross thought his nightmare preferable to this godforsaken scene. Its unreality made him wonder if he wasn't part of an enormous collective dream of which the whole country was a projection: sullen fields as old as the struggle itself. Perhaps it was the destiny of this landscape, with its infinite possibilities of ambush, to be bound by hostility, and its people condemned by a decision of geography to a history of feuding, covert manoeuvres, field-craft and infiltration.

The distant lights of approaching buses became visible, making their way downhill before disappearing behind the hedgerows. Under the instructions of a sergeant they tramped across the muddy field to a gate.

Cross saw the soldiers checking papers and asking passengers the purpose of their journey. He looked back towards the train. Troops were moving through the lit carriages, guns at the ready. This wasn't track damage, he thought, this was a terrorist hunt.

There was a sudden commotion from beyond the train, yelling, then a quick burst of semi-automatic fire, and the shouted command, "Halt! Or we shoot."

At least they were doing it by the book, Cross thought. An excited buzz grew among the crowd. Troops hurried everyone aboard the buses, no longer checking papers. The smell of cordite carried on the breeze.

As Cross got on the bus, a flare went up. It hung in the sky, turning the landscape phosphorescent. He heard a longer burst from further away. As the light fell to a dull glow, he imagined the quarry zig-zagging, making for the trees, hit by a burst that whipped his feet from under him and turned his legs as suddenly rubbery as one of his children's Mr Spongee toys. He didn't care what anyone said, it was hard not to identify with the fox.

IT WAS after ten by the time he got back. The buses had ended up driving all the way to Belfast in an erratic convoy, stopping off at stations in search of the promised train that never materialized.

After being dropped in the centre, Cross decided to walk before getting a taxi. The rain had stopped and there was still time for a beer.

He had a great love of Belfast. He loved it like an ugly child, less assured and more awkward than its capital sisters in England and the Republic. It was one of the divided cities of the century, along with Berlin and Beirut, except that everyone chose to forget Belfast. Cross relished its streets, the dirty weather, the bars, the unexpected friendliness of the people with their harsh accent, and the special flavour of its fierce history, so strong sometimes that Cross felt he could taste it.

The night streets were empty, apart from the occasional patrol. For all the daily reminders of danger, Cross enjoyed roaming the city, drawing inspiration from the ebb and flow of its movement, from the wonderment of so many lives going about their separate businesses. Streets as memory; brief snapshot moments kept his mind alive. Nothing thrilled his romantic side more than a second's eye-contact in a crowd, a relationship made and lost in a moment.

Robinson's was crowded so he drank in the Crown two doors down. The booths were full and he stood at the long mahogany bar, and wondered if these little epiphanies added up to anything. He was not religious, but he sometimes wondered if they weren't evidence of a grander design. His agnosticism worried him. Of all places, this country was not one for sitting on the fence.

This time tomorrow, he would know. Everyone said that the result of the hearing was a foregone conclusion. The woman's medical records showed a history of mental illness, stemming from an earlier incident of sexual assault by a soldier, and Cross's counsellor told him that his acquittal would result in her being put in psychiatric care. This left Cross feeling obscurely guilty, as though he were responsible in some way.

Two

THE FOLLOWING day was quiet by Belfast standards. No one got shot, there were no explosions, no security alerts; everything ran on time. By nightfall it was another Friday like anywhere else, with the town going about its business, blowing off steam after the week. The bars in the city centre, where it was possible to mix without fear, and the barricaded sectarian drinking clubs in their respective enclaves all throbbed with a compulsive mixture of loud music, beery warmth and the din of loose talk which swelled to a crescendo in the hour before closing. Outside was foul and squally, which made drinkers all the more reluctant to leave the security of their bars. At ten past ten the Duke of York, a large pub in Donegall Road, was full to bursting when a white Range Rover with a rusted back panel and a smashed tail light pulled into the car park, the reflection of its brake lights flaring on the wet tarmac. Three men got out.

None of them spotted an old blue Triumph Toledo pulling in behind them and parking on the other side of the car park. There was nothing to show that the two men inside were on surveillance, except that British soldiers tended to adopt a regulation dress that was as obvious as a full uniform—leather jackets, jeans and sneakers, hair worn long.

They had followed the Range Rover from Woodvale in the north-west of the city, down the Crumlin Road. The men they were tailing were Protestant paramilitaries and the driver was under observation from an army team hidden in an attic across the road from his house.

The Toledo was alerted as the three men left, and at the next intersection it slipped in behind the Range Rover. It remained inconspicuous in the late-night traffic, following through the city centre and across the Lagan, then down Mountpottinger Road before looping back again over the river via East Bridge Street. The Range Rover continued at the same sedate speed, the three men drinking from cans, oblivious to what was behind.

When the Range Rover pulled up outside the Duke of York the soldier in the passenger seat of the Triumph used the two-way radio to report to base and lit a cigarette to irritate the driver, who lowered his window. Unpleasant gusts of cold air blew into the overheated interior.

They made desultory conversation but the driver was not a talkative man. The forecourt stayed empty, apart from the occasional scurrying figure, hunched against the rain. The driver looked at his watch and sighed. "Last fucking orders, please." His colleague lit another cigarette and amused himself with the night glasses. A couple tottered drunkenly out of the pub.

"What's so funny?" the bored driver asked when the other man started to smirk.

"Bloke having a slash. You can see the steam."

The humourless driver grunted. "Fucking animals."

He took the glasses and a little later spotted a figure crouched down by the door of the Range Rover. He watched, puzzled, then reached for the radio and spoke in the pedantic manner of those whose limited powers of observation have been drummed into them by rote.

"Delta four zero to honeypot. Come in, honeypot. We are in our last reported position. We have what looks like a stoley. The white Range Rover under obs is being broken into. Two persons involved. Weather does not permit full description, but both are wearing dark clothes. Do we follow or not, bearing in mind our orders to stay with the Range Rover? Over."

The last remark set his colleague off laughing. "Rover over."

A crackly voice came back, telling them to stay where they were.

"Understood," said the driver. "Vehicle departed, heading north."

The other man was becoming helpless with laughter.

"I can't wait to see our boys' faces when they find their motor missing."

THE RANGE ROVER avoided the known roadblocks in the area and it was not until fifteen minutes later that a police patrol car spotted it in the vicinity of Ormeau Road. It skirted the west bank of the Lagan before heading north, then east towards a hastily organised trap of two army jeeps and a police car, an unmarked Ford Granada recognizable only by the way it sat so low on the road because of its reinforced armour plating.

The police car was the first to give chase, tucking in behind the stolen car before announcing itself by switching its lights to full beam. The two vehicles wove expertly in and out of the night traffic, and jumped a set of red lights at sixty, causing two intersecting cars to collide.

The police Granada lost the Range Rover in a housing estate and positioned the two army jeeps by the main exits to the estate while it attempted to flush out the stolen vehicle. In spite of an epidemic of joyriding in the city, the driver of the police car had never been involved in a chase before and was nervous.

One of the jeeps spotted the stolen vehicle leaving the estate and set off in pursuit, alerting the second army vehicle, which took up a ramming position but mis-timed its run and narrowly avoided colliding with the first jeep. The two jeeps were still immobile when the Range Rover shot past in the opposite direction after doing a handbrake turn that had spun it around a hundred and eighty degrees.

News of the chase brought clusters of people on to the street, youths mostly, who applauded the getaway car.

"Sticking out!" yelled a lad, chucking a rock at the army cars as they pulled away. It bounced off the side of one vehicle with a dull thud. A cheer went up.

The police car was a quarter of a mile away when told that the Range Rover was heading its way. By then the two policemen had started to enjoy themselves. It made a change from their normal patrol routine of betting on distances and checking them against the milometer, which was usually about as exciting as it got. With luck, this could turn into a biggy.

They headed towards each other down a straight stretch of road. The police driver was thinking about braking and skidding sideways to block the road when the other vehicle switched lanes and drove straight at him. He panicked, and panicked even more when the other car flicked to full beam. Because of the height of the approaching vehicle in relation to the low-slung Granada, the driver could see nothing but a wall of white light. He gripped the wheel helplessly, while his colleague, who was pumped up with adrenalin, yelled at him to stay on course.

"He's not gonna swerve," wailed the driver.

"Ram the fucker!"

"We're all fuckin' mincemeat!"

"Just steer the fucker straight. I'm saying a fiver the other feller's chicken."

As the Range Rover bore down on him, the driver considered his options in the little time left. He was not a hero, he decided, but he had gone close enough to talk it up. So he wrenched the wheel over, hoping that the other driver wouldn't do the same, and shut his eyes. The two cars shot past each other at speed, scraping sides, wing mirrors flying.

"Brilliant!" shouted the other policeman. "But you shouldn'ta swerved."

"And if I hadn't you'd be a fuckin' paraplegic," yelled the driver, who felt a moment's exhilaration at the closeness of the call, then saw he was losing control on the wet surface. In a moment of liquid fear he muddled the controls and floored the accelerator, a silly mistake, but one—he realized as he made it—that could be taken for defiant machismo. They mounted the pavement with a jolt. Bystanders scattered as the car slammed up the grass bank. It was the turn of the other policeman to get nervous.

"Steady up, for Chrissake!"

Blurred figures filled the windscreen and the driver shut his eyes again and waited for the impact that never came. Instead the car shot through empty space, where moments before a crowd had been, leaving behind long, impressive crescents of tyre scars, and rejoined the road some seventy yards later, just avoiding the two army jeeps that were back in the chase.

"Geronimo!" yelled the driver, feeling better now his foot was unstuck and he had seen his colleague's fear. They were half way to being a canteen legend.

* * *

THEY argued later about whether without the helicopter the Range Rover would have got away. By then there was a full alert and the helicopter spotted it on a main road heading towards the M2 that ran north from the city.

It swooped low and settled in over the vehicle, co-ordinating the movements of the ground patrols. A second police car joined the chase as the Range Rover turned away from the motorway for narrower roads that became wooded and harder to monitor from the air.

The helicopter suddenly announced it was losing it. By then the most recent police car in the chase was half a minute behind and the rest a minute and more away. The helicopter observer said he thought the Range Rover was probably driving without lights.

They only found it because the police car at the head of the chase ran over something lying in the road which the Range Rover had also hit with more disastrous consequences. The impact had sent the stolen vehicle careering down a bank and into a large tree, which had smashed the car's electrical system, buckled the bonnet and sent a plume of steam up into the wet night air.

The police car had only skidded after its collision. The driver's first thought was that he had hit a deer.

He got out and went back to look. He noticed an abandoned shoe and didn't at first connect it with whatever was lying in the road. Then, closer to, he saw a trouser leg with a white strip of flesh above the sock. The rest of the figure was harder to make out. There was some sort of grubby coat so soggy with rain that it looked from a distance like the pelt of a dead animal. The driver thought the coat was covering the head, then realized, with a lurch of his stomach, that it was spread all over the tarmac, the scramble of pink and grey-white, squashed flat. He took in the pulp of brains, smashed bits of skull and an object that he couldn't identify, then recognized—between spontaneous heaves of vomiting—as a tongue.

Three

"WHY DO they need me? Why can't traffic deal with it?" Cross was irritable and felt like taking it out on the desk sergeant on the phone.

"Traffic's already there. There's something they think you should see, sir."

The crash site was right on the edge of his district. A couple of miles further and it would have been someone else's problem. He put down the phone and looked at Deidre, annoyed to realize that he still desired her, in spite of everything they'd just said.

He had not suspected, though now he could see the signs had been there for years—in the growing distance between them since Fiona's birth, and in Deidre's exasperation at his lack of ambition. Top promotion, once within his range, would have allowed her the sort of reflected glory she enjoyed. Cross had always admired her social skills. It pleased him to see how wanted she was by other women's husbands. He had felt unthreatened by this until now.

He embraced her before leaving, breathing in her scent and warmth, sensing her resistance.

The garage was accessible from the kitchen. Cross was grateful for this basic security. He took the torch from the shelf and went through the tedious routine of getting down on all fours and peering under the engine, sweeping the beam along the chassis and up into the wheel arches. It was humiliating going through this ritual every time he wanted to use the car and he always felt stupid crouched down on the concrete floor.

The children's bicycles were in the way as usual and had to be moved. He stood staring blankly at Mattie's bike, thinking how ridiculous it was for the boy's grandparents to give him such an expensive one, and far too big for him. He didn't know yet what to think about Deidre, or if it changed everything.

He got in the car, turned the ignition and held his breath. As thorough as his checks were, he always tensed in expectation of the blast that would rip away his legs and most of the rest of him.

CROSS hadn't known what to make of that afternoon's hearing. He had been exonerated, as expected, and the woman who had brought the charge referred to psychiatric care.

Listening to the dreary process of bureaucracy running its course, Cross had an overwhelming desire to scream. The whole thing was an extraordinary waste of time. Markham, the board's senior policeman, admitted as much afterwards. The RUC had become absurdly cautious about internal discipline since the arrival of a special team from England, headed by Deputy Chief Constable Stalker, to investigate accusations of deliberate assassinations carried out by the RUC on members of the Provisional IRA. The official line invariably was that the police had reacted to an armed response, though privately it was openly and gleefully admitted that the victims had been ambushed. Anyway, several of the dead men were wanted for the murders of police officers, so within the force their deaths were seen as fair retaliation.

"Stalker's an idiot and it'll end in tears, mark my words," said Markham. "We're left walking on bloody egg shells. Try getting a surveillance operation mounted and see where that gets you. Try getting anything done, for that matter. And how much is it all costing? They've been here months."

According to Markham, no one had properly defined the Englishman's brief to him.

"The man's blundering around, thinking that he's going to arrive at the truth and expose it to the world. Hah! And he's a Catholic to boot, like you."

Cross caught Markham's crafty glance.

"I think so, sir."

Markham grunted as though this explained everything. Cross was uncomfortably aware that his religious background put him at odds with the rest of the force, and his English origins put him at a further remove. For years he had thought

Deidre was joking when she said, "But, darling, we loathe the Brits."

After the hearing Cross had gone to his divisional barracks, a monument to the city's Victorian prosperity, now desperate and distinguished by peeling paintwork and rising damp. Behind the makeshift shell of grilles and fences and security fortifications that protected the outside from attack, the core was rotten and neglected. It had been due an overhaul for years but with the threat of terrorist reprisals against contractors working for the security forces the work got endlessly delayed. Cross's office—a dark room with bars through which the sun rarely shone—smelt of mildew.

He sat at his desk, too shy to seek out his colleagues and announce his return. That could wait. He phoned Deidre at the tourist board. She was out and he left a message. When she called back he told her the news. She sounded pleased and relieved. "At last things can get back to normal."

Cross wondered what normal was; certainly not going out to celebrate in some fancy new restaurant that Deidre wanted to try. He pleaded exhaustion, making sure not to upset her, and they compromised without too much fuss. Such cautious politeness was a recent feature of their marriage.

"I'll cook us decent steaks and do the potatoes you like," she offered. Dauphinoise or Lyonnaise, he could never remember. He said he would pick up a bottle of wine and promised to be back early.

As he was about to leave, Hargreaves, one of his detective sergeants, stopped off at his office. "They said on the gate you were back. Bloody good thing too, sir. I had a lot of money riding on the verdict."

They laughed. It was no surprise to Cross that there had been an office sweepstake on the outcome.

"We've got a new recruit. A WPC," Hargreaves went on, rolling his eyes. "From Charley's Angels."

Charley's Angels was a unit dealing with sex abuse victims. Cross asked what she was like.

"Bit bright for me." Hargreaves was wary of intelligence, especially in female officers, as it usually came at the expense of common sense.

Cross was never sure how much he liked Hargreaves, but he

felt at ease with him in the security of his dingy office, which seemed far more his than his expensive home.

Hargreaves was a good detective but tended to coast on a reputation acquired from a couple of tough postings, including Crossmaglen, and was clever at bunking off in slack periods. He lived alone and his free time was spent building a boat. There was a wife somewhere and a daughter in a wheelchair, crippled from birth. Hargreaves only mentioned her when he was drunk, and usually added, with tears in his eyes, that he needed all the overtime he could get to pay to have her looked after.

They'd ended up in the bar to celebrate Cross's return and, as he was about to go, were joined by a group of detective constables. He left as one constable was daring another to eat the contents of an ashtray for five pounds.

Cross telephoned Deidre to say that he had been delayed, calculated that he was all right to drive and arrived home to face her disapproval, which increased after smelling the drink on him.

"I don't suppose you remembered the wine."

He hadn't. He worked hard to mollify her while she cooked the steak and he prepared a salad and laid the table. "In here or the dining room?" he asked.

"Oh, in here, don't you think?"

Again this deadly politeness, when neither of them really cared where they ate. Cross saw later that he should have taken more warning of Deidre's initial mood. On what moment of negligence, or look, or careless expression the evening had turned, he was not sure. The ostensible row had been about giving a party to mark the outcome of the hearing, but even then he was aware of more being at stake than a well-rehearsed argument about her gregariousness and his lack. Suspecting that his absence of social commitment was being taken for a lack of deeper devotion, Cross relented. "Go ahead and have the party, then."

He shrank at the prospect. It would be an excuse to invite a lot of Deidre's friends. His colleagues were a cut beneath her.

"I'm just trying to organize us some fun," she said.

"Let's go to bed, then."

She regarded him almost fearfully. He ploughed on, trying to lighten the mood.

"I was rather hoping that part of your celebrations would include an assault on my diminished libido."

The effect of the remark was extraordinary. Deidre seemed to burst apart with anger.

"It's always your fucking needs. Me, me, me. Did you think of me once in all these fuckless weeks? Did you ever think of trying to reassure me?"

She banged the table to emphasize the point. Cross floundered in the wake of her anger, trying to persuade himself that the row might still resolve itself in bed. Fights had become their main way of initiating sex. But Deidre was intransigent.

"You come home late. You forget to bring any wine. You make boring small talk through the meal. You can't see beyond yourself and your own little world and its problems and for the last God knows how long you've been a complete pain in the arse to live with, and now you expect me to come upstairs with you and lie back, open my legs and let you shag me."

Cross smiled, still trying to salvage something.

"Oh, boy. You don't have a clue, do you?"

"What are you talking about?"

Deidre said nothing and he realized he'd known for some time what was coming.

"I'm seeing someone else. You should know that. I hadn't meant to tell you, but now I've said it."

The effect was as abrupt and shocking as if he had been thrown into icy water from a speeding boat. His surprise must have shown. Deidre laughed weakly.

"Fine detective you are."

"What's his name?"

"What difference does it make? It's none of your business."

"It is." He had never seen her so angry.

"The fact I'm fucking another man might be your business, but who he is has nothing to do with you."

"It does if I know him."

"Christ! Me, fuck one of your friends?"

He wondered how often she had done this to him before.

Four

THE GLOW of lights announced the accident site up ahead. The approaching scene revealed enough vehicles to start a carnival, far more than usual. Cross parked and walked the last hundred yards. He reacquainted himself with the familiar sights—the police lights around the tented-off body being attended to by the scene-of-crime squad. Everyone went about their business with a grim-humoured detachment, professional indifference reducing the corpse to an afterthought, to angles of calculation, measurement, geometry and Polaroids.

He felt superfluous and imagined Deidre going to bed, briefly naked as she slipped on her nightdress and into warm sheets—an unwelcome reminder of the tatters of his day.

Doody, in charge of the scene-of-crime team, stood above the rest, enormously tall, enormously bigoted. He had been investigated for passing police files on Catholics to loyalist paramilitaries, and cleared, though the accusation had stuck. Cross wondered if his own charge would give him the reputation of a sex pest, clearance notwithstanding. He had already noticed some WPCs looking at him askance.

Cross found Hargreaves and asked why there were so many vehicles. Hargreaves ticked them off on his fingers. The police and soldiers from the four chase vehicles were still hanging around. Then there were the traffic mob, called in after the accident, and the emergency services, including firemen for the trapped driver of the crashed vehicle, plus scene-of-crime, summoned by the traffic police, and them.

"What about the body?"

"First hit by the stoley, then by a police car and, after that, by an army car in the group behind."

"Three in all," said Cross in disbelief.

27

"There's a dip in the road. It would have been difficult to see. The head's all over the tarmac and in the treads of three separate vehicles."

"Is this a joke?" Cross asked and Hargreaves looked put out. "Never mind. It sounds more like a farce than a murder."

"They say it's not as straightforward as it looks."

Cross felt his patience tested. "Who's responsible for us being here?"

Hargreaves pointed out the sergeant from traffic. The sergeant, sensing Cross's mood, passed him on to a nervous young constable.

"Rees thought you ought to see the body, sir," said the sergeant, sounding unconvinced. "I'd rather have got this lot tidied up and sent home, but Sherlock here had other ideas."

The sergeant moved away, leaving Rees's Adam's apple bobbing up and down as he stammered to find the words.

"In your own time, constable."

"It was the way the body was lying, sir," he eventually managed. "Like it was there when it got run over. If he'd been hit standing he would have been thrown aside or dragged by the vehicle."

Rees had bad breath. Cross wondered about the state of his own. "Is that all?"

"No, sir. I noticed the wrists—"

"Sir!"

It was Hargreaves with the news that the driver had been cut out of the Range Rover and was on the way up. Cross asked Rees to excuse him and followed Hargreaves. A stretcher was being carried up the bank, the ambulancemen cursing as they slithered on wet leaves. Hargreaves told Cross that the driver was still unconscious. Cross took a closer look and turned in surprise to Hargreaves.

"Did you know it was a her?"

"Yes, sir, but I didn't see it made any difference."

Hargreaves was rarely mischievous. Cross had to laugh. "What about the other one. It is a boy?"

"Yes, sir," said Hargreaves with a straight face. "I've already cautioned him."

Cross spotted a pale, skinny youth sitting on the steps of an ambulance, wrapped in a red blanket. One wrist was cuffed to a rail, which let him smoke with his free hand. He drew deeply on the last of his cigarette and flicked it towards them as they approached. The youth looked the kind with a ready excuse. Cross wondered what it would be this time.

"What's your name?" asked Cross.

"O'Connor."

"First name?"

"Vincent. I already told your man."

"What do you remember about the accident?"

"I didn't see."

"What else do you remember?"

"Nothing. I must have got a bang on the head."

They shifted to one side to let the ambulancemen load the stretcher.

"Is she all right?"

"I don't know. You'll be taken to the hospital for a check-up, then if you're fit you'll be transferred to a police station and charged."

Cross sought Rees out again for the rest of his story, which grew increasingly bizarre. Cross shook his head, trying to make sense of it.

"Did you notice any other marks?"

"Well, no. I thought of that and couldn't see anything without disturbing the body."

"Thank you, constable. You did the right thing."

Cross felt the start of a headache and wondered if it was a delayed reaction to Deidre's news. He sighed and walked over to the scene-of-crime squad.

"Nice to have you back, sir," said Doody insincerely.

"Mind if I take a look?"

Why he was bothering to be polite was beyond him. Doody wouldn't think any more of him for a bit of civility.

"Help yourself, sir." Always the supercilious use of "sir," after the insolent pause.

Cross stepped over a puddle of vomit and bent down to inspect the body. At last he was doing what he was there for. He felt calm for the first time since arriving.

He took in the details, the crushed skull fragments, the bits of brain tissue and shattered jaw bone and tongue. None of this told him anything. Turning his attention to the body, Cross guessed from the condition of the hands the man was in his fifties. He looked more closely at the wrists. Each was as Rees

had described, both pierced by a neat puncture about the size
of a large nail. Apart from church crucifixes, Cross could not
recollect seeing anything like it. He asked Doody if anyone had
inspected the man's pockets.

"We were waiting for you"—again the slight pause—"sir."

The man really was the limit. Cross felt a surge of anger at
his own lack of authority. Christ, he thought, this constant
doubt had to stop, and it was getting worse. He stared at
Doody. "After you."

They were behaving like children. Doody relented and put
on a pair of clear polythene gloves and felt his way through the
dead man's pockets. There was nothing in the trousers.

"He isn't wearing a jacket and the shirt hasn't got a pocket,"
said Doody.

"Unbutton the shirt."

Doody gave Cross a quizzical look before doing as he
was told.

"Are there any marks or scars?"

"No," said Doody.

The left coat pocket yielded a handful of coins. They were
placed in an old jubilee-year biscuit tin that served as the
squad's container for the dead's last possessions.

The only other item was a piece of newspaper folded in four.
The constable in charge of the tin, who wore polythene gloves
like Doody, smoothed out the paper and placed it in a cellophane envelope.

Cross asked to see it. The paper measured roughly eight by
five and, though torn at the edges, it had been folded carefully
to suggest it had been kept for a reason. On one side was a
selection of display advertisements, on the other, columns of
classifieds. Cross scanned the cross-headings: PERSONAL, SER-
VICES, TUTORING, WEDDING DAY, LOST & FOUND, KIDDIES'
CORNER. There was no date.

Doody interrupted to ask if they could move the body. Cross
nodded and returned to the classifieds. He became aware of
Hargreaves standing by.

"Why would anyone keep this?" he asked.

He heard Doody mutter, loud enough for him to overhear
but not to challenge, "To wipe his arse with."

Someone sniggered. Cross let it go. He'd have Doody gutted
and fucked in hell one of these days. He turned back to Har-

greaves, who seemed embarrassed by Cross's lack of grip. "Get someone to work through these adverts. There may be a connection."

"What do you think, sir?"

"About what? Whether it's sectarian?"

"Yes, sir."

"I haven't a clue."

A dumped body suggested sectarian. Informers were often tortured, though crucifixion was not something either IRA or loyalists went in for, as far as he knew. In other respects the body displayed none of the usual signs of an informer—money pressed into the palm, or bare feet.

Cross felt his headache slowly working its way down the side of his head, making his teeth throb. The dentist had been on the list of things to do during his suspension, but he had never got round to it.

Driving home, he realized there was something at the accident site that he hadn't been able to identify. He thought back and pictured the mess of pulped flesh and bone until he could see every detail. He listed the separate components of the skull and mentally ticked each off—brain tissue, skull fragments, tongue. What there hadn't been were any teeth.

Five

AFTER being cleared by the hospital, Vinnie had been moved to the police barracks, where they had taken away his things, logging each item in a large red book, and led him down to the galleys. As the mandrax wore off he became aware of the sour smell of fear on himself. He lay alone on a hard plastic mattress under a harsh light that wouldn't switch off and tried thinking about having a wank to see if it would make him feel better, then decided it was the last thing he wanted. Anyway they'd be watching, which made him think of doing it all the same, just to show what he thought of them. Then he remembered the state of the girl after the crash.

He had only met her that evening, introduced by his friend Brendan in the Duke of York. He hadn't caught her name. She was from the Markets and teased Vinnie for being a country boy when he said he was from Andersonstown.

She wore black and looked dead cool to Vinnie, wild and available, if he could impress her. When Brendan moved on because of others to meet, Vinnie stayed, buying her expensive foreign lagers until he was cleaned out. He talked about cars, and noticed her eyes shine at the mention of speed. Cars he knew about, stealing them, at any rate, and he named all the ones he'd ever driven, trying not to make it sound like bragging, but she knew them all and others too.

"Now that's dead sexy," she said of a Cosworth he'd mentioned. "Hail Manta, full of Audi, the Astra is with thee, blessed art thou among Sierras." Vinnie, shocked in spite of himself by such casual blasphemy, laughed too loud. "Did you ever see a car in flames?" she went on. "Best sight in the world. Sex in a car, did you beat that?"

Vinnie smirked, thinking he was into the swing of her mood. "No hard-on like a hard-on at speed."

"If you were half the man you make out, you'd be at the bar getting another drink."

From the way she slurred her words he'd thought at first she was drunk but now he wasn't so sure. She seemed so in control as he watched surreptitiously, waiting for the drinks.

"You're great," he said later, lost in drunken admiration. "I've been waitin' all my life."

"You didn't have a life until tonight."

"Where did you learn to be so smart?"

"What about a takeaway?" she asked, ignoring him.

"A carry-out?" Food was the last thing on his mind.

"A car, dickhead."

"Now you're talking."

Outside they necked in the rain, Vinnie high and itchy with lust, pressing himself against her to show the state of his excitement.

"Christ! Give that dog a bone," she said, laughing.

Vinnie bayed at the sky.

"Are you goin' to stand there barking all night?"

They decided on the Range Rover because neither had been in one and Vinnie claimed ownership by pissing on the wheel.

"Let's see the size of it, then."

"Get away."

"You were all for puttin' it in my pocket a minute ago."

As Vinnie finished up, she grabbed him and they ended up sprawled awkwardly on the bonnet of a car.

"Is it the cold that makes it small? And you were steamin'."

"I'm still steamin'," he said in a thick voice, kissing her hard.

"Showing promise," she said when they broke. She kissed him again. Vinnie was up for it there and then, and her jittery, thrusting motions as she squirmed beneath him made him think she was too, until he saw it was laughter she was helpless with. She rolled away from him.

Vinnie worked the lock of the Range Rover. It took time, being drunk. The girl scratched her crotch with impatience. When he opened the door she pushed in front of him.

"Hey, I'm drivin'," Vinnie protested.

"Are you getting in or not?"

She jammed a pair of nail scissors into the ignition. Vinnie's annoyance gave way to admiration. "You've done this before."

"Beginner's luck."

Vinnie found a four-pack of beer by his feet and flourished it in triumph.

They sped exhilarated through the Belfast night. Vinnie watched her: a real daredevil, foot down and feeling him up as she drove.

"Hey, hands on the wheel."

"I'll drive with my knees if I want."

"Ah, fuck me bendy, if mother could see me now!"

"Give me one of those sexy French kisses," she shouted and didn't even slow down, making Vinnie nervous about chasing this wildest of girls. He felt caught in what Brendan called that old machismo bind, wanting to urge caution, not wishing to lose face.

"Is this as fast as we're going?" he shouted.

His erection was wilting in the face of her recklessness, though with what she was doing with her free hand he might just— Then he heard her swear as the car behind switched its lights to full beam.

"It's the fucking peelers!" she shouted, accelerating away.

CROSS looked at Vinnie, who sat across the table from him in one of the barracks' many interview rooms. The strain of his arrest made him pinched and furtive.

"There's nothing to tell. I was driving with this girl."

"With several vehicles in pursuit."

"I don't know what that was about."

"But you didn't think to stop and find out."

"I told her we should of but I wasn't drivin'."

"What did you see on the road before the crash?"

"She said something like, 'What's that?' and before I could see she'd hit it."

"What did you think it was?"

"I didn't see."

"There was no one standing in the road?"

"I told you, I didn't see."

"Whose was the car?"

"Hers, I suppose."

"You suppose."

"We'd only just met."

"What's her name?"

Vinnie looked concerned for the first time. "Is she all right?"

"Just give me her name."

"Marie or Marian, something like that."

"Why didn't you stop when ordered?"

"She was worried, being over the limit. She freaked."

"And if I told you it wasn't her car, would you be worried at that?"

"I'd have to say I know nothing about that."

"What happened when you got in the car?"

"Nothing. We drove off."

"How did she start it?"

"With a key, of course."

"Weren't you surprised at her having a car like that?"

"I think I thought it was her dad's. I was pretty well staggered."

"What happened after you broke into the car?"

"I'd have to say I don't know about that. I was in the gents', see. She went off to get the car. It was a Range Rover she said, and when I got there she was waiting with the motor running."

"But you already said you saw her start it with a key."

"I didn't see, but what else would she start it with?"

"Then where's the key?"

Vinnie shrugged and looked sulky.

"The girl's in a coma. We're trying to trace her next of kin. You can help us find them."

"I'd tell her name if I knew." He looked at the floor for a long time.

Cross asked, "Is there anything you want to add?"

"I'm telling the truth in all this."

"You were seen breaking into the car by two witnesses."

"I'm sticking to my story."

Cross told the constable with him to take a full statement.

VINNIE was taken back to his cell. The last time he had been arrested he'd been let off with a warning. He wondered what he was facing now: one or two years, plus remission. He thought back to school and what happened between one year and the next and tried to imagine all that time put away.

It was not the peelers or prison he feared, compared to what the IRA would do if they knew he had been joyriding again. Dermot they'd got drunk on scrumpy first because they felt sorry for him, and Chancer was back stealing cars while he was still on crutches and his leg in plaster. It was a point of honour to show you weren't intimidated, but Vinnie was still scared from the last time.

Two of them had come to the house. Vinnie had been still in bed with a hangover. His first thought was it was the police, except it was too early for them. Nevertheless, he was half out of the window when the bedroom door opened and he found himself staring at two armed men wearing black gloves. One carried a CB radio.

They addressed him by his full name and for a moment Vinnie thought they were going to shoot him astride the windowsill, dressed in his underpants.

"You've got the wrong O'Connor," he managed to say.

"We're from the Provisional Irish Republican Army," one of them announced gravely to his mother as she arrived upstairs. His father stood ineffectually behind, the pair of them a pathetic picture of formal anguish. Vinnie's fear was worse for the embarrassment he felt at being seen undressed in front of his mother.

"Listen, Ma, I swear on my life, they're mixing me with another fellow."

The Provisional standing nearest him turned to his mother and spoke politely, making it sound like she had some choice in the matter.

"Go downstairs now and make yourselves a cup of tea. It's just a little talk we're wanting. He'll be back safe in the hour."

With a broken leg, thought Vinnie, or worse.

They stayed in the bedroom and watched him dress, then led him outside to a waiting car with two more men inside. His escorts pushed him into the back and got in on either side and the car pulled away. Everyone's actions seemed perfectly rehearsed.

Vinnie tried to protest his innocence but only a whine came out. The man in the passenger seat turned round and jabbed a gun at his forehead, scaring him like never before. Vinnie was convinced they were going to make an example of him and shoot him dead. The story was that they were going to do it to someone sooner or later. He was even more sure when the man worked the gun housing, feeding a round into the barrel, which left him horribly aware that the bullet in the breech was the one that would drill its way into his brain. He started to sob and didn't care who saw.

Outside everything looked desperately normal—bricks and concrete and the beginnings of an indifferent blue sky. Inside the car the silence felt dreadfully loaded.

"This'll do here," said the gunman.

Vinnie started gabbling the end of the Hail Mary, over and over—"*Now and at the hour of our death*"—praying like never before, promising to live the life of a saint if God or the Blessed Virgin got him out of this. He looked frantically for any sign that he might not be about to be killed and found none. They were parked by an empty space of grass, with two weak saplings protected by wire cages. He could see his own body dumped on the grass, like time had jumped.

The four men sat in silence while Vinnie bawled like a baby until one of them lit a cigarette.

"For God's sake, give him one too if it'll shut him up," said the man with the gun.

Vinnie, thinking this was the condemned man's last cigarette they were offering, shook his head furiously and gulped for air, hoping that refusing might somehow keep him alive.

"Ah, for Christ's sake, stop your snivelling. Take the fucking cigarette and get a grip."

They lit it for him. He was still whimpering and that with the smoke started him coughing.

"You do smoke?" asked the driver laconically, speaking for the first time.

Vinnie nodded, still coughing.

"That's all right, then. We wouldn't want to be encouraging bad habits."

"His first and last cigarette," said the man with the gun, laughing, which was enough to set Vinnie off again.

"Government Warning," said the driver, deadpan, emphasizing every word. "Smoking can damage your health."

The man with the gun turned and smiled, then jammed the pistol point hard against Vinnie's knee, making him yelp. He dug it in harder until Vinnie cried out with fear.

"They say the pain is indescribable."

"Read that," said the driver, producing a folded piece of paper from his pocket.

It was a typed statement with Vinnie's full name and address at the top, followed by a confession of his crimes, namely petty larceny and car theft, a promise to not offend again and, if further offences were discovered, then he should be aware of the consequences. His name looked strange spelt out in full, as though it belonged to someone else. Vincent Gerard Declan O'Connor. He wondered how they knew about the middle names.

A delay followed while a pen was found for Vinnie to sign the paper. He scribbled his name with difficulty because of the trembling.

The gunman said, "If we find you up to your old tricks you know what to expect."

Vinnie said nothing, but they wanted to hear it from him.

"What do you get?"

"Broken bones," mumbled Vinnie.

"At the very least," said the driver. "We come to your house, we take you away, we tie your arms behind your back, we put the sellotape over your mouth and we shoot you—in the elbow or the knee, or maybe just in the back of the leg, if we're feeling lenient. Or we smash your bones with a baseball bat or drop a breeze block on you, which makes a terrible mess. But you know all this. The thing is, are you clear about it?"

They showed him some pictures to underline their point. The man next to Vinnie shoved him forward, making sure he saw each one as it was held up, half a dozen Polaroids of smashed knees and elbows, ghastly nightmare cocktails of gristle and bone. The worst was of a large exit hole that had taken away the whole kneecap, leaving only a soggy, unprotected pulp.

"Colt .45. Make sure that's not you, Vincent."

The man in the passenger seat looked him levelly in the eye, speaking politely, with no need of threat any more, like they were exchanging pleasantries over a shop counter.

"Now mind how you go."

All Vinnie could think was that he wasn't going to die after all. He was aware only of his breathing and his relief. It was a miracle he'd not shat himself. God was understanding in His infinite mercy. He fucking well must be if He was letting him off with a warning. The sun came out from behind a cloud, just for him.

Six

BY LATE morning lack of sleep was telling on Cross. He looked through his window at the barracks' dreary courtyard. Not yet lunchtime and the lights were on. He often felt overwhelmed at the start of a case. With the greater issues so insoluble, it was hardly surprising.

He turned to Hargreaves. "Who's working on the advertisements?"

"Westerby."

Westerby was the new posting, a serious-looking young woman with a face he could imagine belonging to Joan of Arc or one of the saints in the stained-glass windows of the churches of his childhood. He wasn't sure why. There was nothing particularly otherworldly about her. She smiled easily, showing good teeth, and did her blonde hair in a way that reminded him of women in films from the 1950s, and seemed more feminine than many policewomen, without adopting the fluttery manner of some.

Cross looked at a photostat of the relevant page of advertisements, which was from an edition of one of the city's newspapers of the week before. His eye was drawn to a long and rambling Prayer to the Holy Spirit that ended:

> The person may say this prayer for three consecutive days, after the three days the favour will be granted. This prayer must be published after the third day. C.S.

What on earth did that mean?

"Tell Westerby to double-check this," he said to Hargreaves, "and any others that look like they might be religious cranks. It's a possibility. At this stage anything is."

He also told him to contact the two soldiers who had reported the theft of the Range Rover for a statement, and to go through the men's hostels and see if any regulars were missing.

After Hargreaves had gone, Cross went over the other advertisements.

A BIBLE QUESTION: What does God say concerning governments? ANS Read Proverbs Chapter 29 verse 2.

DENTURE GRIEF. Dental implants may solve your problem.

PROFESSIONAL CHINESE MAN, educated, late 30 would like to meet lady, for friendship.

CHRISTIAN WIDOW, 29 would like to meet Christian male.

SOPHISTICATED BUSINESS LADY in my 40s. I drive a very sporty car, sail my own yacht, surf, water and snow ski, hill walk and chase rallies. Own house in it's own grounds. Genuine replies only please.

This hotchpotch of yearning, superstition and dread struck him as uniquely Irish, even the sophisticated business lady with her oversell. He noted the misplaced apostrophe, so characteristic of the North. The next advertisement was more succinct than the Prayer to the Holy Spirit, though just as cryptic and puzzling.

WHEN GOD has forsaken His Mansion the Devil must do His work.

What did that mean? Whose work precisely? God's or the devil's?

WHENEVER Cross met Ricks he was reminded how well some of the community did out of the Troubles, and none more than the pathologist, who did better than most—with little risk to himself—carving up all sides with equanimity.

Ricks was an urbane man, around fifty, with irritating, pedantic manners and pampered skin that he kept carefully talced and after-shaved. A well-fed jowl extended to his neck, bulged over an expensive striped collar and told of long, leisurely dinners in the finest restaurants, testaments to a private income and a lack of any Mrs. Ricks to support.

His upstairs office carefully distanced Ricks from the grisly nature of his work. He surrounded himself with expensive personal furniture that included an enormous, elaborately carved partner's desk that he sat behind, pouring tea into bone china. Everyone else Cross knew made do with mugs. An antique lamp cast a comforting pool of light on to the dark green leather surface of the desk.

Through the window, darkness fell over the city skyline. Rain was forecast. Cross usually enjoyed walking but he didn't relish going back into the cold. A biting north-east wind had chased him all the way there.

Ricks pursed his lips. "Sugar?"

Cross shook his head and tried to bury the thought that one day this fussy man's white hands might cut him up.

"He was dead when the first car hit him," said Ricks as he handed over the tea. "If he had been standing there would be signs of impact, as your chap suggested. Completely crushed head, as you saw, which doesn't make our job any easier."

"Dead rather than unconscious when he was hit?"

"I'll get to that in a minute. He would have snuffed it soon enough anyway. Your man was on his last legs. Cirrhosis of the liver. With such advanced damage to the internal organs it's hard to put an age to him. Between fifty-five and sixty-five? Maybe younger, could be older. What else? Five nine, twelve stone three. No teeth, no dentures. Nothing on the fingerprints yet?"

Cross shook his head and asked the cause of death.

"Hard to say, given the state of the head. The wrist wounds—well, there's no tearing to suggest they were supporting the weight of his body. If he was nailed to anything he was probably nailed to the floor." He paused and gave Cross an arch look. "No other evidence to suggest torture, but I can't say for sure because he's a dog's dinner, frankly."

He made a steeple of his fingers and smiled. Ricks enjoyed his little performances, and Cross indulged him, suspecting that there was more.

Ricks toyed with his half-moon glasses for effect.

"Your man's been as dead as doornails for some time."

Cross obliged with a puzzled look.

"In fact, I'd say he's been dead for weeks."

"What about decomposition? There wasn't any."

"Nor would there be, if?"

"If what?" Cross wished Ricks would get on with it.

"If the body was frozen."

"Frozen?"

"As bizarre as it sounds, yes."

"Frozen?" Cross repeated, in genuine astonishment.

"The brain still was, partly. Lucky for you, a) that I went back to check for any bullet wound: none, by the way; and b) managed to squeeze you in at such short notice. If we'd opened him up much later he would have thawed out completely."

Ricks giggled. It was the first time Cross could remember him showing any sign of mirth.

HARGREAVES showed no surprise when Cross told him to investigate deep freezes.

"Domestic or commercial, sir?"

Hargreaves could be quite a comic when he wanted.

"Domestic first. Big enough to hold a body."

He reported back that there were several such models, and several thousand in all, spread over Northern Ireland.

Cross groaned. The men's hostels had come up with nothing, nor had missing persons. Most murders got solved through some break in the first seventy-two hours, a deadline they were well past.

"By the way, sir," said Hargreaves. "The two witnesses of the vehicle theft. One's on leave in the UK and the other is indefinitely unavailable."

"Why?"

"He's been assigned to another undercover operation."

"I hope you made it clear how much we appreciate the army's co-operation."

"Yes, sir. I told them they were bastards."

Meanwhile, Westerby's check on the personal advertisements had revealed that two of the three religious ones—the Prayer to the Holy Spirit and the one about God's thoughts on business—had been placed by a brother and sister named Wilson. They were in their forties, neither was married and they shared a fanatically neat house in Ballymacarrett. They also published an occasional pamphlet under the name Carriers of Christ, a copy of which Westerby produced for Cross.

He flipped through several folded and stapled sheets of A4, poorly typed photostats whose content was the same infuriating mix of the discursive and the cryptic as the two advertisements in the newspaper.

"What are the Wilsons like?"

Odd, said Westerby. Margery Wilson had answered the door looking like something out of a museum, wearing clothes and make-up at least four decades out of date. Brother Raymond by contrast wore cheap army surplus and went barefoot. Westerby had found his unblinking stare from behind thick lenses as disconcerting as his first words to her: "Many stray from the path of the Lord. Be thou saved."

"Do you think they're fanatics?" asked Cross.

Westerby shook her head and said she thought them highly eccentric and probably harmless. "It's possible, I suppose, that they had contact with the dead man through their pamphlet. They have occasional meetings and Bible sessions with like-minded people. They don't have a deep freeze, by the way, not in the kitchen, and I couldn't see anything like a shed in the garden."

"Garage?"

"No garage. But I can't really see them caught up in anything like this, they're too involved in each other. Except that—"

"Except what?"

"I don't know, sir. Pure supposition. But it could be a reason for blackmail."

She remembered the way the sister had smoothed her skirt and given her brother sly, sidelong glances of adoration.

"Suppose." Cross smiled at her and she smiled back gratefully.

"Suppose they sleep together," said Westerby.

"What? I thought they were brother and sister."

Westerby nodded uncertainly, deciding that she was probably the victim of an overactive imagination. Cross's astonishment seemed to confirm it. Westerby became embarrassed. "It was just a thought, sir."

"No, no," said Cross, suddenly embarrassed too. "I'm sure your instinct is right. Is there anything to back your hunch, beyond supposing?"

"I did take a quick look upstairs when I asked to use the toilet. There's only one bedroom from what I could see—the others were studies or prayer rooms. And there was only one bed in the bedroom. So I suppose I thought blackmail."

"Do you think we should talk to them again?"

Westerby seemed surprised to be asked. "I'm not sure, sir. I suppose they're the only obvious lead."

"What about the sixth advertisement, do you have anything on that?"

"The one about the devil's work?"

"If that's the one about a mansion."

Westerby consulted her notes.

"Oh, yes. The paper is still trying to chase that up. They seem to have mislaid the details."

"Let me know when you know."

As she was leaving, Cross thought of something else.

"How long does food take to defrost?"

"It depends what it is."

"Say a chicken."

"I don't know. Six or seven hours."

"If it takes a chicken seven hours, then how long shall we say for our man?"

They were both amused by the absurdity of their conversation.

"Thirty-six. I'm just guessing," she said.

"Do one more thing for me tomorrow, would you, first thing. Find out from the Electricity Board if there were any power cuts in, say, a two-day period before the discovery of the body."

CROSS and Deidre sat in silence through the whole of *Newsnight*, but when she made a pretence of watching the programme after, Cross got up impatiently.

"Can we have that off?"

"It's interesting."

He turned it off anyway. "Not as interesting as us."

Deidre looked at him in angry surprise.

Cross started on his prepared speech. "I was thinking I should stay somewhere until we or you or I or your friend sort something out. We could tell the children I have to go on a course for a few weeks."

Far from his announcement having the placatory effect that he had anticipated, it enraged Deidre. "What about your affairs?" she snapped.

"What affairs?"

"Come on, you've had affairs."

"It's not true. There haven't been any."

"Men have affairs."

"I'm telling the truth."

"Anyway, you're not walking out now," she said with finality.

He listened to her accuse him of playing the injured party instead of facing up to facts, and realized how unprepared he was for this talk, in spite of initiating it.

"I could face the facts a lot better if I knew who he was," he said bitterly.

"Can you hear how pompous you sound?"

The criticism stung.

"What do you want to do?" he asked.

"Nothing."

"And where does that leave us?"

"You're not breaking up this family."

Cross suspected that it was her parents' disapproval of separation and divorce that was motivating her line. He tried to get angry but couldn't. It was like they were discussing other people's lives.

"Where shall I sleep?" he asked.

"Where you like. It's your bed too."

After they turned out the light, she surprised him by turning to him fiercely and saying, "Hold me."

He did, with mixed feelings, thinking she was testing him. He wanted her and didn't, and suspected she felt the same.

"It's you I want, not just sex," he said and, to his amazement, she laughed and said, "Try separating the two," and kissed him hard, making her need clear.

As she moved beneath him, physically joined but off in a world of her own, Cross found that each thrust took the form of an unwelcome question in his bursting head. How often? Where? For how long? Who? She sometimes went away, more frequently recently, for a night or two at a time, to conferences, she said. He wondered how many of them had been excuses. He drove at her harder, to blot out his despairing thoughts and Deidre responded, locking her legs round his back to take him deeper. Tight anger dominated the building tension to their release. Deidre's loud shrieks of abandon took him by surprise. She was usually quiet because of the children.

Afterwards they avoided each other's eye. Their desperate coupling had left him even more wary.

When Cross found he could not sleep he got up and checked on the children. Fiona was rolled into a ball on the bottom bunk, hardly visible under the blankets. Mattie lay on his back, uncovered. Cross rearranged his bedclothes and stood watching, calmed by their quiet breathing.

He took a whisky and sat in the living room—the drawing room as Deidre preferred. Her family had provided the luxuries. Their money had paid for the Liberty furniture, as it would no doubt pay for the children's education. None of it felt like his. Even the house, in a well-to-do enclave that he could not have afforded on his own, was bought with the help of the O'Neills. It left him feeling like a tenant in his own marriage.

His own background was far more modest. He had been

raised in the drizzle of 1950s suburban lower-middle-class conformity, his father the voice that announced over the tannoy at Bristol's Temple Meads station.

His mother, after the agony of his birth, could never face another. Cross had overheard her say so. In his presence, unspoken conversations hung in the air, restricted to commonplace observations, a habit he had unintentionally carried on into his family. He wondered if his children would grow up feeling that they had been similarly censored. Perhaps his own memories of himself as a child prevented him from loving his parents as he should—watchful, secretive and untrusting, eavesdropping, prying into grown-up drawers, searching for some clue that would explain the tedium of the house to him. He knew his parents were different when he wasn't there, like the time he had found them dancing to Doris Day singing "Que Sera Sera"—evidence of another life, spoiled by his entry.

At night he lay under his blankets listening to Radio Luxembourg on a cheap transistor with an earplug. Station interference made him feel like he was beaming into a forbidden world of American songs that conjured up an infinity of space to set against the confinement of his room. He dreamed of riding the railroads. They would move to Arizona, where his Stetsoned father, marshalling freight in Santa Fe, would become a source of pride.

The radio that fired these dreams was his greatest treasure, stolen off a boy at school. He was never suspected and never confessed, and luxuriated in the guilt, which he accommodated better than the vague sense of shame his parents inspired in him during pointless Sunday afternoon drives—the mobile equivalent of the static boredom of the household. He remembered the shock of once seeing his mother naked, on opening the bathroom door she had forgotten to lock, and not being able to understand what she was doing. Years later he realized she had been sitting on the edge of the bath masturbating. Once or twice a year he heard his parents' bed creaking.

There had been Mass every Sunday with his mother, who went out of Catholic duty, while his father lay in and Cross worried that he wouldn't see him in heaven. He felt a frustration he could never articulate, beyond feeling that life would go on like that always, never getting better or worse. Waiting at bus-stops in the rain.

He became a policeman by chance, through being friendly with a young constable who asked him to make up the numbers in a local cricket team. Cricket was the only sport he ever showed any aptitude for. Cross, bored with school and desperate to leave home, applied for the force and was accepted.

At the scene of his first murder he learnt something about himself. A woman had been brutally knifed to death by her drunken boyfriend in a house in a street that Cross had walked down every day on his way to school. He expected to be horrified by what he saw but found himself quite calm. The sad messiness of an interrupted life, the graphic evacuation of violent death, the aftermath of murder, all drew him until the scene stuck to his mind like glue, as though he had been waiting all his life to find himself in a room like this and for the discovery of such naked emotion. He needed passionately to know what could have caused this dark spill of violence, in such contrast to the bloodlessness of his own existence. He wanted to understand. He wanted to know the man who had done it and, above all, why.

Seven

HIS CHILDHOOD was a solitary one spent in the fields of East Anglia, trapping rabbits and hunting coypu, scanning the horizon for movement. After the big skies and childlike openness of the Fens, where everything could be read from a distance, Belfast was a maze to get lost in, where the darkest deeds stayed secret. After a lifetime outdoors, he found himself drawn to the dark interiors of Belfast. After he had done with Herron he realized there was nowhere else to go.

So lonely baby. It was the only song for him. *I found a new place to dwell.* He remembered the first time he had heard the message, coming to him over the airwaves. It was on his parents' radio while they were out and he had got up and searched through the dial until he found it: *So lonely baby.* His father wouldn't allow it and called it the devil's music and beat him if he caught him listening. *So lonely I could die.*

His background conformed to a pattern often found in his kind: a history of childhood abuse, parental violence, cruelty to animals, an absence of nurture. There were spells in orphanage-type approved schools, hangovers from a stern Victorian tradition of hypocrisy, where he suffered the humiliation of men inserting their things up his anus and beatings, and after that the army, where he fought back. He was the wild card that could result from an institutionalized upbringing: the unreadable and unknowable beneath the surface conformity. Army training, combined with his canny feel for the lie of the land, honed his lethal skills. Being an agent for others he found easy: he felt immune from people anyway, watching them like they were through a window. Lying was easy too, as he didn't understand what truth was beyond what the naked eye took in. A dying animal caught in a gin trap, watched with intense curiosity, was nothing beyond what it was: a dying animal. Sometimes when he looked at these creatures afterwards he realized that they had been damaged, but he had no memory of how they came to be like that. He saw nothing wrong in this behaviour—it was merely an illustration of what he felt others did to him. Just as some people painted or wrote to express themselves, he destroyed things. But it took time to understand that this was his vocation.

When he arrived in Belfast he knew there was something still missing about himself and waited to discover what it was. He wondered if it mightn't connect with the sense of secrecy that pervaded his childhood, the time spent watching, waiting, hidden. He found what he was looking for in the clouded eye of a tortured man. The dumb, uncomprehending pain of the animals he killed was replaced by a terrible sense of recognition in the eye of his beholder that he was facing his nemesis. *Now and at the hour of our death.* He knew then that his destiny was destruction, killing people. Had he stayed in England he might have avoided this awful calling, but let loose in the grand labyrinth of Belfast, with its tortuous history, he became magnificent. Killing was something—the only thing, perhaps— he was very good at and when it worked it was accompanied by an insight so intense that it blinded in its revelation. *Now and at the hour of our death. So lonely baby.*

Nowhere else to go, except in deeper.

Eight

BLAIR was Special Branch, working out of Cross's barracks, a tall, sharp-faced man of thirty whose well-pressed trousers fell short of his over-polished shoes. Cross was in awe of Blair's huge hands and feet, and whatever trick it was that let you see the menace behind his jokes. He wore his rigid plain clothes like a uniform of arrogance, and crowned the ensemble with an unlikely biker's quiff which contradicted the sober double-vented blazer and grey slacks. If anything, Blair looked like an off-duty footballer, the hard man of the defence.

He came to Cross's office, something he had not done before, ostensibly to congratulate him on the outcome of his hearing, which he regarded as an example of the kind of bureaucracy the RUC could do without. Blair was a realist. Given the vacillations of Westminster, someone had to take the war to the IRA.

"What do you think, skip?"

He called everyone that. Cross shrugged and wondered about the real purpose of the visit.

"Who's the wee lass?" asked Blair, pointing to a Polaroid on the notice board. It was a hospital picture of the young woman who had crashed the Range Rover. It showed her clean of make-up, hair flattened by the pillow. She looked about thirteen.

Blair turned to Cross in surprise. "She's the one that led the patrol boys such a dance? She looks like she's about to receive holy orders."

Cross said they were still trying to identify her. He was

surprised no one had come forward. In a tight-knit community like Belfast it was usually only a short time before someone did.

"I hear she ran down some bum," said Blair.

"The bum was already dead. He'd been dumped."

Dumped bodies suggested sectarian, said Blair.

"Unclaimed. Why bother killing some bum?"

"Unless he'd strayed into an army night patrol and got shot by mistake." The possibility struck Blair as funny and he gave a hee-haw laugh.

"He wasn't shot."

"Then it was probably some martial arts cowboy."

Just his luck if the dead man turned out to have been killed by some over-keen psychotic corporal, Cross thought, and tried to reassure himself that army cover-ups did not yet extend to housing corpses in barracks' deep freezes.

"Let me talk to the boy," said Blair with a loose smile, and Cross realized why he was there. He had heard that Blair ran informers and sniffed around the cells for kids to turn. It was a world everyone knew about but preferred to pretend did not exist.

THE TWO detectives that came to Vinnie's cell were not the ones who had questioned him before. They asked if he was going to co-operate and he said yes, without knowing why. They said no more and left.

When they came back Blair told Vinnie to come with them. Instead of taking him to the interview room, they went outside to a car park at the back of the building.

"Here's your things," said Blair. It was the stuff they'd taken away at the desk. Vinnie inspected the scuffed plastic bag cautiously.

"Are you saying I can go?"

"What about a wee drink to celebrate?"

"Is that an offer I can't refuse?"

The two men stood grinning like he was some sharp wit. Blair said, "The spitting image of Al Pacino."

Vinnie felt obscurely pleased. He fancied the resemblance himself.

They drove to a pub near the city centre with Vinnie ducked down on the back seat as they left the barracks. The two men behaved like everything was normal, talking about a film they had seen. They asked if Vinnie had seen it too. He had and didn't remember it very well.

"You can call me Heinz, by the way," said Blair. "Did you like that film? I expect you're not easily scared by a wee bit of horror, a wild boy like yourself. Me, I was peeking through my fingers."

Vinnie wondered what kind of joke name Heinz was. The man's hair reminded him of old Teddy Boy photographs of his father.

The other one said, "After the shite we deal with there's nothing like a horror flick for comic relief."

"This is Eric."

Eric was younger, though the paleness of his eyes gave him a look of weariness that made him seem older. Vinnie tried to remember the name of the girl he had seen the film with.

They toyed with him before getting down to business, drawing him into their idle conversation, letting him get light-headed on lager and appreciate the easy atmosphere of the bar. The word "informer" was not used, but none of them was under any illusions.

"Hey, I'm no tout," said Vinnie, and protested his innocence until Blair interrupted.

"It's not as simple as that. What about the amnesty you signed?"

"I signed no such thing."

He felt queasy. How did they know?

"A wee word to the boys that you were joyriding again and you're limping for the rest of your days."

"Or we lock you up," Eric chipped in. "And there's no telling how long. We can lose you in the system for years. And that's before you even come to trial."

"The Rah'd never let me near them with my record," said Vinnie.

"We'll think of something."

"They despise us hoods."

"Weren't you in the Fianna?"

"And got thrown out."

The Fianna was the boys' section of the IRA. Their knowledge of the amnesty and the Fianna made Vinnie see that they already had him boxed in.

Eric leaned forward. "Spelling it out in simple letters. One, go to prison. Two, you walk out of here, we tell the Provos and you're broken legs. Three, stick with us and mum's the word."

They droned on, as insistent as a couple of metronomes, swapping to let the other take over, each relaxed, like nothing was at stake.

Vinnie tried to remember more about the film they'd been talking about. There had been amphetamines and cider before, and the smell of her shampoo and taste of her mouth in the dark were strong in his memory. In the frightening bits she had buried her face in his chest and squealed, which made him wonder about her Proddy orgasms. It was the only time he had gone out with a Prot, the first he'd kissed.

"How much is it worth?" he heard someone ask, then realized it was himself.

"Depends what you give us," said Eric genially. "The top-quality boys get six hundred a month, sometimes. Tax free."

"Tax free, skipper," echoed Heinz. "No fucking around with the Revenue. Just between us."

"I still can't see it," said Vinnie.

"One more thing you should know."

Vinnie looked at them and saw that the choice had never been his.

"The name of the girl," said Heinz.

"Still in a coma," said Eric.

"What's her name, Vinnie?"

"I told the other peeler, I just met her."

"Maureen?"

"Something like that. Or Marie."

"It's Maureen. And her second name?"

"Kelly?"

"McMahon. Maureen McMahon."

It meant nothing.

"Who's her da, Vinnie?"

"Mr. McMahon."

He wasn't trying to be facetious.

"Try Eamonn McMahon."

Vinnie was still puzzled.

Heinz added, "Maureen McMahon, only beloved daughter of Eamonn McMahon. You know what they say about the Ardoyne Provos."

The sentence hung in the air.

"If McMahon knew, you wouldn't last two days, in prison or on the street," said Eric. "Come in with us and your slate's clean."

"Don't worry, skip. We're safe hands. We've not dropped one yet."

They left the pub and drove to a district Vinnie didn't know, with wide avenues, and stopped in the apron of a large modern hotel on the outskirts of the city, parking in a corner in the shadows, away from the overhead lights. Most of the spaces were empty, showing neat white lines painted on concrete. The remains of the day's rain lay in puddles.

Telephone numbers were given, which he had to commit to memory. They gave him a name and showed him a photograph of a middle-aged man that looked like it had been taken from a surveillance car. Vinnie knew him by sight and the bar where he drank. Blair told him to see what nights the man went there and the sort of people he met.

"Nothing to it," Blair said. "Just sitting in bars, drinking. That's all we're asking."

At least it was a normal bar, thought Vinnie, and not a barricaded republican drinking club.

Vinnie was given twenty pounds for his time. Fuck you, he thought, on your mothers' graves.

Nine

RAYMOND WILSON sat next to his sister in their over-neat front room, staring at them dourly. Cross was struck by the accuracy of Westerby's description of them, particularly of Margery, who really did look like she was in a time warp. Westerby had thought that she was perhaps re-enacting the part of their mother, an observation that Cross was sceptical of, though now saw was shrewd.

"How many members do the Carriers of Christ have?" Cross asked Margery and her brother replied, "You would have to ask each apostle."

"And how many apostles are there?"

Wilson's look said the question was stupid. "Twelve, of course."

"And each apostle has how many disciples?"

Wilson spread his hands in a gesture of infinity.

"How many copies of your pamphlet do you publish?"

"You would have to ask Apostle Barnabus. He is in charge of publication."

Tiring of Raymond, Cross turned to Margery and asked how many members of the Carriers of Christ were known to her personally. She looked flustered and referred the question to her brother, who sat in stubborn silence.

Cross sighed and passed Wilson a copy of the newspaper advertisements. "They were placed by you."

Wilson made a show of pretending the print was too small to read. Cross bluntly pointed out that it was his name on the booking form.

"What does it mean? 'This prayer must be published after the third day,' " Cross asked.

"It was on the third day that Christ rose. We are merely his carriers. Isn't that so, sister Margery?"

Margery Wilson mumbled that it was. Cross was having trouble keeping his temper.

"What do the initials C.S. stand for at the end of the advertisement?"

"Christ Saves. It is the usual form of greeting between the Carriers."

He drew Wilson's attention to the religious advertisement below theirs. Westerby's efforts to trace its placer had drawn a blank. The mislaid copy details had been located by the newspaper but both name and address had turned out to be false. But, like the Wilsons' entries, it had been paid for by postal order, which needed neither signature nor personal details, and Cross wondered if it too mightn't have some connection to the Carriers of Christ.

Wilson lifted his spectacles and squinted, then covered one

eye and held the paper to his face. His expression turned gradually to uncontrolled rage. "What is this? 'When God has forsaken His mansion the Devil must do His work.'" He jumped to his feet, quivering and working his mouth until threads of spittle formed. "Blasphemy! Blasphemy!"

Margery raised her hands in surprised benediction, with an expression that Cross took to be a combination of arousal and fear. Wilson snorted incoherently until she stood and smoothed his forearm with her hand.

"I'm sure the policeman didn't mean to upset you."

Wilson's eyes rolled up to the ceiling and he began muttering. "Save us, O Lord, from the abominations of evil. Deliver us into the valley of peace. Praise the Lord in His wisdom and cast aside the temptations of Satan."

He sank to his knees, hands clasped. Cross turned to Margery, saying that he had no further questions.

"Brother Raymond, I will be back to pray with you after I've shown these people out."

Cross paused on the doorstep and said to Margery, "We're working on the theory that the dead man had some connection with one of the advertisements. Perhaps yours."

"Oh no, we're very select. There's no one who would fit your description. A tramp, you said, oh no, nothing like that." Her eyes were bright with strange excitement, her voice singsong and breathless. "In spite of what my brother told you, we are a very small and dedicated organization and our membership is very respectable. Sometimes I think that we should cast our net wider."

"Why did your brother get so upset just now?"

"Sister Margery!"

She and Cross both started. Neither had heard Raymond enter the hall.

"Leave these people to their business," he announced stiffly.

"Yes, brother Raymond," she replied, her voice hardly a whisper, her expression one of cowed terror.

In the car, Cross reflected on Raymond Wilson's anger, that inflammable mix of bigotry and fear so symptomatic of the country and so quick to explode. He asked Westerby what she thought.

"I thought he was just an old ham, sir, until I saw how scared she was."

"How old do you think they are?"

"She's older, late forties, though it's hard to say with her got up like that. And I think it's part of his thing to pretend to be older because it gives him authority. But all that eye-rolling and claiming he can't see is just faking."

"Why's that?"

"If they are, well, do you mind if I call a spade a spade, sir?"

"Go ahead."

"Well, if they are fucking then they're going to pretend they're not, even to themselves. It would involve a lot of pretending."

"How do you know all this, if you don't mind my asking?"

"Father was a shrink, sir."

Hence calling a fuck a fuck. He had been shocked.

"Whereabouts?"

"Purdysburn."

Purdysburn was the big psychiatric hospital on the outskirts of Belfast.

"Ever tempted to follow him?"

"No future in it. I'm going to be the first woman chief constable."

MAUREEN MCMAHON was gone when they got to the hospital, her bed occupied by a stranger.

"Where the hell is she?" Cross asked the ward nurse.

The nurse knew nothing, having only just come on duty, so Westerby went off in search of a sister.

Cross had been embarrassed by the speed with which Blair had discovered Maureen McMahon's identity. He had simply checked with the city's Catholic schools and found someone who remembered her. He'd also told him that her father was high up in the Provisionals.

"He's blown up half Belfast. And he hates the RUC since we beat up his sister."

Despite misgivings, Cross had arranged to meet McMahon. He regarded it his responsibility as senior officer to inform next-of-kin in person about any death or serious accident. Tracing him had not been easy. The Provisionals were suspicious of the initial contact, and denied knowledge of his whereabouts. In the end Cross had turned again to Blair, who revelled in that sort of fixing. In less than three hours he had a number that would get a message to McMahon.

McMahon had returned the call personally. When Cross said he wanted to talk about his daughter, McMahon announced coldly that she was no longer his responsibility, but when Cross told him of her condition there was a sharp intake of breath.

Westerby returned with the news that Maureen had been moved to a private room on the sixth floor.

"On whose authority?"

"Her father's."

The door to Maureen McMahon's room was closed and a man with the unmistakable look of a bodyguard lounged on a chair outside.

"You're expected," he said. "But she stays out here."

Cross told Westerby to wait and went in.

Eamonn McMahon sat hunched forward by his daughter's bed, staring at her intently as though his will alone could bring her back to consciousness. He looked up as Cross closed the door.

"Ah, the police. Thank you for taking the trouble to contact me personally."

The voice was mocking. McMahon remained seated. Wiry carrot hair and watery eyes made him seem boyish and vulnerable, in contrast to his fearsome reputation. He was neatly dressed in jacket and tie. It was strange inspecting the senior IRA man at such close quarters. He seemed mild mannered and self-effacing, but Blair had warned him not to be fooled.

"You're a hard man to find," said Cross.

"What brings an English policeman to Belfast?" asked McMahon, picking up on his accent.

"My wife."

"Ah, a Protestant?"

Cross ignored him.

"Well, she would be, wouldn't she?" said McMahon. He sat lost in thought for some time before standing up and deliberately planting himself too close to Cross. He was several inches shorter but used his lack of height as a form of control, keeping his voice low so that Cross had to stoop.

"Inspector, knowing the circumstances of my daughter's accident will not help me come to terms with the dreadfulness of what has happened. We were not close lately but that does not diminish the pain I feel. And it is not a pain I wish to share or discuss with a member of the Royal Ulster Constabulary. From what I can see, you are only here to relish the irony of my particular situation, that of an officer of the Republican Army being visited by the sort of random act that I have apparently inflicted on so many others. And no doubt, as you look an intelligent man, the further irony of a man like me having a rebellious daughter has not escaped your attention."

"In the case of serious accident or death most people are reassured by some sort of formal account, preferably from a senior officer," Cross replied, stung.

McMahon clicked his teeth, his loathing of Cross and what he stood for all too evident. Cross—feeling the sharp stab of his own prejudice—advanced, forcing McMahon back, and used his height to bear down on him.

"I don't give a flying fuck about who you are or what you do, and your little whispering tricks. But hear this. Am I speaking loud enough for you?" He was shouting and didn't care. "I do think that the sorry state of your daughter lying there requires some form of proper explanation and if you don't want it that's fine by me."

He turned and walked out, the anger coursing through him. He was vaguely aware of Westerby hurrying after him down the corridor and into the lift. He was glad she had the sense not to say anything.

They were outside before he calmed down. He breathed in a deep lungful of air. The smell of hospital formaldehyde and institutional dinners always depressed him. He noticed it was a fine day for a change and told Westerby to take the car back to the barracks.

"Are you all right, sir?"

"I feel like a walk."

He left her looking puzzled. She drove by a minute or two later and he saw her turn to check that he hadn't changed his mind. He waved her on.

He had gone about a quarter of a mile when his sixth sense warned him of another car slowing down behind him: the moment of every policeman's nightmare. Was it possible McMahon had set him up? He kept walking, fighting panic. A high wall cut off going to his left.

"Inspector."

It was McMahon's voice. For a second Cross thought it was McMahon about to kill him.

"Inspector, can we talk?"

Cross turned warily. McMahon was in the back of the car, window lowered, seemingly unaware of Cross's panic. As he got out, everything returned to normal. Seeing Cross sweating, he asked if anything was wrong. Cross shook his head and McMahon made great play of letting him see the penny drop, looking at the car, then back at Cross.

"Christ, I didn't mean anything by that. I wasn't thinking. I saw you walking and wanted to apologize for my rudeness. You're quite right, you were only doing your job." Cross wondered what had led to this change of heart. "Do you have children, inspector?"

"Yes."

"Then you know what it's like. You want so much for them, too much sometimes. And after a certain age they only see that as interference. Maureen took after her mother in a way. She only wanted what she saw as a normal life and not getting one turned her wild. Do you mind if I ask you a question, inspector?"

Mind or not, McMahon would ask.

"What's a detective from the murder squad doing on this case?"

Cross wondered how McMahon knew which department he worked for. He cautiously explained the body in the road, mentioning the stigmata but not the freezing.

"Did anyone claim it?" The inevitable question.

"No. Though with the wrists being stabbed I thought of torture, and a sectarian connection. IRA informers are usually tortured."

The sentence hung in the air. McMahon decided to ignore it. "If it's a question of identity I know people who could say if he was one of ours or one of theirs, if he was either."

"He was probably nothing to do with anything. The man was dressed like a tramp."

"A tramp? Some of our lot are pretty awful dressers, but they usually just about keep themselves in shape. But I can ask around."

Cross experienced a gnawing anxiety. Had he somehow fallen under the IRA man's influence?

"How do you know which department I work for?"

McMahon gave an enigmatic smile and they parted awkwardly, each unsure how to end their brief truce.

CROSS walked over the Donegall Road and entered the run of streets parallel to Sandy Row and Great Victoria Street. It was all guesswork, he decided, wild stabs in the dark, whether he was dealing with a crazy case of a frozen man or trying to understand the unfathomable motives of Deidre.

He was not sure how to interpret their unexpected resumption of sexual relations, whether to read it as an act of exorcism performed over the ashes of their marriage or a sign of hope.

He walked for a long time until he found himself in the vicinity of the tourist board where Deidre worked. Marketing the unmarketable, as she put it, trying to attract visitors to a country they wouldn't come to if they were paid. She could be very funny about the job, which she attacked with the energy reserved only for the hopeless cause.

When they had first met, Cross had been a policeman for several years and Deidre was attending a course in cordon bleu cookery at a minor Bristol college that was hired to provide and serve the food at a police dance. She kept returning with her tray of vol-au-vents, and because she was beautiful he kept taking them. She wondered what he'd look like with his shirt off, and he was taken by her boisterous un-Englishness, her pale skin and out-of-control hair.

During the disco Cross surprised her by asking her to dance and surprised her again by dancing well. Drink made them bold as they strolled through the dark gardens of the eighteenth-century house where the party was held. When Deidre removed her shoes to walk barefoot on the grass he took it as a sign that he could have her if he wanted. Her mouth was the sweetest he had kissed, her taste and smell unlike anyone else's. He felt liberated, felt like taking risks. They ended up fucking on the lawn under a crescent moon, and when she came unstintingly and joyfully he wondered if it hadn't been she who had seduced him.

Their backgrounds turned out to be remarkably similar, in spite of the difference of wealth: two childhoods stifled by gentility, the difference being that the O'Neills' was the "right" sort.

"They're terrible bigots," Deidre warned.

"Deidre tells me you're a left-footer," Gub O'Neill had said with a hollow cheerfulness that did nothing to disguise his dislike of his prospective son-in-law. "And a Brit."

Gub and Barbara O'Neill were quintessential Unionists, rich Ulster Protestants, a branch of the ruling clan that had run the province for generations. They made it clear that their ambitions for their daughter went further than her ending up with a policeman. But Deidre always did have a rebellious streak and Cross realized that part of her reason for marrying him was to spite her parents. For them it would have been less of a disgrace had Cross been of Ulster stock, but he was English, and, worse, his Catholic origins made him ineligible for the secret societies of freemasonry and Orange Lodges to which all male O'Neills traditionally belonged, by birth and marriage. Cross was the first Catholic to marry into the family.

IT WAS nearly lunchtime, he saw. Deidre came out of the building ten minutes later. Cross was fifty yards down the street, standing in a doorway.

He watched her shopping alone, buying sandwiches, while he tailed her like a suspect and chided himself. In Marks & Spencer she bought lingerie. It struck him that his behaviour was like the start of a murder plan and he laughed off the thought as absurd.

At the cash desk she looked up suddenly. He was sure she had spotted him, but then she turned back to collect her purchase and he melted into the crowd.

The next morning he feigned sleep, watching her dress through half-closed eyes, aware of the stirring in his groin. He wondered if the lingerie had been bought for herself or for the sake of her new man. Whichever, she didn't put it on that morning. After she had gone he looked for it before going downstairs, but there was no sign of it in her cupboard or drawers.

Ten

HE WATCHED secure in the knowledge that she did not know she was being watched. She left the small terraced house and walked in the direction of the taxi place as usual. He waited, then followed in the car, arriving as her taxi set off. He knew most of her movements and where she drank, and wondered what made her select these anonymous Taig bars in urban precincts, barricaded behind their wire cages.

He was careful to avoid following her into them, tempted as he was to get closer, and waited outside. Usually she left with a man. Most of them he had grown to recognize, all Taigs. She occasionally took them to another bar, in Protestant Shankill, a journey that usually involved a change of taxi. There the men ran nervously up the back steps that went to a room on the first floor with its own entrance. Sometimes she drew the curtains, often not. Afterwards, the men left alone, looking nervous, the effect of the fuck already undone by the prospect of hurrying back to safety through loyalist streets.

She never used this bar to pick up men, though sometimes she visited the landlord, to return the favour of being allowed to use the room, he supposed.

It was strange, the feeling of knowing her so well without her knowing him. Knowing her name, her birthday, where she lived, her telephone number, watching sometimes as she walked the kiddies to school. Had it really been a year since he had decided on her? He would be sad when it ended. He liked this stage, feeling like a guardian angel. It was part of the control, this sense of being able to alter destinies.

Seamus, who used to live with her, had been gone seven or eight months now. He had followed him too, from the house to where he worked as a joiner on a building conversion in the city centre and drank sometimes in a big bar nearby.

Seamus had looked suspicious at his approach, which was only to be expected, and frightened, too. He was with the security forces, he said, and there was something urgent he had to pass on concerning his safety.

"Name any bar and I'll meet you there in five minutes, ten minutes, whatever you say. What I have to say won't take long."

Quarter of an hour later Seamus walked into the place he'd named, still looking suspicious.

"You should know your name is on a list," he told him once they were settled with drinks.

"What kind of list?"

"A list of the Ulster Volunteer Force."

Seamus said there had to be a mistake. He was just a carpenter and not even a republican.

"They've mixed you up with another man of the same name, muddled the addresses."

"Jesus." As it dawned on Seamus that he might be killed he began to panic. "Christ, what can I do?"

He asked why his name could not be taken off the list.

"I've no influence in these matters."

"What am I to do?" Seamus kept repeating. "Are you sure?"

"I saw the list myself. With your name and address. And a photograph too."

"What am I supposed to have done?"

"All I know is that your name is on the list."

"Suffering Jesus. This is a nightmare."

They had stayed in the pub until closing time, Seamus using drink as the solution to his problem. He talked about the woman he was living with and her children, which weren't his, and as he rambled on his dissatisfaction with life became evident.

He studied Seamus like a specimen. Tell anyone they have only a short time to live and they see life only in terms of regret. This stupid carpenter was no different, and in the end he welcomed the advice to flee for his own safety and to tell no one. He was to tell his woman that he had work in the South and would send for them when he could. He was to do this immediately, because his safety could not be guaranteed.

Seamus went home and delayed, pretending that what had

happened that evening hadn't taken place. But then the stranger came a second time, to the house, and said he would not warn him again, time was running out, and Seamus panicked and disappeared as he was told.

In the months that followed, the sadness and disappointment grew on Mary's face. He began watching her more closely, following her to the chemist for the pills she hadn't needed until then, and noting the start of the drinking and picking up men. Once or twice he thought of going with her just to hold her and listen to her heartbeat. But he didn't. Only in control was there tenderness.

The day would come soon. He read the Bible and picked out the right bit for her. Soon she would be relieved of her misery. He noticed that about death, the gentler ones at any rate: faces lost all trace of suffering.

The red car would come for her. They could try and trace that but it wouldn't do any good: it would be destroyed by then. She would come to where he was waiting, come willingly because he would have talked to her beforehand, telling her he had news of her man gone to the South.

"It's Mary, isn't it? You're the spitting image of Seamus's description."

Just to be able to say that—to see the hope in her eyes—was why he had sent the man away.

DROWNINGS upset Cross more than other deaths. Everybody felt bad about them, even the usually imperturbable scene-of-crime squad.

Cross stood hunched in his overcoat, feeling miserably exposed to the cold night air. There had been a change in the weather soon after he'd arrived at the lough. Large snowflakes had started to fall and before they were done the ground was white and one of his shoes leaked.

Death by drowning produced its own sluggish rhythm and a profound silence different from other deaths, as though the act of immersion put the corpse at an even further remove. This one had been only a short time in the water, with none of the bloating of the long drowned. She was shoeless, dressed only in a tatty skirt, blouse and extravagantly coloured cardigan. Bruising to the neck indicated that she might have been strangled first. The lack of coat suggested that this had not been done outdoors.

Looking at her mottled skin and sodden clothes, Cross could not picture her ever having been anything but dead. Usually he was only too aware of how alive they had been and his lack of feeling in this case troubled him. He wondered who she was. It was the main sadness of his work, knowing his role was to arrive too late.

Deidre was asleep when he got home, and up and dressed before he woke the next morning. The light beyond the curtains seemed unnaturally bright and clean, and for a moment he could not remember why.

A carpet of white covered the garden. Snow hung from the trees and the sun shone in a clear sky, not yet warm enough to start the thaw that would turn it to slush before lunchtime. The children were already out, wrapped up, and starting a snowman. Cross knocked on the window and waved. He could hear Fiona's squeals of delight beyond the double glazing as she jumped up and down, waving back.

THE DEAD woman was identified as Mary Elam, aged forty-two, when her sister, Josephine Reilly, reported her missing, after hearing of the death on the local news. She duly confirmed to Westerby that the body in the morgue was Mary.

Cross's morning was spent on paperwork for other killings—routine domestic disputes and a pub knifing, all despatched with what felt like unseemly haste, files closed almost as soon as they were opened. He suspected Mary Elam would be the same. Most of his murders were like that, Friday night affairs where drink had been taken. One case on his desk involved a drunken husband who had bludgeoned his wife to death then phoned the police. Cross had arrived to find him cradling the dead woman and bawling like a baby. His own conscience had been troubled by the selfish relief he had felt at being called out instead of having to go home.

By one o'clock the snow was slush and the sun, having done its work, disappeared behind low cloud, leaving Belfast to its customary grey. It was drizzling by the time he went with Westerby to a house in an older part in their district, a mixed neighbourhood of grimy two-ups and two-downs where Mary Elam and her sister lived.

Several children peered anxiously from the end of the dark hallway. Cross counted five, an older boy and the rest four or five years at the most. Three of them turned out to be Mary Elam's and were being looked after by Josephine, a tired-looking woman in her late thirties.

She showed Cross and Westerby into the good room of the house. The children, all too curious to show any grief, gathered in the doorway, drawn by the novelty of a visit from the police.

Josephine said, "It's all right, I've told them but it's not sunk in yet, except maybe with Liam."

Liam, the oldest, was beckoned forward and sat on the arm of Josephine's chair. He told Cross he was eleven.

"And you understand from your aunt what has happened?" asked Cross.

The boy nodded gravely.

"This is WPC Westerby," Cross went on. "Perhaps you could take her and the others into the kitchen while I ask your aunt a few questions. I'll not take long."

Josephine Reilly turned out to be quite precise in her answers and needed little prompting. She seemed to have decided that the best way to deal with her grief was to be as factual as possible.

"I saw Mary on the Monday morning. She lives only two doors away so we saw a lot of each other, but I didn't see her the rest of that day and on the Tuesday she gave the children breakfast as usual, according to Liam. She didn't take them to school that morning. Sometimes she walked with them or she left Liam in charge. He's a responsible boy and there are no roads to cross except one where there's a lollipop patrol, though I don't know why I'm telling you that. When they came back after school Mary was not there but that's not unusual. She has a habit of going off without saying and when that happens the children stop over here."

"How do you mean, she went off?" asked Cross.

"Gallivanting." Josephine smiled wanly. "Mary liked a good time. It's no problem for me to look after the kids."

"She went off without telling you?"

"Not always. But Mary didn't keep the same time as the rest of us. She lived in a different world and that's what we loved about her. With Mary you can feel like you're away from yourself, and for the kids being with her was more of a holiday than

I can ever manage. She was blessed with an imagination. I need to feel the ground under my feet."

She started crying silent tears.

"You've no idea who she went to see on the Tuesday."

"I've no idea who she went to see ever. It was never local."

"And how long was she away on these occasions?"

"A night or so, but, like I said, it was nothing for me to look after the wee ones."

Cross asked to look at Mary's house and said that he could go on his own if it was too upsetting for her. Josephine nodded.

"It's number forty-three. The key's on a string through the letter box."

Mary's house was the mirror image of Josephine's, with rooms to the left rather than the right of the front door. Other than that, it was another world. The hall was a fantasy of drapes, the ceiling a dark blue stuck with stars and crescent moons of gold. As Cross moved to enter the front room he drew back, startled by some peripheral flicker, and waited for the shock to settle. Peering through the crack of the door, he saw that the television set had been left on without the sound. What was it about this country, he thought, that compelled everyone to leave the television on regardless of whether anyone was watching? Even his rich parents-in-law did it.

He switched off the set and looked around. The room was even more startling than the hall, like something out of *The Arabian Nights*, with more drapes, this time fixed to the ceiling, and cushions scattered on the floor. Looking closer, Cross saw that underneath it was like thousands of other rooms in the city, with its three-piece suite, no doubt bought on hire purchase, cheap carpet and Sacred Heart of Jesus above the mantelpiece. An old white telephone, grubby with age, stood on a table beside the sofa and scrawled on the wall behind were numbers, some with names by them, all men's.

The rest of the house showed no evidence of housekeeping. The fridge was unstocked and what looked like six months' supply of empty wine bottles lay around. Upstairs the beds were unmade and in the largest room a cupboard was stuffed with garish clothes, jumble shop bargains by the look of them. Dozens of candles were stuck in wax-encrusted saucers. Cross couldn't help contrasting the orderliness of his own home with the imaginative chaos of Mary Elam's.

It was her, he presumed, in the curled photograph on the dresser—a striking-looking woman, well preserved in spite of poverty, with a look of mischief and defiance. Cross wondered how long it had been since he'd seen the same look in Deidre's eye.

Eleven

Belfast, July 1971

CANDLESTICK had crossed over the water that July, in the summer of Rod Stewart, after falling in with another soldier on leave in Liverpool by the name of Baker. He joined him on the ferry with five others for a drinking spree that ended in Belfast, where Baker had relatives. Baker, with his military swagger, was treated as a local hero among his own kind, a tough man to be bought drinks, who could advise loyalists how best to organize their own defence against the IRA. The mood in Protestant Shankill that summer was one of uncertainty and fear.

After the other soldiers drifted home, Candlestick remained, ostensibly on account of a woman he was seeing. When his leave was nearly up, Baker told him it would be worth staying for the opportunities presented by the paramilitaries' fledgling protection rackets. Teenage gangs called the Tartans were doing most of the collecting, mainly at the instigation of a clamp-jawed fanatic McKeague, dismissed by Baker as a toy soldier. The collections were erratic and badly run.

"These fellows are crying out to be organized."

Candlestick sensed that Baker needed him for an audience and went along with Baker's picture of them as the only reliable elements in a world of intrigue and rumour, forged by their common army bond, professionals among amateurs. It was second nature for them to watch each other's backs, he said, though by then Candlestick had decided Baker was a fantasist, happy to subscribe to Belfast as a cowboy town with himself as the hero. When Baker started to hint that he was on special duty, Candlestick let himself be gradually persuaded, after an initial scepticism. Baker said he had been approached through his regiment on account of knowing Belfast and offered a clandestine operation. He added that he was recruiting, if Candlestick was interested.

Candlestick shrugged and said that was beside the point. He was probably listed as missing from his regiment.

"That's the last thing they care about. I've been given fucking immunity, man. We can rob banks if we want."

Candlestick was curious about Baker's employer. Baker clearly didn't know who was hiring him, though it hardly mattered, from what Candlestick could see. The only clear thing about Belfast that summer was that everyone was operating in the dark-street riots, the erection of barricades turning sections into no-go areas, mass early-morning arrests, the law of the assassin's bullet.

Candlestick made a phone call that night and said, "I'm in."

No QUESTIONS were asked by Baker's handler, Captain Bunty, when he met Candlestick at the Candlelight Inn in Rosemary Street. Belfast was, as Baker said, wide open and Bunty implied that they were free to take what they wanted in exchange for getting in with the Protestants.

"At the moment the Prods couldn't hit a barn door at two feet. On the other hand, we can't be seen to be helping them."

Bunty was a soft man with glasses and a rosebud mouth. He cultivated an air of fastidious detachment, occasionally expressing bewilderment at the stubbornness of the Irish.

He shook hands as they left and said that he would get the two guns Baker wanted. A garage owner named Tommy Herron was the man he wanted them to watch because when the various local defence organizations amalgamated, as they soon would, Herron would come out on top.

Although Baker and Candlestick were familiar figures in Protestant West Belfast, they were not known on Tommy Herron's patch in the east. Baker suggested they announce themselves in style, so they swaggered into a vigilante bar on the Newtownards Road and asked for the man in charge. When no one stepped forward Baker laid his newly acquired Browning on the counter. The room went quiet.

"Tell your man to be here this time tomorrow."

Candlestick found the atmosphere both hostile and demoralized on that first visit. When they returned the next day it was plain mean. The man who introduced himself was a big man going to fat. He was with two dockers and didn't seem impressed.

"Who collects your donations, Mr. Eddoes?" asked Baker.

"What business is it of yours?"

"It's our business all right. We're in the business of charity collection."

The man on Eddoes' right took a step forward and Baker let him see the gun in his waistband. When he hesitated Candlestick flattened him anyway. After that they adjourned with Eddoes to a back room.

"What are your rates?" asked Baker.

"Twenty-five pence a week at least for householders and forty quid a week for businesses."

"And how efficient are your collections?"

Eddoes looked sulky. Baker stood up.

"It's no skin off our noses. You're in a mess. We're trained, you're not. Now answer the question."

"Enough gets back, but I suspect some fellows are out for themselves."

"We'll put a stop to that. You're wasting your time if it's just going into some tearaway's pockets. We'll make everything neat and tidy. We'll arrange your collections and you can work out how to distribute them. The basic rate stays the same but businesses should be fifty quid, with a review of those that can afford more. What I'm proposing will double your money in a month and we'll pay you one per cent for the privilege."

Eddoes made greedy eyes and asked for three. They split the difference. When Baker announced their fee was seven and a half per cent Eddoes yelped in protest.

They took over immediately. Their main rival was McKeague, a violent homosexual who surrounded himself with a cohort of youths. For reasons that Candlestick never understood, Bunty took great interest in spreading word of McKeague's criminal record for buggery, gradually discrediting him until he was isolated from the rest of the UDA.

On his collection rounds Candlestick made a point of being polite, treating those he was extorting like valued customers. Many grumbled that their money was going straight into private pockets. The purchase of seaside caravans was said to have flourished since the introduction of the levy. Candlestick said that was all changing and was careful to cultivate an impression of honesty until his presence on the street brought a sense of security and contributors fooled themselves into believing they were getting value for their money.

The few businesses that were reluctant to cough up did so after Candlestick threw a recalcitrant shop owner through his own window. The story spread until it came to the attention of Tommy Herron, who by then was the leader of the newly formed Ulster Defence Association, as Captain Bunty had predicted.

"What brings a couple of Brits to Belfast?" asked Herron in the upstairs room of the Vulcan bar.

"We're the Magnificent Seven," said Baker.

"You're five short of a full house," said Herron, amused.

"Laugh if you want. It's your town needs protecting."

Herron looked at Candlestick. "Have you got anything against shooting Fenians?"

"Not if I'm paid."

Herron laughed his big laugh and ordered up more drinks. He was drinking Red Heart, a bottled stout made by a Catholic brewery for sale in Protestant areas, and he chased it with Scotch, Candlestick noticed, rather than Irish whisky. He toasted them, saying what excellent fellows they were. "My kind of boys."

Unlike other loyalists they had met, Herron had a plan. He dismissed the rank and file of the association as an ill-disciplined rabble with a propensity for drink and idle threats.

"We should be out fighting the IRA, not sitting in pubs nattering like a bunch of old women."

"What about the Ulster Volunteer Force?" asked Baker.

"The Ulster Volunteer Force has less than half a dozen men with any leadership ability, and one's half mad. And in the last two years it has done absolutely fuck all, apart from rob a few banks, damage a memorial, blow up a bloody pylon and bomb the home of a nationalist MP. What is needed, gentlemen, is a reign of terror. It's the only way to bring those Fenian bastards to their knees. Are we speaking the same language?"

They were. Recognizing their talent for violence, Herron made them bodyguards to the UDA's inner council. He swore them in personally in an upstairs room decorated with the various flags of the union. There was a sword and a Bible on a table and the witnesses wore camouflage and dark glasses. Candlestick found the whole process slightly risible, a bunch of pasty-faced, overweight men pretending to be Hibernian gunslingers. They'd need some teaching, he thought, as he listened to Baker declaiming the oath of allegiance.

"Being convinced in my own conscience that there is a conspiracy to bring about a united Ireland by use of force," Baker recited, "I will actively defend, by any and all means possible, the area under the control of the Council."

"WHO ARE all you guys?" Candlestick asked Bunty when he felt he knew him well enough, not that he expected an answer.

Bunty laughed. He was drunk but not yet indiscreet.

"We're the cowboys. All the rest are the Indians."

Candlestick by then understood that Bunty was using them to encourage Herron and the UDA to operate on two fronts. Bunty wanted the Protestant paramilitaries to fight their own war against the IRA, and also to terrorize the local Catholic population into rejecting its support for the IRA. The message "ALL TAIGS ARE TARGETS" had begun to appear daubed on loyalist walls. Candlestick was left wondering to what extent Herron was a puppet of the British, perhaps even being run by Bunty.

Bunty laughed even harder in December when a bomb went off in McGurk's bar in North Queen Street, killing fifteen Catholics. The security forces announced an IRA own-goal, when it was in fact the work of the UVF, an operation planned by Baker and Candlestick.

"Hell of a bang," said Bunty. "Any retaliation?"

Candlestick said he had heard that the IRA had taken to driving around and shooting Protestants on the streets.

"Fuck me, no. Pardon my indiscretion, it's the Brits doing that."

Candlestick realized he still had a lot to learn.

Twelve

THE BIG clock on the wall said the man was late. Vinnie listened to the noise of traffic bleed into the country music song on the jukebox. He was waiting in the same bar they'd taken him to before. It was large and crowded enough not to attract attention but not yet full, which made him feel exposed.

Most of the time Vinnie was able to persuade himself that he had the cunning to see both sides off. He'd survive. He had always lied well, though he preferred to think of it as making up stories. As a kid he had been good at avoiding punishment.

He sat and waited for the policeman and rued his breaks. Maybe if he hadn't lost his regular girlfriend as a result of the whole business he'd have had the strength to resist getting sucked into the peeler's net. The night he had gone off joyriding he had lost her to Brendan, who was supposed to be his best friend. This girl—not the one he'd been joyriding with— let him have sex without a rubber because of a scam she had of getting the pill from a sister in Manchester.

When Vinnie found out about her and Brendan he was that upset he went out and stole a car, an Astra GL, regardless of any threat of punishment. He drove down to Twinbrook, where he put on a show for a crowd that gathered to watch him burning up the road and doing handbrake turns. He didn't care who saw or if anyone caught him. But nothing happened and soon after eleven he went home, dumping the Astra on the way.

Feeling he had nothing left after losing the girl—both girls, with the McMahon one still in hospital, he'd heard—Vinnie started watching the IRA man, O'Mara, as a way of mourning for the rubber-free girl, who would not even come to the door when he'd gone round. He drank in O'Mara's pub, taking Des, a friend from his Fianna days, who had kept a clean sheet since.

Des knew people in the pub and Vinnie found himself on the fringes of a crowd of more or less decent citizens, most of whom he knew by sight.

O'Mara usually arrived late and drank only a couple of beers. At first Vinnie was not sure if he intended to pass on any of this information, which struck him as pretty pathetic. Anyway, he preferred the look of O'Mara to either Heinz or Eric with their stupid pretend names. O'Mara looked like the jolly farmer in an old children's picture book of his, always laughing and joking.

The meeting Heinz was late for was their third. He hadn't seen Eric since the first.

When Blair arrived twenty minutes late, the bar was full enough for Vinnie to feel less anxious. Blair asked how the job was going.

"Fine," said Vinnie.

"I hear you were ill today."

"That's right," said Vinnie, refusing to be drawn. "Amazing how news gets around."

He'd slept in because of a hangover.

Blair had arranged for Vinnie to do a labouring job on a building site in the north of the city for a contractor who paid cash and asked no questions. Vinnie was suspicious when the offer was made, but, as he had not worked in a year and liked money, he decided to take the job and play dumb with Heinz on the question of information. But it didn't turn out like that. Instead, Vinnie realized he was being outmanoeuvred when the policeman gave him the address of a loyalist arms dump to pass on to O'Mara.

"To give you an in, like," said Blair.

The story was that Vinnie had come by the information during an evening's drinking with another labourer, a Protestant—he was even given a name—who bragged of knowing about the weapons and had taken the sceptical Vinnie along to look.

Vinnie wondered at the extent of Blair's plan, and how the bits were meant to fit together: fixing him with work that gave him access to information to pass on to O'Mara, to what end?

Blair finished his drink quickly.

"No more for me, but get yourself another."

He gave Vinnie twenty pounds. When Vinnie came back from the bar the other man was gone.

Later that evening Vinnie approached O'Mara and asked if he could have a word. O'Mara inclined his head, like a bishop receiving an audience.

"What about, son?"

"In private," said Vinnie, like he was in *The Godfather*. "If you don't mind."

O'Mara nodded to a man across the bar and all three went into a back room, which was empty except for stacked chairs. Vinnie was frisked and declared clean by the minder. O'Mara cocked his head, indicating that Vinnie should step forward, and when he did O'Mara drove his fist into the softness of his stomach.

It was a clinical punch, executed with the minimum of fuss, Vinnie realized, even as he gasped for air, doubled over. He was aware of O'Mara gently holding him by the shoulders, massaging them, and making him stay down until he had got his breath back.

"There, there. You'll be right as rain in a second."

When Vinnie had recovered enough to stand up, O'Mara patted him on the face.

"No more cheek, son. So long as you understand that, we'll get along fine."

Thirteen

CROSS asked for, and got, extra help to carry out a door-to-door inquiry to help reconstruct the missing thirty-six hours in the life of Mary Elam.

Catholic neighbours were reluctant to co-operate, Mary having been one of theirs. Rather than imply criticism of her lax behaviour, they preferred to pretend ignorance, beyond acknowledging her as a bit of a lark and surely the sister of a

saint. Local Protestants were more forthcoming. To them Mary
Elam was a woman of loose morals and an inadequate mother.

"There's several screws missin', for a start," said the woman
living adjacent. But for all her nosy vigilance, she hadn't seen
anything either. "She doesn't do it on her own doorstep, that's
for sure, and she's easy enough to spot skippin' down the road,
but I remember nothing on the Tuesday. Mind, the curtains are
always drawn and half the time she's sleepin' off the drink."

Bennett's, the local taxi firm, was at least able to provide
details of Mary's regular haunts, Catholic bars on the edge of
the district and beyond. But she had not been spotted in any
during the unaccounted-for period.

Cross asked Hargreaves to organize tracing the men connected to the telephone numbers on Mary's living room wall. It
was a job that required more discretion than Cross thought him
capable of. But as most of the men would probably turn out to
be married, he figured they'd probably rather talk to a man, so
he told Westerby to look into Mary's background.

Cross sought relief in working long hours on the case. The
days bled into each other and his domestic problems receded.
Several nights it was after midnight before he finished. Too
tired to drive home and too late to call Deidre, he slept in the
cells.

Hargreaves had little to report on Mary Elam's men. "The
general picture, like one of her casual fellers said, is of a girl
who liked a good time."

"Any suspects?"

Hargreaves shook his head. Cross turned and asked Westerby for her report on Mary.

"She was an affectionate if careless mother, but Josephine
could be relied on to look after the children. There seems to
have been no bad feeling about that. However, Mary's behaviour did come to the attention of the welfare people, who inter-
viewed her. I've not talked to the social worker as she's away,
but Josephine says it caused a lot of resentment because the
local Catholics were sure it was a Protestant neighbour who'd
reported her."

Cross suspected that Mary's promiscuity was the real cause
of affront. Her friendships with men depended on favours or
presents in exchange for sex. The pattern of sexual activity was
interesting, he thought. It took place away from home and

often involved travelling by taxi to one of several pubs. It seemed Mary only had sex with men she knew, though there were at least a dozen of those. Cross asked Hargreaves where they went, given that she didn't take them home.

"They were reluctant about that, sir. One said they used his van or went outside in summer."

"What do you think?" asked Cross.

Hargreaves looked stumped. Cross sensed he was embarrassed by the Elam case. He looked at Westerby.

"I think she must have had a room somewhere."

"Go on."

"She wasn't a prostitute in the usual sense and I can see her being quite fussy about where she took them. Not home, for a start. Her bedroom is, well, untidy but quite romantic, not the sort of place you'd take someone unless you knew them well. It also suggests she'd want some comfort, but I can't see her using a hotel because it'd be money she'd rather have for herself."

Cross nodded and told Hargreaves to find out where Mary went with the men because it may have been where she was killed.

Hargreaves looked irritated and sighed noisily when Westerby added, just as it looked as though the meeting was over, "One more thing, sir. This behaviour with men was quite recent."

Cross was surprised. The messy patterns of Mary's life had suggested long-term habits.

"According to Josephine, Mary's disappearances started less than a year ago. Before that she had been a reliable mother, slightly vague but a good provider. She had a man living with her for about three years, not the children's father."

"Where's the children's father?"

"Zaire, the last anyone heard. He's an engineer and before he left five years ago they lived in a smart house, with a car. According to Josephine, Mary had done well for someone of their background."

What followed with the husband was the usual Irish divorce. He was only supposed to be gone a year but then didn't come back. When the cheques stopped coming, Mary sold the house to be near her sister.

"What happened to the other man?" asked Cross.

"Seamus McGinley. Same sort of thing. He drifted off to the Republic to find work—he's a carpenter—and didn't send for them like he'd promised."

"Run a check on both of them, just to be sure."

"I've checked on McGinley," said Westerby. "He's in Galway living with another woman. He reported to work both days of Mary's disappearance. And on the husband I'm waiting to hear back from the consulate."

MARY ELAM'S autopsy confirmed that death was by strangulation. There was no water in the lungs. The skin on her wrists showed signs of chafing, perhaps the result of being bound. The stomach contents revealed nothing unusual. Her liver showed a history of alcohol abuse. There were no signs of sexual intercourse. Ricks, as fastidious as ever, remarked disdainfully, "Unless of course he masturbated into her underwear." The underwear was missing.

Fourteen

HARGREAVES uncovered the first lead in the Elam case. More questioning had produced a witness, an eight-year-old child. Cross was about to hand the statement back when the name of the witness caught his eye.

"Teresa Reilly? Josephine Reilly's daughter?"

Cross couldn't believe that they'd questioned the whole neighbourhood without bothering to check the immediate family. Hargreaves looked embarrassed.

"It's not quite as bad as it looks. The wee girl was upstairs sick with a fever that day and was still in bed when the Reillys were questioned."

"Give the man who spotted it a medal."

"It was me, sir."

Cross looked at Teresa Reilly's statement again. She described seeing someone from her bedroom window who she thought was her Aunt Mary getting into a red van some time on the Tuesday morning. When shown pictures she picked out a Ford Escort.

"We cross-checked on the Vulcan," said Hargreaves. Vulcan was the high-speed computer log of vehicles registered in Northern Ireland. "There are eight red Escorts in the immediate vicinity, all accounted for. We're working on similar ones in the areas where she drank."

"What was her temperature?"

"Her temperature?"

"The little girl's fever, man. If she had a high fever she might have imagined the whole thing."

Cross had not meant to snap, but his gut told him that the girl's description was unreliable.

HIS MOOD did not improve when he discovered later that Westerby was responsible for discovering the Reilly girl and not Hargreaves as he had claimed.

By then Cross had the feeling that his other investigation into the frozen man was close to a state of complete inertia and soon to be consigned to that limbo of unsolved cases whose only chance of revival was a lucky break. It was not a crime that could be sustained by some larger force—like public outrage—which would lead to resources being thrown at it until a solution was produced. It hadn't even rated a mention in the papers.

He went back to the autopsy report. A note of the missing teeth led him to inquire what percentage of the population in their fifties wore sets of dentures and he wasted several hours finding out the depressing answer before abandoning the idea. Checking dental records would be too time consuming for their limited resources. Unlike vehicles, which were computer logged, teeth were still card indexed.

At the end of a frustrating day, Cross decided that his last option was to call Blair, who surprised him by suggesting a drink in the bar. Cross was puzzled by the invitation, as they had never socialized before.

"How's your man in the road?" Blair asked, not sounding that interested.

"Pretty hopeless, but I wouldn't mind another word with the O'Connor boy."

Blair looked evasive, which Cross took to mean that the boy was now Blair's informer.

"I need to give him one more go," said Cross. "I've got nothing else."

"Hardly seems worth the bother."

"Nevertheless."

"I hear McMahon has taken up permanent watch at his daughter's bedside," said Blair, changing the subject. "He ought to be careful. Word will get out."

Mention of McMahon seemed to loosen him up.

Like many officers in the front line, Blair took the attitude that the IRA was a cancer that had to be destroyed by whatever means necessary. It was the fault of gutless politicians that they were left in the absurd position of bending rules which no one really cared about, then were held accountable. Blair was particularly scathing about the term "shoot to kill."

"Of course it's shoot to kill, it's not going to be anything else with the weapons they give us. There'd be a lot more squealing if the IRA was running around completely out of hand."

Cross let him talk on, unwilling to be drawn.

For Blair there were two codes never to be violated: the protection of operational methods and police sources of information. Cross realized that the Stalker inquiry was the real target of his spleen, poking into areas where it would only do damage. Unarmed men in the field of fire deserved what they got.

"We're not cowboys. We do our homework. We have a pretty good strike rate but we're not infallible." Blair took another gulp of beer and said, "Well, at least Sir Jack's fighting our corner. He can't stand Stalker."

Cross pointed out that it was the chief constable who had called for the inquiry in the first place.

"Daft, isn't it? By the way, how do you find Sergeant Hargreaves?"

"He's a good policeman."

"He's put in for a transfer to SB."

Cross was surprised.

"Don't tell him you know. It's early days yet. We should talk about him some time."

"I can't say I know him beyond the job. He's got a crippled daughter, I believe."

It was Blair's turn to look surprised.

"Crippled by a bomb?"

"Since birth, I think. She lives with the mother. They're separated."

"As for the O'Connor boy, I'll see what I can do. But not at the barracks."

"I'll meet him wherever."

Blair phoned the next day to say that Vinnie would be outside the chemist's near York Road station that night at eight. Cross was uneasy as he put down the phone. He was never comfortable in Blair's orbit.

CROSS arrived early at York Road station and passed the time driving around the block. He spotted Vinnie ten minutes later, walking with shoulders hunched against the cold, underdressed in a denim jacket. He let him wait outside the chemist's while he checked neither of them was being followed then pulled up alongside. Vinnie glanced around nervously before getting into the Volvo.

Neither spoke. The boy blew into his hands to warm them. Eventually Cross said that he wanted to go back to the site of the accident.

The boy lit a cigarette. He seemed frightened to Cross, who had a sudden craving to smoke even though it was years since he had.

"Can I have a cigarette?"

Vinnie seemed surprised by the request and Cross felt obliged to offer an explanation.

"I stopped but the smell of that makes me want one again rather badly."

"It's a danger to your health," said Vinnie, handing one across.

Cross lit it with the dashboard lighter. The cigarette tasted strangely sweet, the sensation as familiar as if he had smoked only yesterday. The sudden invasion of nicotine turned him light-headed and he stalled the car at a set of lights.

He drove on, feeling self-conscious and foolish. The boy was inspecting the car with apparent disapproval.

"Did you ever steal a Volvo?" asked Cross, surprising himself with the question.

Vinnie looked taken aback and Cross laughed.

"Off the record."

"Crap car. Too heavy and no speed."

Cross laughed again. He asked Vinnie about himself, whether he had brothers and sisters and what he did. After an initial wariness, the boy chatted easily enough until Cross asked him if he had a girlfriend.

"What's it to you?"

Cross shrugged and half enjoyed the rest of his cigarette, which tasted alternately foul and wonderful.

"What do you want?" Vinnie eventually asked.

"What do you mean?"

"Why're you asking all these questions?"

"No reason, just to pass the time."

"You're not a queer?" Vinnie looked quite resigned to the prospect.

"No, I'm not."

After the shock of the question, Cross saw why the boy had asked—scrounging cigarettes, the unusual intimacy of driving with a stranger at night, his own uncharacteristic lightness.

"You're a Brit, aren't you?"

"Yes."

"You must be daft coming here."

"Probably."

"What did you do it for?"

"My wife comes from here and got homesick."

He looked at Vinnie, whose expression mixed incredulity with curiosity.

"You came here because of your wife?" The concept seemed beyond him.

"And now," said Cross without knowing why, "I find out she's having an affair."

"Get away."

Cross wondered what he was doing and did not particularly care. Just being able to say it out loud was a relief. "What would you do if you found someone you were with had gone off with another fellow?"

"I'd probably kill the both of them."

Cross was startled by the chord it struck in him.

"You may be right, except I've got the children to think of."

"Well, just him, then."

"That should be enough."

"Why are you telling me this?"

Cross, remembering their earlier exchange, laughed and said again, "No reason. Just to pass the time."

Vinnie lit a second cigarette and Cross had to stop himself from asking for another.

As they neared the scene of the accident Cross was reminded of how remote the location was. Without the lights and the vehicles of the security forces to guide him, it took a while to find the spot.

"The man lying in the road was dead when he was run over. He was probably murdered," Cross told Vinnie, after pulling over. "Look around, try to remember exactly what happened and see if there is anything, any detail, you might have overlooked."

He left the boy to walk up and down the road a few times. The night was overcast and, as usual, rain was not far away. Together they went down the bank to where the Range Rover had crashed, and up again without a word. Vinnie appeared withdrawn, dragging hard on his third cigarette.

He let the boy wander around a bit more, though he could see it was hopeless. Vinnie shook his head at Cross and they returned to the Volvo in silence.

"Can you give me another cigarette?"

Cross asked the boy for a match because the dashboard lighter had gone cold. He dragged deeply, exhaled and leaned forward to turn the ignition, light-headed again. The car was slow to start.

"Wait," Vinnie said, remembering.

Cross paused, willing the boy, who only shook his head. He turned the key again. This time the engine fired.

"There was another car," Vinnie blurted. "I heard a car start up, quite a long way off, after the crash. There was that noise an engine makes turning over."

"Before the others got here?"

"Yes."

"And did you hear it passing?"

Vinnie's face screwed up in concentration. "I don't remember."

Which meant it had probably been parked up ahead and

driven away from the crash. Cross drove slowly, looking for a spot where a car might have waited. To the right was the bank. The left side was thick with fir trees and after about two hundred yards was a bend. Past that it seemed that they had gone too far so he turned back.

They almost missed it, a gap in the trees by the bend. Cross stopped and got out, telling the boy to wait.

The space was just wide and deep enough for a car, and there was no ditch to hamper access. It was a good vantage point: anyone waiting there would have had sight of the accident without being seen.

It felt secure in among the trees, sheltered from the chilly wind which was reduced to a gentle soughing in the tops of the pines. Cross looked up at the sky, just visible through the branches, and absorbed its silence, trying to imagine someone waiting whose thoughts would reveal the mystery, if only Cross could tap into them.

Cross returned to the Volvo for a flashlight. Vinnie pointed out that he had left his key in the ignition.

"Not tempted, are you?"

Vinnie laughed. "Like I said, too heavy and too slow."

Closer inspection of the area showed evidence of tyre marks. For the first time since the start of the case Cross felt that click in his head that told him a connection had been made. He was prepared to bet that, in spite of the time passed, the tracks belonged to the car the boy was talking about. He doubted if any others had pulled in there. It wasn't the sort of spot lovers used. He'd have the area gone over first thing in the morning.

Driving back, Cross was scarcely aware of Vinnie, beyond his chain smoking. Cross's excitement detonated the rest of the case in his head—the stigmata, Raymond Wilson's hand crumpling the copy of the advertisement, his sister's look of submission, Westerby's quiet persistence. He could almost hear the hum of the deep freeze that held the frozen body, imagined too being able to visualize for the first time where it might be.

He was hardly aware of the boy talking, and whatever he said in reply must have sounded vague or insincere because Vinnie clammed up, saying that he was crazy even to think of trusting a policeman, let alone a Brit.

They drove in tense silence, with Cross fumbling to

remember the start of the boy's conversation. Clearly what he'd wanted to say was important. It had begun with him asking if it was Cross who had handed him over to "the other peeler." Cross, in his distraction, had missed the point. He had been thinking of Deidre, with a surge of jealousy and lust that had shattered the kaleidoscope of other images in his head.

Cross tried to start the conversation again, apologizing, but failed. Was it a gift of his, he wondered, to reduce others to silence?

About five minutes from York Road station Vinnie started gabbling, the words spewing out of him, half-formed sentences that made little sense, stitched together by panic.

"I talked to the man—I shouldn't ha'. I talked to the man. I talked to the man."

Vinnie repeated it over like a record stuck in a groove.

"What man?"

"The man I shouldn't ha'."

"Who? I can't help unless you tell me who."

"O'Mara."

"Is this something to do with the other policeman?"

Cross felt a wrench of anxiety, a sense that he was being drawn into something better left alone.

Vinnie nodded. He was hiccoughing, tears pouring down his face as he spilled his pathetic story.

When Cross realized what he was being told he interrupted to say that Vinnie should not carry on because, as a policeman, he could not guarantee his silence. He thought how pompous he sounded.

"You said you'd help," whined the boy.

It was too late. He had the gist of the boy's story and was compromised as it was. Besides, he wanted to hear him out. Vinnie's confusion mirrored his own: perhaps a part of him wanted to see himself bawling out his own helplessness in similar fashion.

He did not stop the boy, as he knew he should, and instead told him to go on. His own separate train of thought ran parallel to the boy's tumbling words, but there was some nugget of self-revelation that lay beyond reach.

Cross gripped the steering wheel tighter after Vinnie was done and turned to him. He felt strangely calm, like a man who had just seen off an attack. He realized what it was about himself, an unacknowledged part lived with too long—his silent companion, self-loathing.

"What you're doing is feeding your policeman what O'Mara tells you?"

Vinnie nodded, spent after the exertion of confession. He was being used by Blair to watch the IRA. That much Cross could have guessed, but not what followed. Vinnie had thrown himself at the mercy of the IRA man, who was using him to pass back false information to Blair.

"What have you been asked to say?" Cross asked.

Vinnie wouldn't tell at first and Cross repeated, "I can't help unless you tell me."

"They told me to say that there was a senior officer, an inspector, who was passing on information to the IRA because of being blackmailed."

"Did they give you a name?"

"No. That's all I was told."

"And how were you supposed to have found this out?"

"Because I work in the bar now and overheard the conversation when I was in the cellar changing the barrels. O'Mara meets sometimes in the room above."

What a mess, thought Cross. He doubted if he had it in him to help the boy. It would be far cleaner to go to Blair but Blair would no doubt pass on Vinnie's name to loyalist gunmen.

"Why are you telling me this?" asked Cross. Their conversation was starting to go round in circles.

"I want you to tell me what to do because you're clever."

"Why trust me?"

"Because you treated me like I was a human being instead of a lump of shite."

Had he? He was aware of a curious atmosphere of heightened intimacy.

"Go home and do nothing for the moment," Cross eventually said. "I don't know what I can do, but give me a couple of days and meet me on Saturday at seven outside the station."

CROSS found the house in darkness when he got home, though it was not late. He sat in the kitchen and poured three fingers of whisky, which he drank too quickly while pretending to read the newspaper. After another whisky and eating nothing, he lay beside the sleeping figure of Deidre and again was confronted by the uncomfortable realization that he still desired her.

In the night he awoke and went to the bathroom and masturbated, trying to think of Deidre.

All he knew was that he should not shop the boy to Blair. He would not have the boy's death on his conscience. He was tempted to tell Blair that he knew from a source that the IRA suspected Vinnie of being a tout. That at least would cause Blair to regard his information as tainted and to call off any investigation into a non-existent informer in the RUC. He seemed to have travelled a long way that night, to what end he did not know.

Fifteen

Belfast, April 1972

CANDLESTICK drove Tommy Herron to a hotel on the outskirts of the city where Herron had hired a meeting room. They were joined by two men, one darkly good looking with greying hair, the other much younger and his bodyguard.

"Francis," said Herron. "How're you doing?"

"Fine, fine, Tommy, you old rascal."

"Any objection if my man stays?"

"None," said the other beadily. "If Pat does too."

Pat and Francis, Candlestick thought. What kind of names were they? Not Protestant. He had assumed the meeting was going to be one of Tommy's regular get-togethers with other loyalist leaders. From the way this man was talking it was clear that he was IRA. But this was no tense encounter with the enemy, Candlestick soon realized, rather a pally hard-drinking affair to sort out their different business interests.

"Ach, I've known Franny for years," said Herron on the

drive back to Belfast. He was drunk and garrulous and happy to entertain Candlestick's astonishment at their meeting with Fenians. Breen was a Sticky, he said, a member of the Official IRA who had stayed with the rump of the movement when the Provisionals had split away in 1969.

"Breen's too canny to get caught up in all that fanatical stuff. There's not much of a life to be had in the Provos."

OVER THE next weeks Candlestick became privy to the extent of the two men's interests. At first they seemed concerned only with defining their respective boundaries and reaching agreement over areas of dispute. But then Candlestick came to see that it was more complicated and sophisticated than that. For all their official hostility, there were pockets held in reserve where Breen and Herron acted together. Property stolen in one man's area could be fenced in the other's.

Candlestick sensed that Breen knew exactly what he wanted from Herron. Herron was crafty enough but no match for Breen, whose lazy, amiable air hid a greater application. Candlestick watched Breen bamboozle Herron, then move in with his own proposal, which was that the Officials be allowed to work a racket on building sites in Herron's area.

"Jesus, Francis, I don't know about that. I can't let a bunch of Micks be seen to be running around my patch."

Both men laughed easily.

"Tommy, Tommy. This is money, big profits. We shouldn't let political differences interfere with business."

By then Candlestick had learned a valuable lesson. Nothing was to be taken at face value. On the surface it seemed straight-forward enough—the oppositions and the barricades and the divisions of life in wartime. But beyond that there was another zone where everything moved freely, where opposite numbers met to discuss common interests in backroom deals, where hidden alliances formed and shifted and regrouped.

Candlestick kept his own counsel. He knew better than most that many were not what they seemed. He wondered if Herron knew that he and Baker had been planted by the British, and, if he did, what difference it would make. Of himself he knew that he knew more than Baker, because unlike Baker he had more than one master.

Sometimes he was surprised by how carelessly secrets were

confided. The temporariness of everything—and the invisibility of the enemy—made people curiously lax. Off-duty hours became an excuse for loud-mouthed celebration. Baker's gang of mercenaries operated in a social climate that drew together a mixture of people from right across the security forces. At Saturday night parties in different houses he met off-duty RUC officers and soldiers from the Ulster Defence Regiment. More than once men were pointed out to him and he was told they were Provos. He was never sure whether to dismiss this as far-fetched. The idea of Provos being at these parties against all the odds seemed in keeping with the strange fraternizations of the time. There was a sense in which out-of-work hours were accepted as a period of truce, a relief from the absurdity of the daily conflict.

He even saw Captain Bunty at one of these parties. It was being held in a large, under-furnished, uncarpeted students' house and he was on the stairs talking to a woman who shouted above the din of loud music, "I tell you, the only way is stick it to the fuckers."

A large, voluptuous Hungarian with a raucous laugh had introduced herself as Lena and later told him in bed, after making him come by rubbing his penis between her oiled breasts, that she worked in a massage parlour run by an ex-republican internee that was a front for army intelligence gathering. She mentioned this casually as though it were all a game to be shared and enjoyed. Candlestick thought of Baker strutting around, and Herron and Breen fixing up deals, while Lena lazily told him, as they lay on her crumpled sheets, that a client of hers was a city councillor who was tight with the Provos and knew the names of the gunmen who had killed three soldiers they had picked up and driven off to what they'd promised was a party.

"They shot the boys while they were standing pissing by the road, with their beer mugs still in their hands."

She liked it when he licked her with his fastidious tongue and liked his body, and the fact that he told her nothing of what he did.

"Most of them you can't shut them up," she said.

Candlestick passed on the information about the councillor to Tommy Herron and heard no more. By then Herron was distracted by a struggle with his apparent ally, the army. It was

Breen who'd first told him that the army was not quite the friend he thought it was.

"They're not nice people, Tommy. But then you've probably not had them in your home. They're like pigs on their house searches, kicking doors down in the middle of the night and dragging families out of bed. How would you feel walking down to the corner for a packet of fags, trying to slide by some squaddie with his rifle pointed at your head and barking out orders and probably not yet nineteen years old?"

Herron shrugged and said it wasn't his problem.

"It is, Tommy. They're using you, Tommy."

"Get away."

"I can tell you of at least three shootings of Prods that were not the work of the IRA, but your friends the Brits—soldiers in plain clothes masquerading."

Herron squinted at him suspiciously. "They're fucking amateurs thinking they can run around like cowboys taking pot shots at anyone."

Candlestick had never seen him so enraged. Later he saw how these deaths fitted the larger pattern. It was clear from what he had picked up from Bunty that he and Baker were there to train the loyalists to take the war to the enemy, and part of that involved terrorizing ordinary Catholics into withdrawing support for the IRA. Undercover soldiers killing Protestants in cold blood and pretending it was the IRA was the same policy in reverse, aimed at hardening Protestant resolve.

He also saw what Tommy didn't see: that by passing on this information Breen drew Herron into conflict with the army and took heat off the IRA.

Herron ordered his men to fire on soldiers patrolling the streets of his patch of East Belfast. Candlestick was quite happy to join in, but Baker, he noticed, was never anywhere to be seen.

In the general confusion there were occasions when the army thought it was fighting the UDA only to discover afterwards that it was their own undercover soldiers they were shooting at. In one such battle, which Candlestick heard about from Lena, over a hundred rounds were fired, two soldiers were shot and a wounded plainclothes man was seen being executed with a bullet to the head.

Herron laughed loudly when Candlestick told him this and

laughed even louder when he retold the story to Breen until there were tears of laughter running down their cheeks. Herron also passed on to Breen the information that the Brits were running a republican massage parlour, just in case he was thinking of using it himself. Breen laughed at that too. Candlestick warned Lena of this, casually and in such a way that she understood he could say no more. He thought she seemed regretful when he left. Afterwards he missed her animal smell.

BELFAST became a city in which Candlestick blossomed like blood in water. He recognized that everything was spiralling out of control. The months ahead would become one long drunken killing spree. The phrase "licenced to kill" would be one of the season's jokes—a reference to Protestant bars being used as interrogation and killing centres.

During that heady vigilante summer he became a law unto himself. He produced a pistol in the Strathaven Bar in the Shankill and stole the till money, which he put in his own pocket. As far as Herron was concerned, Candlestick answered only to him, or so he thought. He answered to Bunty too—and another man Bunty didn't know about—but in the end the only one he answered to was himself.

He carried a fragment of a song in his head, lodged there like a splinter of shrapnel: *Hit him on the head with a rolling pin, Jump back, baby, jump back.*

People stood aside for him these days. He wore his violence like a halo.

He walked purposefully through late-night streets on his way to kill a waiter from an East Belfast hotel where Herron and other loyalists gathered. Herron had him down as an informant, and decided to pursue the matter even though the lad was about to transfer to another hotel.

Candlestick was told that he would receive his instructions from a top UDA man. It turned out to be Eddoes, who had disliked him since their initial disagreement over the protection rackets. Eddoes said to make sure he shot the boy in the head so that even if he lived, brain damage would make identification impossible. Candlestick, who knew about these things, said nothing and measured up Eddoes for when it would be his turn.

Using a .32 pistol taken from a UDA arms dump, he made

his call, banging on the waiter's door, thinking, as he heard the lad get up, how stupid can he be. He suffered a moment's anxiety, wondering what he'd do if it wasn't the boy that answered.

His hair was sticking up where it had been slept on and he was still struggling to put on his dressing gown, which had tartan lapels. He was dopy with sleep and when he turned to run Candlestick grabbed him and with one fluid movement slammed him against the wall, twisting the boy's head sideways to see the eye. He liked watching its little clicks of emotion as it registered growing disbelief, then panic, terror, and the full horror, all in less time than it took for him to level the gun.

Candlestick felt his awareness fine-tuned to an exquisite pitch. It was one of those killings where each detail was so clear that it could be recalled at will and replayed, as fresh as when it was done: the squeeze on the trigger, the muzzle flash and how the skull opened up—with a soft *thwap!* that he swore he could hear beneath the boom of the unsilenced gun—then the way the body collapsed like a felled animal. He took in the missing bits in the floor mosaic by the boy's head, and felt the tingle of the gun's recoil.

He fired twice more, point blank behind the ear. Dead easy, he thought, laughing at his joke. If they were marking out of ten he'd be a gold medal—action, interpretation and execution perfect. The angle of the arm as the coup was delivered, the slight cock of the wrist. He felt the adrenaline pumping through him, hoping that when his turn came he'd get someone as good as him. *Hit him on the head with a rolling pin, Jump back, baby, jump back.*

Sixteen

THE TYRE tracks at the scene of the accident were from an old type that conformed to a comparatively small range of cars. By calling in favours, Cross borrowed enough personnel to reduce the list to a dozen. One of these was an old Austin van registered in the name of Berrigan. The address turned out to be false, but the previous owner was traced through vehicle records and, from there, the garage the van had been sold to. It was in a village near Strabane, close to the Donegal border.

Cross was on the phone to the Republic when Hargreaves walked in, looking grim, with the news that the divisional commander wanted to see him.

DC Nesbitt, widely known as King Billy because of his energetic loyalist views, was a burden that Cross had been spared since reinstatement. He had been away on policing courses in the United States, swotting up on riot control and lecturing on the hazards of Northern Ireland. He liked to point out that his men stood twice the risk of being shot than in El Salvador.

Nesbitt was having a shouting day. He was a big man with the turkey cock mannerisms of someone much shorter than his six foot three. Hitler on Stilts was another of his nicknames.

"We've got a hundred and twenty unsolved murders in this division alone, why not one more?"

Nesbitt always took a pragmatic approach, calculating the importance of any murder to its effect on the community. The Mary Elam case was of some consequence because children had been left parentless. Nesbitt claimed he was not a heartless man. He argued for priorities. With a divisional murder squad of ten detectives and two hundred murders to solve each year, they could not afford to spend long on marginal deaths, and the anonymous vagrant was a case that should have been already closed.

"A murder is a murder, sir."

"That's the whole bloody point. You don't know if it is a murder. Not for sure."

"With respect, if the body was frozen—"

"Cause of death?"

"Sorry, sir?"

"What's the bloody cause of death, man?"

"We don't know."

"Quite. Maybe the bugger fell into a deep freeze when he was drunk and died. Maybe he deliberately shut himself in the bloody thing because he was going to be dead any minute anyway. It's not clear it's a murder and if it's not clear, you're wasting time."

"What about the wrist scars?"

"What scars?"

"In my report."

Nesbitt glanced at Cross's report then dropped it back on his desk. "Three more days, then forget it. And no extra personnel. What about this Elam woman thing?"

"We think she had an arrangement with a landlord who let her use a room over his bar."

"What does that add? I thought she wasn't seen in any of the pubs on the day she disappeared. How many pubs are we talking about?"

God, the old bastard was being difficult. "Three or four."

"Which? Four or three?"

"Four. She used three regularly, which we knew about, then a relief driver at Bennett's Taxis told us just this morning he remembered she once wanted to go to another bar but he refused."

"Why?"

"Because it was over in the Shankill."

Nesbitt groaned. They had all assumed until then that Mary Elam had only hung out in Catholic places, with Catholic men.

The Strathaven bar was a red brick corner building on the edge of Shankill, with a Union Jack painted in the window. There were the usual elaborate murals on the gable-ends of houses with their blunt statements of political allegiance: ONE FAITH/ONE CROWN, IN GOD OUR TRUST, NO SURRENDER. Cross also spotted a familiar bit of loyalist graffiti, 6 INTO 26 WON'T GO, a reference to the six counties of the North standing in defiance of the twenty-six counties of the Republic.

It was soon after morning opening when Cross and Hargreaves arrived, and there were only a couple of old men sat on wooden chairs, their beers in front of them on formica tables. They looked up with watery eyes. Their black suits were baggy and shiny with age, and one had his military medals pinned to his chest.

The landlord was a large man, his frame filled out from drink, his handsome slab of a face smoothly razored and smelling of Brut. He grunted at them and told a German Shepherd that lay growling disagreeably at his feet to shut up.

"Search me," he said dully when Cross showed him the photograph of Mary Elam.

"The dead woman that's been in the papers."

"We think she came in here," added Hargreaves.

"It's not a crime."

Cross noted the tattoo on the man's forearm, a heart and dagger with the words "Ulster Forever" and a separate banner with "Mum & Dad." Another sentimental bully, he thought, with a record probably as long as his arm.

He stonewalled their questions until Cross in exasperation asked to use the telephone and was referred to a pay phone in the corridor.

When he returned he leaned forward, speaking low enough for only the three of them to hear.

"McElwaine, B.D. Grievous bodily harm. Assault. Possession of stolen goods. Need I go on?"

The dog at McElwaine's feet growled up at Cross.

"Shut up, Puzi." He looked at Cross. "I don't remember saying anything about my name."

Cross sighed. "Brian David McElwaine, licenced victualler. You've a sign over the door in big letters for anyone that cares to read."

McElwaine stared at the two policemen huffily. "What you're talking about's ancient history."

"Still enough to hold you for questioning in connection with this woman's death," said Hargreaves.

They were interrupted by the old man with the medals

shuffling to the bar for two more beers, which allowed McElwaine some respite.

"All right now, Billy?"

"Ah, not bad, not bad."

"Billy's our most famous regular," McElwaine announced, suddenly full of landlord's bonhomie. "Survived the Somme. Thirty-sixth Ulster Division. How many went down that day, Billy?"

"What's that?" said Billy and McElwaine, grinning, had to repeat himself.

"July first, 1916," recited the old man in a tremulous voice. "Two thousand of our lads alone and over twenty thousand of us altogether, in the one day."

"It was Billy's birthday that day too."

Cross wondered if Billy had been a member of the original Ulster Volunteer Force, many of whom had fought at the Somme, and in whose memory the present paramilitary outfit was named.

"Puts today's troubles in the shade, eh, Billy?"

But Billy was caught up in a loop of his own.

"There was twenty of us in my class. We all went away and only I came back. It gave me the pick of the girls, I have to say."

He giggled feebly and went off, slopping his pints with shaking hands, leaving thin beer trails on the floor. The interlude let McElwaine forget his humiliation and he continued in his role of expansive landlord.

"She drank here a bit," he volunteered.

"On her own?" asked Cross.

McElwaine made a show of thinking, then nodded.

"Describe her."

"Well, you've seen her."

"Not alive."

"You noticed her. She liked a laugh."

For all McElwaine's false cheer Cross thought he detected a strain beneath.

"Was she friendly with any of your regulars?"

"You'd have to ask them that."

"Did you notice her with anyone in particular?"

"I don't remember."

McElwaine was starting to sound truculent and his mood was visibly eroded.

"What did she call herself?"

"I don't think she did. She was just a face. We called her luv because that's what she called everyone."

"You didn't know she was called Mary?"

"I did not."

"And what would you have done if you had known she was?"

"Names are all the same to me," he replied, unconvincingly.

"I don't suppose you get many Catholic Marys coming in here, do you now?"

McElwaine leaned meaty arms on the counter, his mask slipping to reveal the latent hostility. "I run the bar. I mind my own business, so a fellow can enjoy a drink and forget the cares of the world."

Hargreaves took over. "Did you know she was a left-footer?"

"Like I said, so long as nobody causes trouble, they're welcome. I don't care if they're the Queen of Siam."

"Did she have any arrangement with you?"

McElwaine stared at him with his pale blue eyes and asked exactly what Cross was getting at.

"Mary Elam depended on men for favours."

"There's no law against that."

"Technically not. All I'm saying is that if she was using this bar to pick up regulars then this would not be happening unless you were agreeable."

McElwaine started polishing a pint glass with a cloth. "What my clients get up to is their business."

"Do you have rooms upstairs?"

"It's where I live."

"Married?"

"If you want to look get a warrant."

Afterwards Cross told Hargreaves to do just that and to check on McElwaine for paramilitary links. He wondered if there was more to Mary's movements than met the eye.

CROSS was checking under the Volvo when the telephone rang and Deidre called out that it was for him. She looked annoyed as he took the receiver. It was a Saturday and the family was about to go shopping.

"Yes."

"This is Donnelly."

Cross couldn't place the name.

"In Ballybofey."

It was the Irish policeman he had talked to about the van registered by Berrigan.

"We've located this Berrigan fellow, or at least a fellow by the name of Berrigan."

This was good news, but Cross's excitement was curbed by a background squabble between his children.

"He sounds quite promising," Donnelly went on. "He lives on a farm in pretty remote parts, about ten, fifteen miles from here."

Fiona started crying and Deidre spoke sharply to Matthew, who joined in the chorus of wailing. Donnelly asked if it was a good time to call. Cross said he was just going out but to carry on.

"He lives by himself, from what we can tell, and according to the Revenue he's an upholsterer, though he's not exactly what you'd call a figure in the community. A man up that way had barely heard of him: 'Is that the fellow who lives up on Crosshead Farm?' he said. 'Keeps pretty much to himself.'"

Cross was amused by Donnelly's lazy delivery and accent. He pictured him sitting at his desk at the station, feet up and in no hurry, his Saturday shopping in plastic bags beside him.

"What do you want me to do, sir?"

Deidre, having quelled the children, was rolling her eyes to say that he should get a move on. He was tempted to tell her to go on without him. It was only her parents they were seeing after the supermarket.

"Can you have him picked up?"

"Aye, aye, sir," said Donnelly jauntily and Cross couldn't tell if he was joking.

"I could get over first thing Monday."

"What's murder, Daddy?" asked Fiona in the car.

"Just a part of my work, nothing very interesting."

"It's when you shoot somebody," said Matthew, pointing his finger and making gunfire noises.

"That's enough now, Mattie," said Deidre. Cross caught her sidelong glance: if looks could kill, he thought.

After a fractious trawl round the supermarket he managed to cry off going to Deidre's parents. In his job pressure of work could always be claimed and Deidre knew that she was in no position to object. She seemed relieved at the prospect of his not going with them.

Once he was ensconced in his office, he tried calling Donnelly. Ballybofey police said he was at home. Donnelly was in. Compared to earlier, he sounded brisk.

"I'm pretty sure Berrigan's your man, but he's not there and it looks like he hasn't been for a while."

"How long?"

"Given the state of the place, months even. Your man's not exactly one for the housekeeping. The good news is the van's there and the tyres look right. And I found a deep freeze in a shed at the side of the house."

"Big enough to hold a man?"

"Big enough."

They agreed Monday for him to come over and look.

On the way home Cross got caught in a traffic jam and only then remembered the seven o'clock appointment with Vinnie. He was already late and by the time he cleared the army roadblock that was the cause of the hold-up another half-hour had gone.

There was no sign of Vinnie outside the station. Cross waited, cursing his negligence, then returned to his silent household. A terse note from Deidre said that she and the children were staying the night with her parents.

He felt curiously stranded without her and was annoyed at how much he had come to rely on their ailing relationship. He stayed up drinking and staring at the television without being able to say what it was he was watching. Images of Deidre's infidelity blipped through his mind, as regular as the rhythm on a cardiograph.

Seventeen

ON THE motorway it started to rain. By Omagh poor visibility made driving treacherous and Cross's speed was down to forty. The lorry ahead threw a dirty spray, which his overworked windscreen wipers couldn't clear. He spent several miles nudging the Volvo out from behind the truck, trying to overtake, but the road, usually empty, was busy. He had to pull back when an approaching vehicle loomed out of the murk, headlights flashing and horn blaring.

It had taken longer than he had wanted to get away. Administration and briefings had occupied half the morning. He had also faced the unpleasant task of phoning Blair to say he needed to talk to Vinnie once more. He felt bad about breaking his appointment and not giving the boy's dilemma much thought. He made a hash of calling Blair, who was reluctant to co-operate.

"Things are very delicate in that direction, skip. I can't risk anything."

Given Blair's lack of help, Cross made no mention of what Vinnie had told him, though he had half-intended to when he'd picked up the phone.

Cross's exasperation increased during the drive. If it wasn't a lorry blocking the way it was a bus. He should have been able to do the journey in half the time.

He'd finally told Blair that he would be outside York Road station that night at eight and if Vinnie couldn't make it then he would be there the same time tomorrow. Blair had grunted and hung up, leaving Cross with no indication of whether he would pass on the message.

In Newtownstewart he stopped and bought cigarettes. The dreariness of the place emphasised how uncomfortable he was outside Belfast. He had never learned to interpret the local towns and villages, all of them as hostile as a bandit town in a Wild West film, with their empty streets and hidden eyes.

He sat in the parked car and smoked with the window down, feeling like a guilty schoolboy. Deidre had a crusading zeal against smoking. He wondered what his life would have been like if he had not met her. He flicked the butt away unfinished to show himself he didn't need it.

Donnelly turned out not to be the stout, ruddy fellow of farmer's stock Cross had imagined but a lean, angular man of metropolitan looks in neat suit and jazzy tie. His hair flopped over his brow and his most frequent gesture was a flick of the head to stop it from getting in his eyes.

"You're younger than I imagined," said Cross. He meant it as a compliment.

"And you're older. Welcome to Ballybofey."

It was said pleasantly. Donnelly was clearly direct, which was a relief.

Ballybofey police station was a dirty pebble-dash building in the main street. After the massively fortified barracks of the North, it looked naked. Wire mesh over the windows was the extent of its defences. Most of their work according to Donnelly involved co-operating with customs on border smuggling.

"I've not come up with much on Berrigan, a dark horse altogether. Seems like it turned out nice after all," said Donnelly as they got into his dilapidated Opel Kadett.

During the drive, Cross dozed and awoke to find himself facing a desolate landscape like something from a nightmare. As far as the eye could see, the hillside had been stripped of vegetation, leaving clumps of splintered pines sticking out of the ground like broken bones. There were craters of muddy water where whole trees had been upended and enormous clods of earth thrown up by the upheaval. Cross asked if it was some sort of firing range.

"Christ, no. That's just the forestry people."

They turned off into a forest maze of unsignposted lanes so complex that Cross could not believe they weren't lost.

"I know the way," said Donnelly with a smile, though soon after he announced he had made a wrong turn, by an abandoned burnt-out car, and reversed back.

"Berrigan makes his living from a few animals and a bit of

upholstery," he said, "though, you can imagine, there's not much call for that sort of thing around here. He was a new-comer too, which is unusual in these parts."

"When did he come here?"

"A couple of years ago."

"Married?"

"Not as far as anyone knows, but he could keep a harem up here and none would be the wiser."

The lane narrowed and the tall firs closed in until they brushed the sides of the car, and there was no view beyond the tunnel ahead and the thinnest strip of sky above. Cross had seen only one other vehicle since the town, a tractor they had followed for a mile or so until it had turned off.

The Kadett ground up a track so rutted that Donnelly had to use bottom gear. As they came over the crest of a hill into bright sunlight the trees disappeared and below lay a tiny valley and Berrigan's farmhouse surrounded by steep hills. Its walls sparkled white in the sun, the fields around bright green. Cross got out to open a gate across the track. The air was fresh, though for a moment he thought he smelt something tainted on the breeze.

The farm became distinctly less alluring the nearer they got. Rusting machinery and discarded sacks littered the land.

"Do we know for sure he's not there?" Cross asked.

"If he is I'd be surprised, let's put it like that. At least the van's still where it was," said Donnelly as they parked in the yard.

Cross inspected the van's tyres. Their tread looked similar to the sample.

"Is this the van the body was carried in?" asked Donnelly.

"Pretty definitely."

"I can get it gone over if you like. It might take a while but they're not bad."

Cross looked round. Most windows in the outbuildings were broken and left unrepaired. Several belonging to the house had been patched up with plywood that had become warped by rain.

"Mr. Berrigan was not exactly one for the jobs around the house," said Donnelly.

"He could have been gone for years," said Cross.

"Oh aye. If it wasn't for the farmer who has the fields above the house seeing him from time to time, I'd say the same. The door's open—no great call for security up here."

The interior was dark and musty, the boarded windows making the rooms unnaturally dark. A sitting room and dining room were clearly not used, their furniture covered in dust sheets. The detritus of Berrigan's life centred on a flag-stoned kitchen, with a parlour off it that contained little apart from an armchair and stove, empty gin bottles and a few cans of cheap food. There were not any of the usual things that defined people's existence—newspapers or books, television or radio.

"There's no post," he said to Donnelly. "Do you think he doesn't get any or he comes back for it?"

"They might hold it for him in town. I'll check."

A telephone was the only connection to the outside world. Cross picked up the receiver. It still worked.

Upstairs they found a few old clothes and some basic toiletries. The bath was full of dust. The bedrooms were empty, apart from one room which had been camped in, with a mattress on the floor and a couple of blankets. A sheet was tacked over the window. A cupboard held two old suits and some shoes. Downstairs Cross had noticed some waterproofs and gumboots.

"This fellow has things pretty stripped down," said Donnelly.

"The bare essentials. No Mrs. Berrigan."

"No sign of a woman's touch, I'll grant you."

They were on their way downstairs when the telephone rang, startling them. They looked at each other in surprise, then Donnelly ran to answer. It was for Cross.

"Me?" Cross asked in astonishment.

It was Westerby, who had traced the number through the directory. She sounded breathless. The line was very bad.

"I thought you ought to know, sir, I think I've found two more advertisements. They feel like they belong with the other one."

She had decided to check back-issues of the classifieds on the hunch that there might be more than the one advertisement. Cross marvelled at her dedication but wondered at her keenness. Phoning him felt like a way of seeking his approval. He decided he was being unfair—it was the unpleasant atmosphere of the farm making him sour.

"What makes you think they belong?"

"They both have false names and addresses."

Cross's chest felt tight and he reached for his cigarettes and fished around for a light. Donnelly produced a book of matches from his top pocket—advertising a cocktail bar, Cross noticed.

"And there's a reference to piercing hands," said Westerby.

Cross exhaled. The tightness in his chest persisted. He had the sudden feeling someone knew he was at the farm and was even watching.

"Are you there, sir?"

"Yes," said Cross. "What do these new ones say?"

"The first appeared on the last Friday in February. *'Yea, for thy sake are we killed all the day long; we are counted as sheep for the slaughter.'* "

He wondered if Westerby ever read in church.

"What's the procedure for placing an advert?"

"Write your copy on the coupon in the paper and send the right money."

"And no one need know the address is false?"

"As long as it gets past the scanners. The supervisor told me they turn down some they consider contentious. Otherwise there's no check."

"What about the other one?"

"This was only a couple of days ago. It goes, *'For dogs have compassed me; the assembly of the wicked have inclosed me: they pierced my hands and my feet.'* "

They pierced my hands, he thought. He wondered if Westerby wasn't being over-imaginative. She seemed to sense his reluctance.

"I just thought you ought to know, sir. I'm not so sure now I've told you."

"Why not?"

He was irritated by her sudden backtracking.

"Well, they feel like they belong together, but I could be wrong because I'm pretty sure these are from the Psalms and the first one isn't."

"You did the right thing telling me," Cross said, hanging up, though he did not see why it could not have waited. For the moment he didn't want to consider the implications of what she had told him, and he resented her intrusion.

Outside he was glad of the bright daylight. Donnelly was sitting on a mounting block. He looked content, making the most of the early warm weather.

"Is there anything else you'd like to see?"

"Give me five minutes. Stay there if you want. I'll just be poking around."

"A rat the size of a tank just ran across the yard."

Donnelly smiled his easygoing smile and said he'd sit in the sun if it was all the same.

The farmyard was surrounded by a rectangle of outbuildings. Most were empty or contained rusted machinery. In a smaller shed Cross found the freezer, easily deep and wide enough to hold a man. It had been switched off and the ice had turned to water.

Next door seatless chairs hung from the ceiling. An armchair stood on the floor, its stuffing spilling out, and another lay pushed on its side. Swathes of calico lay on the floor covered in dirt. A bench was littered with tools and old lozenge tins full of upholstery tacks. Berrigan's workshop seemed indecently cluttered after the spareness of the farmhouse. Cross's eye was drawn to what looked like a screwdriver with a snapped-off point. He picked it up, careful not to get his fingerprints on it, and held it to the light. The handle was wooden, like a screwdriver's, but the stem thinner and sharply pointed. He tried to remember what the thing was called as he slipped it into his pocket, wondering if it had been used on the dead man's wrists.

The workshop had a back door that took him out into the fields on the far side of the farm. He stopped, puzzled by a bizarre sight in the distance, between him and the barn—cemetery-straight rows of what looked like tiny garish body bags. Line upon line of dead children, it seemed, ready for burial. Cross couldn't wait to leave.

The barn was much further than it looked. Several times he almost gave up. Ditches not visible from the farm needed negotiating and they shortened his temper. The dead children turned out to be plastic bags full of peat.

He heard Donnelly call and turned: the farm seemed tiny. Cross shouted back and Donnelly waved.

He pressed on. His nostrils caught a whiff of something: manure, or perhaps the sickly smell of silage. Then he recognized the stench of decay. It came from the barn and was so overpowering that he had to cover his nose.

He cautiously pulled open the barn door and stood blinking in the entrance, his eyes adjusting to the dark. He was aware only of the total silence. Then something rose up at him, and he threw his hands in front of his face as the air became furious with a black buzzing. They swarmed around his head, thousands of flies, and Cross understood then what had been nagging him since his arrival. Donnelly had said that Berrigan kept animals. But the farm had none.

He realized he was staring at the remains of the man's livestock—several chickens, a couple of cows, a piglet, some kind of other animal whose head had been removed, and a donkey. He had to force himself to look.

Each animal had been systematically slaughtered, throats hacked from ear to ear, the chickens with their heads snapped off. The belly of each animal was slit up the middle then across. Grey sacks of intestines lolled out of the carcasses on to straw treacle-sticky with blood. Blood was on the walls, sprays of the stuff, looking like it had been hosed on. Cross could imagine only too clearly the jets of it pumping out of the bellowing, thrashing animals in their death throes. Christ, what slaughter. He'd never seen anything like it.

Had it not been for the hammer on the floor he would have left it at that and fled. It was a small mallet. He wondered what it was doing there until he saw the state of one of the cow's legs. The front knees were smashed, bone shards exposed. All four of the donkey's legs had been broken, the other animals' as well.

Out of the corner of his eye Cross sensed movement and spun round, heart thumping. What had disturbed him—a wild cat crouched on top of the stalls—was not what held his eye. The severed head of a goat had been jammed on to the post of the stall and deliberately arranged as a sightless observer of the carnage below.

The cat started gnawing at the goat and Cross yelled in delayed fright, causing it to scurry off. He saw too that the other animals were in the process of being eaten away. He felt rats watching.

Cross fought his way out of the barn, staggered and fell to his knees, then on all fours. He knelt there panting, feeling cold sweat pricking his flesh. He fought the urge to vomit, in the belief that if he won that struggle it would ward off the evil of what he had just seen. But the images of bone and guts swam uncontrolled before his eyes, and his stomach contracted and with a cry of despair he retched in blinding spasms until his eyes burned and the horror of the barn seared itself on to his mind's eye. The cruel detail of the slaughter became ever clearer, and he saw fresh patterns in the killer's method, saw how each animal's belly had been carved up, then across to make a sign of the cross.

With nothing left in his stomach to bring up, he continued to retch until he fell sideways from exhaustion and lay on the grass staring at the sky, a pitiful drooling creature so weak that he doubted if he could stand. He felt blighted by what he had witnessed. The grisly tableau had assaulted his humanity, reduced him to an animal, stripped him of reason. If it was the work of Berrigan, then he was dealing with a monster. *As sheep for the slaughter,* he remembered from the quotation, except there had been no sheep in the barn.

He heard Donnelly call, sounding so close that Cross could not work out how he had got there so fast. He thought he had only been in the barn a minute or two, though it had felt like an eternity.

"Christ, what happened?"

Donnelly moved towards the barn, but Cross shouted at him not to.

"Don't!"

"Jesus, what went on in there?"

"I'll tell you later, just don't go in. How did you get here so fast?"

"I drove. There's a track. Are you all right?"

Cross rose shakily. Donnelly pointed to the top of the car, visible over the hedge. He resisted Donnelly's help, ashamed of the vomit he could smell on himself beneath the general stench.

As he made his way unsteadily towards the car he remembered the hammer and told Donnelly to wait. He forced himself back, keeping his eyes averted from the carnage—a hell to which he had already sworn he would never return—to retrieve it.

Eighteen

IN THE days after the barn Cross felt his grip go. He slept badly, waking at five without fail. Irritable days passed teetering on the edge of exhaustion.

"For Christ's sake, Matthew, will you stop banging that spoon!"

The boy ran from the breakfast table in tears. When Deidre told Cross not to swear at Matthew he snapped back that he had not been swearing at the boy.

"You know what I mean," she said in exasperation. "At, in front of—just don't swear."

"That's rich coming from you."

"I do not do it in front of the children!" she shouted, setting Fiona off.

"We do nothing in front of the children!" Cross yelled as she went after Matthew, leaving him to mollify Fiona.

"Daddy's horrid," was her only verdict.

He looked at his toast and decided he was not hungry. What sleep he had got had ended with a dream where he'd watched Ricks' fastidious white hands perform an autopsy on him, while the barn's sharp-toothed cat picked at his remains.

DONNELLY had taken him back to the farm, where he had cleaned himself up, then driven him to Berrigan's nearest neighbour, who lived on an adjacent smallholding. The farmer was surprisingly young, and told Cross he had taken over the place at sixteen after his father died. Cross wondered what another thirty years of solitude would do to him, or what chance he would have of picking up a wife in such a remote spot.

In spite of being neighbours, he and Berrigan could have been living on different planets. The farmer's sightings were

restricted to the occasional view of a distant figure in the valley
below. Cross understood something that he had not appreciated
until then. He saw how isolation could have sent Berrigan
crazy enough to slaughter his own livestock.

The drive back to Ballybofey seemed quicker than going,
the route less tortuous. Cross was tempted to stay over except
he had to be at York Road station at eight.

Cross said, "I'll have the hammer and the screwdriver thing
looked at by forensic. Get someone to go over the van and look
at the animals before getting rid of them."

Before he left, they talked to several local shopkeepers.
Cross grew impatient with the endless preambles that took in
everything from local match scores to the health of relatives.
All of them had trouble recalling Berrigan. By the end Cross
had no idea whether he was tall, short, fat, thin, forty, fifty or
sixty. ("Well, his hair was white, I'd say, but not an old man's
white, so it might have been a colour like white.")

"He went to Donegal more. There's more of a choice," one
shopkeeper said. They were in a cheap supermarket whose art-
less displays reminded him of the first supermarkets of his
childhood.

"Did he come here much?" Cross asked.

"Oh, never in here, but so I heard."

"Well," said Donnelly afterwards. "Ask five people to describe your man and you come up with five different men."

Cross pointed out that one of the few things he had learned
as a policeman was how unobservant people were, or rather
how stubbornly observant and completely wrong.

ON THE drive back to Belfast he turned off at Newtownstewart and drove fast along the straight road that crossed the
high country in the direction of Maghera and Magherafelt. He
suspected Vinnie wouldn't be waiting and when he got to York
Road, only five minutes late, he was proved right.

He arrived home to find that Deidre had already eaten. She'd
left him some, she said, turning back to the television. When
she came into the kitchen to make a cup of tea she saw he had
not touched his supper and asked what was wrong with it.
Cross said nothing was and saw she didn't believe him. He had
stared at his plate unable to eat in spite of his empty stomach.

"How are the children?" he asked.

"Fine. Fiona's maybe got a bit of a cold."

He tried to think of something to say. The best he could manage was, "I was in the Republic today."

"I may have to go away soon for a few days," said Deidre, sounding bored.

"Work?" he asked, giving her the opportunity to lie.

"Work. Brussels, of all places."

CROSS worked the next Saturday afternoon in an effort to reduce the usual mountain of paperwork, but before he could attack it the phone rang. It was Hargreaves.

"I wonder if you wouldn't mind looking at a body."

"What happened?"

"We're not quite sure, sir. It may be an accident or a suicide. Bloke's a journalist by the name of Warren. A neighbour was alerted by the smell."

Cross was familiar with the name. He was a local crime reporter.

He found Niall Warren's body hanging in a built-in bedroom cupboard, suspended by a leather belt looped around his neck and tied to the clothes rail. The rail had buckled slightly with his weight. It was not high enough to let the body hang freely and the legs were awkwardly bent, the feet dragging on the ground. The stench was overwhelming. Warren had been dead long enough to start turning putrid.

It was the memory of the dead animals rather than the sight of Warren that forced Cross to sit down with his head in his hands. He caught Doody's sneering look and dragged himself up to confront the grotesque apparition in the cupboard.

They had met a few times. Cross vaguely remembered a short, corpulent man around forty, quite nondescript, with the sort of face not looked at twice. In death he was remarkable. The face was rouged and roughly smeared with lipstick. He wore women's high heels, black stockings, suspenders, silk knickers, a camisole and elbow-length cocktail gloves. His hands and ankles were bound.

Even the scene-of-crime squad, who were inured to most things, were shocked. Being conventional men, they felt threatened.

"Sick fuck," said Doody. "Why couldn't he have jerked off

like any other wanker? Fancy cleaning up after this fellow's spunk. I don't suppose he thought of that."

"What's the point?" asked a constable.

"The point is," went on Doody, "to turn your tool as stiff as a crowbar by cutting off oxygen to the brain. The only problem in your case is you've got to have a brain in the first place."

"You sound very knowledgeable, sarge."

"It was once explained to me by a senior officer," said Doody with a smirk in Cross's direction.

"But what's the getting kitted up all about?" asked the persistent constable.

"You'd have to ask a clever man like DI Cross about that."

"Carry on, sergeant," said Cross. "Why do they get dressed up?"

"Because they're perverts, sir."

Cross left them to it and asked Hargreaves about the neighbours.

"You should talk to Mr. Jobson downstairs." Hargreaves rolled his eyes. "Wears a wig and only answers to Winston."

Jobson's wig was orange and in jaunty but hopeless contradiction to the desiccated face below. Cross put him at around sixty.

He endured Jobson's steady drip of complaints—about the police tramping through the building, leaving the front door on the latch—relieved to be away from the fetid smell upstairs. He wondered how much the sound carried and if Jobson had heard anything. From the way he cocked his head, Cross guessed that most of his time was spent monitoring the residents' movements.

"Cup of tea? I'm just making one."

"No, thanks."

"It's Winston, by the way."

Jobson fussed around, moving with the deliberation of someone who knows what it is to fill up the slow hours of a day. Cross asked if Warren had many visitors. Jobson thought he recalled hearing his bell some time in the previous week, which was unusual.

"But you're not sure?"

"Winston. I was in the back at the time."

"The back?"

"The bathroom."

He looked furtive.

"When was this? Winston."

"Some time in the afternoon of the Monday or Tuesday."

Cross asked if he could be sure the visitor was for Warren, and Jobson replied that everyone else was out during the day.

"Why wasn't Warren out? He was a reporter."

Jobson made a drinking motion with his hand. "Never the same since Mrs. Warren left."

Cross was surprised there had been a Mrs. Warren, given the shabby bachelor air of the flat.

"When did she leave?"

"He started drinking some time last autumn, so it would have been then."

"What was she like?"

"I think she might have been a Brit, though sometimes she sounded more like a Yank. Classy bitch, if you don't mind my saying."

"Age?"

"Hard to say. Well preserved. They were only married a few months. Is it true?"

"Is what?"

"That he was found dressed up."

His eyes shone. Cross ignored him, asking instead if he had noticed anything unusual about Warren's behaviour.

"The noise, for a start! Non-stop clatter, banging away on that typewriter, day and night. And then he starts throwing things around, which he does when he's had a few."

"What sort of things?"

"Glasses, by the sound of it. In the end I had to bang on the ceiling."

"When was this?"

"Now that I remember exactly. It was three-thirty in the morning on Tuesday night. He stopped after that."

Whether this was before or after Warren might have had his visitor, Jobson couldn't say.

"Do you have any idea how long this visitor stayed?"

"I'm not saying it was a he," said Jobson craftily. "But I don't know how long because I would have been down the shops then."

Cross suppressed a sigh.

"I thought you said you were in."

"I was. But then I went out."

Cross was almost relieved to get back upstairs.

He looked around Warren's living room, listening to the men in the bedroom grunting and cursing as they manhandled the body out of the cupboard and on to a stretcher. Cigarette burns punctuated an over-padded Draylon three-piece suite. A low coffee table was ringed with stains from carelessly placed glasses. There were unemptied ashtrays.

The only personal touch was a framed photograph next to an IBM electric typewriter. It showed a woman, caught by flash-light, at a formal party. She wore cocktail gloves similar to the ones on the corpse. Her hair was up and she stared at the camera with a look of wild exhilaration. She held a thin-stemmed glass crookedly in one hand. The neckline of her dress was low, revealing a full bosom. She was very beautiful, creamy skinned, indeterminate age.

He watched the covered stretcher being manoeuvred awk-wardly out of the bedroom and through the flat, and heard Jobson's door open as the procession made its way downstairs.

In the bedroom Cross noticed the clothes that Warren must have been wearing before getting dressed up, slung untidily across a hard chair. A balled-up sock lay on the carpet. The shirt had grime on the collar. The trousers were heavy with small change and keys.

These pathetic reminders of Warren's last moments of ordinariness—undressing like he had done thousands of times with no reason to suspect that this time was any different—almost undid him. He sat on the edge of the bed and counted the change from the dead man's pockets as a way of distracting himself. He took the keys in case he needed to get back in downstairs. The flat itself would have to be padlocked because the front door had been smashed by his men gaining entry.

A window had been left open and the stink had lessened. The doors to the wardrobe were shut now. Cross was fairly sure the death was the result of an autoerotic experiment gone wrong, but what had led up to it was probably beyond his understanding.

He looked at his watch. They had missed the football results. He was surprised that the scene-of-crime team had not turned on the television for the final score. They were not the types to let death interrupt them.

"Did you look at the knots on his wrists?" he asked

Hargreaves, who was waiting in the living room, smoking a cigarette. He nodded.

"Could he have tied them himself?"

"Perhaps by using his teeth, though he would have had trouble getting himself undone."

"What do you think? That he did it by himself?"

"Or had a partner who panicked when things went wrong," said Hargreaves.

"Or got carried away and accidentally did him in."

THE WARREN case was unpopular with his team. Those involving sexual difference always were, and his briefing was accompanied by predictable jeering at Warren's expense. He noticed Westerby taking dutiful notes which inattentive colleagues would no doubt filch. These meetings sometimes reminded Cross of the classroom.

The autopsy report was as inconclusive as Cross expected. Death was by strangulation. Ricks thought it was possible—at least not impossible—that Warren had tied his own hands. The body showed an extremely high intake of alcohol, enough, in Ricks' opinion, to cause carelessness.

"But wouldn't the body instinctively react if there wasn't any drop? The rail was hardly five foot high."

"People in prison cells manage to hang themselves without any sort of drop." Ricks gave Cross an arch look. "It becomes strangulation rather than hanging."

"Doesn't the body reject what's being done to it?"

"You have to remember that your Mr. Warren was probably in pursuit of some sensation that was, shall we say, always just beyond his reach, and he pushed himself until he lost consciousness. Are you all right?"

"Yes, fine. Why?"

"You look a bit peaky. Not coming down with anything, I hope."

Cross, aware of his dream, avoided looking at Ricks' hands.

He should have closed the case there and then, he supposed, and wondered later why he didn't: no one would have quarrelled with death by misadventure.

"How's your frozen man?" Ricks asked as they parted.

"Don't ask," replied Cross.

Back in his office he called Donnelly in Ballybofey.

"He's full of interesting blanks, is our Mr. Berrigan," said Donnelly. "I tried turning up the deeds for the farm. The agent who sold him the place is dead. But I did find out that Berrigan paid cash and his previous address is given as his solicitor's. Unfortunately the solicitor keeps himself amused with the bottle and barely remembers the job."

Donnelly had also talked to the Inland Revenue. In contrast to Berrigan's cash purchase of the farm, his income tax returns for the past few years suggested earnings of barely subsistence level.

Cross sent off the mallet from the barn for forensic examination, and the other tool, which he remembered was called a bradawl.

That night he waited in vain again for Vinnie outside York Road station.

WESTERBY seemed subdued and Cross wondered if she was having trouble fitting in. He was aware of Hargreaves' dislike of her. Her keenness, ambition and intelligence marked her out, and Cross suspected they would count against her. Westerby was undeniably bright.

To his shame he ended up condoning the movement against her, even taking part in it. He found his reaction inexplicable, beyond putting it down to exhaustion. His temper was often only kept under control by criticizing those least able to defend themselves—such as his children. With Westerby it began with a reluctance to single her out for praise, in case it was seen as favouritism. He then started to take pleasure in catching her out. She had been uncharacteristically forgetful in failing to get the information he had asked for about power cuts around the time of the Berrigan death. When reminded, she had hung her head, biting her lip, fighting back tears.

She'd reported back later by phone, saying that there had been no power cuts in the week before they'd found the body. This eliminated one possible explanation of why the body might have been dumped. Her voice sounded hurt and remote. He thought of apologizing. He disliked himself for his coldness. He would rather it wasn't directed at her.

HE LAY awake listening to Deidre's breathing. His eyes strained in the dark, and he found himself thinking about

Jobson being kept awake downstairs by the noise of Warren's typing. What was it that Warren had been typing? Cross was suddenly alert.

Nineteen

Belfast, May 1972

VIOLENCE grew as the drunken summer nights lengthened. Candlestick watched the so-called hardmen adjourn to upstairs rooms where the boozing carried on. These long nights of drinking drew to a climax with a baying for blood, but once the peak of intensity had passed, inferiority reasserted itself. For all their hatred of Catholics—"We should feckin' get ourselves a Fenian fucker"—Candlestick saw that they were too scared to act upon their drunken bravado. He found the loyalists a sorry bunch, sloppy and unfocused, ill-disciplined compared to the IRA, and too drunk to do anything except turn their need for violence inward. They moaned that they were both discriminated against and neglected. Their only response was reaction. Candlestick bided his time, waiting to channel this aggression into something more than empty threats.

One night he slipped out of the bar, taking Baker. Baker was in one of his quiet moods. He had days now when he said little.

Candlestick drove nowhere in particular, with his window down, letting the warm night air in. They crossed the Lagan and skirted South-west Catholic Belfast before taking the Springfield Road up into Woodvale. At the top end of the Crumlin Road, where it butts into Catholic Ardoyne, they stopped for Baker to go to a chip shop. Candlestick stayed in the car. A cab turned out of the Ardoyne into the Crumlin Road. Candlestick was struck by the fact that its passenger and driver would be Catholic, simply because of where they were coming from.

While Baker ate his chips, Candlestick explained what he had in mind. Baker, his mouth full, grunted his appreciation, then crunched his chip bag into a ball and lobbed it into the gutter.

They waited until after midnight when the streets were empty. First they looked on the Antrim Road and Clifton Street, but in the end they found their quarry in one of the darkened streets closer to the centre. He was walking with the weaving lurch of the very drunk and spun round startled when Candlestick called out from behind him and announced that there was a bomb down the street, and he was an off-duty member of the bomb squad waiting for the security forces to arrive. The man stood blinking, trying to focus.

"Is that right?"

"What's your name, pal?"

"Sheehan," he said without thinking, so sealing his fate. Candlestick chopped him across the neck and Baker helped stick him in the boot.

They held Sheehan at the rear of the bar until only the paramilitary men were left. Candlestick hit him a few times, to get himself in the mood, but Sheehan's girlish squeals irritated him. He was unhappy with his choice and wanted to return him to the street like you did damaged goods to a shop. Then, seeing the decision was his, he told Baker that Sheehan did not feel right.

"He's too easy."

Baker was still in a sulk and said little beyond asking why. Candlestick said he was going to dump Sheehan and get someone else. Baker was concerned that Sheehan could identify them. Candlestick told him not to worry.

He left Baker and drove around with Sheehan unconscious again in the boot. But he saw no one he fancied and decided Sheehan was fine after all. What he had needed, he realized, was time alone to psych himself up. If he didn't feel right before he'd feel flat afterwards.

It was odd, he thought, how little he—or Baker come to that—were in the mood for what had to be done. His irritation towards Baker grew. Baker was too crude—he thought of him lobbing his greasy chip bag into the street—not the sort to appreciate the subtlety of violence. No finesse.

Candlestick had no respect for the loyalists. They could be dropped to a man into the Irish Sea. Their mottled boozy flesh revolted him. Yet for all his contempt, he was nervous at performing in front of them. Violence had a sacred momentum, like going with a woman. To appreciate both you needed time and privacy. Acting out some charade in front of a drunken crowd was like being asked to do sex in public. He doubted if there would be any pleasure in it.

If Baker was surprised to see Sheehan again he said nothing, and together they dragged him upstairs. A silence fell as Candlestick booted Sheehan to the floor and announced to the assembled drinkers that there was the Fenian fucker they had been talking about.

The crowd stood in stunned disbelief, as gormless as a roomful of idiots at the start of a party. Candlestick saw the extent of their hopelessness. They would have to be shown each step of the way.

He motioned Baker to pick up Sheehan and hold him. Candlestick punched him hard, once to the head and then in the gut, making him yelp and squeak.

"Have mercy on an innocent man," Sheehan pleaded, his arms outstretched.

"Be a man and I'll let you live," whispered Candlestick.

The other man's eyes flickered with hope. Candlestick made a point of two fingers and drove it into Sheehan's solar plexus, doubling him up.

"Ah, the dirty fucker's been sick," said Baker.

Baker rubbed Sheehan's face in his own vomit. That got a simple laugh from the crowd. Candlestick paused and looked at the puddled faces of the onlookers, slack with stupefaction. He felt the room in his control. The audience, after its initial awkwardness, now seemed in boozy good humour.

"Tell us what you know about the Irish Republican Army," he asked Sheehan.

That got a gasp from the crowd. Candlestick's claim that Sheehan had information on the IRA was barely an excuse to give the digging some point. But for the audience it was as though the whimpering victim had been transformed from a helpless drunk into a monster.

IT BECAME an epidemic during that summer of 1972. The killings were known as romperings after an Ulster TV children's programme. Candlestick never knew who was responsible for the name. He knew of similar sessions in other parts of the city and wondered if Bunty was behind them. The fanatical McKeague, who was in the process of forming the Red Hand Commando, was attributed in some quarters with initiating them.

After Sheehan, Candlestick had difficulty remembering if the idea had been his or whether it had been planted in him so subtly by the likes of Bunty that he and others like McKeague claimed it as their own.

Invariably the men seized had no terrorist connections. They were just innocent drunks abducted as they stumbled home. But in Candlestick's increasingly expert hands they confessed anyway.

How much was followed up afterwards he had no idea. The loyalists were unsystematic at best. The point of the sessions was not the information extracted, it was the sense of secret power gained, the feeling of invincibility, of striking at the enemy regardless of the victims' actual innocence, a fact everyone was happy to ignore. But this sense of power soon collapsed into guilt, which was why it became necessary to continue. For Candlestick, who felt no guilt, the ritualized violence became the headiest of drugs.

Among his disciples was the young UVF thug Lenny, who prided himself on being able to hit harder than the rest. Candlestick gave him his head, making him the focus of these sessions. Lenny liked to cut. He also added a final twist, leaving his grisly signature by hacking at the victim's throat until head and body were virtually severed.

All was condoned by Captain Bunty.

"They've got to learn to stand on their own two feet and fight for themselves," he said of the loyalists.

They killed a young Catholic who was with Protestant friends at a disco at a hotel that was a meeting place for UDA leaders. Somebody recognized him as a Catholic and after a scuffle outside the hotel, in which Baker punched a woman in the eye, the young man was taken to Eddoes' house and then on to a club where his jacket and boots were taken away. Nine men interrogated him about belonging to the Provisional IRA. He denied it, saying that he was out celebrating a wedding that was to take place the next day.

"Not yours?" asked Candlestick.

"No, not mine."

"Pity. If you'd said yes I'd have let you go."

By that stage they had loud music playing to mask the screams, a device that Lenny said gave a certain swing to the evening.

"Please allow me to introduce myself, I'm a man of wealth and taste," went the opening line of the song Candlestick played most, timing the victim's screams to coincide with the song's chorus of *whoo-whoo-whoo!*

Candlestick made the young man confess his guilt, like the others, forcing him to name his non-existent comrades. Meanwhile Baker repeatedly hit him on the back with a wooden pickshaft handle until it broke.

Candlestick, fired by the music and exulting in the sharp clarity of it all, produced a commando knife and crucified the lad to the wall, stabbing his palm with the dagger and using another knife on the other hand. Someone suggested cutting the balls off him, but Baker cut his buttock instead, opening up a long shallow incision. Candlestick then tore him free of the wall and picked him up single-handed and swung him round, dropping him on the floor on his head.

He saw the eyes of the other men high on the violence. He looked at the young man, broken on the floor, and felt a surge of tenderness. They always talked, always told him their stories, never mind that they made them up in the end, told him lies just to satisfy him, made a ghastly truth of their lies. He wondered where it came from, this desire to extract people's stories from them. He wanted to know everything. He wanted no secrets between them. Before he had done he would cut him, once up and once across his lily-white chest, leaving the signature of his cross.

Twenty

WHATEVER Warren had been typing was no longer in the flat. Cross searched all the obvious places and some less likely ones too. He was surprised by a drawerful of lingerie in the bedroom, all new and still in cellophane wrappers.

The start of Sunday church bells distracted him and he went to the window. A steady procession of people, dressed in their best, made their way past. The peal of the bells always depressed him. Sundays in Belfast struck him as being more than usually governed by the dead hand of the past.

He had meant to go on from the flat to Deidre's parents, but instead arranged to meet Warren's colleagues. He had only phoned the newspaper on the off-chance someone might answer, then realized from the noise in the background that the office was full of staff preparing the Monday edition. When he called the O'Neills and spoke to Deidre, saying that he might come later, she managed as always to sound both disapproving and relieved.

At the newspaper offices Cross asked for the duty editor and was told he was not available, so had to make do with the author of Warren's obituary, a smug young man who was pointed out to him sitting in the middle of a large open-plan office.

"Ronnie Stevens," he said as they shook hands. "I know, I don't look like a Ronnie."

He was only in his mid-twenties but came with an air of experience, probably because he felt that seeing a dead body or two entitled him to. Horn-rimmed glasses contributed to a spurious gravity. His checked shirt Cross recognized as Marks & Spencer because he had one like it, a Christmas present from the children.

The bizarre circumstances of Warren's death were not being

reported, apart from a brief note on page one. The obituary, which Stevens showed him in proof, made only passing reference to Warren's decline, put down to illness. The photograph was of a younger, thinner Warren, hair neatly combed and fresh faced, more or less how Cross remembered him.

"It could have happened to any of us, poor sod," said Stevens. "Newspapers, you know. Us hacks like a drink, but you learn to control it. Work hard, play hard."

Cross asked if Warren had been popular.

"Not unpopular."

Cross took this to mean that he had not been liked, a suspicion confirmed by Stevens' emerging description of Warren as a gauche figure, tagging along and drinking with the crowd.

"What about his wife?"

Stevens wiped his face with his hand, suppressing a smirk. "We were all dead surprised when he showed up with her. Good old Niall, not exactly a ladies' man, and she was a looker. Made him glow like a Belisha beacon. Bloody hell, we thought, how did he pull that off?"

"And how did he?"

Stevens shrugged. "Well, it's not who he was, it's being here—in the front line, all that crap."

"But she must have been able to take her pick."

"Yeah, sure. You see them in the Europa, war-zone groupies hanging around with the big-shot foreign correspondents, getting shit faced. But I don't think she drank, really, and that's all most of those boys do. Niall didn't in those days and whatever he lacked in social graces he made up for in contacts. Niall knew the stuff that doesn't get in the papers. That goes a long way with some women—they feel they're getting the dirt. Anyway, she looked like she'd signed on for the full ghoul's tour. There was even a rumour that she was intelligence."

Cross raised his eyebrows.

Stevens dismissed the suggestion with a shrug. "They say that about anyone who turns up here without a good reason."

"Hadn't they only been married a few months?"

Stevens scratched his neck and said he'd never fathomed the marriage. "She never struck me as the marrying type. I think it was a joke for her. As far as I know they never lived together."

Cross let the silence ride, curious. Stevens looked reflective for the first time, even slightly out of his depth.

"Then," Stevens went on, "given the circumstances of his death, I suppose she must have found out about his sexual quirks."

"And what do you make of his quirks?"

Stevens gave a worldly shrug that didn't quite come off. "It was news to me. Different strokes for different folks, I suppose."

"What story was he working on when he died?"

"Story? I doubt if there was one. He hadn't written a word in months and had more or less given up coming in by the end."

"What happened to his wife?"

"Haven't the foggiest."

"In spite of her being so intriguing."

"Outside work we don't have much of a social life apart from the pub and once she dropped out we lost sight of her."

Cross asked to be shown where Warren worked and Stevens led him to a space identical to all the rest, with a cheap modern desk surrounded by a low partition stuck with various memos about pay negotiations. Warren's filing cabinet was empty, apart from a few hanging folders with more staff memos, several dozen back issues of the newspaper and a two-year-old *Playboy* magazine stuffed behind. The desk revealed the usual clutter and in the drawers were several bulky cardboard folders full of old drafts of stories, scrappily typed and amended in biro. Muddled in with them were dozens of pages of scrawled notes torn from notepads.

A thinner folder marked "Current" contained only a few incoherent and unfinished notes. Apparently Warren's recent work amounted only to these few pieces of paper. None of it was of interest apart from a striking quotation which read: "When the Nazis took on the government of Poland they flooded the Polish bookstalls with pornography. The theory was that if you permit all things for self-gratification, you are likely to encourage withdrawal from any sort of corporate responsibility."

The quote was circled and arrowed towards a list written in the same hand, under the heading *Drugs: Provs? UDA? INLA? INLA-UDA?* Underneath was an amendment: *Don't be daft.*

Cross wondered if the connection had anything to do with Warren's story. He pocketed it and went off in search of Warren's editor.

Brian McCausland was a corpulent man with a Zapata moustache, a hangover from two decades earlier that looked like a forlorn reminder of his years on the street, before he got soft sitting at a desk. A well-rounded gut pointed to days organized around expense-account lunches.

He took Cross into a private office with an inside window that looked out on to the central working area and another with a view of the Royal Avenue. After expressing perfunctory regret about his colleague's death, he moved on to the story Warren had been working on when he died.

"I've no idea what it was about," said McCausland. "He didn't say and I didn't push it."

"Don't you usually discuss stories with your reporters?"

"Of course I do. Frankly, inspector, I thought it was probably a fantasy. No doubt you've heard the shape Niall was in when he died."

"Where would this story be now, if it wasn't fantasy?"

"In his head, I would imagine, if anywhere."

"Did he not tell you *anything* about the story?"

McCausland blew out his cheeks and shook his head, to indicate the futility of Cross's line of inquiry. "Niall was in a hell of a state by the end, drunk all the time. He was on a formal warning and within an inch of being fired, and he said he had a story that was, well, big, and would I back him. As he wouldn't say what the story was about, it was rather difficult to offer any assurance. But I gave him until today—no, tomorrow—to come back with a full brief."

"Could it have been about this?"

He showed him Warren's note about the pornography. McCausland read it, frowning.

"If it was, he was barking up the wrong tree. Armed robbery, hijacking drinks lorries, extortion, drinking clubs, alternative transport systems, tax fraud and prostitution, yes. We know the terrorists go in for all of them. But drugs and pornography, no. The Provos take a very hard line on drugs, but you know that. Niall was not reliable towards the end."

"How did he seem in the last few weeks?"

McCausland considered the question, sucking his teeth. The gesture reminded Cross of Ronnie Stevens scratching his neck and he wondered if either was hiding something.

"Scared," said McCausland finally.

"Why?"

"Because he was facing the chop and was helpless to do anything about it. I don't believe there was a story."

"Did you like him?"

McCausland seemed thrown by the question. "My patience was sorely tried. I felt sorry for him but had no reason to dislike him."

"But you were about to fire him."

"He was about to fire himself. We'd bent over backwards. We even paid for him to dry out, but he was pissed before he got off the train back."

Like Stevens, McCausland was surprised by the beauty of Warren's wife, not surprised by the break-up of the marriage and totally unprepared for the circumstances of his death.

"Always struck me as completely straight."

"Why do you say that?"

"Because he didn't have the imagination to be anything else."

CROSS had the rest of the day to kill. There was still time to join Deidre. He sat in the car and flipped a coin. Heads he went. It came up heads. He did the best of three and got tails twice, and laughed at his childishness. Now that joining Deidre was out of the question, he didn't feel like going home so he went back to Warren's flat for want of anywhere else. He was curious about Warren. Perhaps McCausland was right and his story was all fantasy. Cross decided he would like to prove him wrong.

He made himself a cup of milkless tea and took it into Warren's living room. He was more thorough than he had been that morning. He moved furniture and looked under carpets. Before he was finished it was getting dark and he had to turn lights on.

Persistence eventually paid off. Lodged between the wall and the desk he found a screwed-up sheet of carbon paper which Warren would have used to make a copy of his work. Cross smoothed the sheet out and excitement gave way to disappointment. The carbon was so used that it was indecipherable. Even if Warren had backed up his last story on to it, what he had written was lost in the maze of print.

Cross was about to throw the sheet away when his eye was

drawn to the margin, where there were some notes added by hand. These were partly decipherable and among them he made out two names. The first was McKeague. The other was Heatherington.

Heatherington meant nothing. The name McKeague did. McKeague had been a notorious fanatic and founder of the Red Hand Commando, a loyalist death squad. His name had been connected with the Kincora Boys' Home scandal that had caused a big stink when the story had broken in the papers some years before.

"Oh, that old chestnut!" said McCausland when Cross called him, on Warren's phone, to ask if McKeague could have been part of Warren's story.

McCausland made it plain from his tone that he did not welcome the interruption and sounded bored by Cross's insistence. The story had been the subject of countless abortive editorial meetings.

"There'd been rumours about this for donkeys' years. Boys servicing local politicians and even boys being sent to England for the amusement of English MPs. No one has made it stand up."

Cross remembered that when the scandal had broken the men in charge of the boys' home were revealed to have loyalist paramilitary connections, hence the suggestion of a vice network involving local politicians. It was widely believed that a cover-up took place because British intelligence was blackmailing some of the politicians involved.

"What do you think?"

McCausland sighed theatrically. "I know the boys in the home were being abused for years and the hardest thing was to get anyone to believe them. Any complaints made by them— dating back to God knows when—were ignored. And it's probable that the men doing the abusing shared the boys with others, but not to the extent suggested. It was pretty small potatoes, a councillor here and there, but beyond that I would be very cautious. Talk to a dozen journalists and you'll hear a dozen versions of the same story, adjusted to suit whoever's telling it."

"And McKeague?"

"He was named as a homosexual contact and a file on the allegations against him was being considered by the DPP when he was shot, either by his own men in the RHC or by the INLA, depending on who you want to believe."

Either way, it struck Cross as oddly appropriate. The INLA was in many ways the republican mirror of the RHC. Both were highly unpredictable, given to feuding and operated on the outer limits of the sectarian conflict.

Something about McKeague nagged at the back of his mind until he remembered. "Wasn't there a murder case?"

He could hear McCausland getting restless. "More your department than mine, I would have thought. Yes, there was. Nothing was proved and no charges were brought, but there was a suspicion that he had been responsible for the death of a ten-year-old boy whose burnt and cut-up body was found later by the Lagan."

It had happened soon after Cross had arrived in Belfast. At the time it had been widely reported that the death was the work of satanists. There had been previous reports of black magic rituals in republican areas and, as the murdered boy had been Protestant, there was a large element of hysteria attached to the case.

"Why was McKeague not charged?" asked Cross.

"From what I know of McKeague he was quite capable of buggering little boys but I'm not sure he was up to murder. The story I heard was that McKeague's name was linked to the killing as a piece of slander by his Protestant colleagues."

"Why?"

"He was an embarrassment. Too queer for their taste." McCausland sighed noisily. "Look, inspector, at the risk of teaching my grandmother to suck eggs, we've all sifted through these stories a hundred times, McKeague and the rest of them. Because of the inefficiency of the various local authorities in exposing the scandal there's the natural tendency to see the whole thing as part of some cover-up. Cock-up is more like it, if you'll excuse the pun. And if Warren believed he was cracking Kincora then it was the act of a desperate man."

McCausland said he didn't know of any Heatherington and quickly excused himself.

Cross went home feeling restless and dissatisfied, to find himself in Deidre's bad books even more than usual for not turning up at her parents'.

"The children hoped you would read them a story."

"There's still time."

"They've been asleep an hour!"

WHEN Cross walked into Nesbitt's office he found another police officer there, with grey hair like iron filings and unblinking eyes of unsettling intensity.

"Sit down," said Nesbitt brusquely. "This is DI Cummings."

They nodded cautiously at each other. Cross was disconcerted to realize that Cummings reminded him of a thin version of his father. The dark green uniform was carefully pressed and starched in a way that made him feel slovenly. He wondered who Cummings was—CID, Special Branch?

"Tell us about Mary Elam," said Nesbitt.

The Elam case was the one Cross had the least desire to discuss. There was the illogical but very real feeling that Mary Elam was not being co-operative: if the dead were so reluctant to reveal their secrets they could hardly expect the police to bend over backwards for them. The investigation had not thrown up a single worthwhile lead. The van Mary Elam had been seen getting into seemed to have vanished into thin air. Hargreaves had gone back to check the Strathaven. There were rooms upstairs and a separate back entrance which Mary could have used. One or two of her men admitted going there with her and said she had regarded it as a bit of a dare, a couple of Taigs doing it in the heart of enemy territory. The landlord McElwaine was the likeliest suspect, but they had nothing on him. The Elam case was turning out like the Berrigan and Warren cases—inquiries that no one wanted. It was a stalemate. The whole fucking country was a stalemate.

Cross dutifully told Nesbitt and Cummings that their inquiries were concentrated on the Strathaven bar.

Cummings made it clear that he doubted Cross's ability. Cross marked him down as one of those handsome policemen who finds himself on camera a lot, with the necessary actorish confidence to make appearances count. They were usually adroit in committees, too, and hell to work for.

"I'm working on the assumption that Mary's killer knew her by sight," said Cross cautiously. "If her death was planned, then he knew where he was going to take her. I don't think she was killed at the Strathaven, unless it was done with the collusion of the landlord."

"A rather nasty piece of work," Cummings said.

If Cummings was so well briefed then why, wondered Cross, go through the whole charade of having to inform him.

"I would sweat that landlord, if I were you," added Cummings.

"He's been sweated," said Cross, thinking he was probably covering for Hargreaves.

"Go on," said Cummings, making it plain that the landlord was still very much in his mind.

Cross continued lamely, explaining that Mary Elam's last movements possibly involved one of her usual haunts and where she was murdered may well be close by, but remote enough not to attract attention. He told them that Hargreaves was in charge of a search of deserted buildings near the Strathaven.

"We're still checking. I feel we're very close to a break."

He wondered why Nesbitt and Cummings were taking such an interest.

"I want DI Cummings to take over the case," Nesbitt said abruptly. "He will, of course, liaise with you and I know you'll give him every co-operation."

He looked at Cross sharply. This was a professional slap on the wrists. Cross realized he had been half-expecting it since being called in. He was prepared to admit to himself, though not to them, that he had handled the case badly. He couldn't decide whether it was laziness or instinct. The latter told him that there was more to the business than met the eye, though for the life of him he couldn't see what. But he was equally prepared to accept that he was guilty of sloppy thinking.

Looking at Cummings' disciplined little mouth and shiny buttons, he realized that since the hearing and the business with Deidre, which were now irrevocably linked in his mind, he had been increasingly haunted by the idea of some other life, one that did not involve looking under his car every day for bombs. Deidre was why he had come to Belfast in the first place and now that their future was in doubt he questioned the point of everything.

Twenty-one

GUB O'NEILL said grace before Sunday lunch, praying that "the Good Lord see to the needs of those less fortunate." Cross bowed his head and stared at one of his mother-in-law's soup concoctions. After his failure to show up the week before, Deidre had made it clear that there would be no excuse this time.

Barbara O'Neill carved the roast, keeping up a running commentary on the state of anything and everything from the quality of the meat to pop songs on Radio 1. She knew the cost of everything to the penny, from a can of beans to the price of a united Ireland. It was her way of keeping up with the times.

"Who'd want to live in Eire—the cost of living. I mean they're nearly bankrupt! And they've nothing like the social services that we do."

Like most women of her class and generation, Barbara O'Neill dressed in pastel woollens and wore her hair in a perm like an iron helmet. Make-up and powder were immaculately applied and she always smelt of perfume. Being a traditionalist, she liked to give the impression of being Gub's "wee woman" and argued that women shouldn't work, though she had a career of her own in local politics, as a magistrate and local councillor.

Although Cross was vaguely included in the conversation he felt like the fourth tennis partner, stuck on the base line while the others rallied round the net. He and the children were largely silent during the meal.

The O'Neills had recently moved from a very large draughty house on the outskirts of Belfast to what they called a modest bungalow, in fact an expensive piece of architect design built on land overlooking Lough Neagh where planning permission regulations were waived because Gub O'Neill had the necessary clout.

130

Cross's father-in-law was officially retired and liked to give the impression that his activities were restricted to chopping kindling and shining shoes, though he continued to earn a good living from private surgery. O'Neill had done well out of medicine but had always managed to pretend that he was merely an ordinary doctor in public service, and cautiously screened the extent of his wealth.

In his carefully pressed cavalry twills and neat checked shirts and cravats, and with his impressive head of silver hair, he cut an imposing figure, reminding Cross more of an admiral or a general. His bearing and posture reflected centuries of breeding, realized in the effortless beauty of Deidre. Their grandchildren's attractiveness—the fact that they took after their mother rather than Cross—was obviously a source of enormous relief. The threat of introducing inferior stock had been averted by the fortitude of the O'Neill genes.

Cross was only starting to realize the extent to which the O'Neills were influencing the direction of his children's lives. Since their birth, Deidre had moved towards accepting her parents' values, previously scorned. As the children grew, they plotted their future, leaving Cross feeling redundant.

Male O'Neills did not become policemen. Government administration, the armed forces, the clergy and medicine were what they did, as well as applying a canny business sense to the stock market. The fact that the family fortune was founded on trade—traditionally disapproved of by landed families like the O'Neills—was conveniently forgotten. Until Gub's grandfather had rebelled against tradition and gone into the munitions business the O'Neills were well bred but never rich landowners. The move paid off handsomely for Austin "Shooter" O'Neill, especially towards the end of his career, when the firm was kept on permanent overtime, providing for the demands of the First World War. After gorging himself on a lifetime of enormous profit, Shooter embarked on a world tour and shocked the family for a second time by marrying—his first wife having died only shortly before—a swarthy Mediterranean adventuress half his age, with few words of English. Fortunately for the O'Neills, Shooter's heart gave out before he could alter his will in her favour. She was never invited to Belfast.

Cross would have found Deidre's family less formidable had the weight of tradition sat more heavily. But they were relentlessly unceremonious, always organizing chaotic family games, where the need to win was barely disguised, and entertaining with cardiganed informality. Social activity was centred around what they called the parlour, an enormous extension that incorporated a ranch-style kitchen, a picture window view of the lough, an open fire, eating space and a large television, which was left permanently on.

Over pudding, Gub O'Neill got on to his pet subject.

"All she"—meaning Mrs. Thatcher—"has to do is let the security forces wipe out the IRA."

"Oh, Daddy, how can you say that?" said Deidre, by way of token objection.

"I fought during the war with an Irish regiment and you couldn't ask for better men—if you lead them. But they're no good without leaders. The IRA is just the same. Remove the leadership and the rest would fall away very quickly. The UDA and the UVF—that'll go by the board if they wipe out the IRA. What do you think?"

O'Neill was looking at Cross, who was reluctant to engage. He sensed Deidre's impatience across the table.

"I really don't know any more," he began laboriously. "I think I thought the British government should take a more decisive line towards withdrawal, a five-year plan after which the troops would leave. And I think I thought that they should appoint a minister of education for Northern Ireland because until you get the children together you'll not get rid of the bigotry."

The O'Neills looked horrified at the prospect. Barbara O'Neill moved smoothly in. After Cross's stumbling, her fluent riposte was a snub.

"I can see the point of what you're saying, but it's not as easy as you think. When I look back on when I was a little girl, you were either very definitely Catholic or very definitely Protestant. Everyone knew what everyone else was. I never played with Roman Catholic children."

"Over my dead body is what you're saying."

Cross heard Deidre's sharp intake of breath. It was the first time he had insulted Barbara O'Neill.

"Is exactly what I'm saying," she said, with a level stare and a smile that disguised a will of steel.

His triumph had barely lasted a second. He was naive to

think that she was unequipped to deal with his attack. In the silence that followed Cross knew that he was supposed to respond, realized too that Barbara O'Neill scented blood. He tried to think of some witty response but was weighed down by the silences of his childhood.

Gub O'Neill took advantage of his slowness and barged in.

"When Merlyn Rees was here as secretary of state, I said to him one day, 'Merlyn, until you really carry out what you know and believe to be right—and that is that the IRA should be taken out—you're never going to get anywhere. There are a whole lot of good bogholes here and you should make use of them.' "

"They're terrible cowards, you know," added Barbara O'Neill.

They weren't, in Cross's opinion, but what was the point in saying so.

"Just a Paddy here and a Seamus there, nobody knows where they are. And if they did that, the boys will soon get cold feet. And you may get one or two wrong ones by mistake, but what's that among so many?"

Cross wanted to say that as far as he was concerned the North could be dumped unceremoniously into the hands of the republicans and that bigots like them should face the choice of martyrdom or conversion to the Church of Rome, and see how they liked that.

Gub O'Neill droned on about some current inquiry.

"Waste of bloody public money if you ask me."

"Not in front of the grandchildren," his wife interjected.

"Does 'em good to hear a bloody now and then, doesn't it, Mattie?" The boy giggled. "Big boys' games, big boys' rules, eh? You'd go along with that, wouldn't you?"

His grandson nodded in bewilderment as O'Neill turned his sights back on Cross.

"If the basic attitude of the government towards the security forces is get on with the job and keep the lid on things, then it should let them get on with it and not enquire too closely about what goes on under the lid. Either they do that and show a bit of responsibility or they have the guts to declare all-out war. What you don't do is let them get on with it and throw up your hands in horror when some mishap comes to light. What about all those colleagues of yours that have been shot or blown up?

Do you think the IRA cared about the Geneva Convention when it was killing them?"

"Now, children, have you all had enough?"

Both Cross and Deidre came under this banner as far as Mrs O'Neill was concerned.

"Who's for coffee?"

THE SITUATION improved a little when they took the children for a walk, which meant that Cross could play with them and avoid Gub O'Neill, who was on to the iniquities of the dole.

"Too many of them look upon it as a payment for a life of doing nothing."

"Now shut up a moment, Gub, and look at that view. Isn't it perfectly charming?"

Perfectly charming was Barbara O'Neill's highest accolade.

"Perfectly charming," echoed her husband. The view was of the lough in pale sunlight. The grey sky of earlier had given way to blue and the day was mild. Without meaning to, Cross found himself standing next to Deidre.

"All right?" he asked.

"Fine. A nice lunch."

The way she said it everything could have been all right.

"I'll take you back, then I must work."

"You work too hard, darling."

The endearment was thrown in for the benefit of Barbara O'Neill, who had joined them.

"Yes, you do," she said. "Why don't you take the rest of the day off?"

"I can't really," he said.

"Surely it can wait till tomorrow? Leave the children with us and go off somewhere nice with your wife."

Deidre looked panicked at the thought, and just to rile her he said, "That would be nice, wouldn't it, darling?"

She appeared annoyed by the returned endearment.

Under the brisk command of Barbara O'Neill, they found themselves being bundled off and told to collect the children in the morning.

"But they haven't got their pyjamas," protested Deidre feebly.

The children, delighted by a break in their routine, were unconcerned by such details.

* * *

CROSS and Deidre found themselves driving back to Belfast, wondering what on earth they were doing.

"Fuck it," said Cross. "Why don't we forget about things for the rest of the day and call a truce."

Deidre glowered, giving no quarter. He'd had enough and braked hard so that she was thrown violently forward in her seat.

"You bloody fool, what was that for?" she said, angry and rattled.

"Shut up and listen. Until you told me about you and whoever it is I thought things were basically OK, not terrific but OK, and once the hearing was over I wanted us to have some time to ourselves to make things better. That's what I thought. I know I haven't been attentive lately—"

"I'm not telling you who he is."

"Stop being so fucking childish. What difference can it make?"

They hammered away at each other, hurling insults until Deidre sank back in her seat, flushed and breathless. Cross experienced an inappropriate stab of desire, and wished he could put aside his self-control and take her in his arms. A fuck was not the solution to all their problems, but it would be a start, he thought grimly. But what he took to be a slackening was her rallying for another screaming onslaught.

"Arsehole! You pompous arsehole! You should have seen yourself at lunchtime. Stuck up, poker up your arse—just because you think my parents look down on you, you feel you have the right to come on all high and mighty, Mr fucking Plod. Arsehole! Arsehole!" With that she was out of the car. "Go solve your fucking murders!"

Cross sat at the wheel, shaken. He nearly went after her but decided he'd not be seen crawling.

Twenty-two

CROSS arrived at Berrigan's farm in the middle of the night, half-expecting to find Berrigan there. When Deidre had not come back by ten he had looked for her in several restaurants she liked, hoping for a showdown. Then he had driven around aimlessly, chain smoking a ten-pack of cigarettes, before deciding. He went via Maghera and Dungiven, crossing the border at Londonderry. He drove fast, concentrating only on his driving.

He got lost several times in the forest lanes and nearly turned back, struck by the pointlessness of his journey, but then found the burnt-out car that had pointed Donnelly in the right direction.

He sat for a long time in the parked car. He wished he still had some cigarettes. The silence of the night was absolute, full of the stillness of the slaughtered animals. He felt scared in a way that he had not since childhood.

He got out slowly, his nerves taut. He didn't know what he was looking for: traces of Berrigan, or through him some confrontation with himself, perhaps.

He had his torch but he didn't want to use it or turn on the house lights because the twilight world he found himself in seemed clearer than an illuminated one. As he went through the rooms he thought of the various compartments of his own life: each drawer of Berrigan's was like a container of his own memories, every door a reminder of different thresholds, first with his parents, then with Deidre, and the doors of his work, as the bearer of bad news.

He lay for a while on the mattress in the makeshift bedroom, trying without success to feel his way into the mind of the man who had once slept there.

Downstairs he found himself staring at a pair of wellington boots in the hall. He put them on. They were too big and he was struck by an absurd thought: had he ever read "Goldilocks and the Three Bears" to Matthew or Fiona? He realized he had put on the boots to go to the barn.

He felt his way through the workshop, which was unnaturally dark after the semi-gloom of the house. He stumbled against an upturned chair and pitched headlong, barking his shins.

He found the door and pushed it open. While he tried to work out the direction of the barn, the moon appeared to reveal it, gaunt and forbidding. The peat sacks looked even eerier by moonlight.

He marched across the fields, head down, and entered the barn without hesitating. The stench had gone. There was nothing there, not even any lingering atmosphere of evil, just a smell of disinfectant. He stayed only a minute, hoping that unconnected details buried in the recesses of his mind might surface. But nothing happened.

The luminous dial of his watch glowed in the dark. It was three-forty. He took the track back to the farm, covering the distance quickly. He looked again at the deep freeze and in the workshop, after propping both doors open so that he could see a little better. Even so he had to let his touch guide him. He worked his way across the surface of the bench, feeling various objects until he recognized them. Inside the cabinet full of tiny drawers that lay propped at the back of the bench he found more tacks, hooks, a few scraps of braid and old tins. He opened the tins to see what was inside: more of the same. He dropped a tin and the nails spilled on to the flagstones in a metallic shower. As he knelt to scoop them back up he was aware of something else. At first he thought it was just paper to line the tin. He picked it up and turned it over and could make out a darker side. He took it outside and saw that it was a photograph.

He used the map light in the car. His first reaction was disappointment. It was an ordinary family snapshot, its colours faded. There was a woman, and two children, boys of about five and six. To one side was a man, older than the woman. It was a bright summer day which made everyone screw up their eyes. Behind them was a kitchen window with washing-up liquid next to a spider plant.

He looked again at the man. He was good looking, middle

aged, stocky and his hair was receding and turning white, which fitted with some of the local descriptions of Berrigan. He looked disappointingly unlike a killer. Cross remembered as a boy seeing a photograph of the Rillington Place murderer, Christie—so ordinary. Part of him had expected and still did, as silly as it was, to see the mark of Cain.

Then it went click click click, like the tumbling numbers of a one-armed bandit falling into place.

It was the vagueness of the man in the photograph that alerted him. The way he'd deliberately positioned himself so that you looked at him last, then hardly at all. The whole case had been dominated by vagueness.

The van was where he'd made his mistake. Once it was linked to Berrigan, he'd jumped to the conclusion that Berrigan's ownership meant that he'd driven it on the night of dumping the body. And that Berrigan was therefore the killer.

What Cross had overlooked in his haste was that the opposite could also be true—that it was Berrigan who'd been frozen in his own deep freeze and transported in the back of his own van. The man Cross was looking at in the photograph was Berrigan all right. But Berrigan the dead man rather than Berrigan the killer.

The woman was presumably his wife. Cross wondered where she was now and what age the boys were. Then, because he was aware of tripping up so badly over Berrigan, he asked himself the opposite: what if they weren't anywhere? What if they were dead? Had he found the picture in a drawer he would have been less inclined to conclude that, but the way it had been carefully hidden—sealed away—left him with the distinct impression that they existed only as memories.

Twenty-three

Belfast, June 1973

CANDLESTICK was told by Herron to wait outside the room and when he was asked in ten minutes later Herron looked grim. "We have a good arrangement here, don't we?" asked Herron. "I look after you well, don't I?"

Candlestick nodded and looked at Breen, wondering what he had been passing on. Candlestick's relationship with Breen had become quite informal with Breen's move into loyalist areas and the expansion of Herron's rackets into republican areas. He often found himself liaising with him and they'd struck up a friendship of sorts, occasionally drinking together. Candlestick even passed on scraps of information about the loyalists and Breen had confided that Herron had asked him to provide two gunmen to shoot his brother-in-law, whom he suspected of being an informer for the Provisionals. Candlestick wondered at the craziness of it all: Herron sub-contracting an assassination to the enemy. Breen was amused as ever and willing to do the job because it would inconvenience a rival in the Provisionals.

As Herron continued to question him it became clear that he had been alerted by Breen to the fact that some of his men were being run by the British, and that Breen was unconcerned about being seen to be the source of this alarm. Candlestick realized that whatever loose alliance he might have with Breen it did not extend to trust.

"I'd just like to clear up a couple of facts here," said Herron. "You came over here when?"

"The July before last."

"What happened? I mean, why did you suddenly decide to come over? It's not exactly Benidorm."

"I came to see a woman. You could ask her except she's married and her husband doesn't know."

"And you came over with Baker."

"I met him in a pub in Liverpool and it turned out we were coming over at the same time. He was with a gang of fellows."

"And did he say what he was doing coming here?"

"Visiting relatives."

"What made you decide to stay on?"

"Well, I was past the date of return to my regiment and Baker said stick around because there was money floating about."

"So you're a deserter."

"You know all this."

"Then tell me why the fucking army hasn't arrested you."

"Because they don't know I'm here."

"And what about Baker? If he's got relatives here wouldn't it be the first place they'd ask?"

"You'd have to ask Baker about that."

"It's a sad day when you have to question the loyalty of your own men."

Candlestick assured Herron that his allegiance was not in question. He had carried out his orders. He had no dealings with other parties. He had not lined his own pockets at the expense of the UDA. (This was not entirely true. Candlestick was in it for himself as much as the next man, and not above the odd "homer.") He had been willing to shoot at soldiers during Herron's war with the army. The last point seemed to persuade Herron.

"Did you see Baker join in any of this?"

"He may have."

"But you didn't see him?"

Candlestick said he could not remember and Herron and Breen exchanged significant looks.

WHEN he next met Breen alone, Breen apologized for putting Candlestick on the spot. Candlestick shrugged and said that he had nothing to hide. Breen gave a sardonic smile.

"Does Tommy know you're seeing a Catholic girl?"

"It's none of his business."

"Then it's true that you are?"

She was a student named Becky and her family had been

republican for generations. He was annoyed with himself for being so easily tricked into admitting it.

"Well, I'm damned if you are not blushing. What are you telling her if you're not telling her you're Tommy Herron's bodyguard?"

"I told her I was working for you."

Breen threw back his head and laughed. "Attaboy! That'll teach me to be nosy."

"What was all that about with Tommy the other day?"

"Nothing, really. I heard some of you fellows were British assets. True or not, it's always useful to me if Tommy conducts a witch hunt in his own ranks. We're friends most of the time but I still have to be seen to be making the odd move."

TWO DAYS later Candlestick arranged to meet a man in a bar off the Malone Road. He took a taxi to the Botanic Gardens and walked the rest of the way, making sure he was not followed. He had been meeting this man since his arrival in Belfast. It was to him that he was known as Candlestick. Their meetings were secret. No one else knew about them, not Baker or Herron or Breen or Bunty.

On that occasion he passed on what had occurred between himself and Herron and Breen and their suspicions about Baker working for the British.

"Do they suspect you?" asked the man.

"I'm pretty sure they don't."

"In that case I think you should tell Baker that he's been rumbled. Stampede him and let's see what happens."

BAKER'S flight was an erratic affair. He fled Belfast and returned to his regiment in England, where his claim that he had been on special duties in Northern Ireland was dismissed when he could produce no supporting evidence. The contact number for Bunty turned out to be a dead line and had been, according to the GPO, for several months. Baker's story was rejected as fantasy and he was court martialled and dismissed from his regiment.

As far as Bunty was concerned, Baker next resurfaced when he was told by a Detective Sergeant Cummings—an RUC contact—that Baker had come to his attention after walking into a Wiltshire police station and announcing that he wished to speak to a police officer about crimes committed in Northern Ireland.

Bunty raised his eyebrows, feigning ignorance, and asked what on earth Baker had been on about. Cummings knew that Bunty understood precisely what Baker was on about. Bunty was a great one for coded conversations.

"He claimed that he had been ordered to kill IRA terrorists but had undergone a religious conversion and wanted the matter off his chest. At that point the Warminster police called us and we flew him back here."

"A religious conversion, you say?"

"It's his way of saying that he wants to do a deal."

"What do you think led to this conversion?"

Cummings said he thought Baker's disappointment stemmed from the way his regiment had treated him. He had expected a hero's welcome, once the real reason for his absence had been established.

"Then panic set in," Cummings went on. "Baker has relatives here in Belfast and realized his running away might lead to reprisals if the loyalists suspected him of working for the Brits."

"So he'll name names in exchange for leniency in court and protection for his family."

"Exactly. But the problem we have is that he is unreliable. Some of the names he's coming up with we know and others we don't know, and some of the ones we know appear—how shall I put it?—a little far-fetched. We'd like a second opinion."

They got down to horse trading, going through Baker's list, so that Bunty could protect his own agents. Candlestick's name was carefully crossed out by Cummings, who then asked about Tommy Herron. He noted that Bunty kept a straight face throughout the process.

"Baker's claiming that Herron authorized all these killings. What do you think?" asked Cummings.

"I'm not sure it'll be relevant by the time you get to court. From what I hear, Herron's days are numbered. I would have thought more of a worry for you is Baker's allegation that the RUC was in on planning half these killings."

"I'm not sure Mr Baker's conversion has left him with all his marbles."

Twenty-four

CROSS arrived back from Berrigan's farm as day broke to find Deidre not at home. He was too tired to know what he felt about that and was sitting drinking coffee in the kitchen when she walked in. She seemed in a good mood.

"It wasn't what you think," she said.

"What am I to think?"

She drifted past, kissing the top of his head. Her offhand affection ambushed him, and he reached out and encircled her with his arms and they stayed like that, his head pressed against her, as she started to talk.

"I went to a film and then I ate alone in an empty restaurant, an escalope and a bottle of wine, and after that I sat in the Europa and watched the foreign correspondents getting drunk. One of them bought me a drink. He was very gentle and concerned that I should be drinking on my own. He wanted me to go upstairs with him."

Cross felt a pang of jealousy.

"I thought about it," she went on. "Quite seriously. But he was too nice and too drunk and it wouldn't have worked and he would have got maudlin, when what I wanted was a plain, straightforward fuck. Can you understand that?"

"Can't you get that anyway?" He felt petty as he said it.

"I wanted a souvenir, something to remember myself by, so that whenever I passed the hotel I would be reminded of taking a stranger to bed for an hour or two, and having something outside the rest of my life, which would be like a marker, unlike all the other stuff which ends up forgotten in the swill."

"And?"

"I didn't. I took a room and even thought about phoning down to see if they could send someone up. Isn't that what men do when they stay alone in hotels, ask the desk for a woman? Can you order a man? Well, I never found out but I got a grand night's sleep."

Cross stared at his coffee. The idea of Deidre having desires independent of him was something he was reluctant to acknowledge. While he criticized her for a certain hardening of attitude over the years, he was slow to accept a similar calcifying in himself. He saw now how much he took her for granted.

"You should have called me," he said. "I would have come."

It was the wrong thing to say. He had missed the point, whatever that was. She gave him a breezy smile.

"You weren't here," she said and walked out whistling.

CROSS asked Westerby to track down Vinnie, telling her that he needed to talk to the boy but didn't want him picked up officially. She said she would go round to his place when she was off duty. She was grateful to be asked. It seemed like a resumption of more normal relations.

Vinnie came to York Road station two evenings later, surly and mistrustful. Whatever confidences had once been shared no longer applied. Cross wondered why he had come. There was no detectable sign of anxiety beneath the taciturn exterior.

"I'm fine," was all he said when Cross asked how he was. "Really fine."

"Last time you asked if I could help."

"I said I'm fine."

"Then why are you here?"

"To tell you I'm fine. OK?"

They went on without getting anywhere until Cross gave Vinnie a number at work where he could be reached if necessary. By doing this he felt absolved of any further responsibility. He was sure—hoped—Vinnie would not call.

Afterwards, he was aware of the sour taste of a bad conscience. He stalked the house grimly. Deidre sensed his mood and avoided him. They had learned to refine their behaviour to intrude on each other as little as possible. Cross felt a seething irritation at the absurdity of it all.

The phone rang late and Deidre hurried to answer it, leaving Cross to wonder how often her lover called her at home. He stood in the sitting room, just out of earshot, straining to hear.

"It's for you," she announced from the hall, and was gone when he got there.

It was Westerby. She apologized for phoning so late, but she had something on the Berrigan affair. Cross's bad mood fell away at the excitement in her voice.

"It's the woman and children in the photograph. They were killed in 1982 when their car was blown up by a bomb. Her name was Bernadette Breen and the children were about the right age for the boys in the photograph. I don't know what happened to Mr. Breen but I have their old address."

WESTERBY collected Cross the following morning and they drove to the Breens' old neighbourhood, a moderately prosperous northern suburb, out towards the zoo. Cross lowered the window and breathed in the damp, warming air. After another night of rain, the morning was mild with a gentle blue sky and the promise of fair weather.

The Breens' house was a white semi. Cross was struck by the contrast between the primitive state of the Donegal farm and the obsessive neatness of these suburbs with their orderly gardens and verges. The tree in front of the house was heavy with early blossom. The transition between the seasons was passing him by.

The woman who answered the door had been there only six months, knew nothing of the Breens and referred them to a neighbour opposite.

There was no answer when they rang the bell and were told by a passerby that the woman was down at the shops and would be back shortly. It seemed a friendly neighbourhood in spite of its fussy air.

They waited in the car. Cross was uncomfortably aware of his earlier unpleasantness to Westerby.

"Mind if I smoke?" he asked.

"Fine. I didn't realize you did, sir."

"I don't, as a rule. How are you settling in? Everything all right?"

He was aware of how stilted he sounded.

"Yes, fine."

"Compared to your previous work?"

"Like a holiday."

She smiled wryly and added that the sex abuse unit was

regarded suspiciously by most departments, because it dealt with what was thought of as welfare work and was staffed almost entirely by women.

"The men thought it was an easy turn. You know, going to the birthday parties of kiddies who'd been victimized. They called it the shopping unit because they thought we spent most of our time in Marks & Spencer."

Cross stubbed out his cigarette. He saw an old woman in the distance walking towards them with the aid of sticks.

"The kids were the hardest to deal with," Westerby went on. "You'd take them down to the canteen and buy them sweets and get them to draw, and try and get them to talk that way. We had these anatomical dolls and you'd get them to show you what had happened. Buggery, rape, oral sex. I used to despair. That's where the real damage goes on, as if anyone cares. In the home. The rest is easy. Sorry, I'm preaching."

It was unusual to have any discussion about work.

"No. I wonder if the whole crisis is not just a larger manifestation of violence in the family."

Westerby did not know what to make of Cross's remark. It sounded uncharacteristic and so formal, more like something she would have expected to see written down. She wondered whether he was happy with his life. At that moment it seemed not.

"Come on," he said, breaking the awkwardness. "There she is."

The arthritic old woman who had been making such painful progress up the road arrived at her gate. After they had introduced themselves, she invited them into her front room, which looked like it had not changed or seen visitors in twenty years.

"That's the Breens," she said, nodding at the photograph Cross showed to her. "It was terrible. To have it happen right outside."

She struggled up from her chair using her sticks, brushing aside Cross's help, and moved to the window, pushing aside the net curtain.

"It was about half past eight. I was in the kitchen. I thought it was my gas that had exploded. We've never had anything like that round here. The poor souls, they didn't stand a chance. They had to re-lay the concrete in front of the garage after."

She returned to her seat, shaking her head. The Breens were Catholic, she thought, pleasant enough but distant.

"You're not sure?" Cross asked.

"With a name like Breen you would have thought so but they were not church-goers."

She knew little more about them, apart from remembering that Breen was some sort of contractor.

"On the morning of the explosion do you know where Mr. Breen was?"

The old woman cocked her head. "Well, I suppose he was there. My first thought was that it was him in the car. After that I was straight on the telephone to the police, but everyone else must have been too because the switchboard was jammed. When I next looked there were fire engines and ambulances and everything. I do remember thinking that I never saw Mr. Breen after that, even when the house was sold."

WESTERBY could find no record of Breen since the deaths of his wife and children.

"Well, almost no record," she told Cross. "I checked the obvious sources. There's an awful lot of Breens in the phone books but none's our man. But he does have a building society savings account with the Nationwide still under his old address. The last deposit was made before his wife died, and there have been various withdrawals since, amounting to about fifteen thousand pounds."

"How much is in the account?"

"Fifty thousand pounds."

Cross whistled. Who the hell was Breen?

"The withdrawals were made from different branches—Strabane, Londonderry, Armagh and Newcastle, so there's no pattern. I only thought of building societies because I had to go to mine yesterday."

"Isn't there a limit he can draw in cash? Cheques would have to go through a bank."

Westerby shook her head. "You can draw cash if you phone up and give notice. His old driving licence would have taken care of any proof of identity. He never changed the address with vehicle licensing."

* * *

"EMPHYSEMA," said Charlie Spencer, a once-big man shrunk to a husk. Cross put him at sixty-five though looking much older. His skin was pitted and pale. Bony wrists hung loosely from frayed shirt cuffs, but his hair was still rigid from years of discipline.

They sat in the small conservatory of a nursing home whose bright colours couldn't mask the smell of institution and sickness. Through an open door Cross could see patients tranquillized into a semi-comatose state, slumped round the afternoon television. Spencer stared at him uncomprehendingly.

"You were in charge of the Breen case," Cross prompted.

Spencer's breath rattled in his chest. He apologized for his failing memory.

"Oh yes, a complete mess," he said after Cross had reminded him. He stared at the garden and blinked at the warm sun. Cross tried to decide if he was contemplating his limited future or dredging a faulty memory.

"I can hardly remember what my wife looks like, even though she comes every day," Spencer eventually said. "What did you say your name was?"

Cross felt he was facing another dead end. He noticed that the lawn outside had just received its first mowing of the year.

Spencer appeared to have drifted off. Cross rose to leave, but then Spencer, his eyes still shut, spoke. "It was Breen who usually took the car, except on that morning his wife was going to use it to drive the children to school because they'd missed the bus. Breen wasn't there."

"Where was he?"

"In a hotel across the border, on business, he said. Some of the staff said he had a woman with him, but I never had a chance to question him again. Mr. Breen was murky waters."

"Do you think he had anything to do with the wife's death?"

"Until I spoke to him. I don't think you can fake shock like that. In my mind there's no doubt the bomb was meant for Breen, and maybe part of his shock was knowing it was."

"Who wanted him dead?"

"At first I thought it was the Provos because Breen was a contractor with at least one company that did maintenance work for the security forces."

"Which would have made him a target."

"Quite. The Provisionals never claimed the bomb, but I

thought that was because they were too embarrassed after blowing the woman and children to smithereens."

Spencer added that he'd heard later from a colleague in Special Branch that Breen's background was more complicated than it appeared. As well as doing work for the security forces, he was also thought by some to have been in the Official IRA.

"An old Sticky is what I heard, dating back to before the riots of 1969. Some said he dropped out in the seventies. Another story went that he was still active but worked out of the Republic and resurfaced in the INLA."

"If he goes that far back wouldn't he be known about?"

Spencer shrugged. "Maybe he was. Maybe his name just didn't appear on any list. Go back to the beginning and you find they were all in each other's pockets."

Cross saw that Spencer thought he didn't believe him. Spencer sighed and his breath wheezed.

"Let me tell you a story, going back to the start of the Troubles. It involves a man from the *Daily Mirror*. Most of the staff on the Belfast desk were young and keen. Then this old drunk was brought in to run the office and none of them could understand why. Anyway, one time the drunk was drunk in the bar of a hotel well known to be neutral. It was also common knowledge that the receptionist was an active republican, so when two soldiers got on the roof and started firing at some commotion, the receptionist went berserk and phoned the barracks to complain, and when the barracks wasn't quick enough he marched into the crowded bar and shouted that unless the soldiers got off the roof there'd be trouble. When nobody moved, here's your receptionist to your man from the *Mirror*: 'You fix it or none of yous is being let into the disco on Saturday.' And the man from the *Mirror* did. He made the call. The soldiers got off the roof and they all went to the disco."

Spencer smiled and gave a painful laugh. Cross wasn't sure what he was supposed to make of the story. Spencer, seeing his confusion, patiently elaborated.

"The receptionist knew that the man was intelligence, which was more than his colleagues did. The thing is, in those days they all went to the disco—the security forces and the IRA, the whole bloody shooting party. Even McGuinness used to put in an appearance. So your man Breen could have been cutting deals in any direction. In with the IRA. In with the security forces. Making sure his name was kept quiet. They all went to the bloody disco and don't let anyone tell you different."

Cross stood up to leave, still not sure what he was supposed to make of the story. "How well did Breen do out of his business?"

"Well enough to support a reasonable standard of living."

"But not rich."

"I don't know what you mean by rich."

"He had over fifty thousand pounds saved away."

Spencer shrugged. He suddenly looked tired. "Not that rich."

WESTERBY lay alone in bed reading, her evening in ruins after a row with her fiancé. It was a word she hated. Or was it the state of being fiancéed she disliked so much? She wondered what she was getting herself into by saying she would marry Martin. There was passion in her, she knew that, though not enough surfaced in their relationship, which seemed too conditioned by caution, especially where sex was concerned. Sex was not what she had expected. Sex, with Martin at least, had turned out to be about not doing things, not getting pregnant, not having sex during her period (his squeamishness, not hers), not doing what he probably wanted her to do, except she didn't know what that was because he never asked. His reticence about his own body blunted her natural curiosity. In her imagination she always thought of sex as something uncomplicated, but her experience so far told her otherwise.

Because she considered herself only marginally attractive she suspected that she drew men that were in some way flawed in their unsureness about themselves. They assumed she was comfortable. They did not see the drive, sexual and professional, beneath the surface.

At work she saw men eyeing her the way they did all women, with their furtive glances, the casual appraisal, quick to dismiss. To judge by their jibes and general attitude, most of them would have been more at ease in a singular world. Women made them defensive and they ignored them or turned them into the butt of their humour. Some WPCs coped with this by becoming more mannish, cracking crude jokes and swearing. For her own part, Westerby had grown used to masculine ways and their abdication of responsibility when dealing with emotional damage. They made themselves scarce when it came to a notification of death or the aftermath of rape, but were happy enough to gawp at a rape victim when she was being examined or read her statement. Most rape cases they dismissed as not real rape, preferring to see them as a combination of enticement, collusion and one too many drinks.

Westerby thumped her pillow in exasperation. She was wide awake and it would be hours before she got to sleep. She decided she hated her duvet cover. It was a present from her mother, and done in the sort of floral design that her mother didn't like but thought she did. Westerby couldn't stand any of it—the floral dish cloths, the floral towels, sheets and curtains. She thought of them as Prevention of the Sex Act sheets, a design so ghastly that it would deter all but the most determined from ever contemplating any form of conjugation, not that her mother, for all her liberal views in other departments, could accept her daughter as anything other than chaste and virginal, at twenty-seven.

The duvet was a single duvet on a double bed, which pretty much summed up the contradictions of her life. How she had explained the bed away to her mother she could no longer remember. Either she had said that it was already in the flat when she'd moved in or she was looking after it for a friend. It was exactly the sort of detail that her mother would remember and trip her up on one day. New sheets, new fiancé—new mother—she resolved before drifting off into uneasy sleep.

WHILE Westerby slept, the body of a young woman was found stabbed to death on a piece of wasteland that Monday night, which was the spring bank holiday. As it was Westerby's day off she only discovered about the murder in the paper, where it made the front page, written up by Ronnie Stevens.

Stevens had been at the murder site and quizzed Cross as he walked back to his Volvo. Cross had spotted him lurking beyond the scene-of-crime tape that cordoned off the area, in the crowd that had gathered, attracted by the lights and the vehicles. He was irritated by Stevens' assumption that their one meeting allowed him a familiarity, and tried to ignore him.

"Any scraps for the hacks?" Stevens asked with a cocky grin.

"A statement will be released."

"Someone said the eyes are missing."

"You'll have to wait for the statement."

"Is it a slasher?"

Stevens' tone said that he scented a big story. Cross wondered how he had found out about the body. Probably one of the ambulancemen had phoned him in exchange for a fee.

"No, it's not a slasher," said Cross, brushing past.

The paper's banner headline was inevitably "Slasher Strikes!" The woman was not named. Stevens had inferred that the motive was sexual. Also included was the detail that the victim's eyes had been gouged out, which had been withheld from the police statement. As a result, Cross spent most of his morning fending various calls about this, including Nesbitt, who wanted to know how Stevens had got hold of the detail and why Cross had withheld it in the first place.

"Because I didn't want the press spreading panic. It's the kind of case that could get out of hand and until we get a full report the less said the better."

Cross let Nesbitt grumble on about press interference.

"Do you have a name on her yet?" Nesbitt asked just before hanging up.

"Mary Ryan, twenty-one years old."

"Christ, the poor child," said Nesbitt, in a rare display of compassion.

Poor child, indeed. Hers was a fate he would not wish on anyone. It was the most gruesome murder of his career. The eyes had been gouged out and there was a puncture in the neck where she had been stabbed. The sockets were strangely bloodless. Either they had been bathed or the eyes had been removed after death, after the flow of blood had stopped. It was clear that she had been killed somewhere else. There would have been more blood if it had been done on the spot. The absence of blood startled Cross almost more than the vicious attack on her eyes. But the detail that persisted—and would not budge however hard he tried—was the sharp contrast of everyone's visible breath on the cold night air, and the lack of any coming from her.

She was a wee slip of a thing, probably plain at best, he thought, with a wrench of his heart, dowdily but sensibly dressed. One shoe was gone, again suggesting that the killing had been done elsewhere. In all of his years he had seen nothing like it. The body had been deliberately arranged into an obscene display of limbs, with legs akimbo to reveal the pubic area. The victim was wearing no underwear—like Mary Elam, Cross remembered, and he wondered at the connection.

* * *

AFTER the autopsy on Mary Ryan, Cross asked Ricks what the chances were of both women being killed by the same person.

"On the face of it, unlikely, because, as you know, once a killer has established his method he usually sticks to it. Creatures of habit, we are. Stabbers stab, stranglers strangle. Also there's the mutilation of Mary Ryan and not of Mary Elam. There again, both women's wrists show signs of having been bound. Absence of underclothing in both cases too, though neither body showed signs of sexual intercourse or interference. Yon Mary was a virgin, by the way. Hymen intacta." Ricks smirked.

"So it's not impossible they were killed by the same man."

"Not impossible," echoed Ricks. "You're certainly talking about a degree of premeditation."

Ricks' report also confirmed that Mary Ryan's blood had been washed off the skin. There was none on her clothes, which suggested that she had been stripped and dressed again afterwards. Ricks also noted that the nails had been carefully cleaned, removing any foreign skin or fibre that might have got caught beneath in a struggle.

Cross wondered if they had enough to link the two deaths, and later said so to Westerby.

"Perhaps the killer had intended to mutilate Mary Elam but was interrupted," she said. "Or he had to kill her before he meant to."

"Go on."

"Just that, really, and the fact that the killer went for the victim's throat in both cases."

Cross hadn't thought of that. Westerby seemed about to point out something else when she stopped herself, blushing. "You don't want me rabbiting, sir."

Cross laughed. He was touched. "Say it anyway."

"Well, I think one might have been a rehearsal for the other."

NESBITT, as Cross could have predicted, was reluctant to have the cases formally linked. "For a start, outside of sectarian deaths, there are very few instances of repeated murders. The average Irishman does not have the imagination to kill more than once."

"What if we're looking for an Irishman who's not average?"

"Don't get smart with me, detective inspector."

Nesbitt's attitude was more to do with an entrenched police mentality than any real appraisal of the facts, Cross realized. Nor was he amused to find his own argument thrown back at him when Nesbitt cautioned against making any public connection between the two deaths because to do so might cause unnecessary panic.

An incident room was set up, which became an excuse for half the cranks in the city to call. Mary Ryan had been seen with a man whose name and address were provided by a caller who wished to remain anonymous. The man turned out to be eighty-six years old. A supermarket packer was questioned as the result of another anonymous call, leading to more time wasting. The man had no alibi and was evasive under interrogation. As the case against him mounted—someone of his description had been seen in the area on the day of Mary Ryan's death and the supermarket where he worked was only half a mile from where her body was found—he offered his excuse. He had been at a meeting of the Ulster Volunteer Force, an outlawed organization.

Mary Ryan turned out to be startlingly ordinary, heartbreakingly plain and the third girl sharing, found through the classifieds.

"She'd sometimes watch the telly with us, but most evenings she'd be in her room," the bossier of her two flatmates told Cross and Westerby.

"What was she like?" asked Westerby.

"We liked her because she was quiet," said the second.

"We make enough noise for half a dozen, so we wanted a bit of a church mouse."

"Och, Mary, that sounds terrible," interjected the other.

"Well, you know what I mean."

Cross and Westerby left them to their banter. Westerby was looking tired, thought Cross. She had drawn the harrowing task of dealing with Mary Ryan's parents. They lived in County Derry in remote countryside and had disapproved of their daughter going to the big city, where they were convinced no good would come of her. From what Westerby had been able to discover, their daughter's passage through Belfast had been virtually unnoticed: a year or so working at Collins and Sullivan, photographic developers, where her presence had barely registered; no boyfriend; and only a month or so sharing in her new flat. Before that she had been in bedsit lodgings, again leading a life so self-contained that she left virtually no trace.

The only irregularity Westerby could find was in Mary's letters home. These said that she was happy and had lots of friends.

Her room revealed as little as everything else. The furnishings came with it. Other than that there were a few clothes, a Bible and a rosary, a framed photograph of her mother and father, an old good luck card from an aunt, dating back to her arrival, a transistor radio, a Catherine Cookson novel, and the cheap suitcase that she had carried them in.

"The mystery is why should anyone want to kill someone as inoffensive as Mary Ryan?" asked Cross. "Are we looking for someone who knew her? I find it impossible to believe that anyone could have held a grudge against her."

"As far as we know," said Westerby, "she walked to and from work, which would have taken her about twenty-five minutes. Sometimes if it was raining she took the bus, but it was fine the night she died so she probably walked. We don't know what route she took but she had the choice of cutting through Ormeau Park."

CROSS felt that so far it had been a year without a break. Although crimes were committed and solved in the usual run of things, he could not remember so much frustration surrounding a handful of cases. He could not think of a murder more pointless than Mary Ryan's. Why on earth should anyone have noticed her? Cross pinched the bridge of his nose. He had a headache coming on. Deidre was going to Brussels the next day. He'd wanted to ask her whether she was meeting her lover. He wanted to ask if she was happy with him, but knew he wouldn't dare.

Instead he went to bed that night, saying nothing, after religiously cleaning his teeth, a ritual that made him feel that everything was still all right. He checked on the children, staring at them in blank wonder, listening to Deidre's hostile movements downstairs.

Twenty-five

Belfast, October 1973

CANDLESTICK got drunk, which he rarely did. He drank because he could see the frame shifting and was afraid of the implications. Back at the beginning it had all seemed so simple.

It had started with a young man with fair hair, pale blue eyes and a weak chin, whose languid public school air and manner of deflecting remarks disguised his true purpose. He'd introduced himself as Davenport but never said what department he was.

Davenport had approached him through his company commander. He wore a check jacket and cavalry twills, yet, in spite of this, did not seem military.

"Are you interested in going to Ireland?" he'd asked.

"I'll go anywhere."

It was all the same to him.

He was taken for training to a large white mansion near Carshalton, which stood in its own grounds surrounded by a high wall and rhododendrons, where he fractured the cheekbone of his self-defence instructor. Sometimes he was woken in the night and questioned and beaten to test his resistance. He never saw Davenport during these interrogations but sensed him close by. He was taught about detonators and explosives, and on the pistol range they increased the rapidity of the moving targets from five seconds to two. They sent him into rooms with live ammunition where men were waiting to test his reflexes. The unspoken understanding was that he was on his own.

When Davenport told him what he wanted it was a disappointment.

"That's Baker."

The photograph showed a man in uniform with a cropped

army haircut and a broken nose. The separate parts of his features looked as though they ought not to belong together, but the overall effect was arresting and almost handsome. A brief dossier showed that Baker had been to Fort Hood in Houston, Texas, for special training and then to the Gulf with 22 SAS.

"Get close. Do what he does. Tell us," said Davenport with the easy air of a man asking a small favour.

Because of Baker's name it amused Davenport to give him the codename Candlestick. "Better than Butcher, don't you think?"

Candlestick signed papers agreeing to monthly payments into a false name account of Barclays Bank in Downham Market, tax to be deducted at source. It was explained that his operation was to be self-financing, after the five hundred pounds they gave him to get started, which again he had to sign for. Davenport made him memorize contact numbers and names. There was a London number where he was to ask for Mr. Tranter only in emergency. His local Belfast contact would approach Candlestick, who was told to drink in Robinson's bar on Mondays between eight and nine. He would introduce himself as Danny Boy. Candlestick wondered if these people were for real.

AFTER Baker's flight Candlestick felt less in control. In spite of a rift with Tommy Herron, who suspected him of tipping off Baker, he carried on killing for him, but wondered if the past wasn't catching up when information given by him to Herron months before was returned in the form of an assassination order. The target was a pro-republican city councillor, once mentioned to him by Lena, the masseuse. According to her story, which he had passed on, Councillor Healey knew the identities of the killers of three soldiers shot while pissing at the roadside, thinking they were on their way to a party.

Four of them snatched Healey outside McGlade's Bar and bundled him into the back of a Cortina, along with the woman that was clinging on to his arm. Healey was drunk from hours of whisky, and argumentative with it, bellowing his innocence in the tight confines of the car while the woman squawked with fright.

When Candlestick produced his gun the man shouted on regardless, the drink still working on him.

"Shoot, then, you fucker! Pull the fucking trigger, cunt!"

He meant it. Healey was staring mad. Then the woman started up a wail that no amount of slapping would stop.

"Shooting's too good for the pair of you!" shouted Candlestick, his nerves on edge.

"Shut that bitch up!" yelled the driver.

An armoured Land Rover trundled past going the other way, oblivious to the chaos in the car.

When they arrived at the spot where it was to be done, Candlestick was out of the car before it had stopped, yanking open the back door and dragging out the nearest volunteer, then the woman. He threw the woman to the volunteer.

"Get the fucker out here!" he ordered the man still in the back with Healey, who swung his feet up and lashed out at Candlestick. It took the driver's help to drag him from the car, with the woman screaming her head off until the volunteer holding her clamped his hand over her mouth. Candlestick made the other two hold Healey down, face up, making sure the woman was watching.

"Are you looking?" he grunted as he straddled the thrashing councillor. "Then here's lookin' at you, buster!"

Healey's teeth were bared, snarling in anger and fear, as the big commando knife swung down. Candlestick in the frenzy of his assault forgot to take account of how the man looked in his last mortal moments.

Afterwards he read in the paper that he'd stabbed him thirty times and the woman over twenty. He had no memory of her, just a dull ache in his wrist and a vague memory of the knife skittering across her breast bone after it had failed to find a path between the ribs. Whatever he had been stabbing in his imagination it hadn't been either of them.

NOW, AFTER more than two years in Belfast, he was no longer sure what his masters' plans were for him, though he had a hunch and did not like the implications. He was sure they'd ultimately been behind the plot to assassinate Tommy Herron—in ways that he could only guess at. The approach to him to kill Herron had been made by a man calling himself Brown. Brown was dark and Spanish-looking and fancied himself. Brown's first plan was to have Herron and Breen killed together during one of their meetings, but Candlestick's handler Danny Boy had put a stop to that by telling him to warn Breen.

"It could be useful to put Breen in your debt," Danny Boy said in his flat Scunthorpe accent.

Anyone less Irish than Danny Boy was hard to imagine. He looked like a dandy—with his pale face and long, smooth red hair—and talked like a trawler man. "I put the cunt in Scunthorpe," he'd told Candlestick when they'd first met.

Candlestick warned Breen and Breen asked why.

"Because I've nothing against you and you might return the favour one day."

When Breen duly avoided the meeting, Candlestick drove back to Belfast with Herron grousing at the other's failure to show. Candlestick wanted to tell Herron how lucky he was to be alive.

He reported back to Brown who wanted to know why he hadn't gone ahead and shot Herron.

"The contract is for Breen and Herron. If one of them isn't there, how can I shoot him?"

The second plan involved getting rid of Herron only. Candlestick was told a woman would help.

He met her twice, once before the shooting and on the day itself. He had never met anyone so cool and self-possessed. This woman with her seen-it-all eyes was light years ahead of him.

Afterwards he missed her very badly. He tried to find her. Their encounter made a nonsense of his relationship with Becky, the young student he was seeing on Danny Boy's instructions. Danny Boy had also told him to start selling information about the loyalists to Breen.

Becky was from a republican family and had been pointed out as one of several possibilities. Candlestick hung around the university haunts, dealing a little hash and grass by way of cover. He liked Becky because her faraway look reminded him of the skies of his childhood.

He didn't see it at first, the overall picture of their plan. It was not until he was missing Maggie, and wondering what he was still doing in Belfast, that he realized what they wanted. Somewhere in the bottom of his fifth glass of Guinness he understood the importance of putting Breen in his debt.

"Fuck," he said, loud enough to attract looks from other drinkers. It was not a bar where anyone talked. His hostile stare deterred any further curiosity and he went back to his brooding.

They wanted him to switch sides. They wanted him to sell himself to the Officials. But why, he could not see.

HE SLIPPED out of Belfast, telling no one, and made his way back to the Fens, where he haunted the landscape of his early years, spending the last of the autumn sleeping rough and stalking his childhood. He stole a car and trapped animals—birds and rabbits—which he hurt before dismembering and eating. He tried to recapture that feeling of blank curiosity that had once driven him.

Frustration bred violence and carelessness. In an empty field he came across a barking dog. The dog was aggressive and suspicious and it took Candlestick a patient quarter of an hour to gain its trust. As the dog reached up to lick his hand, he struck, using the commando knife brought over from Belfast. The look of betrayal in the animal's eyes seemed almost human.

He slung the dog's body in the boot of the car and drove to Ipswich, where he picked up a prostitute and tried to get her to fuck him like Maggie had, in the front seat, but she didn't see the point and didn't like it and wouldn't kiss him on the mouth.

Afterwards he had nowhere else to go. He phoned the London contact number and asked for Mr. Tranter, who passed him on to Davenport.

"I see you've been a busy boy," said Davenport when they met at a house behind Liverpool Street station. "I don't suppose you even know her name."

He referred to a folder in front of him with a photograph of the mutilated prostitute. He closed the file and Candlestick realized that this was Davenport's way of telling him that whatever happened from now on was between them. It was also his way of saying that if Candlestick stepped out of line again he'd be put away for a very long time for the murder of an Ipswich whore.

CANDLESTICK returned to Belfast in November 1973 and resumed his affair with Becky, as instructed. It needed persistence because she had taken up with another student. He held back, restricting their meetings to drinks in pubs, drawing her out, letting her believe that she was drawing him. But after Maggie his conversations with Becky were like cardboard and he felt his own distance and reluctance, which, curiously, made him more attractive to her. She seemed frighteningly innocent and listened with solemn astonishment when he confided that any relationship between them was impossible because of what he was: an army deserter, ashamed of his past, and not right for her. From the look in her eye he saw that he had planted the necessary fatal seed of rebellion and curiosity.

With Breen he was more comfortable, the two of them drinking together, Breen mocking Candlestick's drinking only halves. He told Breen that since the death of Herron he had lost his mentor and was regarded with mistrust by the new leadership.

"So I thought I'd come and work for you."

Breen laughed in disbelief. "Either you're a bigger fool than I thought or you've got a nerve."

Candlestick joined in the laughter, and, still laughing, added that he was serious.

"I can see you are. But what am I to do? There's no call for a Brit in these parts."

"A Brit would give you access to places where your boys can't go, did you think of that?"

"It's a cause, not a game, a question of birthright. Besides, we've a ceasefire with the Brits."

The ceasefire had been in operation nearly eighteen months and had earned the Officials the contempt and enmity of the Provisionals.

Candlestick tried to speak but Breen held up his hand. "There's nothing I can do with a Brit. How do I explain you to the other fellows? Look at you—Her Majesty's services, running around with loyalist hoods and for all I know covered in the blood of republicans, and probably an intelligence asset into the bargain."

"A man can change his mind."

"If you're talking Road to Damascus, son, you're a long way from seeing the light."

Candlestick stared at Breen with his level gaze. "Know thine enemy. Bollocks anyway. There are Prods who are republicans. You need all the help you can get."

"Not if it's tainted. I'm happy to drink with you but I don't see how we take it any further. Let's just keep playing footsie, shall we?" He looked at Candlestick. "Well, if you're disappointed, you're not letting it show. Are you having the other half?"

Candlestick said that it was his turn.

"Well, at least you stand your round, which is more than could be said for Tommy, God rest his soul."

Twenty-six

DEIDRE went away leaving the coolest of kisses on his cheek, after hugs and tears for the children. They all stood outside in the damp early morning air and waved at the departing taxi. She had insisted on a taxi in spite of his offer to take her to the airport, a treat for the children. Matthew and Fiona stood watching for a long time after she had gone, until Cross took them both by the hand and led them back into the warmth of the house. He prepared them for school and handed them over to Sally, the childminder who was staying while Deidre was away because of Cross's erratic hours.

He felt aimless in her absence and found himself inexplicably arrested by mundane details—the smell of coffee in the kitchen, sunlight on the windowsill—stopped in his tracks, unsure of how he had got there or what he was in the process of doing, or even what had caught his attention in the first place. He wondered how much he ignored the surfaces of his life. Everything was drawn inwards into that tangled jungle of emotion and motive, half-motive, indecision, and something too puny to call fantasy.

HE WENT to Niall Warren's memorial service, curious to see who turned up. Journalists, mainly, he guessed from the scruffy assembly which included McCausland and Stevens.

The priest did his best until he got Warren's name muddled and called him Neil instead of Niall and someone got the giggles and an infectious titter spread to several rows.

Heads in front turned as a latecomer announced herself with

a clack of high-heels. Cross glanced round but all he could see was a black hat settling in place as she slipped into a pew.

He recognized her afterwards. She had the same poise as in the photograph in Warren's flat, rearranged to appear suitably sombre. The hat, the high-heels and a simple black dress and coat marked her out as the most elegant person there. She stood smoking, talking to McCausland. He realized he didn't know her name.

She caught his eye. He went over to introduce himself. She told him she had moved to Dublin and by chance had seen the edition of the paper with Warren's obituary.

"Do you believe in fate, inspector?"

He shrugged. The voice was not as husky as he had expected but strangely whispery. She got out another cigarette after carefully grinding the old one into the gravel with the sole of her patent shoe. Cross lit it for her. No one apart from McCausland talked to her, though many stared. She was very beautiful, playing the part of the poised, enigmatic widow, her nerves betrayed only by her staccato smoking. The gaze she had levelled at the camera was misleading, he saw. In life she rarely looked at anything for long. Cross wondered what she did. A provincial journalist like Warren seemed a poor catch. He remembered the description of her as a war-zone groupie.

Her name was Miranda Ramsay and he asked if he could talk to her about Warren's death before she went back. She said she was staying at the Europa and was free for the rest of the day.

SHE WAS waiting in the bar when he arrived that evening.

"Funny things, funerals," she said over her drink. Cross was being abstemious and stuck to tonic water. She smoked her cigarettes, making it look exotic, like someone in an old film, while they made small talk, then finally touched on her marriage. Cross wondered if she was drunk.

"He had nice hands," Miranda said, as if that explained everything. "And a soft smile."

She had changed since the funeral into a dark skirt and white blouse with a single string of pearls, and she smelled of a perfume he could not identify. He ordered her another gin and tried to imagine her naked. She caught him looking at the hollow of her throat and smiled. He smiled back, less certainly. He was reminded uncomfortably of Deidre's story of her recent visit to the Europa. Perhaps it was her fantasy of an anonymous sexual encounter that he was hijacking. Nevertheless, an agreeable tension prevailed. He had not been unfaithful to Deidre and was surprised at how easy it could be.

They finished their drinks and he walked her across the lobby and pressed the lift button. At that awkward moment when he should have said goodbye the lift arrived and she stepped inside, her silence its own invitation. Others followed, making it easier to join her. Even then he hesitated, but her ironic smile reassured him and he moved into the mirrored box. They didn't look at each other or speak during the ascent, or as he walked behind her down the corridor. It would be this transition, Cross thought, from lobby to bedroom, he would remember most clearly.

They kissed, leaning against her door as she shut it behind them. Her tongue was pointed and darting. He wondered at the unfamiliarity of it all, the newness of a different height and weight, the false urgency of her probing tongue, which conveyed a passion not felt, the sweet-sour taste of her gin. He avoided touching her skin with his hands, which were uncomfortably moist. He thought of breaking off and making his excuses, but when she took his lower lip between her teeth desire won out over uncertainty.

They kissed their way towards the bed and twisted awkwardly on its edge as he unbuttoned her blouse. Underneath she wore a camisole, which she lifted over her head. Her ribcage looked surprisingly fragile.

AFTERWARDS he remembered her flattened pubic hair when he had first uncovered it, and the delicate mole on the inside of the top of her thigh. He wondered at what point he had known they would end up in bed and what had made it inevitable, in spite of his doubts about whether she found him attractive. They had met at six and at ten to seven she had taken him upstairs and by ten past he was entering her: she had given a tiny gasp and a low moan. She'd ground herself against him and dug her nails into his back while he tried to make sense of what he was doing. He could not shake off the feeling they were riding different races, with her driving him with such blind ferocity as a way of losing herself, while he clung on diffidently, preoccupied only with delaying ejaculation. He came unsatisfactorily before meaning to, without her noticing, too soon for her. He tried to massage her to orgasm but she seemed restless, and he apologized and she said, rather halfheartedly, "It was nice anyway, wasn't it?"

Cross caught sight of himself in the mirror and avoided looking at where his belly was starting to slacken, a sign of the gut to come. She lit a cigarette, snapping at it angrily with a lighter. Cross stared out of the window. They were high up at the back, overlooking the bus station. He sensed she was already regretting the encounter. He didn't know what he felt. That he had used her to get even with Deidre? That like Deidre he wanted the memory of an encounter, for no other reason than to have that memory?

"You've a wife," she said.

The statement hung in the air like an accusation.

"Why did you get married?" he asked in retaliation.

"Meaning Niall wasn't my type?"

"Something like that."

"For a man who's just fucked me, you're not very tactful, inspector. I told you, I liked his hands." She paused, deciding whether to continue. "Niall and I shat in the same pot. We understood each other because we were running from the same background, the one that's not quite middle-class enough. Know your place and all that."

She gave Cross an ironic look, tinged with contempt. "Familiar?"

There was an aggression in her voice, frustration seeping in. She pulled the sheet up until it covered her breasts, drew deeply on her cigarette and reached for an ashtray. Cross felt self-conscious next to her. He got up and felt even less comfortable. His shirt and trousers lay in a tangle on the floor.

"Yes," he said in answer to her question, "I know all about knowing your place."

He dressed while she talked.

"I was born Mavis Bull, thank you very much. When I was eleven I started to notice how men looked at me. The doctor with his soft hands probing where he shouldn't. 'And how does that feel?' Even then I knew enough to know which was preferable—the soft hands of the doctor, with his smell of shaving cream and leather in his car, or some yob with callouses whose idea of sex begins and ends with his knob. So I moved on, ideas above my station. The modified accent, the discreet lies about one's—one's!—background. But you know about the minefields of the middle-classes. I rather suspected you did when I first set eyes on you."

Cross wondered if her story was the point of their encounter and that sex was the crash course that permitted this intimate monologue. He imagined her inspecting herself naked in the mirror after he had gone.

"Perhaps that's what you and I recognized about each other. One counter jumper to another. It's very hard to acquire what's not given naturally—the easy gesture, the familiarity that goes with the upbringing, knowing instinctively what note to adopt. Oh, I know it isn't the whole picture. As a class the middle-classes are probably more neurotic than most, and spiteful with it. But I was seriously fucked by them—taken in, turned over and fucked, then laughed at behind my back for saying the wrong thing. Pardon, toilet, serviette, snigger, snigger. It was pathetic. Even more pathetic was how much it hurt."

Cross looked at her. "What happened?"

"I moved up in the world, as they say. The Miranda bit I made up. It seemed right at the time. Only afterwards did it strike me as the kind of name a ten-year-old would give to a doll. The Ramsay was acquired. Fifty, kindly, comfortably off, impotent, a bottle of Scotch a day, leather patches on his elbows, called himself Major. Still boyish but had worn badly, him not the jacket. That was in London. I was twenty-three. He was something in the government—he never said what. I liked him, and was terrified of him too, although he did his best to protect me from his friends, who all saw through me and carried on witty conversations in a higher language that went right over my head. 'Poppet,' one of them called me. They drank Scotch and played bridge, which I was hopeless at, and they swore casually in an unaffected way. If they had wives they didn't bring them. Once, trying to impress, I swore too, a nonchalant use of the word 'fuck,' strategically placed, expecting them to laugh. The one that called me poppet said, 'Not funny, dear,' and it was then I realized three things. That there are certain counters you can never jump, however good you get. That for these men women are quite insignificant. You could be the Duchess of Athlone, for all they cared. I also understood, because of the way I was brushed aside and the way the poppet man continued to play his cards without the slightest hesitation after squashing me, that these men controlled lives."

Cross sat on the edge of the bed, wondering why she had chosen him. Some change in her tone made him turn round. Her eyes were moist and he was moved for the first time. He reached out and took her in his arms. She cradled herself against him and went on.

"The whole thing seems quite unreal now. We could have been living in 1910, not the 1960s—the flat with the mahogany bookcases, the housekeeper who came every day. There had been another Mrs Ramsay who'd died ten years before in the Far East, in a car smash. Sometimes when he was alone with me he used to cry. He would never say what it was about and blamed the whisky. Did I say how we met?"

Cross shook his head.

"He picked me up in St. James's Park. Came and sat on the bench next to me when I was eating my sandwiches and started naming the ducks. 'I only live just around the corner,' he said. He was kind and I liked his whisky breath and he was quite alone in the world, no relatives at all, and was endearingly old fashioned in a fatherly sort of way. It was probably a question of fucking daddy as far as I was concerned, not that I got to fuck very often. Even his orgasms were sad, half-erect affairs that wept gently when the moment came. He tried hard to make sure I was satisfied. I wasn't very often but appreciated the gesture."

"What happened to him?"

"One breakfast he just stood up with a look of terrible surprise, put his hand to his throat and keeled over. I don't know what I felt. Whatever it was it wasn't what I was supposed to feel. Some time later the one that called me poppet came round and asked if I was interested in going to Belfast, which was when I realized what their work involved. He also made a pass and out of spite I let him because I fancied he was a lousy lay and relished the prospect of telling him."

She looked up at Cross and pulled a face.

"Lesson one: don't take these people on. They beat you hands down every time. He was determined to fuck me until I came and I was just as determined not to give him the satisfaction. In spite of it all being so personal there was something quite the opposite about it. He fucked me like I was a lump of meat and, yes, in the end he won. He pushed me on my front and holding my head into the pillow so I could hardly breathe he entered me from behind and used his free hand to fuck my arse. And afterwards, when he could see my humiliation, he came himself, withdrawing to deposit his sperm on me as a way of finally defiling me. And that basically is how I became an intelligence asset, which is not something I should be telling you at all, but never mind."

She lit another cigarette. A silence fell over the room and they stayed there a long time not talking. In the end Cross got up and phoned the childminder to say that he wouldn't be home until after the children's bedtime. He hung up and said that he would have to go soon.

"I'll be going back to Dublin in the morning. Funny things, funerals," she added again, sourly. "It's all right, you don't have to say anything. Ships in the night and all that."

"Do you live there now?"

"What's to keep me here?"

He felt strangely unreleased by her story and incapable of asking the questions he felt he ought to. In the end, she did it for him.

"What do you think happened to Niall?"

"I don't know. According to the pathologist—"

"I asked what you thought."

"Technically there is nothing suspicious, but—"

"God, you sound like a policeman. Brian McCausland told me how Niall died. I don't believe it."

"That he could have done such a thing?"

"I've known enough men to know what they're capable of. I don't know what Niall got up to in his own company. There was nothing between us to suggest that's what he liked, but if he did I can see why he was too shy to say. That's not the point. The point is, whatever his private sexual preferences were, he is not likely to have pursued them in a cupboard."

"What do you mean?"

"Niall suffered from claustrophobia."

"He was very drunk when he died. That might explain it."

"I doubt it, but there's something else. He spoke to me about a month ago. He was scared."

She lit another cigarette.

"He thought he was being watched. He said he was calling

from a public phone box. It sounded like he had got himself in a terrible muddle over some story."

He realized Miranda Ramsay was trying to steer him.

"Are you saying he was killed?"

"I'm not sure what I'm saying, beyond saying he was scared. And his death doesn't fit what I know about him."

"Did he say anything about this story?"

"Nothing, apart from it involving a cover-up. Niall was in a state and none of it made much sense."

"Did he mention anyone called Heatherington?"

"Not that I remember."

"McKeague?"

"Yes, he mentioned him. He said the real point was who killed him."

"I thought it was either his own men or the INLA."

Miranda Ramsay shrugged. "If you say so. All he said was that if you looked at who really killed McKeague it started to make sense. He said it also tied in with a death on the mainland, one of the biggest of the last ten years."

"Any idea who?"

"I'm giving you a very structured version of what was a rambling and incoherent speech."

Cross didn't know how to leave, whether to kiss her or to refer to what had just happened between them. They ended up shaking hands, which seemed the most equal thing to do.

"Don't regret it," she said, with a wry smile.

As he left, she added, "Did you say Heatherington?"

"Yes. Why?"

"He's dead now, I think. I don't remember any more than that. Did you ever play that game, Dead or Alive? Name someone and the other person has to say which they are. It's not as easy as it sounds. Anyway, if you said Heatherington, I'd say dead. I'm sure Niall's story dealt mostly with the dead."

When Cross got home Sally was coming downstairs. "I've just been settling Fiona. Mrs Cross rang earlier."

He thought he probably still smelt of Miranda Ramsay and stepped back as Sally passed. He went upstairs and showered. After towelling himself dry he inspected himself with distaste in the mirror and thought about her hardness.

"The men I fuck and the men I marry are quite different," she had said. "I liked Niall. There was something nicely vulnerable about him. You could still see the child that had got bullied. For some reason for me husbands are not there to be good in bed. Some faceless fuck with a crowbar for a tool I can have when I want, and, yes, I probably am just out to humiliate myself. You too, perhaps? I saw you caught in two minds, pretending to be the faceless fuck but not sure."

She had laughed as he looked caught out.

"You've nice hands, though, like Niall," she'd said.

"HEATHERINGTON was abducted from his girlfriend's flat in Andersonstown in 1976 and his hooded body was found two days later less than a mile away in Colin Glen. He was twenty years old. The Provisional IRA claimed they executed him for complicity with the security forces."

Westerby was reading from a cutting from the *Irish Times*. They were in Cross's office, drinking thin coffee in plastic mugs that buckled from the heat of the liquid. It was not yet lunchtime and the lights were on again.

"So what have we got?" he asked. "Heatherington shot by the Provos in 1976? McKeague shot in 1982 by any number of people, it seems."

The wind rattled the window sashes so hard that he had to get up and jam them with tissue while Westerby consulted her notes.

"McKeague was shot either by the INLA, the UDA or even by his own men in the Red Hand Commando. It wouldn't surprise me if they'd all ganged together to do the job. He seems to have been an exceptionally nasty piece of work."

"What about mainland deaths?"

"The biggest ones are last year's Brighton bomb casualties and Airey Neave, who was blown up in 1979 as he left the House of Commons. They were the most spectacular unless you count Lord Mountbatten, but that was in Sligo."

"What else is there on Heatherington?"

"He was one of six young men acquitted of shooting two RUC constables in Finaghy Road North in 1974. After his death, two years later, the *Irish Times* ran this article."

She handed it to Cross, who glanced at the headline, "Murdered Man in Herron Death Cycle." The article noted Heatherington's death and went on to say that the story was more complicated than the Provisionals' claim that Heatherington had been a British agent and that it had its roots in the still unsolved killing of Tommy Herron in 1973.

Cross sighed. He remembered Herron—short and belligerent, with an ebullient quiff. He read on.

"Who's this Brown mentioned?"

Westerby checked her notes again. "Gregory Brown, shot May 1976 in Cregagh Road from a passing Cortina. The Ulster Freedom Fighters claimed it, saying that Brown, who was a Protestant, had been involved in Herron's murder."

The UFF were a paramilitary arm of the UDA, which would make sense, Cross thought, if they'd carried out Brown's killing in revenge for killing one of their leaders.

"The *Times* carried a report after Brown's death," Westerby went on, "claiming that he had been part of a gang involving an RUC detective constable, a UVF or UDA gunman, a Catholic and a woman."

"What's all this got to do with Heatherington?"

"Search me, sir. And the journalist who wrote it is on holiday for three weeks. Barbados."

Twenty-seven

Belfast, May 1974

CANDLESTICK'S defection was planned by Davenport as part of a wider strategy whose results would take several years to reach fruition. Davenport discussed the matter only with his superior, known behind his back as the Man Who Fucked Younger Women, and to his face as G. No one knew exactly what G did. Some whispered that he was there for Anglophile Americans who liked the fact that he looked the part, to the extent that in film and television thrillers his equivalent was often played by the actor he most resembled: the same ramrod back, moustache and tightly packed, tamed hair that looked like a surreal collaboration between René Magritte and the British public school system. Davenport knew that deep down G was quite mad.

G had first been alerted to the Bunty–Baker operation over lunch with a governor of the BBC, a friend of various intelligence departments and reliably indiscreet. That lunchtime's rumour concerned G's intelligence rivals moving into Northern Ireland behind his back. G was angry but hardly surprised. The status of Northern Ireland had always been contentious. Technically, as part of the United Kingdom, its security was an internal affair. But its proximity to the Irish Republic and susceptibility to infiltration from across the border meant that in practice, and despite much protest, it had fallen into G's domain.

G passed on this tidbit to Davenport. He also left him to come up with an effective response. G was such an excellent delegator that he left the office at five sharp, four-thirty on Fridays, confident that Davenport would cope. Davenport worked in an office known as F4 and was thought to be an analyst, assessing data and evaluating it for future projections. To an extent this was true, but most of that work was delegated in turn, leaving him free to concentrate on strategy.

Davenport's assessment of Northern Ireland led him to two conclusions, reinforced after consulting American analysts about mistakes made in Vietnam. The conflict would go on for at least a decade because guerrilla movements with significant local support do not get defeated, however hard they are hit, and that in the long run they must be negotiated with.

These views put Davenport's organization at odds with the rest of the security forces. The army, or influential sections of it, believed that Northern Ireland was just another colonial war to be won by intelligence gathering and covert operations, until the terrorists were hammered into unconditional surrender.

Such a fundamental disagreement of approach led to a growing strain between Davenport's outfit and army intelligence. By 1972 their policy of joint information gathering amounted in practice to little more than frosty silence.

G's gossip-gathering lunch with the man from the BBC alerted Davenport to the fact that their rivals—known as Internal within the department for some inexplicable reason, rather than by the initial and number that everyone else called them by—were secretly moving into Northern Ireland on the invitation of the army to conduct a joint operation.

Thanks to Candlestick, Davenport was able to monitor the Baker–Bunty operation from the start and, when the time came, to break it up by using Candlestick to stampede Baker back to England. Davenport derived mild amusement from watching the Baker case end in farce. In court Baker had proved such an unreliable witness that the exasperated judge had thrown out his evidence and given him twenty-five years instead. But his enjoyment at his rival's misfortunes was tempered by the fact that his own department had recently suffered an enormous setback because of similar illegal activities. One of their agents had gone on trial for bank robbery and queered the pitch by announcing that the raid was part of his brief as a British spy. The immediate prognosis was extremely gloomy, which was why G was making an unheard-of exception and breaking the sanctity of his weekend for a Saturday meeting.

G kept rooms in Albany and entertained at the RAC Club, which he preferred to more established ones for its anonymity, and occasionally condescended to drink in the Red Lion in Duke of York Street when with Americans seeking London atmosphere. It struck Davenport as slightly silly that G, whose work covered the globe, confined his activities to less than half a square mile of London. There were occasional speculations about a home in the country and even a wife, but neither had been sighted.

They met at the RAC Club, which Davenport found inconvenient as it meant coming in from Stanmore.

"God, is it that gloomy?" said G, after Davenport's assessment.

Davenport had concluded that because of basic differences of opinion between themselves and the army, and the damaging publicity they had suffered in the last year, the department would almost certainly have to cede Northern Ireland to MI5.

"I'm buggered if I'll see them in there," said G.

Davenport caught him taking an approving look at himself in one of the wall mirrors. Dangerously vain, dangerously stupid, he thought.

"What do you suggest?" he asked, turning his attention back to Davenport with a smile prompted by the reassuring sight of his own reflection.

"We capitulate. Pull out and let them take over."

"Wait a minute!"

"Let me explain, sir."

It took Davenport ten minutes of fluent talking to outline his plan. G tugged at his chin and Davenport wondered how much he was taking in.

"Bully for you if you can get it to work," said G afterwards. "Three questions."

"Yes, sir."

"Why the Officials and not the Provisionals?"

"Softer target, more mercenary and almost certainly more susceptible to splits."

"Are you sure you can get the Candlestick defection to work?"

"We've been laying the seeds for some months, and there's a surprise on hand which should ease his passage. He may find the crossing rough but I can more or less guarantee he'll end up on the beach."

"Do you really think you'll have a ceasefire by next year?"

Davenport could see from the eager gleam in G's eye that his knighthood was the real issue here.

"If the Provisionals swallow this Heatherington laddie, there's a chance. We should know any day now. With luck, everyone's attention will be taken up by the strike."

"That's not us behind it, is it?" asked G, suddenly looking as though he ought to be paying more attention.

"Internal."

A national strike was being threatened by Protestant workers in protest against the recent Westminster-Dublin power-sharing agreement. Both Unionists and large sections of the British government were panicked by the implications of the agreement. The usual cry had gone up that Ulster was being sold down the river. Davenport thought it was a pity it hadn't been dumped years ago. He remembered his father saying that Churchill had offered it to the South in exchange for it getting off the fence and joining the war.

"How much is Internal involved?" asked G.

"Up to their necks."

G studied his nails. "I thought they probably were."

"Incidentally, if our little sting works, there ought to be an added bonus in the form of the final dismantling of the Baker–Bunty network. Watch this space."

"What about this surprise you've got lined up for Candlestick? None of my business, but what are the chances?"

"Risky, but worth it if it comes off."

"Yes, but what are the chances of not killing the bugger?"

Davenport laughed. "Rather depends whose finger's on the trig."

BECAUSE of the strike whole areas of the city were without electricity and none of the street lamps were on. There should have been no danger walking in such a secure district. They were strolling down a wide avenue close to the university near where Becky lived, past safe suburban gardens. She was just saying that it was the first proper warm night of the year and how romantic it was when Candlestick saw the silver Cortina. Cortinas were gunmen's cars. He had used one himself for Tommy Herron and his first thought was the illogical one that it was the same car resprayed.

He had only seconds to throw her to the ground. Her scream was as high as a cat's, and strangely exciting. Then came the dull crump of bullets raking the pavement. He felt nothing, only anticipation of the end, and in his mind's eye saw the oil stains on the workshop floor from the day he'd shot Tommy Herron.

He was aware of the car accelerating away and the firing stopping. He risked raising his head. They were lying by a low front wall. He hauled Becky into the garden behind, which at least afforded some protection, and waited for the Cortina to come back and finish the job. It was stationary about a hundred yards down the road, engine idling.

At least they were helped by the power cut. Candlestick could hear the residents starting to react to the shooting, calling out. He could see the car's reversing lights come on as it started to move towards them. Then, to his surprise, it paused and drove away at high speed.

Becky bit her lip and was greenly pale. She had been hit twice, from what he could tell, in the shoulder and in the arm. The wounds felt clean and there was very little blood. His only concern was to get away before the security forces arrived. Because of his status as a deserter, hospital was out of the question.

When he tried to help her up his own leg buckled under him and he realized that the wet in his shoe was blood. Adrenaline had stopped him from registering that he had been hit. He managed to hobble and support Becky at the same time and got them through the garden and into the next, without attracting attention. From there it was a short walk to the Lisburn Road, close to where Becky lived, which was fortunate as there was no transport because of the strike.

He got Becky upstairs to bed, relieved that her flatmates were out. The electricity was still off but the gas worked and he boiled water, then cleaned and bandaged her wounds. He found some aspirin and a cleanish dishcloth that he used as a tourniquet on his leg to cut out the worst of the pain. The bullet had entered below the ankle. He couldn't understand why they hadn't come back to finish off the job.

"Where's the nearest phone?" he asked her.

There wasn't one in the flat. He could tell from the panic in her voice that she did not want him to go.

He took her bicycle, which was downstairs in the hall. Pedaling hurt less than walking, any wobbliness down to how long it was since he had ridden a bike.

His worry that the phone system would be out of order too turned out to be groundless, but there was no answer from his contact's number, nor Tranter's London number, which was supposed to be permanently manned. It looked like they were deliberately cutting him loose, driving him into the arms of Breen. Breen was probably why he had been shot at. The UDA must have found out or been told—who by, he wondered bitterly—that they had been cutting deals.

He tried the only number he knew for Breen, a daytime one, and got no answer. A couple of bars Breen used were listed in the book and he left messages at both. It was all he could do, he decided, other than wait.

She was asleep when he got back. He sat in the window watching the street, resting his leg, trying to ease the throbbing. The pain made it hard to think.

Just before midnight, Becky's flatmates returned and he listened to them moving around, preparing for bed, giggling in the dark.

The sound of a car drawing up woke him from his doze. It was two o'clock. Candlestick moved to the window and saw the silhouette of a man getting out. The street lamps were still off and he could not be sure if it was Breen. There seemed to be a second man too. Candlestick risked knocking on the window to draw their attention and was relieved to be greeted by a cautious wave.

He hobbled downstairs and let them into the house.

"What the fuck's going on?" asked Breen with no sign of his usual humour.

Candlestick explained.

"And what the fuck am I supposed to do?"

"Get the girl seen to for a start. I can take my own chances."

"I thought we had enough trouble with this bloody strike without you getting yourself shot up. Did you get a look at them?"

"It was a UVF fellow I've seen around."

He decided it was safer if he told Breen that.

"Jesus. I suppose you'd better come with us."

Becky started when he woke her.

"There are some men here who'll look after us."

She looked at him, puzzled. "I have lectures in the morning."

Her eyes were feverish. He told her that it was just for the night and that she'd be back in the morning. Becky started sucking her thumb and burrowed deeper into the bed. In the end Breen and the other man had to carry her, wrapped in bedclothes. Candlestick heard Breen curse under his breath as they stumbled in the dark.

They put Becky on the back seat and covered her head with a blanket, and Breen told Candlestick to lie on the floor in front of her. He hesitated, looking for some sign of sympathy from Breen and found none.

"Or you can go in the fucking boot like you did for Tommy Herron."

He hoped the jolt he felt when Breen spoke didn't show. Breen's eyes burned bright with anger.

"Christ, son, you've a nerve coming to me. I hope you know what you're letting yourself in for."

Twenty-eight

MARY RYAN continued to take up her share of headlines, more than anything because of her transparent innocence. Harder-hearted officers referred to her as the Virgin Mary. In spite of her Catholicism even loyalists jumped on the bandwagon. Cross listened to one on the radio as he shaved, thundering on. "This country has become a country of murder. Violence is our virus and when a poor wee girl becomes the innocent victim of such uncontrolled terror then it is up to us to stand up and ask: who are the real perpetrators of this evil?"

Cross disagreed. Violence in the North had always struck him as controlled. The unusual thing about Mary Ryan's death was that it threatened middle-class security. Middle-class Belfast had it pretty cushy, which was why it was so outraged. Mary might not have been one of them as such, but she was respectable and the last person—in their eyes—who deserved to be murdered.

He turned off the radio as the minister cranked himself up for an onslaught against the Papist terrorists at the root of it all. The real enemy, Cross thought, was bigotry. He had worked that much out years ago, along with most others. Not that this understanding made any difference. People were proud of their bigotry. It went across the board, from his parents-in-law down. The Brits were the worst. For all they cared they could have been talking about events in Tierra del Fuego.

When he arrived at the barracks he got out a clean sheet of paper and took the phone off the hook. The frenzied attack on Mary Ryan, the mutilations, all suggested a killing with a sexual motive. Poor Mary, he thought, never looked at twice until then. He pictured her attending Sunday Mass and hurrying home afterwards alone for want of anyone to talk to.

* * *

"You'd expect us to be dealing with a sex maniac," said Westerby, echoing Cross's hunch.

"How do you mean?" asked Cross.

They were in the barracks' canteen. Cross had been surprised when Westerby had come over with her tray and asked if she could join him. The ranks didn't usually mix. Her behaviour would probably be interpreted as pushiness, she realized, but it was too late to change her mind. She was aware of one or two strange looks as she sat down.

"I've been thinking about Mary Elam, sir."

"In that case you'd better speak to DI Cummings. He's in charge of the case now."

Westerby hesitated, then confessed that she had nothing definite to offer beyond speculation.

"You're fond of speculation, aren't you?"

She couldn't tell if he was being unkind.

"Go on," he said eventually. "Speculate."

Again she could not decide if he was annoyed. She ploughed on, feeling that she was stating her case badly.

The way she saw it, she said, Mary Elam was vulnerable on two fronts. Casual sex might have resulted in her meeting her killer. Plus she was running around in a hardcore loyalist area where her very presence was enough to get her killed.

"Which rather rules out the sex maniac."

"I know. Besides, the two killings aren't similar enough. Except—"

Cross looked at her inquiringly.

"Both cases involved abduction. The two Marys were both taken somewhere. What do you think the killer did with them, between seizing them and dumping their bodies?"

She'd asked the question without really being sure whether there was any connection between the two deaths, but Cross leaned forward, interested. He hadn't thought of either case in terms of abduction before. Westerby repeated that she'd been struck by the fact that both women had been held somewhere. What had happened in those missing hours?

Cross's mind kept returning to the Strathaven Bar. Mary Elam's connection with the place was the greatest anomaly in what they'd been able to discover about her. She'd probably liked the risk of taking men there, for the extra sense of danger it added—a Catholic sneaking into a Protestant stronghold. Privately Cross was fairly sure that's why she'd been killed but he had no evidence. Hargreaves had turned over the Strathaven and questioned McElwaine to no avail. From what he'd heard, Cummings was making no progress either, which gave him a certain satisfaction.

He asked Westerby to try and picture what might have happened to Mary Elam if things had gone wrong at the Strathaven.

"What do you mean?" she asked.

"Use your imagination."

"You mean speculate?"

"Yes." Cross laughed.

"Oh, well." She pulled a face as though the idea seemed funny to her. "We know she was picked up by someone in a van, on the Tuesday. Her killer, perhaps? The fact that we can't trace the van suggests he's covering his tracks. Like I said, you'd expect a sex maniac, except there are no signs of interference."

"Unless he didn't touch her."

"You mean he was a looker?"

"It's possible. The likelier possibility is that someone in the Strathaven found out she was Catholic."

"That might explain the delay. If she was interrogated before she was killed."

They agreed that Mary's daring excursions into loyalist territory could have backfired horribly. Once she'd been discovered, it would be assumed she was a spy.

"What do you know," he asked slowly, "about the Shankill Butchers?"

Westerby took a long time answering. "Do you think what we're dealing with is anything to do with them? It was a long time ago."

"Twelve years."

"I thought they'd all been locked up."

"Most of them were, about eight years ago."

Lenny Murphy, the most notorious of the Butchers, had been shot in an ambush a few years earlier, Cross remembered. His death had not been mourned and the police had made no great effort to catch his killers. Murphy's abrupt departure had been seen by most as his just desserts. He had been responsible for the abduction, torture and murder of any number of Catholics. Cross knew from other policemen that the investigation had been a harrowing affair—a seemingly endless catalogue of unparalleled brutality. The savagery of the violence had been bad enough. What had made it even more barbaric was that it had been watched—and applauded—by an audience. Cross suddenly wondered how many witnesses to that sickening violence were still at large.

"Let's suppose," he said to Westerby, "Mary was in the Strathaven when she was challenged about being a Catholic. What then?"

"Maybe they would have taken her upstairs and slapped her around a bit and then it got out of hand."

"Or maybe it was more deliberate and someone remembered how they did it all those years ago."

Westerby considered. "Yes and no," she said. It was always a surprise to find herself discussing revolting crimes so calmly. "Let's say Mary Elam was killed more or less as we've said. It got out of hand and perhaps someone squeezed too hard. Let's also say there were several men in the room when it happened."

Cross nodded and told her to go on.

"Let's say that her murder acted as a trigger on one of the men in the room. Someone not necessarily directly involved, but just watching."

"Your looker?"

Westerby nodded.

Cross realized what she was getting at. "And this man was a witness to the previous murders of twelve years earlier?"

Westerby nodded again and said she thought that Mary Elam's death might have prompted this man to go off and murder Mary Ryan, which fitted the style of the previous Shankill killings.

"But is he acting alone or with others?" asked Cross.

"I'd say we're dealing with a man with a kink. He's imitating the earlier killings—which he witnessed—but for his own gratification."

It was a bold theory, he had to hand her that. He wondered whether he should tell Cummings, in case it had any bearing on the Elam investigation. He decided not, partly because it was pure speculation, and because he neither liked nor trusted Cummings. Let him stew. Instead he told Westerby to look up the records on the Shankill murders and to make a list of anyone who had been questioned in connection with them and not charged.

He decided to visit the Strathaven by himself early that evening. He went and sat at the bar. McElwaine glowered at him, saying nothing, and served him with bad grace. Cross's presence cast a spell over the place. As the bar filled up there were sullen whispers and stares in his direction, and silence. In spite of what McElwaine had told him, strangers were distinctly unwelcome. He lasted half an hour, then left. The beer left a nasty taste.

THEY whittled it down to several names, the likeliest being a man called Willcox, a known UDA member with suspected connections to the UVF, current whereabouts unknown.

Cross scanned Westerby's neatly typed report on Willcox. Born 1953. Mechanic. He'd worked for his uncle, who owned a lock-up workshop, between 1969 and 1972, taking over the business after the uncle's death. In 1977 he was questioned during the Shankill inquiry. No charges were brought, though it was believed that Willcox had been present at several of the killings. He had been questioned in 1979 about receiving a stolen car and again the case was dropped. The last note of him was in 1983, when the police were called in after a domestic dispute, but Willcox's wife had refused to press charges. The WPC calling round a week later to check that she was all right—because Willcox was thought capable of further violence—had been verbally abused by her and accused of snooping.

The last listed address for him was not far from the Strathaven bar, though his regular was a pub called the Windsor. Cross knew the Windsor. It was a mean dive that people crossed the street to avoid. Any stranger going in was taking his life in his own hands, but this seldom happened as there was usually a gang of skinhead toughs hanging around outside to deter entry to anyone other than the elect.

"BIG JOHN wouldn't hurt a fly," was the landlord's verdict on Willcox to Hargreaves.

They went through the usual rigmarole, with the landlord keen to express support for the police. Hargreaves knew the way it went off by heart—first a family history of distinguished service in the British army, followed by the declaration that though there were some bad people about they did not come from around there. This was invariably followed by remarks about what a dirty lot the Papists were. The landlord knew nothing of Willcox's whereabouts, of course.

"He was never in here much."

And so it went on, from everyone Hargreaves questioned—the false show of concentration, the shifty eyes, the flat denials, interspersed with looping, meaningless pleasantries.

No one had seen Willcox since he'd left his wife eighteen months earlier, though Hargreaves was under the impression that several of his old acquaintances still did on the quiet.

"Do we have the slightest idea where Willcox is?" Cross asked Hargreaves, who appeared restless and distracted.

"His wife hasn't seen him since he went. There's a brother in the British army. He says he's lost touch too. There's an ancient mother who makes no sense and denies having a son called John."

Cross caught Hargreaves glancing at the clock.

"What do you think the effect would be on someone attending those Romper Room sessions?" he asked.

"I don't know, sir. Nightmares, probably."

Hargreaves looked keen to get away, although it was only half past four. No doubt he wanted to beat the traffic and get to his boat.

"Were the Shankill victims always men?" Cross asked.

"As far as I can remember, sir."

Hargreaves looked relieved when he was told he could go. As he left he asked, in a way that suggested he was only humouring Cross, if he thought Willcox was really a throwback to the Shankill murders, killing women this time.

"It's the first thing we've come across which might explain why Mary Ryan was killed."

MRS. WILLCOX was a tiny, haggard woman, with a hatchet mouth and an ash-blonde rinse. She was making heavy weather of her thirties but in spite of that her manner was feisty. Cross found it hard to picture her with her husband. The police photograph of Willcox showed a big surly man, with a thin moustache and a look of cunning, well over six foot and running to fat. His wife by contrast was rake thin and not five foot.

Her first remark, made on the doorstep, repeated verbatim

what she had told Hargreaves: she did not care if her dead-hopeless-fuck of a husband was upside down in shit. She invited Cross and Westerby in warily, torn between a natural mistrust of being seen with the police and a desire to pour out her bile.

"The fellows'll tell you Big John was as nice as the day was long, laughing and joking. I dare say, but he wiped the smile off his face when he came through that door."

Cross remarked clumsily that they knew about Willcox's violence. He watched her mouth tighten.

"Just like any other fellow that's had a skinful. I don't know where he is or what he's doing, if that's what you're after."

Cross found her bitterness too painful and stared instead at the impoverished room, leaving Westerby to do the questioning. He admired the way she gradually drew the woman out, encouraging her to admit the extent of her husband's violence and how it dominated her life. Even with him gone, she still seemed curiously resigned to its inevitability.

"It's not like it's only me."

She ground out her cigarette, dragging the pinched butt across the ashtray long after it was out, then lit another.

"It's not exactly news, is it?" she went on. "When the boys run around punching each other up in the air it's on the telly, but when they come home and give the wee woman a diggin' who cares?"

She lapsed into sullen silence. Cross realized that his presence was inhibiting her. He excused himself, telling Westerby that he had papers to check in the car.

She joined him twenty minutes later.

"Tuesdays and Fridays without fail," she said. "And sometimes he beat her on Saturdays, for good measure."

"Badly?"

"He pulled her around the house by her hair."

"And she never complained, or only the once," he said. "Is it just fear that stopped her complaining?"

"And a lack of self-esteem. These women often believe the violence is their fault. Even more shameful than the violence is others knowing about it."

She turned to Cross, her face tense with anger.

"He poured a kettle of boiling water over her vagina, when

she was pregnant, and afterwards he just laughed and told her to stop making a fuss."

Cross found it difficult to hold her eye.

"Mrs. Willcox is right. It would be more terrifying if it weren't so common," she went on. "Who cares? We don't. We don't even keep a record of cases of domestic violence, and nor do the hospitals. Can you tell me why that is, sir?"

Cross knew the answer but did not say. Cases of domestic violence were not considered important and happened too often. He had sat on a committee where the matter had come up and nothing had been done.

"I've got one lead," said Westerby. "The address of Willcox's lock-up garage."

IT WAS a dilapidated lock-up in a row of several under some railway arches. Most of them had an air of being permanently shut. One or two were open, little makeshift repair shops surrounded by gutted vehicles and guarded by malevolent dogs. None of the mechanics remembered the last time Willcox's lock-up had been in use.

They returned with a search warrant. Once inside the dingy, vaulted space, Cross found himself in what had once been a workshop, with a hydraulic lift and a space for a second car. There were old oil stains on the floor, like black blood. At the back was an office partitioned off by a glass screen and next to it a dirty toilet and a tap with running water. A train rumbled overhead.

In spite of the general filth, Cross noticed that the basin had been recently wiped and the surface of the office desk was unnaturally clean. Stuffed into a cupboard he found what looked like a recently purchased bottle of disinfectant and some rags. On the strength of that he told Westerby to get forensic to go over the whole garage.

ON THE way back to town Cross asked to be dropped off at the City Hospital. He went up to the sixth floor where Maureen McMahon still lay in her coma. He half expected a man on the door but there wasn't. When there was no answer to his knock he went in and left a note for McMahon. Maureen lay perfectly still. It was unsettling to think of her being in exactly the same state as when all this had started sixteen weeks before or more.

McMahon called the next day. He warily agreed to meet Cross in the hospital canteen.

They sat in a corner and drank tea. Cross watched McMahon spooning sugar into his cup and thought he didn't look like a sugar man. The bodyguard sat separately, next to the double swing doors, watching anyone who entered without being seen.

"I have two murder victims, both women, both Catholic," said Cross. "You probably read about the second in the papers."

"The one that was stabbed?"

Cross nodded and went on. "The other was a semi-prostitute, possibly working on the fringes of sectarian activity, which might have brought her into contact with the sharp end of your business."

McMahon smiled, refusing to rise to the bait. "Your point, inspector?"

"It's just conceivable both women were killed by the same man. This is not a theory shared by my superiors, so I am out on a limb. But if I'm right, he'll kill again, and he's not one of your ODCs."

ODCs were Ordinary Decent Criminals, a term used to distinguish them from terrorists. Cross looked at McMahon. They both knew that the paramilitaries ran crime in the city, and policed it. Between them there was not much that went on that they did not know about.

"Are you saying it's a Prot killing these girls?"

"All I'm saying is that this man may be operating within your general boundaries."

"But you've no leads?"

Cross spread his hands. He did not want to tell McMahon about the lock-up or his suspicions of Willcox.

"What do you want me to do? Apart from give you a long list of UVF activists you could start by questioning."

Cross was momentarily thrown by McMahon's mischievousness. He was starting to like the man.

"I'm outside my brief even talking to you. I'm just passing this on for what it's worth."

"And what is it that you want from me, inspector?"

Cross raised his eyebrows.

"How can I help you?" repeated McMahon. "I assume we're trading."

McMahon was nobody's fool.

"Does the name Breen mean anything? He was a Sticky."

"Stickies I steer clear of."

The answer was no surprise. Antipathy between the Officials and Provisionals had been permanent since the 1970 split.

"Someone tried to kill him a few years ago with a car bomb, and we have to put the Provisional IRA near the top of the list."

"The name of the Provisional IRA is used to cover a multitude of sins, you know that. If we'd been responsible for every bombing we've been blamed for . . . This Breen, is he your man in the road?"

"Yes."

"I asked around about him. Not a whisper. Are you saying someone caught up with him?"

"I don't know yet. I don't know whether his death was the pay-off of the earlier attempt or something else. What about the name Heatherington?"

McMahon looked at Cross with narrowed eyes. "What exactly is it you're investigating?"

"Heatherington's name came up."

McMahon shrugged. "He's long dead."

Cross nodded.

"Shot for collaborating with the security forces," McMahon said brusquely, and Cross sensed him withdrawing.

"Why was he shot?" he asked.

"I just told you."

McMahon finished his tea.

"Yes, but what did he do?" asked Cross, seeing time was running out.

"He told us a pack of lies."

"About Tommy Herron?"

"No. He told us the truth about Herron, and about Dublin. The lies came after."

McMahon stood up. The interview was over. "Finish your tea, inspector."

They walked in awkward silence to the hospital reception, with the bodyguard two paces behind.

"What about pornography?" Cross asked as they reached the lobby.

"I've no use for it myself," McMahon said facetiously.

"A man told me there's more of it about. And drugs."

McMahon shrugged. They reached the lift and while they

waited McMahon leaned towards Cross, fixing him with his stare, and spoke so no one could overhear.

"Two things make a man greedy. Pornography and drugs. They're difficult to control and they're too easy to fall out over. Now, I'm going this way."

He disappeared into the lift, followed by his man, leaving Cross with the feeling that he had been told nothing.

Twenty-nine

DEIDRE returned from Brussels with Belgian chocolates for the children. She looked well, Cross thought, and well fucked, which was more than he could say for himself. They resumed their egg-shell lives.

At work the bureaucratic machine ground its inexorable way, impervious to any string-pulling on Cross's part. Forensic would take its own sweet time getting round to inspecting Willcox's lock-up. A backlog of work meant several days at least, he was primly told, before anything could be done.

Breen's contracting company turned out to be one of several firms he had been involved in. Questioning of employees revealed that he had been conspicuous by his absence, working at the depot only a morning or so a week and spending most of that time closeted with an accountant. The accountant no longer worked for the firm and it took Westerby several days to trace him.

SHE FOUND him in a flat off the Malone Road and her first thought when Patrick Rintoul opened the door was that he was a sick man. Rintoul was waxy pale and emaciated, and had about him an aura of profound resignation rarely seen outside the terminal ward.

He apologized for being so hard to find. He worked for himself these days, he explained, as he showed her into a tiny kitchen with just enough room for both of them to sit. Even in the littlest things he moved with the ponderous air of a man conserving energy. After making tea he looked in the fridge and apologized for not having milk.

"Black with plenty of sugar. That's the best way without milk. There might be a slice of lemon somewhere. I'm sorry, I don't seem to get out much."

Westerby, sensing that visitors were rare and that Rintoul needed time, chatted casually until they had finished their tea. He appeared eerily calm and was slow to be drawn. From the window she could see a communal garden that clearly no one cared for, and a line of angry black beeches that cut out most of the light. The view was matched by the weather. There was an oppressive stillness, made more so by a grey dankness that had hung over the city for days. Westerby warmed her hands on her mug of tea, glad to be indoors—June already and the heating still on. She listened to Rintoul explaining how he had stopped working full time because of his health but had kept a few freelance clients. She realized with a shock that he was probably not yet forty. He caught her looking at him.

"Yes," he said. "I'm waiting for the sky to fall in. What is it you want to know?"

"Francis Breen."

He lowered his head and fiddled with his cup. "There's nothing to say about Francis Breen."

Rintoul agreed that he had worked for Breen and remembered him well and knew of his disappearance, but beyond that he would say nothing. Westerby sighed. What was it about Breen that turned everyone as silent as the grave?

"Francis Breen is dead," she said. "So anything you say now doesn't matter."

Rintoul looked up. "Is he? Then I'm glad, but it still doesn't alter anything."

"Did you know that he was a member of the IRA?"

Rintoul looked at her for a long time, smiling oddly, then placed his hands over his eyes, his ears and his mouth.

"Hear nothing, see nothing, say nothing," said Westerby.

"If you want to spell it out," said Rintoul with another strained smile. "More tea?"

He seemed reluctant to let her leave in spite of having

nothing to say. She wondered when he had last had human company.

"Is there anyone you know who might talk to me about Francis Breen?"

"I dare say his wife might have a thing or two to say, if she were still alive."

"What do you mean?"

"I think you should let the dead rest. Breen, Mrs. Breen, the children—they're gone now."

"There's a difference between being dead and being murdered. Murder always leaves questions."

Rintoul shrugged and stood up to show her out. She allowed time at the front door for him to change his mind, but he just stood with his hands in the pockets of his shapeless grey trousers and stared at the floor. She left a card with her number in case he thought of anything.

His flat had its own steps down the side of the house and Westerby could still see him standing by his open door as she got into the car. Had he killed Breen? she suddenly wondered. He'd have had nothing to lose. Rintoul was dying, she was sure of that. Whether he would have had the strength to slaughter Breen's animals was another matter. He didn't strike her as having the energy to start roaming the countryside in search of anyone, unless—and the thought drew her up short—he had known where Breen was all the time.

As she got into the car Rintoul started down the steps as though he had just thought of something. She waited.

"Could you give me a lift to the shops?"

It was not a question Westerby had expected.

"You'll need a coat."

Rintoul was wearing only a shirt, a white one in need of a wash, she noticed with a domestic eye.

"I don't feel the cold."

Westerby agreed to take him and said she would wait and run him back again if he wasn't long. Rintoul looked surprised by the offer. She wondered why she was behaving like the welfare services. Stringing him along, she supposed, in the hope that he might talk.

Afterwards she agreed to another cup of tea.

"I know what you're thinking," he said. "If you stick around long enough I'll decide to get it off my chest."

She smiled, beaten by his perception.

"There's only one person who knows more about a man than his accountant and that's his confessor, if you're a Catholic, that is."

"Does that mean you know about Breen's dirty laundry?"

They sat at the kitchen table again. His hands had gone bluish in spite of saying that he didn't feel the cold.

"I'm telling you this where I might not tell someone else, maybe because you're the first woman who has been here in a long time. Oh, don't worry, this is not conditional. There are no strings attached, though I would be very happy if you came round once in a while for a chat."

Rintoul sat for a long time without speaking. He seemed embarrassed. Westerby was left with the strange but distinct feeling that her own life had been spent in pointless waiting. Waiting for what, she did not know. Waiting for the wrong thing, probably.

"Since the doctors told me, I promised myself that I wouldn't hide or pretend or not say what I thought, and here I am doing it again. There is a condition. You can refuse, of course, and I'll forget I ever said it."

"What do you mean?" Westerby looked up at him sharply. His Adam's apple bobbed awkwardly as he swallowed.

"Take off your top and I'll tell you what you want."

Westerby gave an incredulous laugh. "You've got to be kidding, mister."

She was even more astonished when he joined in with her laughter. Now his proposition was out in the open, he seemed relaxed. She realized that she should have left already.

"You can trust me. That's all I'm asking."

Westerby shook her head in disbelief. "All?"

"Don't be embarrassed. If you don't want to, don't. I'll tell you anyway. I'm past caring. Don't worry, I'm not asking you as an officer of the law."

The last remark struck them as ridiculous and set them off laughing again. Westerby was suddenly reminded of a forgotten incident from her childhood. She had been seven and had agreed to undress for two boys if they waited that evening beneath her window. She had, standing on the ledge every time she removed a piece of clothing. It had been summer and hot, she remembered, and had not taken long as she was not wearing much. She remembered how unashamed and powerful she had felt. The memory reminded her of a sense of daring since lost.

She watched herself in some disbelief as she started to take off her jacket. She told herself that there was something essentially innocent about the process, like that time from her childhood, though a nagging part of her wondered at her motives. Was it just compassion for a sick man, combined with an impatience at her usual staidness, or a harder ambition to do with Rintoul giving her what she wanted?

She unbuttoned her blouse while Rintoul began to tell her what she needed to know, then took off her brassière and sat with them on her lap, pretending she was posing as an artist's model. She felt less self-conscious than she thought she would until becoming aware of the marks the brassière had left on her skin. She decided her body looked unattractively pale and wondered if Rintoul was disappointed. He appeared more embarrassed than she was, and glanced up only occasionally. She decided she must be mad. Think of it as succour to the dying, she told herself, hanging on to every word Rintoul said.

"Most of the time I worked for Breen I laundered his money and cooked his books, and made it my business not to know any more. Oh, for sure Breen was in deep with one lot or another, and again I didn't ask. The Provisionals, I assumed. Anyway, he was friendly enough and took a liking to me and probably told me more about himself than he did most people, but never about his business, always about himself. I thought he was a shit, frankly. He could charm the birds off the trees but he didn't give a fuck about anyone. It was like talking to a mirror. You were only there as a reflection of his vanity."

WESTERBY drove up the Malone Road afterwards not sure whether to berate or congratulate herself.

She phoned Cross to pass on what she had learned, wondering what his reaction would be if he knew how she had got her information. Cross was a bit of a stuffed shirt, though less of a pain than most officers. At least he treated her like she had a mind of her own, capable of putting two thoughts together.

"You remember Breen was away on the morning his wife died," she said.

"At some hotel."

"With a woman."

She hoped Cross would ask who the woman was so she could deliver her trump, but he didn't, spoiling the effect.

"The woman was his sister-in-law."

"Say again," said Cross.

"The woman was Bernadette Breen's sister. Breen was having an affair with his wife's sister."

"Where is she now?"

"I'm trying to find out."

Cross wondered how Breen had felt on learning that his family had been blown up while he had been cavorting with his dead wife's sister.

Thirty

South Armagh, May 1974

"How SERIOUS are you about this, son?" Breen asked, his humour better than when he had last seen him.

"Dead serious," replied Candlestick.

"One or the other, you can't have both."

He was slow to get Breen's little joke.

Breen left a few minutes later and after that Candlestick saw only the masked man who brought food to the locked attic where he was being kept alone.

He had no idea where they were. His watch and shoes had been removed. His foot was less painful since the doctor had dug out the bullet and patched him up. He told him a couple of bones were chipped and apart from that he was lucky.

"Kimo sabe," he said when the masked man next came, and thought he detected the slightest of laughs.

On the night of the second day two masked men came carrying guns and hooded and handcuffed him and led him to a van.

It banged emptily as he was thrown in the back and wrapped in what felt like a heavy rug that prevented any movement.

He calculated they drove for an hour before he was taken out. His disorientated senses told him he was in deep countryside, but when he was taken into a strange metallic space he could not say where he was. The whoosh of rotor blades made him wonder if there was a helicopter nearby.

The next thing he knew he was lying on the ground, his head ringing.

"Stand up, cunt."

He tried and was kicked down again. Boots thudded into his body. He was then hauled to his feet and spreadeagled against the wall. He knew from his SAS training that this pre-interrogation position soon became excruciating. In Castle-reagh IRA men had been made to stand like that for sixteen hours. He knew too that any movement was likely to be rewarded with a blow to the kidneys. He now recognized what he had thought was the whirr of helicopter blades as white noise.

He risked testing the situation by moving. Nothing happened. No one hit him. He removed his hood. The space was empty. It looked like a metal shipment container, lit by a solitary bulb and furnished with a mattress, blanket and an empty plastic bucket.

He alternated brisk press-ups and sit-ups with periods of trance-like stillness, until he achieved a state where time and noise no longer mattered. He listed ways in which he could be more troubled. At least he was dry. His captors' methods did not extend to heat control or noise variation. He countered the noise by imagining that he was on a long flight. Nor did they switch the electricity on and off to confuse him further.

Nobody came and he was given nothing. From the state of his beard he guessed that he was in the container for two days. In that time the noise didn't stop once.

Eventually he was given food—a pallid stew out of a tin—and allowed to slop out. He was taken hooded from the container, clutching his bucket, and directed where to throw it. He felt cool air on his hands, and even through the hood he was aware of its sweetness after the fetid stillness of the container.

Sometimes he was put against the wall with the hood over his head and punched until he vomited up the food he had just been given. Sometimes he was tied to a chair. His interrogators overlooked his wounded foot, which was a mercy. Like their crude punches, their questions were unimaginative and unde-viating, accusing him over and over of being a British agent in league with Baker. They wanted to know who had controlled them and the nature of their operations. Candlestick repeated that he was an army deserter who had fallen in with Baker.

He varied his resistance. After several sessions he deliber-ately broke down and confessed that he had been conned by Baker and threatened with exposure as a deserter. He had acted as a mercenary, until he saw what Baker was getting into.

"I want to talk to Breen," he said.

They ignored him and went over his history in Belfast to the point of exhaustion. He stuck to a version of events until he believed it himself. He named Bunty and Eddoes and all the rest of them. Breen he said had impressed him more than any of the loyalists and had contributed to his change of heart, especially after he had been told by Herron to shoot a waiter he realized later was an innocent Catholic.

They shifted their line of questioning to his relationship with Becky, what he felt for her and what they talked about. He knew she was the weakest link in his story and treated it with some puzzlement, saying that it had not been his intention to get involved.

Candlestick felt sorry for his interrogators. The more he stuck to his story the more sluggish their questioning and beat-ings became.

"Tell Breen I'll only talk to him from now on," he told them at the end of one session.

"We're the ones asking the questions, mister."

"And I'm only talking if you bring news of Becky."

The next time they came his silence provoked one of his interrogators to lose his temper and to throw at him what he took a second or two to realize was his own shit. Screaming obscenities all the while, the man kicked him until his ribs cracked and the other one had to drag him away.

"Christ, Seamus!"

A name, Candlestick thought.

After they had gone he lay down, covered in his own excre-ment, nursing his damaged ribs. He had seen them off but he was not sure how much more he could stand.

* * *

"You're more trouble than you're worth," was Breen's line. "What use are you to us?"

"For a start I know how the army mind works, and with my accent I can go places you can't."

"Since when did you become an idealist, anyway?"

"Under the circumstances I can't afford not to be," said Candlestick, spreading his hands.

Breen threw back his head and laughed. "Such a cool baby."

Their session was being conducted alone in the curtained kitchen of the main farmhouse. Candlestick had been allowed to remove his hood.

"Just what is it that you're after?" asked Breen.

"I need someone to take me in, you know that. I can't go back to England because of the army. I can't go back to the UDA."

"Why don't you just fuck off to Tangiers?"

"There's the girl."

"There's always another girl. What's the big deal about this one?"

"I don't know yet."

"Well," said Breen, "at least you're not trying any of that romantic crap on me. Look, I'll be straight. You've got everybody's knickers in a twist. Your information is of limited value. My pals say you're a British asset."

Candlestick shook his head and smiled.

"What do you want me to do to prove I'm not?"

"Frankly, the matter is out of my hands. You'll face a Court of Inquiry."

THEY took him to a barn where three men, all masked, sat behind a table. Candlestick didn't think that Breen was among them. The general charge amounted to conspiring with the British army to murder Roman Catholics, with particular reference to the shooting of the waiter on Tommy Herron's instructions. It became increasingly clear that there were no mitigating circumstances.

Candlestick made a short speech saying that he had seen the error of his ways. In his opinion his growing belief in the justification of the republican cause was reason enough to spare him, as he could be of value to it. His death would serve no one.

He thought of Becky while his judges conferred. There was something between them, he thought; on his part a desire to see her protected, a feeling new to him. He felt sorry for her, again an unfamiliar feeling. He wondered what their future would have been like.

The verdict was a foregone conclusion. He could hardly find it in himself to feel angry or afraid. He was offered a priest, and refused.

The almost soporific formality of the trial was replaced by abrupt urgency. There was to be no appeal or reconsideration, he realized, as masked guards hustled him to his feet. He felt his first real stab of panic as they pulled the hood over his head and bound his hands. He struggled in vain, silently cursing Davenport. They spun him round until he was giddy, then dragged him tottering from the building. He was aware of moving from concrete to grass, climbing a short slope, and going through a gate.

"Mind the cow shite," said one of them, pulling him aside. "We don't want to be spoiling good shoes."

The significance of the remark was brought home to him when he was told to remove his shoes. This was the way they shot informers. He wondered what would happen to the shoes.

His heart beat too fast. His mouth tasted rusty and his bowels turned as liquid as his mouth was dry. He hoped they would get it over with quickly.

"Tell us that it's the Brits you're working for and you'll be spared," one of them whispered temptingly.

Candlestick shook his head, alone as he ever would be, panting now, open mouthed, counting down. They would shoot him whatever. Ninety-five. Ninety-four. He wondered how far he would get before they shot him. He remembered the birds flying away from the trees after he had killed Tommy Herron. It had been autumn then. He tried to recall Becky's fluttering heart under his chest and the feel of her ribcage, but the image would not materialize in the dead black of the hood. He could feel its coarse material each time he breathed in. Seventy-seven. Seventy-six. His breathing became a rapid whimper. Something hit him in the back and he recoiled in fright. It was only a shove, he realized, to push him forward on to his knees. Damp earth seeped through his trousers. Fifty-seven, fifty-six. He was gabbling now, going too fast, close to grovelling.

"Take the hood off," he said. "I don't want the hood."

They surprised him by obliging. He knelt, blinking in the grey light, taking in the feminine curve of the field's horizon, the trees coming to full leaf. He counted slower now, feeling the sweat on his face dry in the coolness. For a second or two he felt himself in a pool of calm, just long enough to draw strength.

He recognized Seamus in spite of his mask and saw the revolver in his hand. Seamus was nervous.

"Take your mask off, Seamus."

Seamus fumbled with the gun, ignoring him.

"You're scared, Seamus."

"Shut your gob," said one of the others.

The fear returned, hammering at him. He willed Seamus through clenched teeth to get on with it. Thirty-three. Thirty-two.

"Last chance," said one of the voices behind him. "Tell us what you know and this stops."

"Fuck you," he managed to say. "And the mother you rode in on."

Seamus moved round behind him.

Twenty-seven, twenty-six. His vision clouded. The black tunnel was waiting. Would it ever end? This field felt longer than the rest of his life together. He tried and failed to think of anything good to take with him. Twenty-five. Twenty—

The report banged in his ears and he was hit in the middle of the back. He pitched forward and tasted earth. They had botched the job. He was still alive.

Twenty-four. Twenty-three.

He couldn't tell where he'd been hit. There was no pain. The wet warmth he thought was blood was liquid shit. He had voided himself. It wasn't right that this shame should be the last thing he experienced. Now he knew how the others had felt.

The muzzle of Seamus's barrel scraped the side of his head and he braced himself for the explosion. There was a scream. He squeezed his eyes shut and had a clear, high-up picture of himself lying there squealing. He was no different from the rest, after all. Then came a series of clicks—the gun jamming, he thought. Click click click. Then he realized Seamus was spinning the chamber between clicks and he understood what they were doing. They were playing Russian roulette with him.

His brain was sweating like nitroglycerine. Click click click. He gritted his teeth in a supreme effort to keep back the words building in his throat, waiting to pour out: Davenport, Tranter, phone numbers and all the rest. He swallowed the words back down with the bile that was rising in him. In the everlasting second before the hammer fell again he experienced the fear that until then he had only seen in others.

Then he felt warm breath on his ear, a voice saying, "April fool."

He rolled over and lay staring at the sky, in wild search of the heavens, for some sign of understanding. He wondered if he wasn't dead anyway, if this was not the start of an afterlife.

His heartbeat gradually settled. With it came a new resolve, a pure hatred born out of a shame revealed to him by his shit, by his screams.

From now there would be no mercy. They would have been better off killing him. One day they would pay.

His would-be executioners were embarrassed and unsure what to do next. They kept their masks on, adding to the unreality of everything. One put his shoes back on and they all walked back to the farm in silence. Candlestick had trouble with his balance. The sharpness of everything made him dizzy. Seamus carried the hood. Who had made it? Candlestick wondered.

They took him to an outside wash house and cut the twine that bound his hands and went outside while he stripped off his soiled clothes and washed himself down. His mind was blank, his hands steady. He waited for the shock to kick in.

He asked for fresh clothes and stood shivering until they fetched a pair of trousers several sizes too big and a vee-neck jersey with holes in the elbows. They led him back to the container. The noise was no longer there. He lay on the mattress, shaking uncontrollably, until by will alone he dragged himself up and started exercising hard, counting off the minutes, counting upwards this time until he reached twelve hundred. Then he lay down and slept like a dog, secure in the knowledge that they would not break him now.

BREEN got him drunk after that, both of them downing quantities of vodka. He was sure Breen had been behind the hoax execution. It was a test of Candlestick's true knowledge, a way of finally deciding whether he was who he said he was. Breen's cleverness was a slipperiness that was hard to contend with, his vodka yet another test. Drinking with the devil, Candlestick thought, grimly: one devil to another.

As the bottle became emptier Breen's gentle enticements to confess became harder to resist.

"Now it's over, you can tell me," he said with a laugh.

Nothing would be easier than to tell Breen everything, just to experience the feeling of lightness it would bring.

"The girl was part of the set-up, surely?"

"The trouble with you people is you see things where there's nothing to be seen."

"Well, you've got her wrapped round your little finger. She's been pleading on your behalf, and her da's more than convinced too. It worries me that she's not prettier."

"She's fair enough."

Candlestick's lips felt thick and clumsy from the vodka.

"Here's me: this boy could do better, I'm thinking. So why's he bothering with a lass like her, unless there's more to it than meets the eye?"

Candlestick watched Breen fill up his glass until it was level with the top.

"Do you have an answer to that?" he added.

"I bet your wife's no oil painting."

Breen threw back his head and laughed.

"True, true."

"Was it your idea to have me shot?"

"It was my idea *not* to have you shot. The others were all for sticking a bullet in your ear. I told them it was the way to decide if you were telling the full story. There's not many who wouldn't start gabbling in the face of that. Congratulations, comrade."

Breen raised his glass in mock salute. The vodka appeared to have little effect on him. Candlestick was sure that Breen still didn't believe him. He knocked back his drink and Breen poured him another. Candlestick tried refusing.

"There's no defaulting here. It's the end of the bottle or nothing. What do you think of Mr. Davenport now?"

The reference to Davenport nearly threw him.

"What are you talking about?"

Breen shook his head, to say never mind.

For a moment Candlestick saw again into the abyss of his own fear. He started to nurse a hatred of Breen, a murderousness of the kind usually reserved by sons for their fathers.

After the bottle was finished Candlestick offered a confession of sorts, a sour, dank admission of childhood lovelessness.

"I spent my childhood getting fucked. I think that entitles me to fight for who I want to fight for."

He added that you didn't have to be not a Brit to hate the Brits.

Breen raised his empty glass. "Amen to that."

Thirty-one

CROSS reread the forensic report on the lock-up where blood tracings matching Mary Ryan's had been found. They had a murder site. As for John Willcox, he was still nowhere to be found.

The phone rang. It was Donnelly calling from the Republic to say that he had located Bernadette Breen's sister, Molly Connors, living in West Meath under her maiden name.

"So she never married, by the looks of it," said Donnelly. "Do you want me to call her?"

Cross called her himself. The phone was a long time ringing. There was a silence when he said who he was and what he wanted to talk about.

"I thought someone would come asking sooner or later," she finally said.

Molly Connors had an attractive voice, deep, perhaps even a contralto, he thought. He asked to come down in the following week. Saturdays were easiest, she replied, and in the end they agreed on the following day, Molly perhaps because she wanted to get the meeting over with, Cross because it would mean not spending the day at home.

* * *

AT THE next morning's breakfast he announced his intention to spend the day working.

"I hope you're not taking the car," said Deidre, spooning egg into Fiona's mouth.

Her car was being repaired, it turned out, and she needed the Volvo as Saturday was the only day she could do the shopping.

"We can all go, then I can take the car after," volunteered Cross.

The argument lapsed into a stubborn silence once it became clear that Deidre was not prepared to relinquish the Volvo.

"We shouldn't be having this row in front of the children," she said.

"Do you want to step outside?"

She pulled a face that told him not to be so childish. Cross felt a blinding desire to hit her and stalked out of the room to escape his anger. It showed how far things had broken down, he thought. Pride prevented him from going back to apologize.

He phoned the barracks and found no vehicle available. The main hire company had nothing either, at such short notice, so he tried Hargreaves on the off-chance, without getting any reply, then rang Westerby. She took her time answering and he wondered if he was getting her out of bed.

He explained what he wanted, wondering why he wasn't taking the train.

"Don't worry if it's inconvenient," he said, but Westerby announced that she could drive him to West Meath, though she sounded doubtful and he started to make excuses. Perhaps he should spend the day with his family after all, he thought. Someone was moving around in the background at Westerby's end of the line and there was the sound of a pop-up toaster.

"No, really, it's fine," she said. "Martin's playing rugby anyway, so it gets me out of watching."

She told him not to thank her until he had seen the car.

DEIDRE was already gone, with a final glare of anger, before Westerby arrived. It was the first time he had noticed her clothes, he realized. She was wearing jeans and a loose sweater.

The car was small, slow and uncomfortable. Even with the seat pushed right back Cross had trouble with his legs. As they turned on to the Malone Road and headed south, Westerby said she had managed to speak to the *Irish Times* journalist in Barbados.

"About Heatherington?"

She nodded. After his arrest for his apparent part in the shooting of two policemen, Heatherington had been taken to the Crumlin Road gaol. Cross asked to be reminded of when this had happened.

"May 1974, sir."

Westerby went on to explain how in gaol Heatherington had exercised his right to select which prisoners he was put in with and elected to be billeted with the IRA, claiming that he had once been a member of the IRA's youth movement.

"The Provisionals questioned him as a matter of course and he struck them as shifty. So they checked with their people outside and found out he'd had nothing to do with the shooting. Well, alarm bells started to ring. When they asked him why he had requested to be put in the IRA wing he quite reasonably answered that it offered protection from loyalist reprisals. As far as they were concerned he'd just shot a couple of policemen. Nevertheless, the Provisionals became convinced they had a plant on their hands and Heatherington behaved like he had something to hide."

"So they sweated him?"

"Exactly. Until he told them he was working for the Brits and backed that up by spilling stuff that could only have come from them. He named the gang that had killed Tommy Herron the year before, which confirmed IRA suspicions that the Brits were behind Herron's murder. He also had up-to-the-minute information on that month's bombings in Dublin, again confirming the Provisionals' belief that the British had been involved. Can this be right, sir? Surely the Brits can't be condoning the slaughter of civilians."

"What did your man in Barbados say?" asked Cross.

"He said it was generally thought, even then, that the loyalists did not have the expertise to carry out such a sophisticated operation by themselves. Surely this can't really be true?"

She took her eye off the road and looked at Cross, perplexed.

"Hard to believe," he said lamely.

Like most people he blanked out the nastier stories: the torture in Castlereagh, the dirty ops and the black propaganda.

These things went on of necessity but it was best not to inquire too closely. These things were wrong in theory, but he could see how in practice they became enmeshed in a complex psychological war where moral considerations had no place. He remembered the indignation of the Dublin officer—he couldn't remember his name—who had told him about the bombings just mentioned by Westerby. Twenty-eight dead altogether. It *was* hard to believe.

They moved on to the motorway. Westerby broke off her account to coax the car past an army convoy. Cross had never grown used to these faceless, sinister processions of khaki camouflage.

Once past the vehicles, Westerby explained that Heatherington's interrogators had pushed him into confessing to being part of a pseudo-gang run by British intelligence.

"Pseudo-gang?"

"Counter-propaganda outfits is how they were described to me, acting like wild cards. They'd carry out a bank raid, which was then blamed on the Provos, to trick them into hunting through their own ranks for culprits."

Homers, they were called: unofficial freelance raids done by activists to line their own pockets. The paranoid, discipline-crazy Provos were hard on anyone found carrying them out.

Heatherington's gang had also been told to undertake "no warning" bomb attacks, again to discredit the IRA. Westerby, after recounting this with a mixture of disbelief and wonder, again looked at Cross.

"Is it really that dirty?"

"Probably," he said cautiously.

"Well, it seems like Heatherington was being used for pretty high stakes. The point of his operation, he finally confessed, was to get inside the Provisional wing of the Crum and poison three of its leaders. Once this was discovered *and* they found where the poison was hidden, all hell was let loose because on top of that Heatherington had named a whole string of Provos who were informers for the Brits."

"And the Provos didn't know whether to believe him?"

"Not until they learned about the plot to kill the leaders and found the poison. Then they swallowed the lot."

The Crumlin Road leadership had panicked and ordered a

massive internal hunt for the traitors. In the chaos that followed many forced confessions were extracted from innocent men.

"Are you saying the whole thing was a hoax?" Cross asked. "And he wasn't there to poison anyone."

"That was a decoy to get them to believe everything else."

Cross was amazed at the elaborate nature of the plot. If Westerby was right then it was someone's intention that Heatherington should have been suspected of being a British agent from the start, exposed and under interrogation should have passed on crucially damaging false information. The operation was a classic sting.

"What happened to Heatherington?"

"After the poison was found someone spirited him into protective custody. He then went on trial for the shooting of the policemen, was acquitted and stayed in Belfast in the belief that he was not on any IRA hit list, which struck me as pretty daft until the man from the *Times* explained to me that there had been a change in the Provisionals' leadership as a direct result of the Heatherington operation. And the new men had nothing against him, believe it or not."

"But his luck ran out."

"Two years later. He was shot, presumably on the orders of the men he'd duped."

Cross shook his head in disbelief at the whole story.

"It's amazing," said Westerby. "What people have minds like that, sir?"

"People who like to play games."

Westerby turned off the motorway, and they drove in silence through Protestant Portadown with its brickwork and kerbstones painted in the colours of the Union Jack, and on towards Catholic Newry. Cross's back was starting to ache, which took the pleasure out of the journey. He thought about lunch but decided to press on. They were in republican country and he felt exposed and apprehensive.

The rolling fields and hedgerows reminded him of his childhood. The last time he had been in England he had been struck by how few hedges were left, uprooted in the general move towards open farming. South Armagh by contrast was still a countryside of entrenched smallholdings and roadside wild flowers. In the distance he could see the railway line and wondered if it was near where they had been evacuated from the train.

Gazing at the sun-dappled fields, Cross was overtaken by his usual surprise at the contrast between the sleepy landscape and its fearsome reputation. The clatter of an army helicopter, rearing up suddenly from behind a hill, was a sharp reminder of where they were. He watched it head south-west in the direction of Crossmaglen, where the army patrols were ferried to and from by air.

Between Newry and the border they ran into a roadblock. The first warning was a long tailback of traffic. Westerby groaned as they joined the queue. Twenty minutes, said Cross. Half an hour, said Westerby, who turned out to be right.

The stop-start of the traffic eroded what was left of his good mood. He thought of barging to the head of the queue, but a steady stream of cars coming the other way left them boxed in. He got out to stretch his legs. Up ahead he could see soldiers checking each vehicle, letting some pass and pulling others over. Two soldiers approached, inspecting the line of cars, their rifles held down at forty-five degrees. Their arrogance failed to hide their anxiety. They would have seen the local road signs saying *Sniper at work.*

Thirty-two

South Armagh, June 1974

THOUGH no longer a prisoner Candlestick realized he might as well be. He had been taken to a farm in remote countryside, somewhere well south of Belfast, he guessed, where he was reunited with Becky. She moved cautiously, with a wariness that pricked at his new pity for her. Some vital spark had been lost since the shooting. She trembled at every noise. He spent long hours holding her, saying little. Her horizons shrank until she was entirely dependent on him. He felt the unqualified affection he would feel for an injured animal, which she returned with docile gratitude.

The one disturbance to their solitude was a man who delivered groceries twice a week. He said they were paid for. The telephone only rang when her father called, and she always said, "Yes, I'm feeling much better."

Sometimes he missed the unpredictability of violence and was driven from his bed in the middle of the night to roam the farm in a frenzy, until he learned to absorb the quietness of the land, and remembered the watchfulness of his childhood.

He made her presents whittled from wood, and tamed one of the farm's wild cats for her. Under her guidance he started to read, and devoured republican texts. He wondered occasionally if she were not his gaoler, Becky with her dark hair pulled tight from her brow and her pale skin, graver now that the shadow of death had brushed her and was never far from her thoughts. He learned to smile because she said she liked it.

She slept late and rested in the afternoon while he tidied up around the smallholding with its couple of outbuildings. The house itself was small and damp, and ingrained with decades of poverty. He did his best to make it habitable.

Her slow recovery kept them from the outside world. In three months he had not been to the nearest town, even learned its name. The farm's isolation was complete. There were no other buildings or road in sight. That they never saw anyone did not seem strange.

Only the occasional army helicopter flying low overhead broke the silence. Once in the distance he saw an army patrol making its careless way across fields, lulled into false security by the bewitched, uninhabited remoteness of the landscape. Sometimes as he moved around he had the feeling he was being watched. Once or twice he walked down the narrow lanes as it grew dark, taking in the lie of the land and noting where there was a telephone box. He thought of calling one of Davenport's numbers but never did.

From time to time he found her weeping uncontrollably and asked what the matter was but she only shook her head and buried her face in her hands. These episodes puzzled him and he wondered how this sombre woman connected with the young student he had first met in laughing, crowded bars. Only in sex did she lose her self-consciousness, and then not often. Sometimes when he looked at her and saw the slashed belly or slit throat of those he had killed he wondered if his time of slaughter was over. These zero days, in which he did no wrong, were what he supposed adult life was about.

ONE DAY a man came to see Becky and afterwards she said she was taking a job in the local library.

"Is this what you want?" he asked.

"It's what I want," she replied simply.

He was surprised by his question. He had never thought of the future before and he was uncertain how to take her decision. Until then she had given no sign of feeling imprisoned by his fierce protection.

During the long days Becky was away he experienced a gnawing ache he could not identify until he realized it was to do with missing her. She had been going to the library for several weeks when the next-door farmer, a man with a round, guileless face and shock of white hair, approached him saying that he needed a labourer. Candlestick nodded slowly at the offer, wanting to believe that the rest of their life would be like this, with her at the library while he worked in the fields.

She told him she loved him and he said he did too, not sure if he was saying it because she wanted him to. He saw himself as a young boy standing before a wood at dusk, pines blackening in the gathering darkness, knowing that if he went in he would be lost. Words left him feeling like that. Gestures he could imitate, simple acts, doing something and giving it to Becky, even holding her. Words he mistrusted. He still muddled the letters, and remembered the sharp edge of a ruler on the back of his hand.

Becky phoned her father and asked him to come over. He was a bluff and congenial man and when Becky—for she did the talking—solemnly said that she wished to marry he looked bemused.

"You don't look very happy about it," he said.

"It's what we want," she replied simply.

"There's many'll disapprove, marrying a Brit. And you, son, what have you to offer?"

She interrupted. "We're happy here, doing what we're doing."

"I said you don't look it."

"I'm happy just to be alive," she said earnestly.

THEY had a sad wedding to which no one came because there was no one to invite except her parents and a few relatives. It took place in a small town church and afterwards there was an awkward meal in a room over a bar. Becky's father made the best man's speech to which Candlestick replied briefly, formally thanking everyone and saying that he was a very lucky man. He could see their disappointment. He and Becky danced the first dance, accompanied by a fiddler, moving awkwardly at first, then with growing ease, until the room was spinning and he saw only the two of them and no one else.

Their honeymoon was several days in Killeen on Lough Erne. It was the first time he had left the farm, except for going to the town for his religious instruction before the wedding and for the ceremony itself. They ate formal meals in the dining room of the guest house, where they were the only ones staying, and during the days they walked. He wondered what her silences hid. He pointed out birds, which he could name, and once she froze when an army patrol passed, the only intrusion from the outside world in their time there.

On their last day they bought supplies from a grocer and walked to a pine wood. By a black lake he built a fire from twigs, and cooked sausages and afterwards they lay back and looked at the tops of the pines swaying in the wind and he wondered if this was what other people thought of as happiness.

On their return to the farm they continued to live simply in a house of silence and small conversations that seemed to satisfy their needs. At night she sometimes held him fiercely and let out a thin cry at the end that left him wondering if he was not hurting her. When she was asleep he held her tight, wanting to leave his impression on her, like a stamp.

"Are you happy here?" he'd once asked, curious because he sought her guidance in this area.

"Yes, I'm happy."

When she announced she was going away for a bit he did not know what to think. He thought he had offended her.

"It's Mother. She's not well."

* * *

WHILE she was gone they came, early one evening. He heard the car grinding its way up the track to the farm and slipped from the house into the barn.

After the flatness of the last months he was slow and out of practice, his mouth dry with anxiety. When the car drew up he heard doors slamming and men moving into the house, calling his name.

He edged round the corner of the barn and walked stealthily, heel to toe, until he could see through the kitchen window. There was Breen and another man waiting at the table, looking relaxed.

Neither of them noticed him enter the room until he was standing there like an apparition.

"Where the fuck did you come from?" said Breen.

"Call first, otherwise you won't know what welcome to expect."

Breen had lost weight in the intervening months and his hair was greyer.

"Congratulations," he finally said. "I hear you got married."

It had never crossed his mind that he would see Breen again, just as it had never really occurred to him to telephone any of Davenport's numbers. Since the mock execution he had been in limbo. Only Breen's arrival showed him for what he was: a man in hiding.

"There's a job to do. You'll be back before daybreak," said Breen, standing up.

They drove to the city and he was taken to a safe house for briefing. There on a child's blackboard the interior of a bar had been drawn in yellow chalk. Candlestick was careful to show no surprise. He recognized the bar from his own meetings with Captain Bunty.

Breen told him the plan. He would be dropped outside the bar and the escape route was through a back exit to where a car would be waiting.

Candlestick looked again at the blackboard. The bar area was in the centre of the room, with seats all around and the back exit to the right.

"What if he's sitting on the left? I'll have to go all the way round the bar to get out."

"He won't be," said Breen. "He'll be at the back on the right, by the door you're leaving by."

"How long is the run-back?"

"Five minutes to the wash house."

The wash house was where his clothes would be taken and burned and he would hand over his gun and remove any forensic traces.

The photograph of the man he was to shoot came as no surprise. He had already guessed as much and was careful to keep his face a mask, aware of Breen studying his reaction.

He was given a pair of workman's brown overalls and a Browning automatic. He said he would have preferred a revolver.

"Next time I'll get you a six shooter."

THEY dropped him off at the corner just before closing time. He watched the car disappear. The streets were damp with the finest of drizzles and the night was sharp after a mild day, with a wind blowing off the sea. He found himself hanging around instead of going in, wondering if he had lost his nerve. It was the lack of rehearsal he didn't like. What if the back door was locked? It felt too much like a set-up. He told himself to walk in and have done with it.

Bunty was half rising out of his seat, with a silly look of recognition on his face, when the first bullet hit him in the chest, punching him backwards. A neat crimson stain blotted his shirtfront as he slid sideways on the banquette, his unfinished lager still in his hand. He looked like he was trying not to spill it as he fell, a touch that struck Candlestick as absurd as the once-bitten sandwich lying on the table. Bunty crumpled on to the swirled carpet, beer spilling down him, mixing with blood. His head bent awkwardly against the banquette and he made little hep-hep noises as the blood bubbled from his mouth. Candlestick leant forward and stuck the gun behind Bunty's ear, twisted it sideways and fired. The plump body jerked as if tugged by wires. He fired again, straight into the ear: that'd put him to sleep even if the others hadn't.

He smelt the panic rising as people realized what was happening, not all at once because the jukebox was too loud. It was an old Brenda Lee record. "I'm Sorry." Wrong song, he thought. The shocked silence worked its way out from the killing point to the edge of the room until there was only the noise of the music, but by then he was gone. *So lonely baby*.

His heart was thumping, not because of the shooting. It was Bunty's companion who'd almost stopped him in his tracks, getting up to go, as cool as you like, the moment she saw him, brushing past, leaving a trace of her perfume in the air. He caught a glimpse of the same red skirt she had worn last time. For a fraction of a second their eyes met, hers dead cool. Did she smile?

Maggie was gone by the time he had finished with Bunty, gone the way he came in, he presumed. He thought of running after her until he saw there was no way through the crowd, gun or no gun.

Within twenty minutes he was washed and changed and on his way back home.

That night he spent a long time sitting in the field overlooking the farm, growing gradually colder, thinking about the wrong woman.

IN THE New Year Breen used him more. There was a haphazard feel to the shootings that he learned to accept. They were done with little preparation and involved himself and Breen roaming the city by car, stopping off at various bars where Breen would pause long enough to drink a glass of Guinness and inquire after the man he wanted, while Candlestick waited in the car.

He shot a drunken man pointed out to him outside a pub in the Markets, sending him staggering back into a doorway down which he slowly collapsed, arms aloft, caught between surrender and surprise.

He shot others in the following weeks, on the same hasty basis. Candlestick undertook these assassinations without the slightest curiosity. He felt immune. He was the trigger, nothing more. The deaths were of no consequence to him. But as the killings mounted—sometimes as many as three a month—he grew puzzled. The Markets, Ardoyne, the Falls, Whiterock and Ballymurphy. Always Catholic areas. Which made no sense as Breen was IRA. Why was Breen using him to shoot Catholics? He didn't like being kept in the dark. The dark room of his childhood, the varying screams of his mother next door—pain and pleasure. He wanted control.

Thirty-three

MOLLY CONNORS turned out to be a tall, handsome woman who lived on a small farm whose neatness was in pointed contrast to the desolation of Breen's. The farm had a paddock where a couple of horses strolled, and a tranquil view made more peaceful by the late-afternoon sun that bathed everything in a golden light.

"I baked some soda bread in your honour," she said on coming out to meet them.

Molly listened to Cross's explanation for their delay. Her mocking manner suggested she was enjoying some private joke, probably at his expense. She looked in her mid-thirties, which would make her some fifteen years younger than Breen. She was far more striking than her sister, to judge by the photograph of Bernadette, less anaemic and darker, with a hint of recklessness.

It was clear from her air of sturdy independence that she lived alone and supported herself. Her hands were rough from work. She looked altogether strong and without vanity.

"Do you manage all this by yourself?" asked Cross.

"Pretty much. Do you know anything about farming?" she asked, again with the hint of mockery.

"Not a thing."

"This is small enough to manage, just. I have a man come in. But it's the stud that is my real passion."

She took them into a kitchen with a range and a table large enough to seat a dozen and only four chairs to go with it. Like Breen, Molly obviously got by with a minimum, except with her it looked more like choice than neglect.

"Well," she said, after pouring tea. "What is it you want to know? Is it Bernadette? They've not found the men who did it?"

There was no expectation in her voice or disappointment when Cross said they had not.

"I've never expected a solution. From the moment I heard I knew there would never be an answer."

"It's Francis Breen we want to talk about."

Molly stared at the table. "Is Francis dead too?"

"Why do you ask?"

"Just a feeling."

There was no curiosity about his fate, which struck Cross as odd. "Breen was murdered," he said.

Molly considered this, again showing no surprise.

"By the same people that killed Bernadette," she said.

It was a statement not a question. Cross asked what had happened to Breen after her sister's death.

"I never saw him or spoke to him again. He didn't even come to the funeral. His own wife and children."

"Because he was scared?"

"I'd say."

"Do you have any idea who killed Bernadette?"

Molly shrugged. Cross looked at Westerby, a sign for her to take over.

"You were with Francis Breen the morning your sister died," she said.

Molly looked up with what seemed like relief.

"I was with Francis the morning Bernadette died, yes. In bed with him, is the answer to your next question."

"Do you know what happened to him after that?"

"No. Nor did I try to find out. Whatever feelings I might have had for Francis—and they were mixed at best—died with Bernadette."

Molly showed no reluctance to answer their questions. She had waited a long time to make her statement. Cross admired her self-possession and control. She had formidable powers of concentration and would not speak until she had each word arranged.

She told them how she was the sister that had got the education and gone to Queen's and become politicized, unlike Bernadette, who did nursing. The sisters had often argued about Molly's politics. Bernadette dismissed her going on marches and making noises about civil rights as an affectation of higher education.

"Bernadette was right in a way. But it all changed, for me, on the fourteenth of August 1969. I was in Catholic West Belfast when the Shankill gangs moved in and burned out more than two hundred Catholic families from their homes. I've never seen such chaos or carnage. The RUC took Browning machine guns into the Falls Road. Browning machine guns in an area like that! They shot at anything that moved. Those things fired ten high-velocity bullets a second and had a range of over two miles. They killed a sleeping nine-year-old boy, and a British soldier home on leave was shot dead on a balcony in the Divis Flats while he watched the rioting. And then they sent the army in, kids in camouflage who couldn't tell the two sides apart. Well, I met Francis Breen on the afternoon of the fifteenth. He was in the thick of it. I know they said that IRA stood for I Ran Away, but not Francis. We became lovers that night."

She paused, far away, lost in her memories, before dismissing them with a sardonic smile.

"I was very young and it was all very wild and romantic, I dare say, running around with revolutionaries and manning the barricades. Anyway, it all seemed a lot more real than studying. You know, it was our turn, after Paris '68. Mao, Che, Cuba. All the slogans, you probably remember."

"From what we've been able to discover, Francis Breen was a man with several sides to him," said Westerby.

"And several women. I take it you're talking about the rackets?"

Cross nodded.

"Business enterprises, he called them. Raising funds was always a problem for the organization and in the beginning I think it was a real concern for Francis. I even helped him organize a student subscription and university discos. All for the cause, I thought. Francis was a hero to me. Don't forget my first sight of him was at the barricades helping the wounded. And Francis was silver tongued and larger than life, unlike most of the Provos. He dismissed the lot of them as small-minded reactionaries, and it was difficult not to agree. The Officials were far more progressive, enough for the Provos to accuse them of being riddled with Communist agents. Francis laughed at that too and said that as good Catholics the Provvies had been brainwashed into thinking of Lenin as the devil incarnate."

"What made you change your mind about him?"

"A woman's intuition," she said sardonically. "Francis's wallet got fatter, his clothes better and his passion for political debate got less. Once when he was in the bath I went through his pockets and found a huge wad of money and that's when I realized."

Also in her own role of student activist she picked up hints of his unreliability—meetings cancelled without warning and growing rumours that some were making tidy profits out of the struggle—and she came to see that behind his glibness lay a profound cynicism. Nevertheless, she found it hard to break from him. She was naive and besotted, and Breen, seeing that, broke the relationship in the obvious way, by sexual betrayal.

"I was heartbroken, inconsolable."

The end of the affair led to her dropping out of her studies and going abroad to Ethiopia to work in famine relief. When she came back fourteen months later she found her sister Bernadette married to Breen.

"Which was a surprise, to say the least. You could have knocked me over with a feather. And not a word from Bernadette. If she wrote, which she said she did, I never got the letter."

Molly found herself hardened by her time away, she said. Exposure to natural disaster made her less tolerant of what she found back at home.

"I realized that, along with my ideals, I'd lost that sense of the good person I once thought I was. I hated Bernadette—passionately—because she had taken my man, never mind that I was done with him, and, yes, I wished her dead. I took up with Francis again, not because I wanted him, more to spite poor Bernie behind her back. I was jealous, there's no two ways. The affair was my revenge against her and a way of getting back at Francis for undermining my youthful ideals."

Molly watched Westerby in the long silence that followed. Cross studied her hands lying on the top of the table. They were large, practical hands, mannish almost. He thought of Breen lying dead in the road and tried to imagine him alive being caressed by those hands. Molly looked at him oddly, as if reading his thoughts.

"Bernadette never knew about us," she went on. "So in the end the real damage was the harm I did to myself. Since her death I suppose I have spent the years trying to atone, a situation not made any easier by her making me the beneficiary of one of her life insurance policies. I'm living off the proceeds at this moment. It was Bernadette's money that paid for the farm."

She smiled wanly at them. "Sometimes I wonder if I haven't grown comfortable with the pain."

"Do you know anyone who wanted Breen dead?" Cross asked.

Molly threw her head back and gave a hoot of laughter. The darkening shadows emphasized the hollow of her cheekbones.

"It was never easy to get to the bottom of what Francis was up to, but he did talk more towards the end. I think he was afraid of something."

"Or someone?" asked Cross.

"Or someone. When I came back he was very caught up in something. This would have been around the end of 1974. Do you remember the Planet of the Erps?"

Her face lit up unexpectedly at the memory. Planet of the Erps was the nickname of the Divis Flats headquarters of the Irish Republican Socialist Party. The IRSP, or Erps as they were known, had formed after a break in the ranks of the Officials.

"When was that?" Cross asked.

"At the time I'm talking about, around the Christmas of 1974," said Molly. "A lot of Belfast Officials were dead unhappy. They regarded the '72 ceasefire as a Dublin initiative and, as it was still showing no signs of being broken, they took away their toys and started their own party."

"And Breen went with them?" asked Cross.

"I'm sure Francis was his usual canny self and played all ends against the middle before making up his mind. He was certainly involved in the civil war that broke out between the Officials and the Erps in the New Year, though in those early days I don't suppose anyone was quite sure which side he was on."

The situation was complicated by IRSP denials of the existence of any paramilitary wing and the refusal of this new organization to declare itself.

"At the start it was pretty much a free-for-all. There were God knows how many kneecappings in those first months. The Stickies carried out over forty in as many days, I heard. Then the Provos came to the help of the Erps because many of them had old scores to settle with the Officials. Any excuse for a pot shot. For a while there was some mob calling itself the People's Liberation Army, which might have been dreamt up by Francis himself. It was a loose gang of ex-Officials and Provos looking for a bit of action. By then of course the Provos had also called a ceasefire with the Brits, which meant they had no one left to fight, so they did the next best thing and started scrapping with each other. Well, that was Francis, and no doubt lining his pockets all the while. Then of course there was the INLA."

"Which Breen joined."

Molly stood up. "Started. Joined. Ran. Who knows? Francis had learned to move in deep waters by then. I doubt if you'll find many who could say exactly what it was that he did."

She went to turn on a light, a gas lamp on a wall bracket. Though there was electricity, the old gas lights were still there and she preferred them, she said.

While lighting the lamp she remarked casually, "Francis was the man who blew up that Tory Party MP in 1979 as he drove out of the Houses of Parliament."

"Airey Neave?" asked Cross in astonishment.

"So he said, but he may have been joking. Francis was quite capable of fibbing when it suited him. But he was always boasting that the Provos had never pulled off anything like that."

Cross wondered why he was so disconcerted. Neave had been killed by the INLA, so Breen's involvement should have come as no surprise. It was the unexpected mention of Neave, he realized. His name had come up recently after Miranda Ramsay had mentioned Warren's claim that he had stumbled across something to do with a political assassination on the mainland. He wondered at the coincidence of the name cropping up twice in such a short space of time.

"What else did he say?" asked Westerby.

"Always boasting is an exaggeration. He mentioned it twice. The second time he was nervous because several INLA people, including the man who had authorized the Neave operation, had been killed in retaliation, either by the Brits or by loyalist killers in cahoots with them."

"How do you know this?" asked Westerby.

"Francis. He was worried he was next, so when Bernadette and the boys got killed he must have thought it was him they were after and decided it was time to go. Francis was always well aware on which side his bread was buttered and he knew he was getting lazy and careless. He was drinking a lot by then."

"After he went, did anyone approach you or question you about him?" asked Cross.

Molly shook her head.

"Does the name Berrigan mean anything?"

Molly moved her head again, slowly from side to side. Her implacable stare told him how much her hatred of Breen still dominated her life. Cross was curious about the sharp focus of her obsession, and wondered if her hatred could have hardened enough to make her kill. She certainly looked physically capable of it, especially with Breen a drunken, physical wreck by the end.

When she shook hands goodbye Cross noted the firmness of her grip.

Thirty-four

THEY were still well in the Republic when it started to rain so heavily that they had to pull over. When the storm showed some sign of letting up Cross suggested they push on at least to find a telephone to call home and explain their delay. He caught Westerby's dubious look.

"We're still far enough south," he said.

She nodded slowly and pulled a face. The wide stretch on either side of the border was known as bandit country with good reason. It was staunchly republican and any member of the RUC who strayed into it was a target. Cross's own English accent and Westerby's Belfast one would mark them out for immediate attention. The rules were straightforward. In the run-up to the border and through South Armagh they were: stick to main roads and don't stop. The alternative was spelled out for all concerned when an RUC man who had broken down in a lay-by had been found shot in the head. Cross looked at the map again. The nearest place appeared to be somewhere called Clonmellon.

The rain drove hard against the windscreen until even with the wipers on full they could barely see. Westerby's face grew tense. Once or twice the lights of another vehicle splashed over their faces, otherwise they nudged their way forward alone.

They were almost through Clonmellon before realizing it was there. A few pinpricks of light blurred in the wet darkness. Westerby slowed to a crawl while Cross tried to see if any of the buildings was still open or, best of all, a police station. They drove down the main street twice before spotting a bar.

The place looked shut but turned out to be open and full. Beefy farm lads smelling of wet clothes and tobacco greeted their arrival with a heavy silence. Westerby, as the only woman in the place, was an object of sullen curiosity. Cross, painfully aware of his accent, asked the young barman for the phone. They were allowed to use one in a parlour behind.

Deidre sounded brisk and told him she was busy bathing the children. Cross wondered if his not being there made any difference. When Westerby made her call she sounded perfunctory and strained.

The bar fell quiet again as they made their way back. "Mind how you go," said a voice in a mock British accent. Laughter and a few cat-calls followed them out.

As Cross listened to Westerby trying to coax the engine back to life he sensed her blaming him for a day that was ending in disaster. He bit back his own irritation, at Deidre for taking the Volvo and at Westerby for having such an unreliable car. He sighed and told her to wait there.

Back in the bar he was greeted by another silence, more hostile than before, while he explained about the car.

"You're not from around these parts?" said the barman, deadpan. He was a dark, handsome lad with an air of mischief that looked like it could turn dangerous. A few sniggered. Cross was aware of everyone listening.

"I can't remember when we last had a foreigner in here. Where's your lady friend from?"

"Belfast," said Cross.

They probably thought he was army. He tried to think what he would say if they asked.

"At least you're not in a ditch somewhere," the barman went on. "On a terrible night like this who knows where you could have ended up. But you'll not get your car mended now. I think Donny's the man for you, but don't bend over if you drop your change."

There were a few chuckles.

"Oi, Tony!" shouted the barman.

Tony came shuffling forward. He had the bleary look of a man who had been drinking since lunchtime.

"Now, Tony, are you all right to drive?"

"With my eyes shut."

"Take this feller down to Donny's."

The barman turned back to Cross.

"Donny'll put you up for the night, but any drink you're needing, you'll have to buy now because Donny'll only send you back if you start asking for it."

Cross settled on a quarter of whisky and a bottle of wine. There wasn't a lot of call for wine, the barman said, producing a dusty bottle of Valpolicella that he passed on for an exorbitant sum.

"Is that the colour of your money?" he said, inspecting Cross's sterling note. "Are we taking the crown's shilling tonight?"

Cross felt himself redden as the barman took the note.

"I'll call Donny and tell him you're on your way," he said, handing Cross a handful of Irish change with a wink.

Tony went for his car while Cross collected Westerby and explained what was happening. She looked thoroughly fed up and even more so at the sight of the battered Datsun Sunny. Its interior smelt of wet dog and boozy breath. Only one headlight worked but that did not deter Tony from driving at sixty into a blind tunnel of driving rain.

"Can you not drive so fast, man," ordered Cross, who immediately felt that he was being over-anxious.

"Don't you worry, sir, the road's as straight as it's long."

Bloody comedian, thought Cross.

They drove several miles at the same breakneck speed before the Datsun pulled up at an isolated bungalow. When Cross protested at the size of the fare Tony muttered something about an excess charge.

"What for, the weather?" asked Cross.

"Right enough, the weather."

Again Cross had to hand over a British note. Tony had no change.

Donny was waiting in the porch, looking like a vision that had answered the wrong cue. He teetered towards them dressed in a cerise shirt and white jeans. He was florid, paunchy and pigeon-toed, with hair scraped up and over to hide his baldness, and was wearing what was probably the only charm bracelet in County Louth.

"You poor dears! Welcome, welcome!"

He ushered them through rooms that were a defiant assault on plain good taste, all clashing colours and rioting fabrics, the customary Irish way of showing that poverty had been beaten.

Cross avoided looking at Westerby as they went upstairs. Donny proudly ushered them into a room not much bigger than its large bed with a quilted headboard. "Queen size!" he exclaimed before manoeuvring an awkward concertina door to reveal a tiny pink bathroom.

When Cross explained that he would be needing a second room Donny wrung his hands.

"I've none spare. Mooney's boy said nothing about a second room. The other's gone to a lad who's decorating for me. Is sharing out of the question? I've got a little put-u-up we can squeeze in here."

Donny pointed towards the narrow space at the end of the bed. He was so outrageously camp that it was hard not to laugh. Westerby was evidently amused.

Cross told her to take the first bath and went downstairs with Donny to use the phone, which was in a little confessional-like booth beneath the stairs. He called Deidre again to say he was now stranded. Cross had the feeling she didn't believe him. In Belfast it was a clear moonlit night after a sunny day.

"Are you on your own?" she asked.

"With Hargreaves."

He wondered afterwards if she had overheard him calling Westerby that morning, wondered too why he had lied. It was too late now.

As they sat down to dinner, he decided it was better to be in good humour, and he raised his glass.

"Well, cheers," said Westerby.

Donny insisted they dine by candlelight, which made them amused in a self-conscious way. They were both too aware of being off duty, he thought.

Donny fussed over them with outrageous stories of his peripatetic love life, thanks to ten years in the navy.

"Every dish a memory," he sighed, serving cous cous. "I can't help noticing, dear, that's a lovely lipstick you're wearing. What is it, if you don't mind my asking?"

Westerby said it was a Yardley.

"The choice you have up there, it's worth all the troubles. We've nothing like it, not even in Dublin. The last time I was in Belfast I spent the whole day in Boots. Paradise! And the pronunciations too, so fetching. Butes the Chaymist. Doesn't she have beautiful eyes?"

Cross agreed out of politeness.

"You're very quiet."

Cross realized Donny was talking to him. "Just tired."

He was wondering about Westerby. He had not let himself notice her eyes before: the clearest of clear blues; cornflower, he thought.

WESTERBY appeared to be already asleep when he got upstairs. Cross had given Donny a hand with clearing up to allow her time to prepare for bed. She had taken the put-u-up, leaving him the large bed. He turned out the light and undressed in the dark. The sheets were cool and crisp. He was pleasantly surprised. He had been expecting nylon.

An hour later he was still awake, listening to a wind that had got up and the rain still beating against the window. Westerby stirred in her sleep, her presence an uncomfortable reminder of his loveless life.

He counted off the quarter-hours on the luminous dial of his watch, and fell to brooding. At some point he found himself wondering about Breen's missing teeth. He saw again the dumped bodies of Breen, Mary Elam and Mary Ryan, thrown out like discarded trash. His own negligence bled into the picture. His failure to resolve his relationship with Deidre. His casualness towards Vinnie, so like Heatherington. They would be the same age roughly. He wondered what Blair had in mind for Vinnie. He shut his eyes and tried to escape the confusion.

A quarter to three crawled to a quarter past. In his exhaustion

Cross's thoughts became a kaleidoscope of waking dreams and random thoughts in collision.

In his clearer moments he felt like a man trapped in a maze of the past—Mary Ryan's murder, reminiscent of the brutality of the Shankill murders thirteen years before; Breen's subterranean meanderings suggesting God knows what collusions; then there was Miranda Ramsay's strange confession with its hints of a different labyrinth. How many mazes were there? And even if he found the centre how would he recognize it?

When he awoke something outside passed for daylight and Westerby's bed was empty. He found her downstairs cheerfully tackling a full breakfast.

"Sleep well?" asked Cross, sticking to toast and coffee in spite of Donny's protestations.

"Like a top," she answered.

It looked like it. He wondered if his own appearance was as ragged as he felt.

THE RAIN was still falling when Donny drove them through sodden countryside back to the village and Westerby's car, which still would not start. A local mechanic who had reluctantly agreed to meet them there pronounced it sick.

"It's your water pump, which is a joke considerin' all the rain like."

The part would not be available until Tuesday, he said. Tuesday week, more like it, thought Cross.

Donny then drove them back to the guest house—which was called Donnybrook, Cross noticed—where he phoned about the trains and told them there was one in an hour from Dundalk.

"You're lucky. None ran yesterday," he said. "I'll take you down there because you'll not get Tony the taxi before three on a Sunday."

The rain, which had let up briefly, returned during the drive to the station. Donny took them via back roads, which Cross would have avoided, and he grew more nervous the nearer they got to the border. Every few moments Donny wiped condensation off the inside of the windscreen.

"Will you look at this bloody car. Now the demister's up the spout. Who'd want to live here if it was the last place on earth? Terrible weather, dreadful people, and hardly a boy to be found that doesn't make you feel guilty for wanting him. Christ, what's this?"

He slowed down. Three men were standing in the middle of the narrow road carrying shotguns and wearing masks. One of them waved the car down. Cross held his breath as Donny opened the window a crack.

"What the fuck are yous boys playin' at?" Donny asked, his accent broader.

"Where are you goin', Donny?"

"Driving a couple of innocent Christians to the station. Should you be wavin' those guns around?"

"On you go," said the man, with a laugh.

Cross looked at Westerby. The bizarre incident had shaken them both.

"Now what was that all about?" said Donny, who turned to Cross. "I'm glad you kept your mouth shut. I thought for a minute those fellows were there for you."

Cross and Westerby laughed with nervous relief. It was the first reference Donny had made to Cross's Englishness. Nor had he asked what they did.

The seething crowd outside Dundalk station was a shock after the emptiness of the last day. Donny stuck his head out of the window and asked if the Belfast train was delayed and was told that it was the Dublin service that had been disrupted. Everyone had been bussed from Lurgan.

Cross insisted on paying for the lift, after pointing out that Tony would have charged three times what he was offering. Donny accepted reluctantly and gave them his card, looking almost tearful at their departure.

"Be sure to ring me, pet, when you're coming back," he said to Westerby, who had to arrange to collect the car.

They waved Donny goodbye while a cluster of people behind them negotiated with a taxi driver.

"Thirty pounds to Dublin," the cry went up and the crowd grew larger with people waving notes.

The station finally cleared when the grumbling Dublin passengers were herded back on to the buses in search of their elusive train.

Theirs, when it came, much later than announced, sat there, its failure to depart unexplained. No doubt the rest of the journey would involve the usual stubborn delays bereft of information, thought Cross. It was like a metaphor for the whole country. In the face of such opacity it was easy to see the attractions of a hard line.

HE WOKE, briefly unable to work out where he was or why Westerby was opposite him, staring out of the window at a featureless field. Both the train and the rain had stopped, he noticed before drifting off again, this time to dream of walking back to the barn, past peat bags full of old bones. Then Westerby was shaking him awake. Donny was right about her eyes.

"You were shouting," she said, looking concerned.

He remembered the flies swarming round his head. He was embarrassed about dreaming in front of Westerby and went into the corridor for a smoke.

"Why do you think Mary Ryan was killed?" he asked on his return.

Westerby hesitated before answering. "Any reason at all?"

"Any reason."

"Because she was meant to be," she said in a strange, tight voice.

"What do you mean?"

"I don't know. It's the only way I can put it. For some reason someone wanted Mary dead. Mary as opposed to someone else."

"So it was personal?"

"Not altogether. I don't think Mary necessarily knew her killer."

"Why do you say that?"

"I don't know, I really don't. But there's something about her death that seems quite chosen."

They went over all possible reasons for killing Mary Ryan, until they started to sound like schoolchildren reciting their tables.

"You end up going round in circles," Westerby announced after half an hour of exasperation.

The train slowed, stopped, moved forward again with a jolt, shuddered and came to a halt a few yards further on.

"Unless . . ." she said.

"Unless what?"

Since she had volunteered the information that Mary had been deliberately selected to be killed, Cross had felt that she was on the edge of some discovery. He watched her forming her thoughts, with a look that he could not identify.

"What if the deaths all belong? What if they're all connected?" she asked, carefully emphasizing each word.

"How? Even trying to link two cases doesn't work, beyond the odd tenuous connection."

Westerby was shaking her head, clearly ahead of him.

"We're looking for patterns where there aren't any. Logically, if Mary Elam and Mary Ryan were murdered by the same man, you'd expect them to have been killed in the same way. What I'm saying is that *all* these deaths somehow belong together."

"Don't tell me Breen's killer murdered Mary Elam."

"But there are similarities between Breen's and Mary Ryan's deaths, and between hers and Mary Elam's. Look at what was done to Mary's eyes and Breen's wrists, and to those poor animals. Take those as the starting point."

Cross now recognized her expression as one of dread.

"So," he said, with a feeling of a man lowering himself into icy water, "what you're saying is, instead of narrowing everything down, broaden it out and ask: what if the deaths are all somehow connected?"

Westerby nodded slowly.

"It did occur to me that— Oh, I don't know. It's just I remember a man from Special Branch moaning about not being allowed to get on with the job of getting rid of terrorists. 'We know who they are,' he kept saying. They all say that. But afterwards, I kept thinking how his remark made sense: everything here is terribly local, like when we walked into that bar last night and we were immediately strangers. What's odd about all these killings is that none of them feels local."

It was true. The elements of Irish crime, whether ordinary or sectarian, were usually simple and on the whole the authorities did know who "they" were, even if they could do nothing about it.

The train staggered and started to move forward again, the carriages creaking and protesting. He looked across at Westerby, who was lost in fierce thought.

"I'm sure it's like when I was at the sex abuse unit," she said. "The cases always turned out to be a nightmare, but the elements involved were usually very simple in the starkest possible way."

"The complications occur because there are too many different ways of things turning out," said Cross.

"Like that game where you have to get all the different colours on the same side of the cube: it looks simple but it's almost impossible to do, like this bloody country. You'd think someone would have worked out a way of getting the orange and green to fit together like they're supposed to."

"Maybe it's the same with our murders. Perhaps they link to this idea of things being both complicated and frighteningly simple at the same time. Not unlike the journey we're on now."

Westerby laughed. "Exactly. The whole thing becomes such a distraction that you end up missing the point. The point of this trip was Molly Connors, and what she told us was quite straightforward, but it's easy to forget that in among—"

"Donny's and Mooney's and breakdowns and gunmen in the middle of the road."

"And endless train journeys and roadblocks."

They laughed, glad of a moment's light relief. What a bizarre sequence of events had led to this detour, Cross thought: a series of connections and half-connections that could not have been guessed at the outset.

"What's the straightforward version of these killings, then?" he asked, serious again.

Westerby puffed out her cheeks, exhaled and then laughed.

"I didn't say it was that straightforward!"

"OK. Where do you want to start?"

"Let's start with Willcox, saying for the sake of argument he's our man. He owns the lock-up where Mary Ryan was killed and has possible connections with the Shankill murderers. Let's say for the moment he's acting alone, though it's possible Breen and Mary Ryan were killed in front of an audience. What do we know about Breen that would make him a suitable victim for Willcox?"

"He goes back a long way. He was an active republican which is enough to put him on most death lists."

"Say the original plot to blow up Breen was a loyalist one, and Willcox a part of it. Then a couple of years later he learns Breen is Mr. Berrigan, resident of Donegal."

"We're still stuck with why anyone should want to freeze him."

"We'll get side-tracked if we get into that."

Cross was surprised by how abrupt she sounded. Mary Elam, she suggested, was a possible Willcox victim because of her association with the Strathaven.

"What about Warren?" Cross asked.

"Warren was asking questions and digging up stuff on McKeague, who was a loyalist extremist. Enough maybe to bring him to the notice of Willcox. Was McKeague killed before Breen disappeared?"

"Yes. A month or so before."

"McKeague was killed by the INLA and Breen was INLA—"

"—so the attempt on Breen's life could have been a reprisal."

"Though there's another argument that McKeague was got rid of by his own side. If that's the case and McKeague was killed by the UVF, where does that leave us?"

"Then Willcox was involved in McKeague's death. Which means that Warren could have put himself into the frame by asking too many questions, and turned himself into a target."

THERE was more rain waiting in Belfast. Back in the city, Cross felt a vague depression settle. They shared a taxi and went to Westerby's first. When they got there she invited him in for a cup of tea as neither of them had had anything since breakfast.

Her flat was several storeys up, on the top floor of an enormous Victorian house, under the eaves. She called out as they went in but there was no reply. While she made tea in the kitchen, Cross looked around at the main room, which was sparsely furnished, suggesting that she hadn't lived there long. It felt like a student flat, with its simple furniture and rows of books. He noted the volumes of psychology. On a long table stood a computer. It was the first time he had seen one in a private home.

"Is the computer yours?" Cross asked.

"Martin's."

He wondered who and where Martin was, as he stared at the machine. He felt useless in the face of technology. Even the new press-button phones made him clumsy.

"Do you understand them?" he asked.

Westerby came through with tea and biscuits on a plate.

"Computers? Up to a point. The biscuits are only digestives, I'm afraid. Shopping, you know."

They sat on pine chairs at a round wooden table. Westerby warmed her hands on her mug, then got up to turn on a gas fire. She seemed comfortable in her own space, more than at work, and easy about Cross being there. He felt awkward. The last twenty-four hours had been strange. She had put on fresh lipstick at some point, which made him feel old.

"If you can spare me tomorrow," she said, "I could take a copy of the files and put all the data we have on that beast over there."

Westerby nodded towards the computer and said that it might pick up patterns they had missed.

"Maybe dates, locations. Maybe the advertisements. We haven't talked about those. Perhaps they're some sort of link between each death."

Cross wondered why they had not examined the advertisements more closely before. It was always the same. Only at a certain point in an investigation did things fall into place, and then floating elements suddenly attached themselves to facts.

"If the killer is advertising these murders by placing quotations in the papers, what's his reasoning? Do you think he wants us to know?"

Westerby thought hard.

"Yes and no. If he was killing out of a compulsion and wanted to draw attention to the fact then he would develop a consistent signature. A way of killing that says: this is me. After leaving the quotation on Breen, you'd expect him to continue with the others. Instead he seems to be disguising himself as he goes along. I think he's leaving traces of clues in the hope that someone will pick up on them."

"Why?"

"To show that he's cleverer than us."

"Then we're not talking about Willcox, are we?"

Westerby laughed at the idea of Willcox as mastermind.

"Maybe he's just the executioner and not the brains," she said. "I'm sure we're dealing with a smart man. My father—the shrink—once said that most murderers want to get caught. The desire for punishment is as great as the need to kill. That may be hooey for all I know, and we may be pushing this thing so far out that we're trying to walk on water, but my feeling is this one is different."

"He has no intention of getting caught."

Cross wasn't sure even as he said it. Westerby was moving too fast for him. He frowned while she traced patterns on the table with her finger.

"Most killers you come across, sir, they're not exactly the jack of spades, are they?"

"No."

"Well, I think this one is an ace."

Cross was still contemplating what she had just said, again wondering if they weren't overstretching the argument, when the front door opened. He didn't know what to make of the sight that greeted him. It was human, but beyond that he wasn't sure. Westerby, seeing his expression, burst out laughing. Cross looked again and realized that the stranger was covered from head to toe in mud. Westerby, still laughing, introduced them.

"Martin's been playing rugby. All weekend, by the look of it."

"Football. The rugby season's over. Excuse me if I don't shake hands."

He padded off towards the bathroom, leaving Cross with no idea of what he looked like. He wondered when it had started to rain. Deidre had said on the telephone the night before that it had been clear and dry. He sighed. He supposed he had better be getting back.

Thirty-five

THE NEXT morning Westerby collected the files on the various cases, copied them and took them home and logged every possible detail and variation she could think of, from dates of birth to national insurance numbers. A thought occurred while she was doing this and she took half an hour to track down

Francis Breen's dentist. She learned that when Breen had last attended, just before his disappearance, he'd had a full set of teeth. It was unlikely, given his dental record, that he'd lost them between then and his death. Westerby put down the phone, wondering what had happened.

She worked all day, apart from pausing for a stale sandwich. The phone rang only once. It was Martin to say that he was going out for a drink after work.

By the time she was finished it was dark. She had a headache and her shoulders were stiff. She looked again at her analysis and shook her head, wondering what to make of it.

Cross was still in his office when she rang. He thought she sounded tired.

"I think you'd better come and have a look, sir. It's too weird to explain on the phone."

WESTERBY didn't answer the door when Cross rang. Instead she stuck her head out of the window and threw down the keys. The offhand familiarity of the gesture surprised him. It was like a scene from another relationship—not theirs—he thought as he stuck out his hand and caught the keys cleanly, which cheered him up.

Westerby answered the upstairs door looking neat and fresh, her skin rosy from a hot bath. She smelt of soap. She pointed to the computer, which was still on.

"I'll show you what I've got."

The screen glowed green as she scrolled through the material.

"I tried the obvious things like grouping addresses according to postal codes and telephone exchanges to see if anything emerged. I thought maybe the killings were particular to one part of the city. I used Breen's old address for this, by the way. But apart from the bodies ending up in our area, there was nothing there."

Cross noticed her hair was still damp from her bath.

"I noted the approximate times of death, but they were too random. I checked the dates of each killing for patterns. Possible. Breen was found on the first of February, Mary Elam on the first of March. Both Fridays. Mary Ryan was found on the twenty-seventh of May, a Monday."

"So the murders took place around the weekend. What about Warren?"

"I'll get to him in a minute. They also took place around the turn of the month."

Sensing Cross's gaze, Westerby turned and looked at him quizzically before continuing.

"The victims are all Catholic. I know that's obvious, but it's just as well to remind ourselves."

"Warren as well?"

"Warren as well, though Mr. Warren is turning out to be a bit of a problem. For a start, his date of death was in the middle of the month and there's no advertisement to go with it."

"The rest have?"

"I re-checked. Exactly a week before, in the case of Breen and Elam, and ten days before with Ryan. There is the other Psalm I found ages ago when I phoned you at Breen's farm— Psalm 22, verse 16: *They pierced my hands and my feet*— which I thought might relate to Warren, but I can't see how it does. The dates are all wrong."

"What else?"

"There is one other thing. I don't know what to make of it. There *is* a pattern, almost two, in fact."

He wondered if she was spinning things out because she had too little to go on. Then, seeing the gravity of her expression, it occurred to him that the knowledge in her possession was making her hesitate, even a little afraid.

She pressed the keyboard and a set of numbers came up on the screen. Cross looked at them: 49, 42, 21.

He looked at Westerby and shrugged.

"Ages of the victims," she said.

He looked at her blankly.

"The computer seems to think it's important. Breen, Elam and Ryan's ages are all divisible by seven."

"By seven? What kind of pattern is that?"

Cross felt stupid and a little angered, partly at Westerby's ease with technology, partly at the thought of telling this to Nesbitt.

"This is not a joke, sir. I've analysed the data for any possible combination. Dates of birth. Dates of death. Last known addresses. Death sites. You asked for patterns. Well, here they are."

"Yes, I'm sorry. Go on."

"There's a further age pattern. Breen, Elam and Ryan were

killed in descending order. Breen was forty-nine, Mary Ryan twenty-one. There's a gap at thirty-five and twenty-eight."

"Warren?"

"Forty-one. Nearly forty-two." She hit the computer keyboard hard enough to register her frustration. "Nearly isn't good enough. I'm sure we're dealing with something quite precise."

"So what are you saying?"

"If this is not just a question of chance, and I've seen stranger coincidences, then the killer must have known their ages. Which means he selected them. Very carefully."

A chill passed over him.

"How do you explain the absence of victims of thirty-five and twenty-eight?"

"I can't, unless there are deaths we don't know about."

"Do you believe the pattern?"

Westerby shrugged. "What I believe and what I can prove are two different things, but, yes, I believe there's something there and it's deliberate."

"But why?"

"I'm sure there is a logic to these deaths. The more I go through the material the more I have the feeling that someone else has gone through it too: names, addresses, ages, religions."

Cross decided to give her instinct the benefit of the doubt. She turned to face him.

"I'm still not sure if the death of Mary Ryan wasn't the work of a gang, but even if it was, I'm pretty sure that the organization behind the killings is the work of one man. With a plan."

"Thank you," he said, feeling stupid. Thanks seemed quite inappropriate and inadequate.

"It's a start," she said. "There are a couple of other things, to do with Breen. There's his teeth."

"I assumed he wore dentures and they got lost."

She told him about Breen's dentist.

"Which means someone pulled them out," she said. "I don't know how I can say that so calmly. Anyway, Breen was tortured more than we thought."

"Which again says sectarian."

"Yes, except why go on to kill to some bizarre pattern? Why the elaboration?"

"I don't know. You said there were a couple of things."

"Breen's birthday was at the end of January only seven days

before his body was found, so technically he was forty-nine by the time he came to be lying in the road. I know this sounds pretty crazy, but if this business of age is crucial, then it could explain keeping the body on ice. If it was vital that Breen was forty-nine not forty-eight."

Thirty-six

HARGREAVES found someone who was willing to talk about Willcox, a man named Catterick who bore a grudge over a dud car he'd been sold, with a clocked milometer and mongrel bodywork.

"Some Taig ought to knock that man's cunt in and see if I care," Catterick had told Hargreaves, who cheerfully mimicked Catterick's Ballymena accent for Cross. "I've seen the fucker swanning around with that child."

Catterick had given Hargreaves a probable address for Willcox off the Newtownards Road, where he lived with a nineteen-year-old. Cross ordered a watch to be put on the house.

Westerby spent the rest of the day on the phone checking unsolved deaths, looking at all victims aged thirty-five or twenty-eight in the period between the deaths of the two Marys. There weren't any in their area.

She wasted hours talking to clerks in other divisions. The calls were yielding nothing and she was starting to doubt herself.

"Why thirty-five and twenty-eight?" asked an unhelpful clerk, a bitter-sounding man she decided was a reservist. Westerby sighed and explained it wasn't for her to say, she was only following orders. The man grunted and went off. It took fifteen minutes of impatient waiting before he came back empty handed.

The last clerk she spoke to was a woman who sounded

bright and efficient for a change. She was gone a much shorter time than the rest.

"Here's something," she said. "Shot twice in the head and dumped in his own boot. No witnesses. No one claimed it, but it looks like a professional job."

Westerby asked his age and name.

"Wheen, Patrick, thirty-five. Married, four children and another on the way."

Wheen was a Roman Catholic. Westerby felt no elation adding his name to the list.

But she failed to find any victim in the whole of Belfast to fill the gap between Wheen and Mary Ryan. There were three twenty-seven-year-olds and a couple of twenty-nines but none at twenty-eight. Westerby cursed. She supposed she would have to extend her search to outside the city.

She broke off for a coffee, and as she stood watching the machine tip the powder into the plastic cup she realized that there was still one possibility left. She hurried back to her desk and rang back the friendliest of the clerks and asked if there were any deaths whose files had been passed on to the security services.

"It's possible," said the clerk, who went off to look.

After finishing with the clerk, Westerby worked swiftly for an hour, making further calls. Then, with mounting excitement, she checked through everything and called Cross at home. His wife answered. Her precise accent left Westerby feeling mildly grubby. Cross sounded cautious when he came to the phone, like she had telephoned in the middle of a row.

"Is it a bad time to phone?" she asked.

"No, no, go ahead."

She started with Wheen. Cross listened in silence then asked if there were any others.

"There's also a twenty-eight-year-old. He didn't show up at first."

"Why not?" asked Cross.

"Because Special Branch have the file. He was an off-duty soldier. Arnold, Roger, a sergeant in the Ulster Defence Regiment."

"How did you get this if it's with Special Branch?"

"Let's just say I have a friend, sir."

She did not. It had taken a fair amount of ingenuity. The

helpful clerk had come back with the information that an army sergeant had been killed off duty. She knew his name was Arnold and that Special Branch had everything else of relevance.

Westerby did not call Special Branch. Caution advised her against it. Instead she had telephoned the Army Pay Corps. This established some basic information about Arnold—including his full name and regiment. She'd then phoned the army press office at Lisburn and, saying she was Special Branch, asked to check what information had been released about Arnold's death. Whoever she had spoken to had been bored and chatty and quite happy to while away ten minutes of a dull afternoon gossiping about a dead soldier. Last of all, she'd called his regiment to fit the missing pieces.

Arnold had been beaten to death in an alley and no one was saying very much about it. According to witnesses, he had been seen drinking prior to that in off-limits pubs. Westerby thought it was possible that Arnold had been on some sort of undercover operation. More important to her was his religion. Sergeant Arnold—surprisingly for a member of the heavily Protestant Ulster Defence Regiment—was listed as Roman Catholic.

"If you add these names to the others," Westerby said to Cross, "you now have five victims of the same religion, whose ages descend in multiples of seven."

She took a deep breath before going on. She noticed her coffee, several hours old and untouched.

"There's another pattern too now, if you put the first letter of each name together."

Cross scribbled each name in order:

> Berrigan (Breen)
> Elam
> Wheen
> Arnold
> Ryan

"Beware? Be warned?" Westerby said over the phone.
Cross stared at the letters. His brow felt clammy.
"If we're right, you know what this means, sir?"
He shook his head, forgetting that she could not see.
"It means the next one will be fourteen."

* * *

SEVERAL hours later, Cross was still brooding on the implications of Westerby's news while waiting for an armed unit to pick up Willcox, who had been spotted at the address Hargreaves had been given. Cross sat squashed with Hargreaves in the back of an armoured patrol car, listening to an Action Man sergeant rehearse several beefy constables from the Special Support group.

"Suspect has been in the house since 22.45. Lights out at 23.27. It's now 23.40. Give him another five minutes to finish his shag and in we'll go, sir," the sergeant said, deferring to Cross.

"You're the one who's done the course, sergeant," he said sourly. Anyone would think the man was organizing the D-Day landings.

The sergeant was on his walkie-talkie, alerting the other men positioned and waiting in the lanes at the back of the house.

The vehicle braked to a halt and the sergeant and his three constables were out at the double and taking a sledgehammer to the front door. Judging by how long it was taking them they were having trouble.

"Cowboys," Cross remarked to Hargreaves as they got out.

They walked through the splintered front door, which was backed by some kind of steel reinforcement, in time to see the constables clattering up the stairs and shoving aside Willcox's screaming girlfriend, who hissed at them, "Shite-faced bastards!"

Cross ignored her. As he turned the bend in the stairs he saw the constables banging in and out of doors, while the squawk of the sergeant's walkie-talkie told him that there was no sign of Willcox at the back.

Typical balls-up, he thought, looking in the bedroom. The bed was still warm, and there were indentations in both pillows. Out on the landing a constable was standing on a ladder, sweeping the attic with a torch.

"Not up here, sarge," he called down.

Everyone stood around getting in each other's way, still pumped up with surplus adrenaline. One constable started accusing those outside of not doing their job.

"Cunt got out the back," he said.

"How about a cup of tea, love," said another to the girlfriend, who was trying to hide in the bathroom. The sergeant shouted at her in exasperation, asking where Willcox was.

"I was asleep, I'm tellin' you, until you noisy bastards woke me up!"

Cross asked for a torch and looked in the loft. He hauled himself up into the dusty space and swept the area with the beam. He missed it the first time—a hole in the brickwork giving access to next door. He trained the torch through the gap. The pattern was repeated for several houses along, allowing a crawl path of escape.

"Right, let's go," said the sergeant when Cross told him and they all clattered downstairs and into the street, where Cross watched the bully-boys vent their frustration on the neighbours of adjoining houses, rousing them from their beds and noisily searching rooms for the missing man.

They did not find him, nor did Cross expect them to. It was easy enough for Willcox to have slipped away. Even at that time of night enough of a crowd had gathered to have hidden his disappearance.

Cross took his temper out on Hargreaves.

"Why did the whole thing have to be conducted like some half-assed military operation? Why not just pick the fucker up? Instead we wake up half the street and lose our man. Go and talk to the girlfriend."

Cross went off to find the sergeant to tell him to call the operation off. The sergeant, he was glad to see, was shifty in defeat. Cross, as much as he wanted to, failed to come up with a crushing remark.

Hargreaves returned and announced, "She knows fuck all about him, or says she does."

"She must know what Willcox does."

Hargreaves shrugged. "Willcox never said where he was going. Whatever he did he kept to himself."

"Is there any evidence he has a job?" asked Cross.

"Only in that he isn't in much. The girl's as thick as shit. Her curiosity doesn't extend beyond getting a shag and a bit of money for herself."

Cross thought that she was probably playing dumb, knowing what Willcox would do if he found out that she had been talking to the police. Given what he was capable of, Cross could hardly blame her.

* * *

"THE FUCKING man was in and you missed him!"

Cross endured Nesbitt's rant in silence, putting up with the flying spittle and counting the broken veins in the other man's cheeks. Like a lot of officers, Nesbitt was a big drinker. At some senior functions Cross had been to, everyone had ended up too paralytic to speak. Most of them had their ways of keeping going, either drink or Dexedrine or caffeine pills. You needed something to get through fourteen hours at a stretch. There were even rooms in the barracks unofficially designated for sleeping off binges. They invariably smelled of vomit.

"Well, what's your excuse?" Nesbitt finally asked.

"None, sir."

Nesbitt grunted.

Cross took a deep breath. "I still think the Mary Ryan murder is connected to several others, sir."

Cross caught Nesbitt's look of sceptical anger, a familiar trick of his. His brusque dismissal of any connection between the deaths was entirely predictable.

"For a start, Military Intelligence and Special Branch would know from their informers if there's a sectarian killer working on this scale."

"With respect, sir, I still think—"

"Bollocks. Come back and convince me of the connections between—what?—an old Sticky, a single mother, a taxi driver, an army sergeant and a wee girl who worked in a photographic lab, and I'll believe you all you want."

"The connections are age and religion."

"Why? Why?" shouted Nesbitt. "Tell me that."

Cross tried explaining that their killer might be a resurfaced survivor of the old Shankill gang.

"Willcox, you mean?" asked Nesbitt, grudgingly.

"Forensic says Mary Ryan was almost certainly murdered in a garage belonging to Willcox."

"Find Willcox, then!"

THEY DID, after Cross had the bright idea of phoning Willcox's mother. To his astonishment, she announced that her son was staying there but was out.

Cross took Hargreaves and a couple of reliable constables. Willcox seemed quite unperturbed and put up no resistance when they picked him up, shambling back from the shops laden with plastic bags of groceries. He had merely asked for the shopping to be taken inside, kissed his mother goodbye and told her that he would be back soon.

Willcox in the flesh had a Slavic appearance not apparent from his photograph. His left eye was lazy, which also didn't show in his mug shot.

Once they were settled in the interview room Cross asked him why there had been all the bother the other night.

"There's a banging on my door, how am I to know it's not the Rah?"

"Do you have a reason to fear the IRA?"

"Is my name Paddy or Seamus?"

"But when you saw it was the police why didn't you go back, if you've nothing to hide?"

"I'm not a pillock and I didn't like what you did to my front door."

Cross led Willcox on to his ownership of the garage. Willcox looked puzzled.

"I haven't been there in years."

"When was the last time?"

Willcox made a show of frowning and lit a cigarette.

"A year or more."

"What does the name Mary Ryan mean to you?"

"It's a common enough name."

He vaguely knew of the murder, he said, when Cross told him about it, but hadn't known the girl's name. As it dawned on him that Cross was trying to connect him with Mary Ryan's murder, he stayed unconcerned and denied any knowledge of it. But he did have trouble remembering where he had been around the time of her death.

"Not at the garage, that's for sure," he said with a laugh. He scratched his head and smoked his cigarette and looked at Cross with profound indifference. Cross caught his gaze and held it. He tried to picture him pouring a kettle of boiling water on his wife. Anyone capable of that would be capable of pretty much anything.

Cross was the first to look away. He was uneasy. Part of him understood only too well Willcox's violence. It was probably only a combination of upbringing and cowardice that prevented him from taking his fists to those weaker than himself.

How tempted he was sometimes to thump the more miserable specimens dragged in for interrogation.

Cross tried to organize his thoughts. He pushed cautiously back into the past, to establish how well Willcox had known the men convicted of the Shankill killings. Willcox took on an air of superiority, as though to say Cross couldn't touch him.

"If you're trying to fit me into the killing of this Taig bitch you're barking up the wrong tree. I've remembered, I was at me mam's all week."

At the mention of his mother, Cross realized that Willcox idolized her, like so many of his kind.

"Daytime too?"

"Too right. She was ill."

The octogenarian Mrs. Willcox duly confirmed that her dutiful son had indeed been with her during the entire week of Mary Ryan's murder and left the house only long enough to go to the shops to fetch her food and medicine.

Cross remembered that the woman's memory was faulty and pressed her on the dates of her son's stay.

"I remember it quite well, thank you, because it was the week of my birthday, and Johnny was here for that."

"Shit," said Cross, after hanging up. "Shit, shit, shit!"

Willcox's mother had effectively blown his hopes. Even allowing Willcox a certain amount of clandestine leeway, there was no proof of his responsibility for Mary Ryan's death beyond the circumstantial connection to his old garage.

Cross fumed as he watched Willcox stroll out of the cell unconcerned.

"Abyssinia, I don't think," said Willcox with a big smirk to Cross, who was then forced to crawl to Nesbitt.

"And what does that do to your theory?" asked Nesbitt nastily.

Cross had no answer.

THE NEXT day he came downstairs and found Deidre in the hall with a letter in her hand.

"What's this?" she asked tersely, holding out a pink envelope addressed to him. It was scented, the writing feminine. Deidre had opened it and he felt a stab of guilt, thinking it was from Miranda Ramsay.

"I don't know," he said.

He looked again at the envelope and saw this time that the writing was uneducated. Embarrassment gave way to anger that Deidre had opened his mail.

"What business is it of yours, anyway?"

He stared at Deidre. She seemed brittle and defensive.

"The children need their breakfast," she said, handing him the contents of the envelope and turning away.

Cross looked at the folded piece of pink paper. He opened it and his hand trembled as he read:

They know not, neither will they understand; they walk on in darkness: all the foundations of the earth are out of course.

It was written in the same hand as the envelope. He checked the post mark. It had been posted the previous evening, after Willcox's release. Coincidence? Maybe he'd made his girlfriend write it.

He was still brooding on the matter several hours later in his office and staring at the note when he realized whose writing it reminded him of. He picked up the phone to Westerby.

She came back several hours later with the copy of Mary Ryan's Catherine Cookson novel. Mary had written her name on the fly leaf. That's what Cross had remembered.

"Would you say her writing matches the letter?" asked Cross.

Westerby agreed that they looked similar.

Which meant that Mary's killer had forced her at some point before she died to write the letter. Which meant that the killer knew Cross would be the investigating officer *before* the murder. And, most unsettling, knew where he lived.

Thirty-seven

BETWEEN themselves they had started calling him the Psalm Killer. It was Westerby's name, first used in Cross's office while discussing the advertisement sent to him and the ones that had appeared so far in the newspaper. The latest one puzzled them. There was still no sign of it in the paper.

"Why the Psalms, do you think?"

"Because he's the Psalm Killer," Westerby had said in a voice that didn't sound like her. She looked nonplussed and added, "I don't know why I said that."

She was puzzled that this latest quotation had been sent to Cross first. She checked herself, reluctant to go on.

"What?" asked Cross.

She appeared annoyingly reticent, and eventually said, "It's just a wild guess, sir. It's not fair to say."

"Oh, for God's sake, come on."

"It occurred to me that he might not need to send them to the paper anymore. This latest is his way of saying he knows where you live."

"I know, but where does that get us?"

Whichever way they looked at the problem it was like beating their heads against a brick wall. Westerby had been tense and fractious from the start of the meeting and Cross felt he'd caught her mood.

"I'd say it's his idea of a sick joke. He's saying he knows you now. He's also saying he knows more than you."

"And what do I know?" he snapped.

Westerby rode out his angry silence, studying her papers.

"I'm sorry," he finally said. "Go on."

"Until now," she said coolly, "the advertisements have appeared seven days before the body, with the exception of Niall Warren. The pattern holds for the deaths of Arnold and Wheen."

She passed over copies of the advertisements relating to them. For Wheen it was the one she had found earlier: *For dogs have compassed me; the assembly of the wicked have inclosed me: they pierced my hands and my feet.*

"It's from Psalm 22. The other one is Psalm 69," said Westerby.

Arnold's read: *Let not the waterflood overflow me, neither let the deep swallow me up, and let not the pit shut her mouth upon me.*

The Wheen killing was straightforward enough. The man appeared to have been abducted by one of his fares, shot and his body left in the boot of his car. The Arnold murder was harder to unravel because of the silence surrounding the case. Cross had tried Blair, who said he'd ask around as a favour—in return for what? Cross wondered—and came back with the fact that Arnold had been off duty at the time of his death and not on any undercover assignment.

"What's your angle on this?" Blair had asked, on the phone.

"His death might connect to another case."

"Well, good luck," Blair announced breezily. "The army are as paranoid as hell about this one."

Cross asked what Special Branch's involvement was.

"Nothing, really," said Blair disingenuously. "We were just asked to cast an eye over it. Few irregularities. I can tell you his death was personal not business."

AFTER getting the necessary clearance, Cross had driven out to Arnold's barracks to interview his commanding officer, Colonel Greenfield, who blandly confirmed that Arnold had been off duty at the time of his death and not undertaking military work.

On the parade ground outside the colonel's window Cross could see a squad being drilled by an NCO with a theatrical roar. Greenfield by contrast spoke so softly that he had to strain to hear. Compared to the sharply creased and starched soldier who had authorized his entry, Greenfield looked casual, even scruffy in his khaki jumper. A scrap of dried tissue was stuck to his jaw where he'd cut himself shaving.

"Sarn't Arnold was a first-rate soldier, inspector," said Colonel Greenfield. "First rate and a man of great bravery. I can't see how the sarn't's death could connect with anything you're investigating."

"Nevertheless, perhaps you could tell me the facts."

"Frankly, inspector, they are a mystery to us. The sergeant was off duty when he was set upon."

"And off limits."

Greenfield shrugged. "Like I say, a mystery."

Cross inspected the regimental lists behind the colonel's head, a careful roll of honour for fallen heroes to which Sergeant Arnold would no doubt be added, killed on active service. Arnold was one of the regiment's star soldiers, Greenfield told Cross, and, with a look of warning, added that he was keen to preserve that reputation, for its own sake and for that of his mother and father.

THE TRUTH of the matter was somewhat less glorious, as Cross found out that afternoon from Ricks' autopsy.

"For a start," said Ricks, "Sergeant Arnold was stocious when he died, having drunk something in excess of ten pints."

Ricks made it clear that he did not care for Sergeant Arnold. It was one of his quirks that he had likes and dislikes among the dead he cut up. Reminded of past cases, he would say, "I remember him. Rather disagreeable, I thought," or, "She was nice."

Over the usual ritual of fussily served tea in china cups, Ricks explained that Arnold had been beaten and kicked around the head. His spleen was ruptured, several ribs cracked, the left collarbone smashed. One tooth had been dislodged (and swallowed).

"The skull was a tracery of multiple fractures and death was caused by one or several blows to the head by an assailant or assailants unknown, as you people say. Have another bikky."

Ricks was in an unusually flippant mood and quite unconcerned speaking about a Special Branch case to Cross after making it clear that he didn't care for the officer he was dealing with. Cross wondered if it was Blair and glanced again at Ricks' report. At least it cleared up why Special Branch had been involved and why Sergeant Arnold's commanding officer was so keen on discretion.

"That sort of dilation you'd expect from regular anal intercourse over a period of years," said Ricks. "So yon Tommy was as queer as a coot. Of course, it's still illegal in the forces. Hence your chums in SB, I suppose. There's a lot of squaddies shitting themselves, no doubt."

WESTERBY was always aware of having too little time to follow up matters properly. Most of her work for Cross was being done out of hours at home. She went to bed dog tired and woke up feeling the same. She found herself thinking up ways of not seeing Martin. Her period was late too.

Cross, looking for an excuse not to go home, phoned Niall Warren's colleague, Ronnie Stevens. The Warren case had been nagging away in the back of his mind. He was aware of neglecting Miranda Ramsay's doubts about his death.

Stevens was evasive on the phone but finally relented and agreed to meet in a bar close to his newspaper. He was already waiting when Cross arrived, sitting alone—in forlorn contrast to the earlier sociable picture he had painted of himself—and several drinks to the good.

Cross was shocked at how rough Stevens looked. The smug, purposeful air was gone, replaced by a puffy face and blood-shot eyes. He sat down and decided to skip the pleasantries.

"Did you know that someone killed Niall Warren?"

Stevens' eyes flickered suspiciously around the room. He shook his head as he dragged on his cigarette. Cross thought he seemed scared.

"Because of the story he was working on," Cross added.

Stevens shrugged sceptically, his poise recovered.

"Who told you this?"

"When did you last see Warren?"

"A couple of weeks before he died."

"At the office?"

"No, at his flat, as a matter of fact. He asked me to go round."

"Why?"

"I never found out. He was pissed as a fart when I got there and so out of it that I left."

"Was he scared?"

"He was dead drunk." Stevens giggled and held up his glass. "And now he's a dead drunk, end of story."

"What was he afraid of?"

Stevens emptied his glass, looked at it ruefully and an-nounced that he needed another. Cross leaned forward, taking hold of his wrist, and told him to answer the question. Stevens' gaze swam. He was drunker than Cross had thought.

"Niall was scared because he had scared himself. It was a way of getting attention."

"How had he scared himself?"

"When you can't find out the truth it's very easy to start imagining it," Stevens mumbled.

Cross let go of his wrist and told him to get his drink. He appeared more collected when he returned.

"Off the record, inspector?"

Cross shrugged and agreed.

"What do you remember about Kincora?"

Just what he'd read, Cross said. Boys were abused by the staff and the staff had paramilitary connections and that had given rise to gossip about boys being provided for a vice ring that involved loyalist politicians.

Stevens looked bored, like he'd heard it before and started waving his hand like a conductor, in time to what Cross was saying. Cross waited for him to stop.

"Yeah, I know, not funny," said Stevens. "Except sometimes you have to know when to laugh and walk away. I told Niall, forget it, but he wouldn't listen."

"Warren said his phone was tapped and his flat had been searched."

Stevens gave a harsh bark of laughter.

"Inspector, we've all had that. It comes with the job."

"What did he tell you about Kincora? Specifically."

Stevens sighed. "That people had been killed because of it. He named John McKeague. McKeague knew where a lot of skeletons were buried and was about to blow the whistle. He was also a puppet of the Brits."

"How would the security forces react to Warren trying to get to the bottom of such a story?"

"Simply deny it. That's what they're best at. They wouldn't have to go as far as killing him. All it needed was a word in the right ear and the story would have been buried and Niall given the push."

"When was McKeague killed?"

"January 1982. Shot in his shop. What amazes me about these guys is how they make out they're such big potatoes and it turns out they run some fucking electrical store in the Shankill Road."

Cross asked if Stevens had any idea what angle Warren had been pursuing. Stevens lazily flicked ash at the ashtray and missed.

"McKeague was a fucking fanatic and a queer to boot. If he was such an embarrassment that the security forces wanted to shut him up they might have subcontracted the job to the UVF. That's your conspiracy, if you're looking for one. Anyway, it's all hogwash. Knocking off a washed-up drunk like Niall wasn't going to be on anyone's list of things to do, whatever Niall thought."

"How can you be so sure?"

"Inspector, the security forces daren't fart at the moment for fear of getting into trouble, what with your British copper's inquiry. Surveillance ops are almost at a standstill and the message we're getting is that your lot and everyone else are sitting on their fannies. Now, if you don't mind, I have a date."

Stevens stood unsteadily, said goodbye and wandered off to the toilets. Cross decided the man was scared, for all his bluff.

He stayed for a second beer and was debating whether to have another when Westerby walked in. He had left a message without knowing quite why, saying where he was.

"It's turned up, sir!" she said.

"What?"

"The advertisement."

The advertisement had arrived at the newspaper in the afternoon post. Westerby had been monitoring forthcoming classifieds as they arrived at the paper. The message was identical to the letter sent to Cross.

"When's it due?" asked Cross.

Westerby pointed to the box where the date of publication was written in. Cross counted off the days on his fingers. Westerby looked tensely expectant and Cross found himself vaguely irritated. He would far rather be sitting drinking his beer in peace, feeling the evening slide away. He reluctantly pushed his glass aside.

He offered Westerby a lift home. It was a pleasant evening. The sky was a perfect blue and as there was at least another hour of daylight he asked if it was all right just to drive around a bit and headed out towards Carrickfergus, along the coast road, the light-flecked sea to their right.

"Are you sure?" he asked slowly. "About the next one being fourteen."

Westerby was silent. She eventually nodded. They drove in silence. The atmosphere in the car had turned strange because of something unspoken between them. He decided the drive was a mistake and turned back.

Westerby looked out of her window, shading her eyes so that he could not read her expression. Cross was still shocked by his initial indifference to her news and how he'd wanted her to leave him alone, except that was not quite true. What he'd really wanted was to enjoy a drink with her without having to talk about work.

He found her idea of the killer moving on to teenagers hard to accept, which was probably why they ended up quarrelling over the date of the next murder. The advertisement was due on the fourteenth, which meant that the body ought to be found a week later.

"It's too soon," said Westerby. "All the others have been in the last week of the month or on the first day of the new month. The twenty-first is wrong, I'm sure of it."

"What should it be?"

"The twenty-eighth."

"Then why isn't the ad being placed later?"

"I don't know," she said defensively.

"And I'm sure I don't," he added caustically.

They drove in angry silence until Cross said, "Until now the advertisements have appeared a week before the murder. There's no point in trying to double-guess him."

"No, sir."

"And anyway, if we're so fucking clever, why was Mary Ryan dumped on a Monday not the Friday?"

Westerby seemed to shrink in her seat. Cross hadn't meant to sound so nasty.

"It was a bank holiday," she eventually said.

"What's that got to do with it?"

"That weekend was a holiday weekend." She sounded fed up and sarcastic. "Maybe something prevented him from dumping the body on the Friday. Maybe his fucking mother came to stay, I don't know. Maybe he had to wait until the Monday. As it was a holiday he probably hadn't been working that day."

Cross wanted to apologize, but pressed on.

"So the body should have appeared on, what, the twenty-fourth?"

"Yes," she agreed warily.

"Which is not in the last week of the month."

"If you say so, sir."

He said sorry eventually and she accepted his apology with better grace than it had been given.

"It's either the twenty-first or the twenty-eighth. We are at least agreed on that?" he said, sounding better tempered, he hoped.

Westerby nodded.

"In that case we put out a full alert for both days."

He pulled up outside her house and left the motor idling.

"We've ten days. We know the age. We know the surname probably begins with an E, or maybe an N. And we know the date."

"One way or the other," Westerby said drily.

"Phone all the schools with Catholic pupils in the greater Belfast area and check those with the relevant names and ages. At least that way we'll have an idea of how many we're talking about."

ON THE strength of this latest discovery Cross got his meeting with Nesbitt. Nesbitt always responded well to a deadline.

"How many days to catch this bugger?"

"Eight, sir."

It had taken two days of bureaucratic nonsense to sort out an initial audience with Nesbitt, who had been away at another of his country house hotel conferences, and a further twenty-four hours to organize a larger meeting involving other departments.

Cross recognized a couple of the faces among the dozen or so in the room. Cummings, for a start, and a Special Branch officer. There was a plainclothes Brit who was introduced as Peter Moffat. Fat faced, thirtyish and very public school, thought Cross, as he watched him standing at the trolley pouring himself a coffee from a silver thermos jug. He helped himself to a biscuit, a shortbread sandwich with a diamond of jam.

Nesbitt summarized the situation briskly, taking a no-nonsense approach that brooked no argument.

"DI Cross thinks we've got a killer who advertises his murders in the papers and the next killing is due in a week."

Cross was surprised at Nesbitt's succinct grasp of his material, in contrast to his own weeks of agonizing. The DCI's brusque appraisal made it sound like he had worked the whole thing out for himself in five minutes. At one point Cross was aware of Cummings regarding him sardonically. He ignored him and turned his attention to Moffat as Nesbitt continued with the panache of a TV presenter reading an autocue. Moffat's eyes were a guileless brown, his expression impenetrable. By calling in Moffat Nesbitt was probably covering himself, Cross decided. Moffat was there in an advisory capacity, though no one was saying what he was advising on or who he represented.

When Nesbitt was finished, Moffat cleared his throat and asked why it had taken so many deaths before anyone had connected them.

Nesbitt coughed loudly, blew his nose, then inspected the contents of his handkerchief.

"There was nothing obvious to connect the deaths. None of them was the same type of murder and two took place outside the divisional area," he said, looking at Cross for confirmation.

Cross nodded, uncomfortably aware of Moffat's scrutiny.

"It didn't occur to you that recurring newspaper advertisements might mean recurring murders?"

"It wasn't that straightforward," said Cross. "There was no reason to think that the initial murder connected with any of the others."

Moffat looked unimpressed. From what he went on to say, it emerged that his speciality was Protestant paramilitary gangs. He probably ran most of them, Cross thought.

"It's possible you're dealing with a loyalist terrorist," Moffat told the meeting, with enough hesitation to make plain his reservations.

Cross asked Moffat who he thought might be behind the killings.

"Let's wait and see what happens next Friday," replied Moffat archly.

"DI Cross," said Nesbitt. "What *is* going to happen next Friday?"

Cross explained that there were nearly a hundred possible targets in the area of greater Belfast.

"Short of putting the city under curfew, it's going to be impossible to keep an eye on them all, but we're going to try. We'll step up patrols in the districts where the killer has struck before."

During his summary, Cross caught Moffat saying something out of the side of his mouth to Cummings, who smiled in agreement. He was sure they were laughing at him.

After the conference broke up, Nesbitt asked Cross to stay behind.

"Moffat thinks your theory is a load of balls, so you'd better be right about this or I'll hang you out to dry. Moffat may be a Brit but he knows Belfast like the back of his hand and he says it doesn't work the way you say."

"Before, I would have agreed. I'm only going on what we've found."

"That WPC of yours, by the way, what's her name?"

Cross felt a twinge of panic at the turn in the conversation.

"Westerby."

"There's nothing going on between the two of you?"

"Between us?"

Seeing Cross's astonishment, Nesbitt relented.

"All right, all right, but I needn't remind you of the consequences."

Cross felt anger well up inside him. He asked who had made the allegation.

"Let's just say that it has come to my attention and it's my duty to remind you of the official line on the three Ds."

The three Ds were drink, dames and debt, all of them rife in the force. Punishment, when applied, could be severe: immediate transfer, a heavy fine, a return to uniform and even dismissal.

Cross felt caught out. He had deliberately guarded from himself any feelings he had towards Westerby. What was not obvious to him was apparently clear to someone else.

"Everything all right at home?" asked Nesbitt.

"Yes, sir. Fine, thank you, sir."

"Good. Keep it that way. At the rate we're going we'll soon have to open a fucking marriage counselling service."

Cross left the room wondering if he was still under investigation.

THE INSECURITY he felt at work followed him home. He got the nagging feeling his house was being watched. He dismissed the thought, putting it down to nerves and lack of sleep. His insomnia was the reason agreed to with Deidre for his move into the spare room. There, instead of being unable to fall asleep as before, he slept for a couple of hours before waking sharply and lying there anxiously until morning.

Exhaustion frayed his nerves and on successive days he found himself lifting his hand to Matthew, then to Deidre. He had resisted slapping the boy but when Deidre kicked him in exasperation during a squabble over the washing-up he had lashed out. In the astonished silence that followed they stared dully at each other until she had made a dignified exit. Cross squirmed with shame and thought of Willcox.

Deidre never referred to the slapping, which had left him with the feeling that his life was increasingly blemished. Even his children started to avoid him.

The room he now slept in so badly was at the side of the house and overlooked fields that were hidden downstairs by the garden fence. The view from upstairs showed how exposed the flank of the house was.

Cross stood for a long time in the uncurtained window, putting off the moment of going to bed, staring out, seeing nothing beyond his reflection but black, wondering if anyone was watching. Playing softly on the radio was an old song whose silly words stuck in his mind: *I wonder wonder wonder who who who wrote the book of love?*

He imagined the memory of that particular moment returning with his death. Cross emptied his glass and told himself to pull himself together. He tried not to notice that he'd drunk the best part of a bottle of Scotch.

THE WATCHER was curious about the sad-looking man keeping his vigil in the lit-up window. He wanted to know how much he knew, how far he had got. He wondered about this policeman, so slight and uncertain, hovering in his night-time window.

He had first seen him when they had come to reclaim the body of Mary Ryan, watching from a derelict house, with night glasses, making careful note of the man who appeared to be in charge, and the registration of his car. It was part of the control, knowing them and watching.

He had followed the Volvo afterwards to a smart new estate in the south of the city. Later, he was able to pinpoint the exact house. There were fields beyond the estate and a playground nearby, and a wind-break of fir trees that screened him from view. The policeman's wife was beautiful. None of them looked happy.

Later that night he pasted together another message, which he put to one side, ready to send: *Deliver my darling from the power of the dog.*

Secrecy, then revelation. Establish the pattern, then reveal it, to show up the stupidity for what it was. If a couple of hundred terrorists could tie up thousands in a grinding war of attrition, why shouldn't one man take it upon himself to reveal the absurdity of it all?

He opened the dossier on the table in front of him. It listed her address and school, the names of her parents and their professions. A nice middle-class girl, he could tell from the photograph. The line of the song came back to him: *Heard the little girl dropped something on her way back home from school.*

He imagined the policeman in his window, trying to picture him. Had he even begun to guess that things had to get a lot worse before they got better?

He returned to the dossier. On Tuesdays and Fridays she went to a youth club, leaving the house and returning three hours later. She lived in a nice quiet part of the city. *Way up on, way up on, way up on, way up on, way up on the avenue of trees.*

So lonely baby.

"THOSE fellows you've got following me, tell them to get off my back."

Cross had not expected to hear from Stevens again. Stevens said he was calling from a phone box, his voice slurred.

"Who?"

"It only happened since talking to you," Stevens said accusingly.

"Why would I have you followed?"

"I haven't talked to anyone else. Unsolicited mail in the post, is that your idea of a joke?"

"What mail?" asked Cross, puzzled.

"Brochures, inspector. One from a clinic that specializes in rebuilding faces, with a letter thanking me for my interest and asking me to make an appointment. Another from a firm making wheelchairs, and a third from an artificial limb company. Some of your people have a funny sense of humour."

"I don't understand," said Cross.

"Because I've got his fucking story, why else?"

"Warren's story?"

"Too right."

"Why didn't you say?"

"Because it's too hot and anyway why trust a peeler?"

Trust, thought Cross grimly. That's what Vinnie had wanted.

"This is between us. I give my word I'm not having you followed."

"Bollocks and shite to your trust."

"Meet me later. We have to talk." Cross was in danger of gabbling. "I'll be in the Horseshoe Bar in the Europa from seven. I'll be alone and I'll wait until nine."

There was a long silence. Cross hung on, waiting.

"There are enough hot cocks to give Paisley a heart attack," Stevens finally mumbled.

"What?"

"Mucky pix. Boys. Young boys, very young boys, some with men. Men in masks looking like a fucking bunch of Lone Rangers at a nudist convention. And I always thought Niall was a crap journalist!"

CROSS was at the Europa early. An hour later there was still no sign of Stevens. He used a telephone in the lobby to call the newspaper. Stevens wasn't there and the bad-tempered sounding woman at the other end said no one could remember when they had last seen him.

Cross waited another hour in the bar, drinking enough to feel maudlin about Miranda Ramsay. He was about to leave when two whisky-sodden foreign correspondents engaged him in barely coherent conversation.

Gavin had silver hair, a leathery face that was gradually collapsing under the assault of alcohol, and he wore a grubby sky-blue safari jacket that labelled him as exotic, while Bas, sporting the remains of a black eye, was a keen young prop forward, fond of a maul.

They asked Cross if he was taking part in the ugly night competition and expressed astonishment that he didn't know what they were talking about. This, they explained, involved a prize for picking up the least attractive woman in the bar, who had to be paraded at the next morning's breakfast as proof.

"You should've seen Bas's last week. *Quelle vache*."

"At least she had a cunt, which was more than yours did."

Bas's roar of laughter boomed round the bar and Gavin shook his head in disbelief at the memory.

"Couldn't bloody find it. Down on my hands and knees for a bit of a sniff and I couldn't bloody find it!"

Cross joined in their laughter, ashamed of himself, and drank away his awkwardness until all trace of Miranda Ramsay was gone.

They ended up in either Gavin or Bas's room, drinking someone else's duty-free Scotch. As the night fell in on itself, Cross tried to hang on to Gavin's urgent listings of the world's danger spots and the corresponding quality of the whores, which he pronounced who-urs.

Cross shut one eye to bring the room into focus, just in time to catch Gavin slump sideways. Bas carried on with the story without missing a beat. Who the others in the room were Cross had no idea.

He awoke to find himself sprawled on the bed, blinded by daylight. The room stank of Scotch and stale smoke. Gavin was snoring gently, still in the chair where he had passed out in mid-sentence. Cross left without waking him, pausing only to rinse out his mouth and take a squeeze of toothpaste which he worked round his gums with a finger.

His head throbbed and his stomach threatened to bring up something, though what he didn't know as he hadn't eaten. Unable to face the hotel breakfast, he had made do with too much coffee, charged to Gavin's room. It added a purposeless buzz to his morning. He was in his office before eight, which was remarkable, given the state of his hangover. All he wanted was to spend the day in bed.

He phoned McIlvenna. McIlvenna was the first policeman he had met in Belfast thirteen years earlier. They were still technically friends, though it was a year since they had seen each other. Deidre wouldn't have him in the house after he had passed out in the toilet. Thinking of his own hangover Cross decided he was in no position to criticize.

They wasted a couple of minutes on pleasantries and McIlvenna said he now had a second home on the Antrim coast which he hoped Cross would soon visit. A sign of the times: policemen with second homes.

When they got down to business and Cross described the photographs Stevens had told him about, and their possible provenance, McIlvenna was sceptical.

"How good's your source?"

"Good, I'd say," Cross said with more conviction than he felt.

"Is he offering any proof of a Kincora link?"

"Yes, but until I've seen the photos on the table—"

"You've not seen them?"

"No. That's why I'm checking. I thought you'd maybe heard of them."

Cross cursed Stevens for his hangover. He could hear McIlvenna slurping a cup of something.

"I've heard the stories, but I'll bet you anything the pictures are fakes. Someone's pulling a fast one on your man, or he's pulling a fast one on you. I'd say they're from the mainland— they're easy enough to come by—unless you can specifically identify those involved."

Cross wished he'd waited until he had something more concrete.

"Is there anyone who knows about this sort of stuff?"

"I'd know, I'd say," said McIlvenna tightly, sounding miffed.

Cross sighed and looked at his watch. He doubted if Stevens would be in the office yet. He hung on, hoping for some scrap from McIlvenna.

"Do you know a councillor called Eddoes?" McIlvenna supplied.

The name was vaguely familiar.

"A right little moral watchdog, always on about sex magazines in newsagents, and so on. He was giving me an earful the other day about the morale of respectable Protestant communities being undermined by Catholic pornography. Which is news to me. And drugs, he said."

"Drugs. The Provos are scared stiff of drugs."

"Sanctimonious fuckers, aren't they?" McIlvenna laughed. "Be careful with Eddoes, by the way. He's not as lily-white as he makes out. Once they've gone respectable, they come up with any excuse to get on their high horse."

EDDOES ran a dry-cleaning business in East Belfast and Cross found him in an office over the shop. McIlvenna had said that he had worked at Harland and Wolff shipyards until injury had forced him to take early retirement. Cross couldn't remember when he'd seen such a big man. Eddoes reminded him of a side of beef and looked uncomfortable in a suit. When he stood up he wasn't as tall as Cross was expecting, but the impression of bigness remained.

"I won't waste your time, inspector," said Eddoes, apparently unaware that it was Cross interviewing him. "The facts of the matter are simple enough. In spite of the miseries that afflict us, we're a blessedly clean city in some respects."

Cross nodded. As a result of the political anomaly Belfast was a curious case of arrested development.

"Until now!" said Eddoes, thumping his desk for emphasis and startling Cross.

"Pornography?" prompted Cross.

"And worse. Drugs."

"What kind of drugs?"

"The worst kind. Oh, if you're asking me to produce some dead lad with a needle in his arm, I can't. Yet. But it'll come, mark my words. The Taigs are moving in. Drugs and pornography, and not just any pornography—I'm talking about boys, some not much more than wee children."

Cross pointed out that republican terrorists had always been against drugs and pornography.

"They *say* they have nothing to do with drugs. What they say and what they do are two different things. A man of your position knows that. They *say* Sinn Fein has no connection with the Provisional IRA. They *say*."

Cross let Eddoes ramble on. The man was a soap box orator, too fond of his own voice and probably crazy.

"They're taking the war to the middle-classes!" Eddoes bellowed. "And unless something is done there'll be drugs handed out in the playgrounds!"

He would not reveal his source, which left Cross thinking that he was probably dealing with another case of Chinese whispers.

Before leaving he used Eddoes' phone to try to track down Stevens. Stevens had not been at the paper when he had tried earlier, nor at home. Whoever he spoke to this time said Stevens was out on a story and no one was sure when he would be back.

Cross became increasingly irritable as the day wore on. His hangover refused to budge. He realized he had forgotten to ask Eddoes if he had known Warren.

THE SIGHT of Moffat hanging round the coffee machine did nothing for his mood. They nodded at each other and stood in uncomfortable silence while Cross made a show of being fascinated by the machine's liquid spurt into a plastic cup.

Moffat was wearing a velvet burgundy waistcoat and a bold check tweed jacket that made him look like he was dressed for a stay in the country, which, thought Cross, was probably how he regarded his Belfast assignment. Friday planes were always full of Brits going back for the weekend. He wondered how often Moffat went home.

Cross could think of nothing to say. It was ridiculous, he thought. They were supposed to be working as a team.

He thought it was probably his antipathy to Moffat that made him decide to go out on a limb and talk to McMahon. He left a message at the hospital. To judge by the speed with which it was returned, McMahon was indeed spending most of his time there.

They met in the canteen after evening visiting hours. McMahon looked ill, paler than before, with dark circles under his eyes. His minder, a different one, sat behind the canteen door as usual.

Cross gave McMahon a rudimentary version of what he knew about the next killing. When he mentioned the likely day and the age of the victim McMahon asked how he could be so specific.

"I'm not in a position to say."

McMahon nodded and thought for a moment.

"Is this anything to do with those two women that were killed?"

"I'm way off the record even telling you this much."

He passed over a list of children of the right age so that the Provisionals policing their various areas could at least give the relevant parents some warning. With luck a lot of irate teenagers would be kept in that evening.

McMahon studied the list and put it away, thanking Cross.

"I presume we've never had this conversation. Now what is it that you want?"

Cross was reminded of McMahon's ability to wrong-foot him and smiled.

"I need to know who killed John McKeague."

McMahon spread his hands, as if to say who mightn't have killed him.

"We all remember McKeague. His gangs evicted hundreds

of Catholics from their homes in the 1969 riots. Of all the Prots he was the likeliest for a public lynching."

"Was he an asset of the Brits?"

"Name me a Prod that isn't," McMahon said sourly. "In answer to your question, it was the INLA."

"But they didn't identify themselves in the usual way when they reported the killing."

"I dare say, but it was the INLA. I know of the men who shot him."

So much for a conspiracy between the UVF and the security forces, thought Cross. Without that, there was a big hole in what Stevens had surmised was Warren's argument.

"What about Heatherington?"

"Why are you so interested in Heatherington?"

"I don't understand the reason behind the Heatherington operation."

McMahon stared at his tea.

"Why?" asked Cross, with a feeling that for the first time in ages he was reaching towards some kind of truth. "Why go to all that length of putting an agent on the inside just for the sake of mischief?"

"It depends on your definition of mischief. There are those who say, and I would be one, that the Heatherington operation did more harm to the Provisional IRA than any other single event of that time."

Cross frowned, sure that McMahon was exaggerating. "But you knew pretty much straight away it was a hoax."

"You have to ask yourself, what in the end did the Heatherington operation achieve? What was its goal?"

"Panic, destabilization."

"And the result—"

Cross shrugged. He didn't know. McMahon continued slowly, like he was spelling out a lesson to a backward child.

"At the end of that year there was the usual Christmas truce, which at the beginning of 1975 was extended into February and from there on indefinitely. It held until the following year."

This was the truce Molly Connors had talked about, though she had discussed it in terms of its incidental results: the Provisionals had ganged up with the emerging INLA to settle old scores with the Officials. Cross still wasn't sure of McMahon's point and said he couldn't see what the truce had to do with Heatherington.

"When Heatherington turned up in the Crumlin Road gaol, the Provisional leadership had no interest in negotiating, not that the Brits were by any means agreed between themselves on the question of negotiation. But some did want it and were putting out feelers. We weren't interested at the time. Categorically."

"But you were after the Heatherington operation?"

"There are many who say that that time was the Provisionals' darkest hour. It led to four years of feuds and sectarianism."

"All because of Heatherington?"

"The Heatherington operation discredited a hard-line leadership. The men that took over were older, with less of a stomach for the long struggle. They were prepared to deal."

"Who were they dealing with?"

"The politicians, ostensibly, but we all know they're not the real men. Part of the problem with the Brits is that they are divided among themselves. We think of them as being united, but most of the time the left hand's feuding with the right."

Cross wondered if McMahon was telling the truth or offering a subtle lesson in propaganda.

"One lot wants unconditional surrender," McMahon continued, "while another group, much smaller, seeks a negotiated settlement."

"Who?"

"MI6, I'd say."

"And MI5?"

"They want to grind us to bonemeal."

Cross was starting to see how seriously Warren might have got himself out of his depth. He thought of something else that had been troubling him.

"Do you remember Gregory Brown?"

McMahon cocked his head. "Heatherington named him as part of the gang that killed Tommy Herron."

"A gang run by the British?"

"Yes."

"Brown's name was passed on by you to the loyalists."

McMahon shrugged, neither confirming nor denying it.

"So Brown's name was used to help establish Heatherington's credentials."

McMahon nodded.

"But," Cross continued, "why jeopardize another agent?"

McMahon shrugged again and stood up. "That's easy," he said. "Either Brown had become expendable or he was deliberately sacrificed for the sake of Heatherington's cover."

"Tell me," said Cross. "Were you part of Heatherington's debriefing team?"

McMahon looked around, pretending he hadn't heard. When he returned his attention to Cross he tapped his lapel with the rolled-up newspaper he was carrying.

"There is, of course, another explanation about your Mr. Brown." McMahon looked mischievous.

"What?" asked Cross.

"His name might have been planted deliberately." He milked the pause, making the most of Cross's curiosity. "To discredit someone else's operation."

Thirty-eight

Belfast, April 1975

"HERE you are working for me and still shooting Taigs," Breen said to Candlestick with a laugh and continued laughing all the way to Belfast.

Breen was using him as an assassin in a sectarian war. Candlestick knew that now and confronted him during one of their drives to the city. Breen just laughed, as usual, and blamed the ceasefire. With the Provisionals' Christmas ceasefire extended there was no one left to fight, except each other.

"It's a fuckin' mess out there," said Breen. "You don't know how well off you are."

It was true, his own position could not have been more straightforward. He lived in something resembling harmonious isolation with Becky. She continued to work in the library and he on the next-door farm. He'd bought an unreliable rusted old Datsun which he sometimes drove up to Belfast where he spoke to his intelligence handler, Danny. It had been several months before he had been confident enough to contact him. He suspected that local telephone boxes were monitored by various parties in the area where he lived.

From Danny he learned that Breen was deeply involved in the foundation of a new terrorist group whose existence was still secret. It was, as far as anyone could tell, the military arm of the Irish Republican Socialist Party, a breakaway from the Officials. The split had quickly turned acrimonious. By his own reckoning Candlestick was responsible for eight retaliatory killings, not including Bunty.

Candlestick looked out of the car window. He liked these drives. Breen always kept the car well heated. Not that he minded the coldness of the farm, though once in a while it was a relief to escape its damp.

"You've an away match today," said Breen.

"A Proddy?"

"Not just a Proddy, a peeler Proddy."

He had not shot a policeman yet. It was to be a doorstep job, his first since the young Catholic barman he had killed for Tommy Herron.

"The great thing about a doorstep killing," said Breen, "is that it violates the sanctuary of a man's home."

He was full of the fact that Protestants went in for them much more than Catholics.

"At the start of the Troubles the Orangies used to stiff whoever came to answer the door. Your Provie preferred to shoot a fellow getting in and out of his car, or just bomb the fuck out of him and have done with it, but then you have to watch and see if he drives the kids to school. The problem with a doorstep job is that if your man doesn't come to the door then you're having to go in after him and that involves his family, which is no good. Are you superstitious?"

Lots of gunmen were about entering the house. They saw it as bad luck.

"No," said Candlestick.

"Good, because if you can get away with it and stiff the copper in his home, that's really the ticket. It demoralizes all the other peelers each time they put their feet up, thinking that if the doorbell rings it's going to be a bullet with their name on. Me, I think they're stupid to even think of answering the door."

They drove to a safe house where Candlestick was given a change of clothing—a denim jacket, jeans and Doc Marten boots.

"They always wear them Beatle boots," said Breen, looking at Candlestick with approval. The jacket was covered with Rangers football badges, another detail that announced what he was. "You look a right little Prod."

He was shown a photograph of a man in uniform. Candlestick thought he looked a bit clumsy, or maybe it was the crooked way the picture had been taken.

THE CONSTABLE'S home was on a neat estate of houses with green roofs and tidy front lawns running down to the road. It was a place of such little activity that any passing car was an event. His driver, an agitated youth, was convinced that everyone was staring at them.

"We're dead obvious. They'll see us a mile off."

It was strange, thought Candlestick, this belief that Catholics and Protestants looked different. He remembered it from his loyalist days, the business of smelling a Taig, of just being able to tell. It was all rubbish. Several of the Shankill victims who had been snatched off the streets turned out to have been Prods.

The driver was reluctant to park and wanted to circle the block while Candlestick did the job. Candlestick made him stop right outside the house, and stuck the gun in his ribs to see him sweat.

"And lead us not into temptation," he said, taking the keys.

Candlestick rang the bell. He could have been the milkman, he thought, for all the nerves he felt these days. Pulse and breathing normal.

The man who answered was in shirtsleeves and Candlestick did not recognize him at first out of uniform. He was carrying a newspaper, his thumb stuck in the middle to mark his place, and showed no surprise at the stranger on his doorstep. In the kitchen at the end of the hall his wife and noisy kiddies sat at the table. The smell of fried tea hung in the air and the television was on.

"Lights out, mister," said Candlestick.

He swung up his arm. Two shots to the body and the coup to

the head straight after he was down. The doormat next to the fallen body had written on it: NOT YOU AGAIN. Now that was funny, he thought.

No one did it better. It was over so fast that the wife and children hardly had time to scream. That night he would have scrupulous sex with Becky. She would approach him cautiously and he would treat her gently. Their sex, like their relationship, was modest, like he was protecting her from the thoughts that lay at the back of his mind, thoughts of Maggie and how it had been after shooting Tommy Herron, and how he missed the vibrant chaos of the long nights of the summer of 1972.

Thirty-nine

STEVENS phoned, sounding edgy, to apologize for missing their Europa appointment.

"We can meet later tonight?" he asked.

"Not if you're wasting my time," Cross answered tetchily.

"I'm not. I'm bringing Niall's stuff."

There were traffic delays because of roadblocks. Sirens wailed in the distance and, closer to, Cross could hear burglar alarms ringing shrilly. He hoped Stevens was held up too.

He arrived ten minutes late. Stevens wasn't there so he waited in the car. It was parked facing the deserted wasteland where Mary Ryan had been found. It was an odd choice of rendezvous, he thought.

Poor Mary Ryan. There were no neat conclusions, he decided, unlike in the detective stories of his boyhood with their mended destinies. Reality was different, a loose amalgamation of dangling relationships, unspoken conversations, injustices, omissions, a gradual falling away of interest. Even his outrage at Mary Ryan's death was ebbing.

Half an hour went by and still Stevens had not come.

Cross wanted a cigarette but not in the car so he strolled to where Mary had been found, to pay his respects. If life were fair, he thought, this would be where he found the clue that would lead to her killer.

It was a starless night, cold and dry. He scuffed the earth with the toe of his shoe and smoked. Unusually it had not rained in a week. A car passed slowly in the background. He resolved to sort things out with Deidre, to cut away everything that had become atrophied. It was a time for resolutions. Giving up smoking would be a start. He threw his cigarette away unfinished.

He didn't remember locking the car and took it as a sign of his increasing forgetfulness. As he reached for his keys some peripheral movement alerted him. Then his head exploded and he thought he'd been shot. A second burning pain dug deep into his back. As he fell he took with him a brief glimpse of ski masks. Two, he thought, but the blood in his eyes made it hard to tell. He tried to say something and a boot smashed into his face, then into his throat.

THE NEXT morning, the Friday when the killer was due to strike, Westerby reported to the special operations room that had been set aside for the day. Extra phone lines had been installed and there were maps on trestle tables, with little wooden bricks that Moffat could move around to show where patrols and roadblocks were set up. Moffat looked pleased at having so many troops at his disposal. By the time Westerby's shift started the operation had already been in progress since the previous midnight. The windowless room smelt of smoke and male sweat. She watched Moffat and Cummings in whispered conference, along with an army colonel acting as military co-ordinator, and was wondering why Cross was late when Nesbitt arrived and said he had an announcement.

He described the attack on Cross as an act of unparalleled brutality. Cross had been found just before midnight, he said, and his condition was critical though stable. Westerby was aware of one or two people looking at her. She thought she might faint. Even Nesbitt appeared shocked by the severity of the beating.

Soon afterwards she was relegated to the main office with a couple of dozy reservists while everyone else was absorbed by

Moffat's operation. Her demotion to message-taker felt like punishment. She was dazed and did not know how she would get through the day.

At the end of her shift, aching with anxiety and boredom, she was about to leave when Hargreaves told her that she was needed in the operations room. Her first task was to organize tea and coffee for everyone. Moffat had his jacket off and had loosened his tie. The atmosphere was both stale and tense. There had been no murder and the feeling now was that there wasn't going to be. Events had reached that stage where everyone was subconsciously wishing for one, just to break the monotony.

When she served Moffat his coffee, he glanced at her and spoke out of the side of his mouth. "Of course, you realize that if nothing happens there's no way of proving this isn't all a wild goose chase."

"DI Cross always said that it could be either this Friday or next."

Moffat snorted. "Or the one after that or the one after."

He closed down the operation at quarter past midnight and thanked everyone for a successful day.

"Come with me," he said to Westerby.

He took her to an office next door. A desk was covered with copies of the classified pages, ringed in red ink.

"There never was going to be a murder," he said.

"If you say so, sir." She was too tired for Moffat's games.

"Look at the fucking papers. They're full of religious advertisements, three or four every day, sometimes as many as six. Of course there's going to be one on the Friday before the murder or the day before or the day after or even on the fucking day itself."

"Are any of the others from the Psalms, sir?"

"Are all yours from the Psalms? Well, are they?"

"That's not—"

"Well?" Moffat was shouting now, red in the face. "How many are from the Psalms?"

"Five, sir."

"And how many aren't?"

Moffat looked hopped-up on something, a combination of caffeine, nicotine and Benzedrine, probably, and would vent his frustration on her regardless.

"One, sir."

"Which one?"

"The first."

"The first! And what kind of theory do you call that?"

He turned away in disgust before she could answer and picked up a fistful of papers and waved them at her.

"Psalms are two a penny. Go back to last year and you find the fucking Psalms cropping up at least three or four times a month. Are you trying to tell me *they're* related to the killings?" Moffat banged his fist on the table.

"But these are all false addresses!"

Westerby was shouting too. Moffat stepped forward until his face was inches from hers. She could see his carotid artery pulsing with anger.

"And what do you make of that? That they're the work of the same person?"

"Of course, sir."

"And how many people has this person killed?" Moffat asked facetiously in a sing-song voice.

"Six," said Westerby in a whisper, knowing what was coming.

"You have nothing to connect Breen's death to any of the others except a hotchpotch of initials and a coincidence of age. Breen's is the only body where any advertisement was found. Am I right?"

"Yes, sir."

"Now I'm asking again, how many people has this person killed?"

"Five, sir." She was getting muddled herself now. "Six."

"ONE! ONE! ONE! How many?"

"One, sir."

"Who?"

"Breen, sir."

There was no point in arguing. Without Cross she had no protection. She felt her eyes pricking with tears. She hoped Moffat did not notice. His triumph would be complete.

"That's better. Now get out and stop wasting my time. Give my condolences to DI Cross when you next see him."

Moffat enjoyed humiliating her, she realized. It was like a rape. She could imagine him using the memory to give himself a hard-on. Maybe he even had one already, she thought, as she turned on her heel and walked out.

Forty

BREEN sent him to England in 1977 and again the following year. He wandered in and out of the House of Commons dressed as a telephone engineer, his English accent taking him into places where an Irishman would be challenged, even by security guards as lazy as these. The cordon around the House was tight enough, but once inside he was astonished by the laxity.

His evenings were spent in meetings in a room above a shop in Museum Street with an Irishman and a horsy-looking Scot with tombstone teeth. He wondered who the Scot worked for. No names were mentioned. Conversations remained entirely to order. Nothing was discussed beyond the job in hand.

Close-range shooting was dismissed because of the uncertainty of escape. Sniping with a telescopic sight was given serious consideration, though, for propaganda purposes, a big bang was thought best of all.

Candlestick looked out of the window as the Scot droned on in a flat, technical voice. Across the road was the British Museum. He could not remember when life had last seemed ordinary and without edge. Perhaps the edge had always been there. Since the beginning. Since lying awake in the dark for as long as he could remember.

The Scot pointed out that whatever kind of bomb was used, it had to allow the bombers time to escape. The usual pre-timed device was no good, as the target's movements were not predictable enough to guarantee that he would be in his car at the time of explosion. The Scot recommended a mercury-tilt switch. It was small and portable, and had the advantage of self-detonation. The explosion was triggered by the car's movement.

Candlestick reported back to Breen, then went back to working on the farm. Neither Becky nor the farmer who employed him ever asked where he had been. His absence was taken for granted. He passed on the information about his London trip to Danny and heard no more.

TWO YEARS later, at the end of March 1979, he read in the newspapers how Airey Neave had been blown up in his own car as he was driving out of the House of Commons. Neave, who was close to the new Conservative prime minister, was about to become secretary of state for Northern Ireland, a post he had actively sought, unlike all but one of his predecessors. Neave had wanted tougher anti-terrorist measures and a war with the IRA. That was what Candlestick gathered from reading between the lines of the British press, which made much of Neave's heroic war record.

The Provisionals were first off the mark to claim the killing, followed by the INLA. Breen told Candlestick that whoever had phoned Ulster Television to put in a bid for the INLA had been told to fuck off. Tears of mirth ran down Breen's cheeks.

Still laughing, he added, "I hope that fucker Neave died screaming for his mother."

But shortly after the assassination Breen's euphoria gave way to edginess. He became more like Tommy Herron in his indiscretion and paranoia, leaving Candlestick with the feeling that life was starting to repeat itself.

THE NEXT run up to Belfast did not end in a shooting as Candlestick expected but inside the maze of the Divis Flats, a crumbling labyrinth of public housing in the middle of the Falls. They'd parked on the outskirts of the city and taken a taxi.

"Just keep your eyes open and your mouth shut," said Breen. They were walking down an endless darkened corridor, one of several they'd taken. "I tell you, this lot make the plot in *Julius Caesar* look like a kiddies' playground."

There were half a dozen waiting in a stripped-out flat, all men, much younger than Breen, and cocky.

"Who's he?"

The one asking was a pale man with a Zapata moustache.

"Never mind him," said Breen. "He's mine."

The meeting was a fractious affair dominated by squabbles

and suspicion. Lack of funds seemed to be a constant worry and Breen came in for criticism.

"You're a rich man, Franny, that's what I'm told." It was Zapata again. He did most of the talking while the others sat in sullen silence, smoking. "Maybe you should put your money where your mouth is."

Breen tried to keep the meeting light. It was clear that he was the only one with any proper sense of organization.

"Steeney's out soon, then we'll see some action," said Zapata, needling Breen.

"You think you're fucking cowboys in some Wild West shoot-up."

"Come on, pops, away to your deckchair."

Breen gave Zapata a look of malevolence which Candlestick caught.

Nothing else was discussed beyond fantasies of lucrative bank robberies, which they all joined in.

AT THE next meeting there was something to talk about. It was hastily convened because one of the organization's leaders had been gunned down by two men wearing military-style uniform. The man's widow, who had been wounded, was accusing the SAS of carrying out the killing. She'd heard one of the assassins call out in an English accent.

The dead man was unusual in that his background was Protestant, his father an army major and a friend of Paisley.

"The odd thing about Ronnie," Breen told Candlestick, "is that some of these wee Proddies are more enamoured of the cause than the staunchest republican. They think it's dead romantic."

It didn't make Ronnie's life any easier, he added, because the Officials had tried to kill him at least three times, and he was on the loyalist death list as a traitor.

Candlestick studied Breen during the meeting after Ronnie's death, shaping the despondency of the rest and whipping up their desire for revenge against the security forces. The man was extraordinary. He gave nothing away. No one would have suspected for a moment that he had been instrumental in the assassination.

Candlestick had no idea who it was he'd shot until he read about it in the papers and realized it was one of the leaders of the organization he did most of his work for. Breen had merely passed him on to another man, leaving him with the impression that it was for a freelance contract.

There were four of them on the operation: himself, the planner, a second gun and a driver. The planner had drawings of the house and details of its inhabitants. There were two adults and three children and on the night in question a guest was due to stay, also to be shot. Only the driver knew the address. The planner told them that as long as they kept strictly to their schedule there would be no trouble with army or police patrols. This information told Candlestick that their target was almost certainly a republican of some prominence if the job was being carried out with the tacit approval of the security forces.

A single blow from a sledgehammer had taken care of the front door, and from there it was straight up the stairs. They knew which room to go to, but when they got there the occupants were already trying to jam the door. Candlestick got his arm through the crack and started firing until the door gave. A woman lay back injured on the bed, her nightdress stained with blood. The man was naked and crouched ready to ward off any attack. His adrenalin was up and the first three or four shots seemed to make no difference. Then with his next shot Candlestick saw the hole appear in the man's forehead and the eyes go. He left the other gunman to finish him off while he went after the guest, who was cowering in the youngest child's bedroom. The man waved in the direction of a screaming infant, as though the presence of the child was enough to prevent any further violence. Candlestick shot him anyway and walked out of the room and downstairs, calling after the other man as he left.

At the bottom of the stairs he looked round just as the wife ran out of the bedroom and threw herself on the back of his colleague. Candlestick had only her arm and shoulder to hit. It was a risky shot but he fired twice and saw her fall back.

"Jesus fuck, you were taking a risk shooting like that. You could've hit me," said the other man, hurrying downstairs.

"I couldn't care if I did," said Candlestick, laughing as he stood aside to let him pass.

Within minutes they were whooping it up on the Monagh bypass, swigging from a bottle of brandy thoughtfully provided by the driver.

"I couldn't half do with a shag," said the other gunman.

"You should've done his missus while you had the chance," replied the driver.

Candlestick stared out of the window and did not join in the laughter.

When they parted the other gunman shook him by the hand, winked and said, "Nice one," which made Candlestick wish he had been less careful with his aim.

Several days later, after the meeting, he asked Breen, "What was that all about, shooting Major Bunting's son?"

"Cleaning out the stables," said Breen tersely. "Strictly between you and me."

Forty-one

THE FOLLOWING Friday—the twenty-eighth—Cross was still in hospital and not allowed visitors until the next day. In spite of there having been no murder on the twenty-first, Moffat had refused to repeat the previous Friday's operation. Westerby felt crushed.

On the Saturday she bought flowers from a stall outside the hospital. She had spent the morning trying not to think about whether there had been another killing. Martin had come round and she'd sent him away, pleading exhaustion. He'd hovered, looking concerned and put out, and afterwards she felt bad.

She found Cross up in one of the private rooms on the same floor as Maureen McMahon. In spite of steeling herself, she was shocked. The bruising to his head was bad enough to make her draw breath. One eye was black and still swollen. Even more distressing was his air of shrunken defeat. He looked like a man who'd had the spirit beaten out of him. He gestured feebly to show where he had been kicked in the throat.

They made sick-room small talk: thank you for the flowers;

it's good of you to come; are you all right?; yes, I'm being watched.

"What did you say?"

"I said I'm being watched."

"What, here?"

"No, before."

"Did you see anyone?"

Cross shook his head gingerly, rolling it from side to side across the pillow. "Just a feeling."

"Was it the same people who, you know—" She could not bring herself to say attacked him.

Cross shut his eyes and was still rolling his head. When he stopped he appeared to be asleep. Hospitals, thought Westerby, how she hated them.

IT WAS the siren that made her think of it, the urgent hee-haw making its way down the Donegall Road. She dismissed the thought, walked on, then turned and went back. The two big hospitals alternated casualty days, she knew that. She checked with the main desk that it had been their turn the Friday before.

An hour passed before the casualty sister could give her any time. She had the hurried, distracted air of someone who deals with too many crises. She nodded curtly at Westerby's request and said she would see what she could do. For the forty-five minutes it took her to return, Westerby sat with the casualty out-patients: two beaten women, a crying child with a broken arm, greasy, long distance drunks nursing bad cuts and a raving man with a messianic beard.

The sister returned with a list, scrappily written in various hands. Westerby's shoulders slumped as she read down it. Then, at the bottom of the page, she saw something that made her heart leap.

"Is there anyone who can tell me how old this one was?" she asked the sister.

The sister said she hadn't been on duty at the time, but would try to find the records, if Westerby didn't mind a further delay.

The answer was worth waiting for.

She was torn between sharing the news and being patient, out of consideration for Cross's weakened state. Several times she took the lift up to his floor, each time losing her nerve, before excitement got the better of her. There *had been* a fatality, so fuck Moffat.

Hit and run. No witness. Aged fourteen. Catherine Edge.

She hadn't died straight away. She'd hung on until the Sunday. Therefore she wouldn't have come to Moffat's attention. Perhaps because it was too normal anyway—everyone had been expecting something with guns or knives, dramatic enough to flatter the importance of the operation. Perhaps without all the hoo-ha on the streets he would have killed her differently. Instead he'd just run her over and nobody had noticed. Clever. That meant, Westerby realized as she hurried down the corridor towards Cross's room, the pattern was more important than the method.

She knocked and apologized, at first thinking she'd got the wrong room. The woman sitting by the bed stared at her. Westerby took in the fine red hair and green eyes. His wife, she supposed, and so good looking too (herself no rival). She mumbled an excuse and closed the door before Cross could see her.

She walked down the corridor, trembling. From the flustered state of her, anyone would have thought that she had just caught them in the middle of having sex.

WESTERBY saw her again in the canteen from her position at a table behind the swing doors, out of sight of anyone coming in. Her first thought was to sneak out unspotted. Instead she watched her standing in the queue, an effortless cut above everyone else. Curiosity got the better of her and after the wife had bought her tea, Westerby went over and introduced herself.

"I'm sorry," she said, "I didn't mean to barge in upstairs."

She wondered why she was apologizing. Deidre blinked a couple of times, signalling distracted recognition.

"Are you a doctor?" she asked.

"I work for your husband."

"Oh," said Deidre. "He's asleep now, poor man."

Westerby asked if there was anything she could do. Deidre sounded surprised and grateful. Nobody else from the police had bothered to ask. There had only been the one call from them, breaking the news.

Westerby realized what an isolated figure Cross was in the force. She wondered if it had always been like that.

"I suppose it's my fault for being so stuck up with them."
Deidre laughed, desperately trying to sound cheerful.

They were still standing awkwardly in the middle of the canteen. Westerby pointed to her table by the door and as she followed her she could not help cast an envious eye over her expensive clothes. The jersey was cashmere.

"Does anyone know why it happened?" Deidre asked as they sat down.

Westerby shook her head.

"Do you think I was right not to let the children see him yet?"

Westerby was surprised. Deidre didn't look the sort to seek approval.

They made small talk about the long hours involved in police work and the strain on the family, and Westerby realized how little Cross discussed work at home. This strict division between the job and the rest she'd noticed with herself too.

If Westerby were honest, she had initiated the meeting only out of nosiness and that had backfired. Deidre's thoroughbred beauty was a reprimand to her curiosity.

Deidre asked if she was married. Westerby shook her head. She didn't want to admit to being engaged.

"We weren't very happy," announced Deidre unprompted. "In fact, we were so fucking miserable I've been seeing someone else."

Westerby registered the astonishment that she felt was required of her, but deep down she was not surprised by this abrupt revelation. Perhaps she had sensed it all along. Something about Cross hinted at a shadow over his life. She wondered at Deidre's use of the past tense, like the man was dead.

"Did he know?"

Deidre did not answer and instead dabbed her eyes with a fresh handkerchief. Westerby couldn't remember when she'd last carried a proper one. Usually she had to make do with a tissue, and often a used one at that.

"Part of him wanted something like this to happen," Deidre said with sudden fierceness.

"That's not true!" Westerby was startled by the strength of her reaction. "He's not one of the ones who go looking for trouble. God knows, there are enough of those. What happened can happen to any of us. It's the risk we take."

Forty-two

WESTERBY sat on her information about Catherine Edge because she did not trust Moffat. The feeling in the barracks, implied rather than stated, was that she had screwed up and it was her fault for having made out she was so smart. She was now paying the price by being ostracized.

During Cross's slow recovery most of the force's energies were taken up with preparations for the Orange Parades. It would be the annual marching season soon when Belfast resounded to the blood-rousing beat of the Lambeg drum. The bonfires and the drinking, the pipes and drums and baton-twirling, and the litter: Westerby remembered it all as faintly tawdry from her own childhood. The Lambegs had been pounded so hard that the noise made her feel sick and she had been anxious in crowds ever since.

She visited Cross once with Hargreaves, who sat awkwardly with hands on knees.

"Done yourself well with the room, sir."

"It's the influence of my father-in-law. He used to be a surgeon here. How's the boat going?"

Hargreaves looked pleased to be asked and they spent the rest of the visit talking about that. Westerby was glad of not having to make the effort to talk. She looked at Cross. He was improved but still deathly tired.

THE NEXT time she went alone. She'd thought better of telling him about Catherine Edge. She also desperately wanted to confide her own fears about where the murders were going, but Cross was clearly in no state to cope with her anxieties. He even seemed profoundly uninterested in the identity of the men who'd put him in hospital. When Hargreaves had tried to talk about it, Cross had shrugged indifferently and said he hadn't seen anything. Wait till he recovers, Westerby told herself.

She was surprised to find Cross up and dressed.

"Are you better, sir?" she found herself asking inanely.

"They let me down to the canteen, which is enough to stop anyone getting better."

She laughed politely. At least he looked in reasonable spirits.

"Were the police still downstairs when you arrived? Great drama."

"No. What happened?"

"There was a big theft of drugs from the dispensary." He looked distracted.

"Are you all right, sir?"

"Oh yes, fine. Can you check for me if anyone knows who did it." He seemed to lose his thread. "Moffat came to see me the other day. Yesterday, I think."

"Moffat!"

"Oh, all very polite. He can be quite pleasant when he wants, but he was here to gloat. He told me there wasn't another murder on that Friday."

"But there was!"

Cross looked at her uncertainly. "What?"

Westerby told him what she had discovered.

"Did you tell Moffat?"

"No, sir. Moffat tore me off such a strip the last time. He's convinced the killings are unrelated, so I thought I'd wait and tell you when you were better."

Cross thought for a long time.

"All right, let's play it Moffat's way. Forget about the killings being linked."

Westerby was disappointed by Cross's capitulation. Then she saw him smile.

"We carry on looking for Breen's killer," he said. "We can do that. And when we have Breen's killer we have the Psalm Killer."

Westerby grinned back at him.

"When do they let you out?"

"God knows," said Cross.

* * *

WESTERBY was alone in the main office apart from some reservists who had been drafted in. Everyone else was taken up with the Orange Parades.

Telephones rang endlessly and the only way they could answer half of them was by ignoring the rest. She snatched up the receiver and was about to hang up, thinking no one was there, when she heard a clearing of the throat at the other end.

"This is Seamus McGinley calling from Galway."

Westerby tried to place the name.

"I'm in Galway," he repeated. "And it's about Mary Elam that I'm calling."

She remembered now: Mary's last boyfriend, the one who had gone off and never sent for her.

He was in a call box, he said, and wanted her to call back, which she did. Then he said he would only talk to a senior officer. She told him that none was available.

"I'm working on Mary's case," she said. "You can talk to me now or I can get another officer to call you back later."

"I don't want anyone calling at home."

McGinley sounded difficult.

"Is there something you want to say about Mary?"

"Do you have any news of the man that killed Mary?" he eventually said.

She replied that they were no closer to finding him, but she very much wanted to hear what he had to say. She hoped she sounded sincere.

McGinley started to speak then stuttered to a halt. He was clearly unused to the telephone and probably feeling doubly awkward because he'd rather be talking to a man. Westerby decided that any attempt to break down his hesitancy would sound like cajoling so she counted a silent thirty, praying he wouldn't hang up.

"Well, it's like it's to do with Mary, I think, but I can't be sure," he finally managed. "You see, I left because I was told to."

"Told to?" queried Westerby, fearing she had a nutter on her hands.

McGinley went on slowly. "This man told me to clear out. A Brit."

"A Brit?"

"That's what I just said." McGinley sounded defensive.

"What did he look like?" she prompted.

"He had film star hair, and blue eyes, not tall."

They embarked on a fruitless game of name the film star: fair, acted in Westerns. Robert Redford was the only one she could think of, but it wasn't him.

"Was he thin? Or fat?"

"Thin, I'd say, definitely thin."

McGinley was hopeless on description, so Westerby, rather than lose him, changed tack.

"Tell me what happened when you met this man."

McGinley laboriously explained how he had been approached and told that he was on a loyalist death list. He still sounded bewildered by the incident.

"I'm just a carpenter."

She wondered why he had waited so long to make this call.

"Has anything happened to make you telephone now?"

"I'm not with you."

"Have you seen this man again?"

There was a silence at the other end. Whether it was suspicion or stupidity that prompted it she couldn't tell.

"The man who told you this, did he tell you to go away?"

"He did, so he did. He even came to the house. And now I can't get it out of my head he had something to do with Mary's death."

"This is important. We need to meet so you can tell me what this man looked like. Your description is the only one we have."

She listened to the dead line and cursed loudly and fluently enough for a couple of reservists to look up.

McGINLEY, it turned out, was no longer in Galway as he'd said. His employer, whom Westerby had spoken to when initially clearing him of Mary Elam's murder, thought he'd moved down to Cork.

Westerby traced the woman McGinley had set up house with in Galway and gathered from her that he was up to his usual tricks. He had moved on, promising to send for her and the children. She had no number for McGinley. He was, he said, in difficult lodgings and always called her. She added that the idea of Seamus McGinley in difficult anything was a joke.

The woman thought that he had gone south. That's what

he'd told her. But the number he'd given Westerby to call her back on turned out to be in Leitrim, up near the border.

She wondered why McGinley had bothered to call. A delayed guilty conscience, perhaps, over Mary Elam. Making some gesture in her direction might have been a way of distracting himself from the unpleasant business of dumping her successor.

She didn't think they'd be hearing from McGinley again. He probably believed that he had discharged his responsibility with that phone call. But Westerby was curious enough about McGinley's motive to call Mary's sister Josephine, who told her that McGinley's leaving had coincided with the holiday season. He'd left more or less a year ago to the day.

CROSS came out of hospital, collected by Deidre and the children, who were sweet and considerate, fussing over him. Deidre made a special effort and Cross wondered if the dramatic intervention of the beating had made her see sense and re-evaluate things. She invited him back into their bed, saying that it was silly to continue sleeping apart.

Most of the time he wasn't sure what he felt. The pills he was taking meant that the days drifted by emptily. Whatever he took at night punched him out until he emerged groggily and the day pills kicked in for the cycle to begin again. He decided to stop taking them.

He was supposed to rest but found himself drifting back to work. The bruising was still there and Cross countered it with a pair of dark glasses that probably resulted in him being stared at all the more.

Deidre, laughing for the first time in weeks, said, "Darling, you look like a drummer in a third-rate jazz band."

"A third-rate drummer or a third-rate jazz band?"

She kissed him and added, "I could quite go for you, but at least let me buy you a decent pair of glasses."

Was this the start of the thaw? Cross wondered.

In bed they stroked each other but nothing happened. Cross didn't know if that was all she wanted. His own body failed to respond and both of them feigned tiredness.

"When you're better," said Deidre, still considerate.

Forty-three

"I'M NOT the man's nanny," said McCausland. "I don't know what Stevens and Warren were up to. Stevens told me nothing."

Cross asked where Stevens was now.

"He's in the Republic."

They were sitting in McCausland's office. The bright weather outside seemed quite unconnected with the sunless cool of the room. Cross watched the crowds in their summer clothes drifting below. The shops were full. Belfast centre was starting to look almost normal. He remembered McIlvenna in vice once saying that shopping was the one thing that would unite Northern Ireland. "We're great shoppers," he'd said.

"I need to speak to Stevens," Cross said.

McCausland appeared not to be listening. He seemed more interested in opening his mail.

"You can't," he eventually said. "Unless he phones us. He's on leave."

Stevens had left ten days earlier, while Cross was in hospital. He wondered if it was Stevens who had found him on the wasteland. Whoever had called the police had left no name.

According to personnel—whom Cross rang on McCausland's phone just to irritate the man—Stevens wasn't due back until the following Monday and had only given twenty-four hours' notice before leaving. McCausland said he didn't think this unusual. Stevens had probably hit a quiet patch.

Cross snorted. Quiet patch! The annual holiday season was traditionally one of the most volatile times of the year. It was when the Protestants celebrated the anniversary of their ascendancy over Roman Catholicism.

Cross was about to get up and leave but was suddenly so

tired that he didn't have the energy. He sat watching McCausland ignoring him, sifting through the waiting pile of letters. McCausland looked up, surprised that Cross was still there.

"I was sorry to hear about the attack on you, inspector. Have they got the fellows that did it?"

His question was clearly a dismissal. Cross struggled up and left without bothering to answer.

The identity of his attackers vexed him. Someone didn't want him digging too deep into Warren's story and raking up the past. He thought the loyalists were probably behind it. It had also occurred to him that Stevens had been bought off and had set him up. Also, they knew where he lived.

After coming out of hospital he had taken the precaution of removing his father-in-law's service revolver from the trunk where it had been kept since he'd been given the thing. Cross's own gun had vanished with his attackers. It was part of standard issue to detectives working in Northern Ireland and he dreaded the endless paperwork that would face him back at work to account for its disappearance. Until that was done he would not be issued with another. He had not realized until then how much he had taken the weapon for granted even though he was lazy about carrying it with him much of the time.

The old revolver was heavy and cumbersome and until then he'd had no use for it and had only taken it on Gub O'Neill's insistence that he have it in the house for Deidre's sake. Deidre had been taught to fire the thing—potting at old cans as a teenager—and, although she disapproved of guns, part of her accepted it comfortably as a family heirloom. Cross wondered if his father-in-law had a licence for it. Probably not; he was remarkably casual about such things.

"You never know who might come to the door while you're out," he'd said. "And you should have something extra to protect the family, just in case."

Cross was about to take the lift when he heard his name called. It was McCausland again, suddenly keen.

"Inspector, what do you make of this?"

He showed Cross a letter. It was properly typed on notepaper and addressed to the news editor.

"Dear sir," he read. "Why has no one connected up the recent spate of killings in this city? Roman Catholics are being systimatically murdered. The two Marys for a start. Seven times Seven and a Plague on your House. Yours faithfully (not loyally), A Friend."

Cross read the letter twice, noting the typing slip, his scalp pricking when he came to the numerical references: seven again.

"You must get a lot of this stuff," said Cross.

"Yes, but they're usually written in maniac's ink. You can spot the nutters a mile off."

"Is this the first one like this you've had?"

McCausland said it was.

Cross took the letter, copied it and passed on the original to Moffat with some glee, as it was the first support he'd found for the theory of linked killings.

Moffat read the letter coolly, giving nothing away.

"Mmm, interesting," he said. "Maybe I owe you an apology. I'll deal with this straight away." He looked up and gave a watery smile. His concessions were even harder to take than his usual objections, Cross decided. The thought of proving Moffat wrong was one thing that was helping him mend.

CROSS wondered if Blair was being asked to act as a messenger. The call came several hours after Cross had passed on the McCausland letter. Blair was affable, ostensibly inquiring after Cross's health.

"Good to have you back, skip."

The call resulted in a drink that evening, suggested by Blair. Cross had forgotten about drink. He'd not had one since being in hospital and his last cigarette had been the one he'd smoked at the scene of Mary Ryan's murder. Cured of the weed: that was something. He did not miss it.

He sipped soda water while Blair sank a couple of pints. In among the chat, Blair delivered what Cross presumed was Moffat's message. It was not a time to go rocking the boat. In spite of his earlier resolve, Cross wondered if he shouldn't heed the warning. Blair was probably right. He would gain nothing from sticking his neck out.

Cross drained his glass. He wanted to go but Blair hadn't finished. Blair would presumably report to Moffat that he was a lame duck. So much for his resolution of revenge.

"By the way, I'd advise against spending too much time with McMahon," Blair said.

"He was a useful contact," replied Cross with more assurance than he felt.

Blair downed the last of his drink and said, "The man's a viper."

Cross wondered how Blair knew about him and McMahon. Sometimes he had the impression that they all knew.

TALK of the devil. McMahon called just after Cross had got to his office the following morning. There was no introduction, just his soft voice saying, "Do you know who this is?"

"Yes," said Cross.

"Then can you tell me who, in so many words?"

"You're the man with the bonny daughter."

McMahon said he wanted to meet. After Blair's warning, Cross was reluctant.

"Why can't we talk now?"

"I don't like to talk on the phone."

Of course not. Stupid. Cross remembered his medical check that afternoon and told McMahon he could be in the hospital canteen afterwards. Then, thinking of the prying eyes that might be there, he said he would meet him in Maureen's room instead.

"I heard you were up there yourself recently," said McMahon. Again Cross was left with the feeling that everybody knew.

THE DOCTOR who did his check-up told him to take a holiday. "The head mends slower than the body."

"When did you last take one?" asked Cross.

"Years ago, so I know what I'm talking about."

She was still young, perhaps not even thirty. In spite of her competent and reassuring air, Cross could see the fatigue eating at her. Another one locked in Belfast's vice.

McMahon was waiting, sitting as Cross first remembered him, staring intently at his daughter. There were fresh flowers in a vase and sunlight slanted into the room. McMahon was a pocket of agitation in the stillness. There had been no sign of his bodyguard, though his chair was outside.

McMahon surprised Cross by standing and shaking his hand.

"Clean bill of health?"

"I was told to take a holiday."

"That's something we could all do with. I used to go to

Belleek myself when I was a boy. Are you one for mucking about on boats?"

"I was warned about talking to you," said Cross.

McMahon's expression darkened. "Well, tell whoever gave you the warning that I have a warning for him. Feelings are running high in the nationalist community. Word's going round that several of the recent killings we've discussed are the work of loyalists. Innocent victims, we're talking about. And from what I hear, the constabulary is doing nothing, maybe even condoning them."

Cross wondered about the different degrees of innocence when applied to the word victim, and how they could be twisted to suit the speaker.

McMahon seemed to read Cross's thoughts.

"This war has its own rules. Quite often not very nice rules but rules nevertheless, not spelled out but clear enough."

He went on to say that the Provisional IRA was not prepared to tolerate a return to the random brutality of earlier years, with innocent Catholics being picked off by loyalist killers.

"Do you think it's that?" asked Cross.

"I think you yourself once voiced the same suspicion."

"What do you know of the theft from the dispensary downstairs?"

McMahon looked taken aback and said it was news to him. As Cross explained the extent of the theft—a whole van load of pure cocaine and heroin—McMahon shook his head in disbelief. He said he did not know who was responsible and was gravely concerned because if those drugs hit the streets there would be a war of quite a different kind.

"People shooting each other for profit." He noted Cross's scepticism. "You may despise us, inspector, but we've kept out the gangsters."

"I thought *you* were the gangsters." He couldn't resist the dig.

"The pushers and the pimps, I mean. The scum."

"Maybe you should look around, Mr. McMahon. The rules might be changing behind your back."

McMahon nodded curtly and said, "In the meantime, tell your people that unless some positive action is taken about these killings the Provisional IRA will step up its campaign against the RUC."

"End of message?"

"End of message."

Cross thought he should leave but sensed McMahon still had something to say.

"Can you imagine what it's like, your life on a switch?" McMahon eventually said. "Sometimes I think she'll only wake when this is all over and who can say how long that will be?"

There was nothing for Cross to say.

"You know, the doctor asked me the other day if I wanted her switched off. What do you say to that? Switch her off?"

"As long as there's hope," Cross said lamely.

"They say there isn't, but you hope against hope, at least you do in my business. Of course, the Roman Catholic Church forbids me to authorize it, and I suppose there's enough of the remains of her teaching in me to make me pause."

He leaned down and kissed his daughter on the forehead and walked out, followed by Cross. McMahon paused outside for a moment, frowning, then walked off towards the lift.

They travelled down together in silence. Cross caught some of McMahon's ill ease.

Again in the foyer McMahon seemed distracted. Cross was suddenly reluctant to be seen leaving the building with him and used the toilet as an excuse.

Standing at the urinal he realized what was worrying him. It was the bodyguard's empty chair upstairs—empty when he'd arrived, empty when they'd left. He was half way across the foyer when he heard the crackle of gunfire.

McMahon lay in a pool of blood in the car park. His assailants had fled. An attendant ran past shouting for a doctor. Cross knelt down. Sensing a shadow fall across him, McMahon opened his eyes.

"Cunt," he spat.

McMahon clearly thought he'd been set up.

"I didn't know, I swear."

"Cunt," he repeated and shut his eyes.

Cross could not tell if he was still alive by the time the paramedics arrived.

"Well, at least you don't have far to go," said one as they lifted McMahon on to the stretcher. "We'll have you fitted up in no time."

He watched McMahon being trundled off and wondered

about Blair's warning. Had Blair been behind the shooting, and used Cross? And what would have happened if he and McMahon had left the hospital together? Would anyone have cared if he'd been caught in the crossfire?

The car park asphalt was sticky with McMahon's blood.

AFTER the murder of McMahon, Cross was carpeted by Moffat, who asked what on earth he had been doing letting himself be seen in public with an IRA man.

Cross replied that he'd only bumped into him in the foyer and had asked out of politeness about his daughter.

Cross could not understand why Moffat was so irate. Moffat should have been beside himself at the death of a top IRA man.

The real source of Moffat's anger became clear when he produced a magazine and asked Cross if he knew it. Cross shook his head. At first glance it looked like the usual poorly produced radical journal that got peddled to an obscure but tenacious readership. It was called *The Limit*.

"Turn to the page marked with the paperclip," said Moffat brusquely.

Cross was not sure what he was supposed to be looking for.

"Well?" said Moffat.

"It's the same letter that was sent to McCausland."

He handed back the magazine to Moffat, who chucked it on the desk with an air of disdain.

"And how did this rag get hold of it, do you suppose?"

He couldn't see what Moffat was getting at.

"Oh, come on, man," Moffat snapped. "I wasn't born yesterday."

"You mean you think—"

"Precisely."

"—that I did it?"

Cross couldn't believe what he was hearing and asked why he should do anything like that.

"Obvious," said Moffat. "You resent my being brought in over your head. We disagree radically over a string of murders—"

"And you think I leaked the letter?"

"May have written it for all I know," said Moffat casually.

"Can I ask," Cross replied equally casually, "if you're taking the letter seriously?"

"I take everything seriously, but—"

He picked up the copy of *The Limit* and, holding it fastidiously between thumb and forefinger, dropped it in the bin.

"I think you'll find," he went on, dusting his hands, "that it's rather academic. We've arrested Willcox."

Cross opened his mouth. Nothing came out. He panicked like a dried actor.

Willcox's alibi, provided by his mother, was not as watertight as Cross had thought, Moffat said. He pointed to her history of mental illness.

"Basic homework, I'd have thought. To check that."

Cross remembered how, when they were first looking for Willcox, the mother had denied even having a son. But when he'd talked to her later she had sounded quite lucid. Still, Moffat was right.

The crux of the case against Willcox was that the weapon that had killed Mary Ryan had been found. In Willcox's lock-up.

Cross was stunned. They'd been over the place thoroughly and apart from blood traces had found nothing.

"What was the weapon?"

"A screwdriver sort of thing, with blood on it."

"And prints?"

"Doesn't matter. He's confessed anyway."

"What?"

"Confessed to the murder of Mary Ryan, and he'll cough up for Mary Elam too, we think."

All along Moffat had denied the possibility of linked murders and now he was saying they were on the point of charging Willcox with two of them.

CROSS only gradually saw the gaps in Moffat's story. What had led him back to the garage? It had already been gone over, so why was the weapon not found then? And without Willcox's prints there was still nothing to tie him specifically to Mary's death, so why confess?

He drove out to the Scientific Support Unit. He had been to the Unit before and knew that outside immediately sensitive areas the security was casual. Most of what was kept out there belonged to the dead and was of no use to anyone.

Cross showed his card at the main desk and they let him through the barrier without asking any questions. He walked down two flights. With his descent everything became tattier and scuffed.

The basement security man was not at his desk. Cross called out a couple of times and nobody replied. There were two of them, from what he remembered, fifty-year-old time-servers, officious and dead lazy.

Under the pretext of looking for them, Cross strolled through the double doors by the desk. There was still no one around. Down a short corridor and through another set of doors lay what he was looking for.

The victims' belongings, murder weapons and incidental scene-of-crime material was kept in this huge stack room of the dead in cardboard boxes on metal shelves. Some were no larger than shoe boxes. Others were as big as packing cases. Cross walked down the aisles until he found the Rs. There were several boxes marked Ryan M, and he checked through the dates until he had the right one.

The box was a standard commercial cardboard one with the vintner's name stamped on the outside. Inside were Mary's clothes, each item wrapped in its own plastic bag. There was her one shoe. The other had never been found. The weapon that had killed her wasn't there. Cross thought it was probably still at the scene-of-crime office. He hadn't really expected to find it there.

Ever since Moffat's description of the weapon, Cross had had an inkling of what was going on. It corresponded exactly to the bradawl Cross had found in Berrigan's workshop. But what Cross could not understand was why, if such a similar weapon was used on Breen, Moffat didn't connect Willcox to Breen's murder.

He panicked when he could not find Breen's box. It wasn't there. He decided Moffat must have it.

He felt foolish when he remembered that it would still be filed under Berrigan. But when it appeared not to be there either he started to panic again.

He found it eventually, out of order, on a top shelf.

The bradawl should still be there, he told himself. He had sent it over to the SSU himself. There was no reason why it should not be there.

It wasn't.

Cross was still staring at the contents of the box when he

heard a shout. It was one of the security men at the end of the aisle. Cross ignored him.

"This is off limits," the security man said, his body puffed up with indignation. "You don't just walk in here and help yourself."

Cross slowly closed Berrigan's box. The jobsworth was not one he recognized.

"Have you heard of D3T?" Cross asked.

"What's that got to do with anything?" the man said nastily, now standing at the foot of the ladder Cross was on.

"And nor should you have done. We're so secret no one has. We go where we like, and it has come to our attention that you are slack, inefficient, leave your desk unmanned and can't even file your boxes properly. What was this doing on the top shelf?" He thrust it at the man.

"I just wasted forty-five minutes because of you," he said and marched off. At the end of the corridor he turned and called back, "It's in my report."

McMAHON'S funeral took place at Milltown Cemetery, watched from a distance by a heavy police and military presence. Since the shooting the atmosphere in republican areas had been extremely tense, and coming during the marching season the whole city felt like it was on the brink. One spark was all it would take. The funeral had been organized with great haste to take place before the holiday weekend. The RUC had sent word to the Provisionals that holding it on the volatile weekend of the twelfth—the main date in the Protestant calendar—would be foolhardy and there could be no guarantee of security against loyalist marchers.

In spite of the short notice a crowd of several thousand mourners turned out to follow the cortège. McMahon was buried with full military honours. It was rumoured that Provisional leaders who had not shown their faces in years were among the crowd.

McMahon's killing had gone unclaimed. The loyalists said it wasn't them, perhaps because they realized that if they had, it would lead to reprisals that would far outweigh the publicity coup of claiming McMahon's death.

Forty-four

A JOKE was going round the barracks about how Willcox had denied killing Mary Ryan until her gouged-out eyes were presented to him on a plate after being found in his fridge. It had done nothing to improve Cross's mood.

Walking through the main office towards the end of the day he was aware of a pocket of hilarity. Several men grouped round a desk were laughing at one of them wearing joke-shop glasses with crazy eyes painted on ping pong balls that dangled on springs. The glasses disappeared when they saw Cross. There were a few suppressed sniggers.

"Sir," said one of the group, calling after him.

"What?"

"Sherlock Holmes wants you."

He turned and saw Westerby gesturing frantically at him. She was alone in the corner on the telephone. He went over, aware of the sullen silence his presence was imposing on the room. Westerby put her hand over the receiver and mouthed, "I think it's him."

Cross gently picked up the telephone on a nearby desk and dialled the switchboard and told them to tell the engineers to trace the call. Westerby was shaking her head, which he took to mean that she was not going to be able to keep him long enough.

"I can't tell you that," she was saying into the phone. "It's confidential."

She was being too negative, he thought. Westerby's face was screwed up with concentration.

"No, don't hang up," she blurted, taking a deep breath before going on. "Yes, someone is being questioned. I can't give you his name."

She listened intently for several moments, scribbling notes.

Cross, who was keeping an open line with the switchboard, quietly urged them to get on with tracing the call. He saw the others in the room watching, aware that something was going on. Suddenly Westerby deflated visibly and looked at her dead receiver.

"He's gone," she said dully.

"What did he say?"

"He told the switchboard he wanted to talk about the lock-up where Mary Ryan was killed. Then he asked me if we'd questioned anyone and what their name was. When I told him I couldn't say, he just laughed— Oh, yes, the first thing he'd said was there wouldn't be time to trace the call and he'd laughed at that too." She consulted her notes. "He said if it was Willcox we'd got the wrong man, then what he said next was: 'I wondered how stupid you were.' Just as he hung up he laughed a third time and said, 'Ask Willcox who killed Tommy Herron.' "

Tommy Herron again, thought Cross.

"What did he sound like?"

"Flat and very in control." She paused, considering, and suppressed a shudder. "I've never heard a voice that gave so little away."

"Do you think it was him?"

Westerby appeared reluctant to commit herself. She eventually said, "There's one thing. It's hard to be sure with him sounding so deadpan, but I'd say that he was a Brit."

"British!" That was the last thing Cross had been expecting.

NESBITT had agreed to see Cross only reluctantly. His secretary, an expert at blocking his door, had gone for the day, and it was clear that Nesbitt was not doing very much. He fiddled with his cuffs, glanced at the clock on the wall and reached into a desk drawer and produced a bottle of Scotch and a glass. As an afterthought he offered one to Cross. Cross shook his head.

"I can understand your beef," he said, after holding an appreciative mouthful of whisky. "Listen, Mr. Moffat is an expert in counter-terrorism. He was brought in over my head. Do you think I'm any happier than you with the idea of Brits coming in and running our show? We've got Willcox, be happy with that. Don't worry, your contribution will be recognized."

"I need permission to speak to Willcox, sir."

"What on earth for?"

Now for the difficult part, thought Cross, keeping Moffat out of it.

"We're still trying to find Francis Breen's killer."

"Yes," said Nesbitt cautiously, stretching the word. "I thought I told you to stop wasting your time there. What's he to do with Willcox?"

"Breen goes back to the beginning and he was cutting deals with the loyalists when Willcox was around. He might know if there was anyone particular that Breen dealt with."

Nesbitt rubbed his eyes with his thumb and forefinger.

"You'd better talk to Moffat."

"I can't find him, sir."

"Then it'll have to wait."

CROSS waited, but only until Nesbitt had gone for the day. He went down to the cells and told one of the constables to bring Willcox to an interview room once everyone was settled for the night. The less chance of being seen the better, he hoped. He was risking a reprimand but he could not think of any other way.

He went to the canteen to sit out the wait and was surprised to see Hargreaves there, reading a newspaper. His shift should have ended. Hargreaves said he'd had too many drinks in the bar and was trying to sober up by eating something.

"What do you think of Moffat?" Cross wondered why he was asking, though he suspected a glimmer of a plan was forming in his head.

Hargreaves belched, politely putting his hand over his mouth. "Well, who is he, for a start? Besides being a Brit."

Quite, thought Cross. Moffat belonged in the shadows to one of those string-pulling groups behind the scenes, the ones with the give-nothing-away names—E4A, 141NT, Resources Development, Field Obs.

Cross could see why men like Hargreaves loathed the British, for their effortless sense of superiority, accumulated through centuries of careful breeding, blood sports and defensive irony. Most Brits in the North displayed a complete ignorance about the country and exacerbated the situation by showing no guilt at not improving that ignorance. No wonder they were despised.

"I thought they stitched us up pretty badly," Hargreaves said. "Bringing him in. We would have worked it out for ourselves."

"Do we trust each other?"

The fact that Hargreaves thought before answering reassured him.

"Anything you want to say, sir, between us is fine by me."

Hargreaves knew how the barracks worked much better than himself, knew all the tricks and dodges. Like any large system, the barracks accommodated deviant behaviour. It was the oil that greased the machine. Asking Hargreaves to accompany him to interview Willcox made him feel better. It would ensure that anyone who saw them would be more likely to keep quiet. His only remaining worry was whether he could trust Hargreaves to keep his mouth shut.

"OFF THE record."

"Says who?"

"Says us."

Willcox sat slouched on the other side of the table, chain smoking.

"I've got to say, it's all been said to the Brit."

"I'm not interested in that. I want to talk to you about Tommy Herron."

Willcox gave him a quizzical look. "Fuck off. I only talk to the Brit."

Only now, faced by Willcox, was Cross aware of a potential flaw to his plan. There was no guarantee that Willcox would not report their conversation to Moffat.

Paralysed by the thought of that, Cross knew he was losing it. Hargreaves seemed to sense as much and indicated that he wanted a word outside.

"How important is this to you, sir?" Hargreaves asked in the corridor.

"It's important."

"And how off the record are we?"

"None of this is happening."

Hargreaves laughed. "Permission to carry on?"

Cross knew he was at the point of no return.

"Permission to carry on."

They went back and Hargreaves told Willcox to stand up and when he refused he yanked him up by the hair and threw two swift punches into his gut. Willcox collapsed to the floor where he lay squirming with pain. Cross found himself torn between watching and looking away. He enjoyed seeing the sullen fear in Willcox's eyes.

"Shut up and co-operate and we'll make life easy for you," Hargreaves told Willcox as he hauled him back into his seat. "Forget this is happening and you'll be looked after. You'll get hot meals and four-star service. Fuck us and we fuck you. Stick a truncheon right up your fat arse. One word from me is all it takes, so do we understand each other?"

With the psychological boundaries of the room redrawn, Willcox seemed to understand his place and the atmosphere changed. Cross was secretly thrilled by this turn of events. After the briefest of flurries, the change required was brought about swiftly and without mess. Part of him was appalled by his condoning of violence, but this pin-prick of conscience was overridden by a more excited voice that said: we can get away with this. Deep down, it told him: isn't that what it's always about? What you can get away with.

Cross repeated to Willcox that their talk was not official. Even so Willcox took a long time deciding. Cross hoped it was face-saving rather than continued resistance. When Willcox took out a cigarette and showed it to Hargreaves, asking permission to smoke, Cross knew he was theirs.

"OK, shoot," Willcox said after lighting the cigarette and expelling a lungful of smoke.

"Tommy Herron," said Cross.

"Tommy? Dead for years."

"Tell me about the man that shot him."

Willcox asked Cross what that had to do with anything. Cross waved the question aside and repeated that nothing Willcox said would be used against him. He wanted to know about this man.

"Yeah, I remember. I saw him on the day he did it."

He went on to explain that—as far as he knew—Herron's killer was one of a number of British mercenaries who ran the loyalists.

"What do you mean, 'ran the loyalists'?"

"There were a few reservists and some fellows in the UDR with army experience, but it wasn't until these Brits turned up that there was any real organization."

Cross had heard rumours but it was the first time anyone had

told him to his face that the British had secretly trained the loyalists to fight the IRA. Hargreaves looked unfazed.

"So who killed Tommy?" asked Cross.

"Who didn't?" answered Willcox, looking crafty. "They
were lining up to shoot him by the end, from what I heard."

"What about the man who pulled the trigger? Was he doing
it for the Brits?"

Willcox shrugged and lit another cigarette. "That's one
story. I also heard that he and Tommy fell out over something
and the Brits had nothing to do with it."

His description of Herron's killer tallied with the one given
by McGinley, Mary Elam's boyfriend: fair hair cut short, blue
eyes, slight but wiry build, not tall.

"You'd not think to look at him that he was dangerous, but I
saw him flatten one of Charlie Eddoes' boys—a big strapping
fellow—with the one blow."

"Eddoes?" asked Cross, looking up.

Willcox was vague about what Eddoes did in those days,
something on the organization side.

"Why would the Brits have been involved in Tommy's
murder?" Cross asked.

"Let's say the Brits didn't miss Tommy when he went.
Tommy knew where the bodies were buried." Willcox laughed.
"Another story I heard was an RUC man was behind it because
Tommy was giving the man's missus a pop, so there you go."

Cross was suddenly having trouble breathing. It was panic,
panic at the realization that Tommy Herron's killer had been
acting to secret orders. And might be still with these latest
killings.

His mind raced uselessly like a revving engine. The room
felt too small and he grew giddy. Finally he managed to ask if
Willcox had talked to Moffat about Tommy Herron.

"Not as such, but we talked a lot about the early days. He
wanted to know about the Brits that were around."

Cross was now even more afraid of Moffat's game. He was
sure now that Moffat was conducting an investigation parallel
to his own, but cutting him out by keeping it secret, perhaps
even using Cross's findings to feed his own. However he
looked at it, he had the feeling he was facing a cover-up. Willcox was the patsy—a curiously willing one—while Moffat got

on with the more serious business of sweeping Cross's investigation under the carpet.

Willcox was staring at him. Cross realized that he must be looking distraught. He pushed his chair back. His breath felt sour.

"This man who shot Tommy, did he have a name?"

"Sinatra—"

"Sinatra?" interrupted Hargreaves in disbelief.

Willcox looked at Hargreaves and sneered at him with some of his old defiance.

"Yeah, Sinatra. Popular singer."

"Why was he called that?" asked Cross quickly.

"Because his name was Francis Albert. Or so he said."

"And Albert was his last name?"

"As far as I know."

Cross took a deep breath. He was still shaky. He needed fresh air. "What happened to him afterwards?"

"I heard he left Belfast."

Willcox ground out another cigarette. "There's another story." He looked amused. Cross waited patiently for him to get on with it.

"There's a story that he came back working as a gunman for the Taigs."

"You mean he changed sides," asked Cross in disbelief. "Come on."

Willcox shrugged. "I've not heard of anyone else doing it, I have to say. Maybe it was just Rah propaganda trying to spook us into thinking one of our own men was running around shooting loyalists. But there were stories that the Taigs had a man with fair hair and blue eyes, like our friend who shot Tommy, and he called himself Dr. Death."

Forty-five

CROSS put out a trace on Albert, Francis, and drew a blank as he'd expected. He had more calls to make and was cutting it fine. It was past noon and he was due at the O'Neills' by one. Each year on the Twelfth of July weekend his parents-in-law held a barbecue for friends with young families. Deidre and the children were already there.

He was about to leave when his phone rang. It was Westerby. She sounded disturbed and apologized for not being able to get hold of him before.

"Have you seen the papers?" she asked.

He hadn't.

"There was another Psalm yesterday. And one today."

"Two in a row?" Cross was sceptical. He asked her to read them out.

"This is the one that appeared yesterday," she said. "*Like sheep they are laid in the grave; death shall feed on them.* And the one from this morning goes, *Behold, I was shapen in iniquity; and in sin did my mother conceive me.* What do you think, sir?"

Cross couldn't get his head round the implications of advertisements on successive days. Nor could he accept what Westerby said next.

"If he's sticking to the pattern that means—"

"I realize what it means. But I can't believe—"

"Catherine Edge was fourteen, sir. Before she was killed we couldn't believe that—"

"Let's concentrate on finding our man rather than speculating what he might do next."

"I thought you found it useful to speculate, sir." Westerby sounded hurt.

"Up to a point."

He excused himself by saying that he was late.

Again he was on the point of leaving and was delayed, this time by a hunch. He contacted Molly Connors, telephoning to ask if she had ever met a fair-haired Englishman in the company of Breen.

When the answer was yes Cross's heart gave a leap.

"What do you remember?"

"He was English, for a start, so he stuck out being married into a republican family. Short sandy hair, like you say, and a level accent. I remember remarking on the accent and he said bluntly: 'It's as flat as where I'm from.'"

Maybe the marriage accounted for the switch, Cross thought, if there were any truth to Willcox's story.

Molly had met him only once.

"Francis told me he'd promised to give the man a ride to Belfast, and sniggered because, like everyone else, he called a fuck a ride."

She remembered the farm they'd collected him from being off the Newtownhamilton to Keady road in South Armagh, near the village of Derrynoose. The name had stuck in her mind. She met the wife, she added, because they stayed for a cup of tea.

"It struck me as odd, this taciturn Englishman who did not bother to introduce his wife."

"What was an Englishman doing in a republican family?"

"That was my first thought too. I was curious enough to ask Francis and I can't remember what he said. Nothing that answered the question, at any rate. I think he said something like: 'He has his uses.'"

She said the wife's family name was Malone and her father an Official of some standing.

Cross wondered if the wife was still on the farm. They might even have their man before the end of the day, he thought with a surge of excitement.

"What do you remember about the Englishman?"

"I didn't really see him. At the farm he disappeared with Francis, leaving me with the wife, and on the drive I sat in the front. I could feel his eyes on the back of my head, and it made me—I don't know the word."

Molly at a rare loss for words, thought Cross.

"He seemed to resent my presence. Francis did all the talking as usual."

"Tell me about this feeling."

"I don't know how to describe it," said Molly. "Well, I do, actually. He made me feel dirty."

Breen had dropped her in Belfast, saying that the boys were going off to play.

THE POLICE at Keady phoned back to say that the farm was empty and had been for some years. However, Becky Malone was easily enough traced through the local library.

Cross checked his watch. He thought the library would be open on Saturday mornings. He had nothing to lose by calling.

"Who shall I say it is?" asked the woman who answered.

"It's a personal matter," said Cross and waited. Becky Malone sounded suspicious when she came to the phone.

"I need to get in touch with your husband," said Cross.

"Who is this?" she asked with an odd, nervous giggle.

"I need to talk to your husband about a man he knew."

"You'll find it hard."

There was a bitterness to the voice. She sounded strange, not altogether there, a bit simple, even. Yet Molly had said she had gone to Queen's.

"Why?"

"Because there's not much of him left."

The line went dead. She had hung up. He rang back. The phone was picked up straight away. It felt like some weird game. He knew it was her behind the silence.

"Please, listen. You don't have to say anything," he said. "I spoke to a woman called Molly who met you a long time ago. She was with the man I need to talk to your husband about. It's important," he added lamely.

He wondered what was going through her head.

"Please," he repeated.

"They blew him up," she said finally.

He heard her quite clearly. It was his turn to be reduced to silence. Christ! Was the man dead after all? Another false trail.

"When?" he asked.

"Three years ago. In his car."

The voice was devoid of feeling.

"I realize this is painful for you, but would you know if this was before or after Francis Breen's wife was killed?"

It was the wrong question.

"Who's Francis Breen's wife when she's at home?"

The voice was sharp and suspicious.

"She was killed by a bomb in her car as well."

"If you say so." Her voice sounded empty.

"There's one last thing. Can you tell me what your husband looked like?"

Shivers down the backbone, I got the shakes in the knee bone. The line was from an old song he'd heard on the jukebox in the bar where he'd met Stevens. It came back to him in the silence after Becky Malone's description.

HE JOINED Westerby in the same bar; "La Cucaracha" was on the jukebox now, full blast. He'd phoned her at home on his way back from the bar-becue, which had been unspeakable, full of smug parents and squabbling children. He'd left before the others, as early as he decently could. As he drove home news came through on the radio of rioting in Portadown.

It was a talk they could have on the phone, he thought, until he realized he'd had enough of the telephone for one day, after the blind feel of his conversation with Becky. He was bursting to discuss his news but was reluctant to go to her place—he was aware of not avoiding her exactly since Nesbitt's warning but of keeping his distance—so he suggested the bar. It turned out to be impossibly crowded and noisy. They were lucky to get a seat when a couple in the corner suddenly stood up and left.

"It wasn't him that got blown up," she said, as quick as a flash. Cross admired her certainty. He had been in a state of gloom since Becky's news.

He shook his head. "She was there."

"She was upstairs, you said. She didn't actually see. I bet there wasn't much left of him afterwards."

Cross remembered Becky saying the same. Maybe Westerby was right.

"Otherwise what have we got?" continued Westerby. "There's a fair-haired Englishman who killed Tommy Herron and talked to me and leaned on Mary Elam's man. But he's not the same one that married Becky Malone and once met Molly Connors because that one's dead."

La cucaracha, la cucaracha.

Don't be a smartarse, thought Cross about Westerby. The truth was that she was much cleverer than him. It was noisy in the bar and the music too loud. Something seemed to amuse her and he asked what.

"Nothing, sir," she said, smiling into her glass.

"What?"

"It's just that you look so bad tempered," she announced cheerfully.

"I am bad tempered," he answered, equally cheerful all of a sudden. "And that record's not helping."

There was a brief lull as "La Cucaracha" came to an end. Cross and Westerby looked at each other, wondering what was coming next.

Cross glanced round at the busy bar and the queues of people lining up to get served.

"Looks like the recession's over," he said, then groaned. "Oh God! 'Sylvia's Mother!'"

And the operator says "forty cents more for the next three minutes." "Please, Missus Avery . . ."

"Why can't it play ordinary records and serve ordinary beer?" He was drinking something fancy out of a bottle.

"I don't know," said Westerby.

With the record and the general noise there wasn't much point in trying to have a proper conversation.

"I've always rather liked Shel Silverstein myself," Westerby announced.

Cross was confused by their banter, and more confused by his going along with it. It seemed uncharacteristic of them both.

"I beg your pardon?"

Westerby grinned. "Never mind."

Now she's getting fresh, Cross thought.

"I'm going down to see Becky Malone tomorrow," he said, without adding, did she want to come? Instead he asked who Shel Silverstein was.

"He wrote most of Dr. Hook's songs." Westerby was having to shout now. There were so many people in the bar that there was hardly any floor space. "And some of Bonnie Tyler. *We're living in a powder keg and giving off sparks.* Do you know that one?"

Very Belfast, he thought, wondering if he was tipsy.

"You'd know it if you heard it. *Once upon a time I was*

falling in love and now I'm only falling apart. What's the title? It's on the tip of my tongue."

Cross shook his head. In spite of the overbearing atmosphere he was reluctant to leave.

"So you think he's alive?" he asked.

"Becky's husband?"

Cross nodded and Westerby nodded back. "What I don't understand," she went on, "is how the man described by Willcox—a Brit that ran with the UDA—ends up in South Armagh in the bosom of republicanism."

Cross shook his head. Talk really was impossible. Westerby was suddenly tugging his sleeve.

"It's that record I was just talking about!"

A new record had come on the jukebox.

" 'Total Eclipse of the Heart'!" shouted Westerby when she remembered the title. "What's the matter?"

Cross was laughing and pulling a face at the same time.

"It's awful."

"A big hit the summer before last. It's awful but it's great."

THEY arrived in Keady at lunchtime. The place was unnervingly empty, even for a Sunday. The library was closed but Becky had told him she would be there all day for the annual stock-taking. Cross had a hangover. He and Westerby had been drunk by the end of the evening.

He recognized Becky straight away, sitting behind the checking desk. She had a put-away look about her, like her life was closed off already. Her hair was up in a bun, which gave her an old-fashioned, spinsterish air. Cross wondered why she had agreed to talk.

The dry squeeze of her handshake made little impression. The brief flicker of her eyes as she looked into his did. There was a force to them not apparent from her normal averted gaze.

"You can go in there," she said, pointing them towards a door. "I'll be with you in a minute."

They waited in a large room. There was sun on warm glass and the dry smell of unread books. The few he glanced at hadn't been taken out in years.

"It'll be all over town by now that I'm talking to the police," she said, shutting the door behind her.

Her remark pointed up their vulnerability. They were a target for any young Turk wanting to notch up a score. For a second, as he looked at the self-possessed woman in front of him, he wondered if she were a siren luring them to destruction.

Bitter Becky, he thought, as she told her story, prefacing it by saying that she had already crossed some forbidden line by marrying an Englishman and was looked on as a witch as a result.

"I live by my own rules now," she said, "and I speak to who I want."

Her account was simple to the point of baldness. She had first met her husband—"Frank"—when she was at Queen's and he was a figure around the university, though not a student. He was English and polite, and older, which she found an attraction, and there was a coolness that contrasted with the callowness of the students. He'd kept his hair short, which she liked, at a time when everyone else let theirs grow.

"He was like a cat."

Cross sensed a confusion in her as to what the relationship was initially about: why had he chosen her when he could have had the pick of others more beautiful? Becky, flattered because no one had singled her out before, said she felt like she was walking on air.

The picture she painted was one that applied to countless young men: semi-dropouts with a history of travel, gravitating towards places where students hung out. He showed no interest in politics or what was going on in Belfast. Life was too short, he said. After her own republican upbringing, which served politics for breakfast, Becky found this a relief.

"He was in and out a lot, coming back with dope, which he dealt."

They'd slept together because Becky wanted to get rid of her virginity and thought his experience would make it easier.

"It wasn't a relationship thing. I guess he went to bed with other girls. We were just part of the same scene. We lost touch over the summer and when I got back he wasn't around at first, and then he was and it started getting serious."

Lulled by her voice and the sun on his back, Cross listened in a semi-trance, and wondered if she was not indeed a witch.

When she went on to explain what had happened to her in the May of 1974 Cross was struck again by how many events had converged that month—the General Strike, the surfacing of Heatherington, and now the shooting that Becky described.

"Afterwards we never talked about it and I didn't want to know. I knew who Francis Breen was through my father, and there was Frank—who'd said he didn't give a toss for anything except a good time—suddenly able to summon up Mr. Breen at the drop of a hat."

"Was Breen some kind of connection in his dealing?" asked Westerby. Becky looked at her, noticing her properly for the first time.

"That's what I told myself. I think. I was sick afterwards. It was a bad time and I was desperate that he didn't leave me. He'd saved my life, you see, and that made me beholden. Frank was why I was alive."

He was also why she'd nearly been killed, Cross thought.

There was a sad account of her marriage and the feeling that she could not shake off that her life had become a lie, though there was no one she could talk to about it, certainly not her father, who would have said: "I told you so."

"Why are you telling us this?" asked Cross clumsily.

"As a way of telling myself, I suppose. I've put too much of my life away in a box, shut it in the dark and forgotten about it. It wasn't until you called that I saw the extent of it. We live on superstition and whispers in these parts: 'There's Becky Malone, the one that married a Brit and look at the good that did her.' And gradually you become the person they say you are."

She described the morning of her husband's death. He had had to go off somewhere early and she remembered waking when he kissed her goodbye.

"The next thing I was aware of was this almighty bang and I was running around the yard in my nightdress with the car blazing away, and thinking to myself: why, why, why?"

She'd phoned her father, who turned up with other men.

"I don't even know where they buried Frank."

"The police were never told?"

Becky shook her head and smiled. "You ought to know that we mind our own business in these parts."

Cross hesitated. "This is not an easy question, but was there any point after the explosion when you could identify your husband?"

Becky looked at him with clear eyes that held his. "I know what you're saying and the answer is no. By the time the fire was done there was nothing to recognize."

Cross stood up to leave.

"It has to have been Frank in the car as far as I'm concerned," Becky said slowly. "Because if it wasn't, then what am I to believe?"

"Was there any suggestion who killed him?"

Breen had come to the farm sometimes, she said, and took her husband off for a day at a time. By then Breen and her father had fallen out, she added. Cross presumed that this was over the splitting of the Officials.

"Frank's the past. It doesn't do to question things too closely, but I suppose it was whatever Francis Breen was up to that got him killed."

A MAN at the desk looked at them oddly as they left.

Cross, suddenly nervous, mumbled goodbye to Becky, and left the building feeling exposed.

They had driven about two miles when, against his better instincts, he turned round and drove back.

"Wait here," he said to Westerby. "I'll only be a minute."

"I'd rather take my chances in the library, if you don't mind," she said with a tight smile.

Cross laughed at his thoughtlessness. "Of course."

The man at the desk was gone and there was just Becky with a trolley of books.

"Listen," he said quietly. "I need to speak to your father. Would he agree, for your sake?"

Becky was afraid of her father, he saw. For the first time he understood the vulnerability she was trying so hard to conceal, and the effort their conversation had cost her. He saw how close she still was to falling to pieces.

"Tell him Franny Breen's dead," Cross added, looking around. He couldn't shake off the feeling that a gunman might burst through the door any minute. Since McMahon, he'd grown increasingly afraid.

Becky told him to call her later. They made another hurried departure, and he did not relax until well on the road to Belfast. Westerby slept most of the way.

He telephoned Becky at the library that evening and she spoke to her father who then rang Cross. But Malone had nothing to say apart from accusing Cross of unsettling his daughter.

"She's not well and easily upset."

Malone's long silences were like granite. Cross wondered what lay behind them.

Cross explained his reasons for talking to Becky and said he was not aware of any distress on her part.

"Still, you upset her and she's easily led."

The only point of the call was a ticking-off, it seemed.

"I need to talk to someone about Francis Breen," said Cross, hoping Malone would bite.

"Ah, Franny Breen."

Shame, he suddenly thought, that's what lay behind those silences.

"Are you an early riser?"

"I can be," said Cross promptly.

"Take the road from Armagh to Monaghan and cross into the Republic. Down that road you'll come to a turning up to Glaslough, a T-junction at Silver Stream. Seven o'clock tomorrow morning. Mine's a red Datsun Sunny. I take it you're coming alone."

It wasn't a question.

THE BEAUTIFUL summer morning lifted his spirits. There was no traffic on the motorway and he made good time. The jaggedness of Belfast felt a long way away.

Cross arrived at the rendezvous five minutes early. He pulled off the main road like Malone had told him. Malone's Datsun was already parked but there was no sign of him. It was too fine a morning to worry, decided Cross. The sun was just coming over the tops of the trees.

An elderly man emerged from behind a hedge, pulling up his trousers. The moment appeared more comical than it probably was. For all his good spirits Cross was starting to worry that Malone's absence was part of a set-up.

Then the man nodded. His face was that of a once-proud lion. He strolled over to the Datsun and leaned inside. Cross realized too late that he was reaching for a shotgun.

"Spread yourself against the car," Malone ordered.

Cross cursed. Of all the things to have walked into. He turned round. The other man's hands frisked him, then the metal of the gun dug into the back of his neck.

"What did you tell her yesterday?"

Very little, he said. She had done the telling.

"What did she say about her husband?"

Cross told him, uncomfortably aware that one wrong word and it would be his last. He could hear the tremor in his voice.

"And is this all you know about the man, or do you know more?"

"I know more," he said carefully.

"What?"

"What he did before he met your daughter."

Malone made Cross turn round. The gun was six inches from his face. If Malone fired it would take his head off altogether. His reserves were ebbing very fast.

"Did you tell Becky any of this?"

Staring down the black holes of the barrels Cross found it hard to remember what he had said.

"It's hard to think with that thing in my face."

Cross saw the gun jab towards him and heard the terrifying boom of it going off. He was surprised when it didn't hurt.

He was crouched forward, with his hands clapped to his head, and it took him a long moment to realize that Malone had shoved the gun past him and fired.

"No one talks to my daughter without my permission. Got that?"

Cross nodded vigorously, guessing what the other man had said. His ears were ringing painfully and he was in no mind to disagree, with the other barrel still loaded.

"A lot of effort has gone into protecting my daughter and your blundering in is not to her advantage."

Cross nodded again.

"It's all right, you can relax now."

Cross found it hard, under the circumstances. Malone appeared more at ease. He produced a packet of tobacco and started rolling a cigarette.

"So Francis is dead?"

Cross nodded.

"Well, three cheers to that. What happened?"

Cross explained. His voice sounded like it was coming from the end of a tunnel.

"Like a tramp? That doesn't sound like Francis. He was always a bit of a natty dresser."

A couple of cars went by on the main road, the first since Cross's arrival.

"Breen came to me—this would be going back to the big strike, so it would have been May '74—and he said, 'There's a bit of a problemo.' That was the exact word he used: problemo. Francis always was a cunt with his little airs and graces. Anyway, he told me that my Becky was seeing this Brit—which was worse than death as far as I was concerned—and this Brit was asking to come over. And Francis did not know if he was to be trusted."

"Why wasn't Breen keen?"

"Because he suspected the lad of being a British asset. It was Breen's idea to put him in front of a mock firing squad. 'That'll loosen his tongue,' he said."

"Did it?"

"It didn't. He kept his mouth shut, so we believed his story."

"Believed what?"

"Believed him when he said he'd been conned into working for the loyalists and that his change of heart came about through Becky. Telling you this now it must sound like we were born yesterday. The lad was given a full interrogation lasting several days which convinced everyone except Francis, who wanted him pushed to the limit. And then there was Becky's pleading, not that she knew what he was being put through. So when it was all over and he hadn't cracked I was only too happy to believe him, for her sake as much as anything."

He flicked away the cigarette, which smouldered in the road.

"I see now it would have been better if I'd been stricter and kept them apart."

"What happened?"

"He married my Becky, against my better judgement, and ended up doing odd jobs for Breen, is what I heard. Breen and I weren't talking by then. Breen was gone from the party when the split came at the end of that year. He took the boy with him, used him as a trigger."

"What about his death?"

"Becky was the only one there. The car blew up while she was still in bed. There was nothing left of him, she said."

"Nothing left of him?"

Malone shook his head.

"How do you know it was him?"

"What's your drift?"

"That it wasn't him in the car. He faked his death, I'm certain of it."

Malone did not look convinced.

"I think your son-in-law is still alive and he killed Francis Breen," Cross added.

"As far as I'm concerned the remains we dumped in the bog were his. Good riddance. I never saw what she saw in the fellow anyway. Maybe that was her rebellion. Marrying him to spite me. The Malones have always been rebellious and you can't get much more rebellious than marrying a Brit."

Malone paused to roll up another cigarette, and added, "But the only person she ended hurting was herself." He sighed before lighting up. "Here's why it was him."

He started walking slowly down the road. Cross fell into step beside him.

"Not long before the boy died Franny Breen called me. As I said, I'd not spoken to him since the split. He said he wanted to meet. I refused until he said it was personal. To do with Becky. So we met and Franny says about Becky's man: 'It seems like I was right about him after all. The fellow's an asset.' "

Malone walked on, letting the implications sink in.

"My daughter married to a British spy, can you imagine?"

Again the shadow play, thought Cross. The acting to secret orders.

"There was a terrible palaver. Breen's lot had been penetrated and suspicion had fallen on my son-in-law. Imagine how that feels, knowing your only daughter is about to become a widow."

Malone looked bleakly at Cross.

Cross said, "But someone got to him first?"

"Obviously. Otherwise Breen would have pulled him in and interrogated him in the usual way."

"How did you feel when Becky telephoned?"

"Relief was the main thing, knowing Becky wouldn't be shamed."

"Did you hear that Breen's wife and children got blown up too, by a bomb that was almost certainly meant for Breen?"

Malone nodded.

"And what did you think?"

"That whoever did for Becky's man went after Breen."

The neatest solution was of course that it had been Malone

who had blown up his son-in-law, then gone on to kill Breen too. Cross filed the thought away.

"Did you ever think it wasn't Becky's man in the car?"

"Whether it was or wasn't is not really the point. The point is he isn't coming back either way, and that's fine by me."

Malone stopped and turned to Cross.

"Becky doesn't know any of this. As far as she knows this fellow just turned up and fell in love with her. But if, as Breen said, he was a British asset, that meant he coldbloodedly used her for cover. Can you imagine what it'd do to her if she found that out?"

Forty-six

"THESE *things hast thou done, and I kept silence; thou thoughtest that I was altogether such an one as thyself: but I will reprove thee, and set them in order before thine eyes.*"

Westerby was reading from that morning's newspaper.

"What the fuck is going on?" asked Cross. It was the third advertisement in a row, not counting the day before when there was no Sunday edition.

Westerby shrugged helplessly. "Why change now?"

"Are we *sure* it is him?"

"The addresses are false like before."

Cross felt utterly helpless in the face of this altered pattern. "From now on any more of these Psalms that are sent in we tell the paper not to run them. Perhaps that'll tempt him to contact the paper personally."

Westerby looked unconvinced. "He's making all the moves and he hasn't made a mistake yet."

"Yes, but we're catching up with him. He has a past and it's only a matter of time before our paths cross."

She looked doubtful. "We're not going to catch him by Friday."

Cross acknowledged the truth of that but didn't say so. He wondered if he should report to Moffat.

"Let's see what happens on Friday," he said.

"Is there anything we can do?"

"Wait," said Cross bleakly.

"MY MAN surfaced as a mercenary in the 1970s working for the loyalists. He was almost certainly run by the British and was the gunman in the plot to kill Tommy Herron. He then— inexplicably—married into a republican family with contacts with the Officials and later died apparently in a car bombing, though, according to some reports, he is still very much alive."

Cross looked at Charlie Spencer. They were sitting in the same conservatory as before. He had the feeling that nothing had changed since he was last there. The same patients sat in the background watching the same television programme repeating itself on an endless loop.

They went through the story detail by detail until Charlie Spencer held up his hand.

"Are you saying your man remained a British agent?"

"According to his father-in-law. Do you know of any other defections?"

Spencer said that it was not unheard of but both Provisionals and Officials were paranoid about penetration, so any conversions to the republican cause were viewed with great suspicion, especially as the loyalists had such close links with the British. But Spencer did remember a case of the Officials parading a defecting British agent in the early 1970s.

"But that was a farce. The agent turned out to be a complete fantasist."

"What happened?" asked Cross.

"I think they lost patience and shot him."

"Which would be easier to penetrate, the Provisionals or the Officials?"

"The Officials every time. More worldly, more corrupt, not as disciplined and, of course, after 1972 they weren't even fighting the Brits."

Spencer was tiring fast.

"What should I do?" Cross asked.

"How cold is your trail?"

"Cold enough."

"Then go back to the beginning. A lot of Brits working for the loyalists were army deserters."

Cross flew out of Belfast on Saturday morning. The plane was full of what looked like English weekenders going home and the mood was light-hearted. Cross half expected to see Moffat among them, sloping off.

Nothing had happened the day before. There had been no murder, at least not of the type they were looking for. After a tense day of waiting, Cross and Westerby had ended up feeling that they were staring defeat in the face.

Evans, A.F., Pte, he thought, wondering if Evans was his man. His Christian names—Albert Francis—suggested he was. Cross restricted himself to a single gin and tonic on the flight and brooded. He had sought no one's permission and had paid for the ticket with his own credit card. He felt he was keeping everything and everyone at bay, hence his flight.

He rented a car at Heathrow and drove to East Anglia. The strangeness of being back in England did not hit him until he was skirting the urban sprawl of London. Its vastness, compared to the tininess of Belfast, felt quite unnegotiable and the volume of traffic, even on a Saturday morning, unnerved him.

He made slow progress and it was not until late morning that he left behind the last of the city, after a stop-start, anti-clockwise crawl around an inner ring road that frequently became clogged by single-file traffic. Even outside the city its influence continued to be felt. He drove through an endless hinterland of suburbs and industrial estates, wondering if the countryside had disappeared altogether.

The army barracks lay on the outskirts of town. It was a gloomy Victorian pile and looked almost indecently naked without the usual fortifications that surrounded barracks in the North.

Colour Sergeant Major Crabtree was already waiting. He was an intense man, and, like a lot of soldiers, not tall. The sergeants' mess was empty in the middle of the afternoon and they sat in red leatherette armchairs beside a trophy cabinet.

Crabtree was not a man to waste words and after two minutes had told Cross all he could remember about Private Evans.

Evans had been a tough and competent soldier but had set himself apart from the others in a way that made him hard to remember.

"Many of your memories about soldiering are social ones, being there for your mates. I have no recollection of Evans joining in with anything."

Cross found it odd how, after talking to Becky and now Crabtree, he felt his quarry was becoming vaguer. Crabtree's memory of Evans was as faded as the old photograph in the regimental museum that showed Evans, F., Pte, a tiny figure in the back row.

Crabtree thought that Evans had transferred to the SAS at some point around 1970 and some time in the following year was reported AWOL. They found a better photograph in the regimental magazine for 1969, an informal picture taken during a break in manoeuvres. It showed Evans eating from a mess tin, and displaying a terse grin among other smiling faces. There were several thumbs-up, but not from Evans. Cross stared at the face. The hair was fair and flat, almost a crew cut, the face not exactly simian but with something of an animal's self-possession. It gave nothing away.

Crabtree accompanied Cross to his car. He had shown no curiosity about Cross's inquiry. His indifference set the seal on Cross's growing depression. He asked the best way back to London and was directed towards Cambridge and told to take the motorway.

The road was flatter than the one he'd taken before and off to his right Cross sensed the levels of the Fens. He turned off the main road without knowing why, beyond realizing that he didn't have to be anywhere. His return flight wasn't until the following night.

"As flat as where I come from," the man had said to Molly Connors about his accent. Cross looked at the pushed-back landscape. By some trick of the eye, trees always appeared on the horizon. The only breaks in the monotony were the occasional line of pylons and the raised banks of the dykes that crisscrossed the fields.

A red phone box by the side of the road announced itself from faraway. It stood entirely alone, surrounded by sky. Cross stopped the car and got out. The scene reminded him of his son's drawings with ruler-straight horizons and giant skies.

He stood feeling the wind on his face. It was stronger than it looked. In the phone box he could see phone books hanging in a row of metal binders. One had been turned over and lay open, its pages greasy with dirt.

The directory was for the letters E to L and Cross flicked through until he found Evans. There were fewer than he was expecting for such a common name, no more than a dozen. He phoned all of them and got answers from most. By the time he was finished he'd used up most of his change. Of those he'd spoken to none had a relative named Francis Albert. There were three left.

He bought a map at the next garage and decided to head north to Downham Market, where a Mrs. D. Evans was listed in a nearby village.

Her address belonged to a run-down housing estate: small semi-detached boxes, again like something Matthew might draw. The size of the sky above contributed to the mean air of the estate, making it look huddled and apologetic.

Cross rang the bell and waited. There was no answer. He was about to leave when he became aware of a woman standing in the next-door front garden watching him. Cross rang again and took a step backwards and looked up at the front of the house.

"She won't answer," said the woman. "She's there because she never goes out, but she won't answer."

The woman told him to go round the back and knock on the living room window. He might get an answer then, but she doubted it. Cross looked at the woman. She was overweight and slovenly. It was hard to imagine anyone being anything else on this desperate estate.

Cross thanked her and went round the back.

Mrs. Evans was a decrepit woman sitting in a sordid living room. She ignored his knocking and continued to sit there, looking straight through him. Cross put her at about eighty. A grimy cardigan was drawn across her thin shoulders and under that she was wearing only a flannel nightdress. The joints of her knuckles were swollen from arthritis. Her white hair was wispy and pale scalp showed through where it had fallen out. As a scene of squalor it was unremitting bleak, and made even more skewed by the bright-red lipstick smeared around her mouth.

Cross knocked once more and got no response. In the next-door garden laundry flapped hard like it was trying to tell him something. To judge from the wind's rawness it was blowing in from the east, straight off the steppes.

The neighbour was still in her front garden when Cross returned, her curiosity barely containable.

"Are you DHSS?" she asked.

Cross took in the cracked veins and missing tooth. He told her he was from the Royal Ulster Constabulary and registered her confusion.

"You'll not get anything out of old Doris. Her memory's gone."

"What about her husband?"

"Long gone. The cancer."

"Who looks after her?"

The woman shrugged. "I tidy up once a week and check each day to see she's still alive."

"It's Francis Evans I really want to talk to."

The woman looked blank and Cross thought he had made another wasted journey, when her expression changed to one of unwelcome recognition.

"You mean Albie. No one called him Francis, at least not round here." She remembered Albie well. He'd killed her cat.

"Never could prove it, mind. Baby-blue eyes like butter wouldn't melt, and always that look that said he was dead amused by something."

Albie had run wild as a child, she told him, and often proved unmanageable. A combination of his unruliness and his parents' negligence led to various spells in care. Cross silently thanked the woman for her years of nosiness. In ten minutes she gave him more than anyone else to date. The weak father who drank and beat his wife and his son and dragged them all off to church on Sundays. The wife—"You wouldn't want Doris for a mother even when she was all there"—who alternated between lavishing affection on her son and thrashing him.

"And I don't know what they got up to some nights. I'm sure he made the boy watch while he punished her."

"What did that involve?"

"I'm sure I don't know," said the woman, this time with a bustling indignation.

* * *

CROSS spent a lonely night in a Holiday Inn, with a mini-bar and third-rate television for company. He drank too much, failed to make it downstairs for dinner, and feeling sorry for himself called Deidre before remembering that his going away at such short notice had sent their relationship crashing into reverse. Cross decided to make amends with the call but Deidre was snappish and irritable.

"You didn't call just now and hang up?" she asked.

"Of course not. Why on earth should I?"

"I don't know what's going on. It's happened twice now."

"When?"

"About an hour ago. You're not seeing anyone I don't know about?" she asked sharply.

It was depressing how quickly Deidre could turn personal. He could hardly rouse himself to sound indignant.

"No, I'm not seeing anyone you don't know about, and while we're on the subject, what about you?"

It crossed his mind that he was actually paying for this long-distance bickering. He should just hang up, he thought, but Deidre beat him to it after getting in the last word. "Well, if you are," she said, "tell her to stop calling you at home."

He swore at Deidre down the dead line, then dialled Westerby. There was no answer.

WESTERBY was still in the office on the phone to one of her former colleagues in the sex abuse unit.

"You're not allowed any brains, you're not allowed any imagination, you're not even allowed any bloody voice," she was saying when she spotted Hargreaves gesturing from the main door and told her friend she had to go. Increasingly she found excuses not to go home—mainly to avoid Martin—and contrived to be still at work several hours into the next shift.

Because they were short staffed, Westerby found herself driving Hargreaves to one of the city's richer suburbs, a leafy area of wide roads and tranquil houses in spacious gardens. A shooting had occurred there. What made the crime immediately extraordinary was that such areas were usually immune.

The body of a middle-aged woman in a floral print dress lay across the threshold of the front door. It was shielded by screens from the crowd of gawpers gathered on the pavement, children with their bikes mainly. Westerby looked round at the organized chaos of the emergency services at work on what should have been a tranquil evening. She took in the neat detached house with its manicured lawn and separate garage, and the last of the sun dipping behind the trees.

"Get some sense out of the husband," Hargreaves said and told her that he was a local councillor with a high profile. Westerby thought the name sounded familiar.

She found him sitting on his own in a large, well-appointed kitchen-diner. Absurdly, the television was still on, playing unwatched in the corner. He looked up as she entered.

"Councillor Eddoes?"

"I asked to be alone," he said.

He was a big man with deep grooves down the side of his face and large hands. Even in his grief there was something calculating about him.

"I know, sir, but we need a statement," she said in her best concerned voice.

Eddoes was suddenly on his feet and shouting. "There's no statement to be made. It's quite clear who the fuckers are, but they didn't have the guts to come in and get me, so they gunned down Betty instead."

He staggered as if punched at the mention of her name.

"Can you tell us who they are, sir?"

Eddoes felt his heart, like a bad actor trying to register shock.

"It's those INLA fuckers."

Westerby made them both a cup of tea, then coaxed the details out of him.

"I heard the shots and ran out," Eddoes said. "The door was open and poor Betty was as you found her."

He held his head in his hands. A policeman walked in whistling and Westerby urgently motioned to him to get out.

"I ran outside," continued Eddoes, "as the car was pulling away. I didn't get the number. It was a family sedan, light blue. A Cortina, perhaps."

"Did you see anyone?"

Eddoes gestured helplessly. "I was more concerned about the state of my wife."

The killing had all the hallmarks of sectarian murder. Eddoes himself was in no doubt that it was the INLA.

"Filth, unchristian filth, that's what they are. Unloading their muck on to the Protestant streets of Belfast because they can't win their fight any other way. You do know about the theft of drugs from the hospital?"

This was the theft that Cross had told her about.

"Mark my words, that stuff will be on the streets and where will it be sold? Not in the Falls Road and not in Andersonstown, you can bet your bottom dollar. Probably not even in the Shankill. They're after the respectable children of hard-working, God-fearing Protestants. Areas like this! They're taking the fight to the middle-classes, not with guns but through the corruption of children."

Eddoes' hectoring sermon was more appropriate to an assembly hall than his kitchen. Westerby wondered whether he was rehearsing the speech for the television cameras that would inevitably come. She was surprised they were not there already.

By the time she left, everything had been tidied away and restored to its former neatness. Apart from a few spots where the lawn had been trampled on, a fine spray of dried blood on the wall by the front door and a stain on the carpet, there was nothing to show that anything had ever happened.

CROSS flew back to Belfast late the next day and arrived home to find Deidre tense and argumentative. His own mood had not been improved by wasting twenty minutes trying to get through to her after landing and finding the number permanently engaged.

She had left the phone off the hook, she told him, because the ringing and hanging up had been carrying on. Cross said he would get the number changed and they had a row about that. Changing the number was not convenient for Deidre.

"I don't like the idea of someone calling up like that," he said.

"It's probably some pervert who'll get bored after a day or so."

"Well, I'll answer the phone when I'm here. That might put him off."

"I'm quite capable of answering the phone," snapped Deidre.

"What, in case *he* calls?" He knew he sounded pathetic.

When the phone rang they both looked at it like it was a charged object about to explode.

"After you," said Deidre with heavy sarcasm.

"Why are we being like this?" Cross asked wearily.

"Are you going to answer the phone or not?"

"It doesn't have to be like this."

"JUST ANSWER THE FUCKING PHONE!"

Cross lifted the receiver and heard only silence.

"Hello?" he said.

There was a soft laugh. "We're coming to fix you, cunt!" a voice with a West Belfast accent whispered.

He didn't tell Deidre what the man had said.

BECAUSE of work it was impossible to disconnect the telephone in case the barracks needed him, so he took the bedside phone into the spare room without further explanation to Deidre and slept there for the first time since his return from hospital. He also put his father-in-law's old revolver beside the bed.

The phone rang once more, some time in the night.

"We're on our way, cunt."

After that he lay awake in tense anticipation. Finally, after it was light, he drifted off uneasily only to be woken by the phone ringing again. He was still half-lost in some dream—the waking part of him was making a mental note to remember to change the number—as he reached groggily for the phone. As he picked up the receiver he realized that it was the front door that was ringing.

"Dear God, no," he said aloud, suddenly fully alert and grabbing the heavy revolver.

He heard Deidre in the hall, calling out, "Coming!"

"No!" Cross shouted. He was about to shout again when he trod painfully on something. Christ, he thought, was the difference between life and death going to be a piece of Matthew's Lego left lying on the landing? There was still the turn in the stairs before the hall came into view. Time seemed to stretch like melting plastic.

"Don't answer the fucking door!"

He threw himself round the corner to see Deidre opening the door, looking for all the world as though she had not heard.

Cross yelled again and she turned and looked at him. He was aware of the children in the hall too, staring at him goggle-eyed.

"What's the matter with Daddy?" asked Fiona.

"Why's he got a gun?" Matthew's voice was excited.

"Thank you," said Deidre, taking a packet from a puzzled-looking postman.

"Are you all right in there, now?" asked the postman uncertainly.

"It's just my husband having a nervous breakdown," answered Deidre with a breezy smile.

Truer than you know, thought Cross as he collapsed on the stairs, a naked man caught between weeping and laughter.

"I thought the door was—" The sentence was never finished. Weak laughter replaced it.

"Why's Daddy not wearing pyjamas?" Fiona asked.

Cross cackled like an idiot, his helplessness increasing in proportion to Deidre's lack of amusement. It was funny. They were still alive, when thirty seconds earlier he would have bet the last remaining moments of his life on the fact that they were all about to die.

"Matthew, Fiona, back and finish your breakfast now." Deidre clapped her hands to hurry them along.

"Hoopla!" said Cross, clapping his hands too, and giggling. "They're not fucking circus animals," he muttered.

"Stop making a spectacle of yourself in front of the children," snapped Deidre.

The tears started without warning.

"Jesus, I thought—" Again the sentence was left unfinished as racking sobs took over his body.

Forty-seven

THE INCIDENT cracked what remained of their fragile relationship. Cross told Deidre that he didn't know what was going on but he believed the house was unsafe.

They decided that it would be best if she and the children stayed with her parents for a while. Both of them tried hard to keep the discussion practical. Cross marvelled at how grown up they sounded.

"Is this the start of a separation?" he asked.

"Why don't you come with us?" Deidre replied.

"It's only for a few days. I'll be all right here."

Their leaving paralysed him. After phoning the barracks and reporting sick, he took the phone off the hook.

CROSS drank away the empty hours of his time alone. His behaviour was a delayed reaction to his beating, he decided. In his few lucid moments the withdrawal felt deliberate. He told himself he was searching for something akin to Breen's final dereliction, and in reaching that state would discover what he might otherwise miss. Whatever, the solution was interior.

He looked haggard in the mirror, unshaven, his eyes smudged with exhaustion. Drink made him reckless. He left the lights on all night, curtains undrawn, and woke on the bathroom floor with no memory of how he'd got there. When he was sober enough he telephoned the children. He felt that he'd never been a real father to them. His work and its residual anxieties were like a screen between them. Even normal activities such as shopping or going to the playground were tinged with an awareness that all of them were potential targets.

He filled exercise books with lists and thoughts, few of which made sense when he read them back. Once or twice he thought he saw things for what they were. He seemed to be caught in some kind of pincer movement involving those wanting Warren's story suppressed and whoever was responsible, via Moffat, for muddying and deflecting his own investigation. Perhaps they were one and the same. Then there were the Provos who wanted him dead because they believed Cross had set up McMahon. And then there was the killer.

He called the Dublin number she had given him, several times, but there was never any answer and no machine to take a message. He'd thought up questions to ask her about Warren that were just an excuse to talk to her. His mind often returned to his infidelity, picking over the details with guilty pleasure. For all the awkwardness of the encounter, there had been an openness, he believed, and a willingness on her part to tell him things she had told no one else.

He wanted to see her. Perhaps he would, he thought, usually around the end of the bottle.

SOMEWHERE in the swirl of his thoughts Cross had a vague memory of fleeing the house to escape his isolation. He'd memorized the address from earlier and thought he was just about undrunk enough to drive. He wondered at the sense of what he was doing.

The boy had answered the door himself and it took him a while to recognize Cross with his stubble and hollow eyes.

"Are you crazy, mister, coming here?"

He hurried him in and shut the door. They stood whispering urgently, Vinnie telling Cross to go away and Cross, half-laughing, saying that he was there to tell Vinnie to do exactly that.

Vinnie said, "You really are crazy, mister."

"Go on. Fuck off to Dublin and get a new life. Your days are numbered if you stay here."

"Who's counting?"

Cross told him about Heatherington. "Touts end up dead. How old are you?"

Vinnie did not reply and Cross answered for him. "Eighteen, nineteen? You're in a high-risk business. I'd say you have the shortest life expectancy of anyone I know. Dead in a ditch at twenty-one, if you last that long."

Afterwards he wondered if he had dreamed the whole thing, but his building society pass book showed a withdrawal of a thousand pounds. He had a vague memory of Vinnie telling him to leave by the back.

CROSS called through the closed door, "Go away, I'm busy."

It was Westerby. She sounded urgent. He tried to stall her. He didn't want her to see the state he was in. But she was insisting.

"Come back in the morning."

He listened to her voice coming through the door, saying it couldn't wait, and reluctantly he let her in.

"Are you all right, sir?"

Cross was swaying unsteadily. Westerby thought he looked worse than in hospital and tried to hide her shock.

They tried sobering him up with pots of black coffee. Cross still felt woozy and her words swam in and out of focus. He frowned, recognizing the name Eddoes.

"Don't you see? It fits. He's still at it," she said.

She was aware of the ridiculousness of talking to a man in Cross's condition. Without thinking, she took his hand and squeezed it, to convey the urgency she felt.

"He's still at work and the same pattern applies."

She explained once more how the murder of Mrs. Eddoes had apparently sparked off a sectarian tit-for-tat and there had been reprisal killings throughout the North. Several Catholics and Protestants had been shot.

"But look," said Westerby, "it starts with Eddoes, forty-nine. Then Caddy, forty-two, and Causley, thirty-five. Caddy was a prison officer and Causley a civil servant. Both shot outside their homes. Caddy was coming back from the night shift too early for anyone to be up, so there were no witnesses. Causley was shot in the face as he leaned down to speak to someone in a car. He's repeating the pattern except this time with Protestants."

Cross stared dully at the floor. It was strange having her there. Westerby wondered how much he was taking in.

"Are you sure?" he asked eventually.

"I do wonder about the names. Taking the first letter from each one doesn't seem to add up to anything: ECC. Eccentric, ecclesiastical? Hardly. They're about the only words I could find."

"Latin," said Cross.

"What?"

"It's Latin. In the Latin Mass the priest held up the host and said, '*Ecce Agnus Dei.*'"

Cross remembered the old Mass of his childhood, before it changed. *Ecce Agnus Dei. Behold the Lamb of God.*

Westerby got up and made more coffee. Cross was starting to think clearly. He was sceptical about the Eddoes killing. Eddoes himself had provided a clear enough motive by saying it was the INLA in retaliation for his public attacks. Cross was momentarily struck by the coincidence of the INLA again. Breen had been INLA—but then his thoughts collapsed.

"These killings are much more in keeping with ordinary sectarian ones, Psalms or no Psalms," he concluded.

Westerby conceded that, but said she was sure the deaths were part of a general plan. What she could not understand was why the rate of killings was accelerating.

"Freezing Breen, taking his time. Then with the first Mary it was like he was courting her. And abducting Mary Ryan, again taking his time. Setting up Catherine Edge. Now it's bang! bang! bang! He's in a hurry."

"But Eddoes," said Cross.

"Eddoes started me off. I saw his age in the paper. Same age as Francis Breen. Forty-nine. And they both go back to the beginning of the Troubles. And the line of killings that began with Breen started with the murder of someone the killer knew. So maybe the Eddoes killing is personal."

"But he didn't kill Eddoes, he killed his wife."

"Yes. That worried me at first."

"I don't follow," he said ponderously.

"What's unusual about this killing?"

Cross felt as dumb as the class dunce.

"Our man goes to the door, rings the bell—" she said and looked at him expectantly.

"But he couldn't know who was going to answer," Cross said.

"Quite."

"So it doesn't make sense. In all the other cases he knew exactly who he was killing."

"Unless?"

"Unless it didn't matter—"

He had it but let her finish.

"—because they were both the right age."

HE WOKE in an armchair, wondering where the blanket had come from. The room felt different. It was tidy, for a start. The curtains were drawn and a table lamp had been left on. His head was splitting and his mouth parched. He went to the kitchen and splashed water on his face, then remembered.

He found her upstairs, asleep on Fiona's bed, and fought the temptation to lie down beside her.

Cross didn't sleep after that. Instead he nursed his hangover and tried to piece together what they had talked about. He remembered with some embarrassment rambling on about Deidre and the children.

By the time Westerby was up and they were having breakfast everything seemed bleak to him. Even if she was right, who did they tell?

"There's only Moffat or Nesbitt to tell," she said.

Cross confessed his growing paranoia. "But you're right. There's only Moffat or Nesbitt to tell."

Westerby asked to speak to Moffat that morning and was predictably blocked, so she badgered Hargreaves to let her speak to Nesbitt.

"You can't just barge in and start talking to the DCI."

She didn't trust Hargreaves to put her case for her but she could hardly say so.

"We already have a suspect in custody. He's admitted the Mary Ryan killing," Hargreaves added.

Westerby couldn't help wondering what they had done to Willcox to get him to confess. Her father had treated men after interrogation in Castlereagh. They had suffered terrible residual damage as a result.

Hargreaves came back at lunchtime and told her that they had an audience with Nesbitt. Hargreaves looked crafty and she realized that if it went well he would take the credit. Otherwise the blame would be hers.

Hargreaves began by putting distance between himself and Westerby, announcing that she had something to say. Nesbitt addressed her with a heavy-lidded stare. Westerby was afraid of Nesbitt. She had always been susceptible to bullies.

He threw her by listening patiently to everything she had to say, his head cocked.

When she was done, he said, "So, it really is your opinion that we have a multiple murderer stalking the streets of Belfast, killing first Catholics and now Protestants?"

"Yes," said Westerby, who seethed at his condescension.

"If what you say is true, this is very alarming. I'll pass it on to Mr. Moffat and if he needs to get back to you he will." He smiled at her brightly.

"Is that all?" she asked.

"Yes, that's all."

"Is that enough, sir?"

"I beg your pardon, constable?"

"I think there's a man running around killing people and you say, 'I'll make a note of it.'"

She saw the look of calculation in Nesbitt's face, weighing up whether to lose his temper or not. He carried on in the same polite vein.

"Why would anyone run around killing Catholics *and* Protestants?"

"Because he's a maniac."

"Maniacs are for the Yanks."

Westerby sensed Hargreaves grinning behind her.

"Why aren't you taking me seriously, sir?"

"I might not be taking *you* seriously, WPC Westerby, because I dislike insubordination, but I am taking what you say seriously. I told you I would pass it on to Mr. Moffat. He will evaluate your material and act accordingly."

Westerby opened her mouth and Nesbitt rose up out of his seat with a roar.

"That's enough! It may have escaped your attention, but because of the circumstances that exist in this country we have one of the most developed and sophisticated police forces in the world. If Mr. Moffat believes that your material is worth acting on it will be acted upon."

"With respect, sir, this force may have its technology, but it is backward and bigoted and run like some nineteenth-century Victorian school."

She had the satisfaction of seeing Nesbitt's jaw drop before she turned and walked out.

Forty-eight

MOFFAT left Belfast that morning and flew to RAF Northolt on the edge of London. He read Jung on the plane, enjoying the fact that he was temporarily out of reach, and occasionally paused to ruminate on the fractured relations between his department and that of the man he was going to see. The balance of power which had been held for so many years by his side was shifting subtly in favour of its old rival, largely because of a greater closeness to the Americans. The Americans were behind the unprecedented Anglo–Irish Agreement due to be signed later in the year. It was their ultimate intention to have an Ireland united at the expense of the Protestant Unionists.

Moffat's own department had always taken a more traditional line, offering covert support to the Protestants while pursuing a policy of unconditional surrender towards the Provisional IRA. He thought of the man he was about to meet and remembered a line from Bob Dylan. *Let us not talk falsely now, the hour is getting late*.

It was raining in England. The waiting car drove him a half-mile along the airfield perimeter to a Nissen hut where a meeting room, smelling of floor wax, had been set aside. Chintz armchairs gave the otherwise spartan room the air of a stage set.

Davenport was already waiting. Moffat knew him slightly but they greeted each other warily. Davenport tried to hide his curiosity. The meeting had been called by Moffat and as he was flying in for it Davenport had arranged to drive out to Northolt.

A thermos of coffee was laid out on a table, with the same regulation biscuits they got in Belfast. Moffat poured them both a cup, fussing over the details of milk and sugar. His fiancée had just left him and since then he often experienced a mild panic in the face of small social rituals.

"It seems we have a multiple killer on the loose in the Province," Moffat said conversationally. "We wondered if it might be one of yours."

Davenport blinked and recovered quickly. He shook his head.

"Nice of you to think it's us," he replied pleasantly.

"I've done you a file."

He handed the dossier to Davenport, who scanned it quickly and pointed out that as his department was now more or less inactive in Northern Ireland he didn't see how he could help. "It's your show," he pointed out. "And has been for the last ten years."

"The thing is, it's no one we know. Our stables are clean."

Davenport rode the silence.

"By the way," Moffat went on, switching tack, "we've been doing a bit of hoovering on your behalf."

"Oh?"

Davenport was clearly a student of the pregnant pause. Moffat swallowed his irritation.

"A journalist. A total alcoholic, but running round asking a lot of awkward questions and rattling old skeletons, yours and mine."

"Such as?"

"Kincora."

"I thought we'd heard the last of that."

"He was threatening to expose—"

"How far back?"

Each was aware that the problem with Kincora was that it affected them both. Several key figures in the scandal had worked for Davenport's department in the early years of the Troubles, before it had lost control to Moffat's side.

"What happened?" asked Davenport.

Moffat drily explained that a couple of visitors who'd been round to see the journalist had got a bit carried away.

"So they made it look like he'd accidentally hanged himself. Um. While dressed in women's underwear."

Davenport was amused. He came from a background that appreciated smut. "Is anyone buying that?"

Moffat inspected his nails. "Um. They made it look pretty pervy. You know, sordid details. Always helps in a cover-up. The man who did the autopsy is a friend of the department and agreed to keep it vague."

Davenport guessed that "friend of the department" was a euphemism for being blackmailed.

"So what's the problem?"

"None, really, except the policeman investigating the case. Unfortunately for us he's also dealing with the murders, and he's on to both. I've included a copy of the journalist's story, by the way."

Davenport sorted through Moffat's file until he found it. This time, as he read through it, his eyebrows shot up in surprise.

"Quite," said Moffat. "If that stuff about McKeague came out, that's egg on your face, not ours."

"Big egg," agreed Davenport, wondering why Moffat was being so co-operative.

"There's another journalist we're in the process of persuading not to touch it," continued Moffat. "Awful balls-up, they got the wrong man at first and beat up the policeman."

The two men snorted with laughter.

"Bloody freelancers," said Moffat.

"How serious is this other business?" asked Davenport.

"Put it this way, we're having a devil of a job sitting on Stalker. He won't be deflected. If there were another scandal—a mass murderer on the loose with some sort of connection with British intelligence—I'd say you could have a civil uprising on your hands."

"Your hands, not mine," said Davenport tartly.

"Um, that depends," replied Moffat cryptically.

"But why is he not declaring his hand?"

"He will, I'm sure of that. In the meantime, I think you should look and see if there are any funny sections in your department that everyone's forgotten about. This man goes back to your time. He was an agent then. You'd better pray to God he's not still one now."

"Your boys haven't got anything up their sleeves for this Anglo–Irish thing, have they?" Davenport asked mischievously.

"Don't know what you're talking about," Moffat said disingenuously.

"Well, you certainly managed to spoil the party last time."

"What are you getting at?" said Moffat, suddenly uneasy.

"You torpedoed the last agreement, we all know that, bombing Dublin and all the rest. Are you sure these killings aren't the first stage of someone's plans to fuck it up this time around?"

"In which case it would be us running this maniac rather than you, is that what you're saying?"

"Exactly. Don't forget we're all in favour of giving the North to the South. Have been for years. You're the ones that have wrecked every initiative between Dublin and Westminster. So perhaps you should take another look in your stables."

Moffat didn't like the turn the meeting had taken. He hadn't expected his argument to be turned against him.

Gotcha, thought Davenport.

NESBITT knew when to call a spade a spade.

"You're talking about a cover-up."

"Yes," said Moffat.

"So what are you going to tell my detective inspector?"

Moffat ducked the question. He had given Cross considerable thought on the way back from Northolt. He could see him being even more difficult if he were told the full circumstances. Cross was the sort of sticky character who would object to a cover-up, less out of principle than cussedness. Moffat knew that Cross did not like or trust him.

"What do we know about your killer?" asked Nesbitt.

Moffat passed over Nesbitt's use of the possessive pronoun.

"Enough to be worried." Moffat handed Nesbitt the dossier he'd been up half the night writing. "I would appreciate it if you read it now."

Nesbitt was a slow reader and his lips moved as he read. Put off by this unedifying sight, Moffat stared out of the window and assessed what Nesbitt had told him about his meeting with Westerby. Moffat recognized that Westerby was much brighter than the average policewoman. In a more enlightened force she would have been singled out for promotion. She and Cross were potentially a formidable team and, in his opinion, the more isolated they were, the more effective they would be, which was why he had taken the precaution of putting taps on their phones, and bugging Cross's office. There was also the smear campaign against them, via Hargreaves putting it about that they were having an affair.

Moffat didn't find Westerby attractive in the usual sense, but there was something about her. She looked like she'd fuck like a stoat for starters, but perhaps that was a projection of his own frustration. Since Sarah he had found himself contemplating propositioning the most unlikely women. At least Westerby looked like a woman, which was more than could be said for most of her colleagues. Anyone half-way decent became the source of feverish collective fantasy in the closed boarding school-like atmosphere in which they worked.

Nesbitt was still reading. Moffat was uncomfortably aware of the beginnings of an erection. The way her colour had risen when she had been humiliated by him at the same time as that defiant look had appeared in her eye had excited him. He wondered how personal his desire was to hurt her. A little kick, perhaps, a little extra humiliation within the larger frame. The point was to set them loose from the main investigation, he mustn't lose sight of that. Two driven and increasingly cut-off people might get further than a larger sweep. Setting the hounds to catch the hare, it was called, and if he managed to pick up Westerby along the way so much the better. He was half way through mentally undressing her and surreptitiously adjusting his trousers when Nesbitt at last surfaced.

"Christ, son, even if half of this is right I can see why you wouldn't want it getting out."

Moffat suppressed a snigger and regarded Nesbitt drily. "That's not even the half of it. That's just the stuff you need to know."

"Don't play the smartarse with me, Mr. Moffat. This is your mess. You get yourself out of it."

CROSS went back to work. He phoned Deidre and they had lunch in a crowded restaurant near the tourist board. She turned up looking brisk and smart.

"You don't look all right," she'd said after he said he was fine. It was true. His eyes were bloodshot and nervousness gave him a haggard air.

Lunch with Deidre reminded him that Belfast was a city of warring factions that nevertheless met occasionally in temporary truce. They were on best behaviour, she showing concern for his safety and lack of appetite. He said he missed the children, which was true, and added that he missed her too, which was true in that he wanted it to be true. He thought she was comfortable staying at her parents and felt better loved by them than him.

"ARE YOU the one I called before?" he asked Westerby and made her prove it by repeating details from the previous conversation.

"You have a nice voice," he said. "Did you find out who killed Tommy Herron?"

"Do you have fair hair and blue eyes?"

"That's for you to find out."

"Are you going to give me a name I can call you by?"

"The butcher, the baker or the candlestick maker? Guess right and you get another question."

"Are you Mr. Butcher?"

The line went suddenly dead.

"Fuck," said Westerby and went off to find Cross.

He wasn't in his office and someone said he was out at lunch. She was worried about him and still shaken by how much he'd lost his grip since the hospital.

Her stomach was wrestling with the effects of a canteen meal when her phone rang. She recognized the voice straight away.

"What's my name?"

"You're the candlestick maker." She held her breath.

"You can call me Candlestick. Now what are you going to give me in return?"

"What would you like?"

"How about a kiss?"

"Well then, why don't you come round to my place?" Keep him talking, she thought, talk crap, say anything.

"I might just."

From the way he said it, she had the sick feeling he knew where she lived. Her gut contracted.

"Tell me your name," the man ordered.

She said the first one that came into her head.

"That's nice," he said. "But don't catch a chill, Jill."

Jill was her mother's name. Westerby was simultaneously appalled and amused by the choice. As for Mr. Candlestick, he sounded too intelligent for such inanities.

"I bet the boys make you do the talking," he continued.

She said she didn't know what he was on about, but carefully, not to offend.

"Talking to the relatives of the dead," he said. "The rape victims. The grieving. Men don't do that sort of stuff."

She wondered how he knew. It was true. The men were notoriously wary of dealing with situations requiring compassion. Hand-holding was seen as a woman's work.

"How did Mr. and Mrs. Ryan take the news of poor Mary's death?"

You sick fuck, she thought, caught off guard.

"How do you think they took it?"

"Answer a question with a question, very clever."

There was a silence.

"Don't go," she blurted.

"Then don't jerk me around, bitch." His voice was harsher. "I ask, you answer. Got that?"

"Yes."

"What happened when you talked to Mr. and Mrs. Ryan?"

"They were very upset." She couldn't stop herself from adding, "What did you expect?"

"How upset?"

"They told me that Mary's death confirmed their worst fears. They'd always thought no good would come of her going to the city."

She felt ashamed passing on this confidence.

"You're cleverer than most peelers, aren't you?"

"Yes, I am," said Westerby, with some defiance.

"Well, in that case, there's something a clever girl should see and see what she makes of that."

Westerby's heart was beating faster. "Me?"

"Yes. I'm starting to build up a picture of you and I like what I see."

"What do you see?" She hoped he couldn't detect the anxiety in her voice.

"Five foot two, eyes of blue."

"What do you want *me* to see?" she asked hurriedly, shutting out the implications of what he'd just said.

He was spooking her, but at the same time she felt a tingle of excitement, like she got when watching the heroine of a horror film going down into the cellar, while the audience hooted at her not to.

"There's a basement," he said, echoing her thoughts.

"What?"

He gave her the address.

"How do I know I can trust you?" she asked.

"You don't, but curiosity will take care of that."

He laughed. She could imagine his sense of humour extending to a tripwire designed to wipe the smile off the face of an over-keen, blundering policewoman.

"CANDLESTICK," said Cross, puzzled. First Francis Albert Evans, then Francis Albert, then Sinatra and Dr. Death, now Candlestick.

"He gave me an address."

Cross was suspicious and asked why the man should want to declare his hand.

"I get the feeling he needs us, in some way," said Westerby.

"You can't go on your own."

"He told me to."

They haggled. Westerby insisted, to prove to herself that she was foolhardy or brave. She also understood that Candlestick had flattered her, treating her with more respect than her colleagues, but she didn't tell Cross that.

In the end they compromised and Westerby agreed to let him drive her there and wait nearby.

"I'm sure he's being quite straight with us for the moment."

Cross shivered, remembering the slaughtered animals.

THE ADDRESS was in an anonymous area of dingy terraced houses in a mixed district that was becoming dilapidated. Cross's hands were damp on the steering wheel. Westerby had forgotten to do up her seatbelt, but he said nothing. It would sound like fussing.

He parked in the street next to the address, again saying he was unhappy about her going in alone.

Westerby sat hunched forward, summoning up her courage.

"We've no back-up," he said.

"We have to see what's there," she said.

They sat in silence, neither moving.

"I'm shaking. Look."

She held up her hand. Cross wanted to take it to reassure her, but was too aware of his own clammy nervous sweat.

"I can't go through with this," she announced.

It was Cross's turn to be positive. He put his hand on her sleeve and squeezed. "If it feels wrong, come back."

"This is unreal," said Westerby.

They looked at each other and laughed nervously.

She reached for the door. His hand was still on her arm.

Westerby paused and turned to Cross. She caught his eye and held it. She seemed calmer, almost amused.

"Kiss me," she said. "For luck."

He had to unsnap his seatbelt to reach across.

He felt her cool lips brush his for a moment, her hand coming up to rest lightly on the back of his head. It was just a good luck kiss she was wanting after all, he thought. He felt like he was poised above a clear blue pool. All he had to do was jump. He thought of the things that held him back.

He continued to hold her while she rested her head on his shoulder and he stroked the nape of her neck, aware only of the touch of her skin and her smell, reminding him of warm summer days. She did not use perfume, unlike Deidre.

He lifted her chin and leaned down towards her, curious to feel again the touch of her lips. Again he kissed her chastely.

She looked up at him, more amusement in her eyes.

"I'll be needing more luck than that."

He felt the sudden surprise of her tongue, sweet and testing, and the clean smoothness of her teeth, and a different taste, like vanilla, which he realized was her lipstick. He didn't want to stop. Passion made them clumsy and their mouths slithered apart. They broke, both of them breathless from the shock of their coming together, then were kissing again. A song line she'd told him about drifted through his head: *We're living in a powder keg and giving off sparks*. He remembered the record in the crowded bar, and Westerby shading her eyes with her hand as they drove back on the road from Carrick-fergus. He felt light-headed for the first time since he couldn't remember when.

They lost all sense of time and suddenly they were moving too fast, driven by desire, sitting in a car in broad daylight. Cross felt her hand slip under his shirt while his own moved across the smoothness of her back. He didn't want to stop, but was afraid to go on. Her urgency matched his. A part of him watched from a distance, marvelling at the strange newness of it all. Then he lost her quite suddenly. One moment she was in his arms and the next she was gone, walking down the street away from him, towards the house.

Reality descended on Cross again like a lid.

As WESTERBY walked down the road she felt more uncertain about what she was walking away from than what she was going towards. *What had that been about?* And where did it leave them? She was unsteady on her feet, like after being ill in bed for too long. The street in front of her jerked about like an old silent film.

She could smell the encroaching poverty. A group of sullen children stood and stared at her. Westerby had dressed down for the occasion, wearing an old pair of jeans and a tatty jersey, and still she felt conspicuous compared to the children in their thrift shop clothes.

She walked past 13A with a sidelong glance. There were

railings in front and steps down to a basement entrance. The single window had a blanket tacked across. Westerby went on to the end of the street. Gulls screeched overhead and she could smell the sea.

She walked round the block to check the back and see if there was an alley between the yards. There was not.

She felt very exposed and wondered if his eyes were watching her. The children were playing with a skipping rope and chanting, "If you hate the British soldiers, clap your hands."

The steps down to the basement were green with mildew. The door was black, with frosted glass panels. To the left was another door, which she checked. It was a cellar that stretched under the pavement and was used for rubbish. She could just make out a couple of dustbins, and beyond that several pieces of abandoned furniture. She checked the bins. Each smelt of refuse but not as if it had been used recently.

The key was where Candlestick had said, under a loose brick by the drainpipe. She had been rather hoping that it would not be there.

She unlocked the door and stepped gingerly inside. The place smelt damp and lifeless, the air stale and undisturbed. The corridor was covered with dingy linoleum and led to a short flight of stairs that was sealed at the top by a nailed-up and padlocked door. In the space underneath the stairs was a makeshift kitchen with a sink and an ancient cooker. A strip of tin plate was nailed to the underside of the stairs above the cooker to prevent burning. The cooker was encrusted with dirt and grease. She moved extra carefully, reluctant to touch any-thing. Mice or rats scratched away behind the wainscoting, and she tried to rid herself of the feeling that she was not alone.

There was a bathroom across from the kitchen, with a free-standing bath, a basin, a wooden chair and nothing else. The window looked out over a tiny walled yard.

Westerby suppressed a shiver and tried to tell herself that this was squalor she was looking at rather than evil. Then she went into the only other room.

She stared, mouth agape. *So this is where the evil is,* she thought. *This is where the evil is.*

* * *

THE WALLS were plastered with images, hundreds of them, making up a demented quilt of death and pain. Westerby recognized many of the pictures—a bound man standing in the street being shot in the head with a pistol; Buddhist monks turning themselves into human torches; charred and twisted corpses; concentration camp bodies in mass graves.

The images were from newspapers or magazines. They were roughly torn, which made them seem even more violent. As Westerby raised her eyes, following the crazed path of one death after another, she realized that the ceiling was pasted with them, the door and window too. Even the floor.

The images danced in front of her eyes, bearing down on her. The horror lay less in the individual pictures than in the obsessive effort of their accumulation. Westerby felt as though she had been transported Alice-like straight inside the killer's head.

She forced herself to look again. Some of the pictures were different from the rest, morgue photos of forensic autopsies— bodies agape, cavities, faces lividly bruised, reminding her of Cross's injuries, or smashed beyond recognition—glossy eight by tens, each a nightmare of colour.

Westerby was paralysed in front of this shrine to atrocity. Every nerve in her body screamed at her to get out. This room was the work of the man who had gouged out Mary Ryan's eyeballs and stabbed Francis Breen through the wrists before slinging him in a deep freeze.

Get out, she told herself, then another voice from deeper inside her whispered that it was too late to turn back now.

Besides the quilt of images covering every available surface there was just a table without a chair. On the table were a dozen or more cardboard wallets. They were dossiers, she saw on opening them, on the killer's victims.

She flicked open the one on Breen. He was listed as both Berrigan and Breen. His date of birth was there, plus both addresses, and a grainy photograph taken on a telephoto lens. Most of the information was scrawled on scraps of paper. The word "Betrayal" was next to Breen's name in a different-coloured ink.

The other dossiers included a snapshot of each victim, but none indicated how the information had been gathered.

At the bottom of the pile was a notebook, a school exercise book with ruled lines, much scribbled in.

She flicked through it quickly, sensing time was running out. She did not want to stay much longer. In the distance she could hear the children chanting.

The book seemed mostly full of statistics, and, as Westerby scanned through the lists, she grew puzzled. The statistics were a catalogue of domestic violence in Northern Ireland—the wife beatings, the batterings, the domestic rapes. *Why would he want to list those?*

Westerby knew about these statistics from her own work in the sex abuse unit. She noted the phrase "plague of domestic violence" in a margin, the word plague underlined. The spelling and lettering were strange, she saw. "Domestic vilence—far gRater than streeT vilence and unremarked on—taken for grantted. The poinT is, *the Two are connecteD*." She found herself agreeing, to her discomfort.

She took the notebook when she left.

The children were still playing in the street. Everything looked strangely normal. Westerby felt she had been away an age, and the innocence of what had happened between her and Cross belonged to another life.

Forty-nine

AFTER double-locking and bolting her front door, Westerby turned the pages of Candlestick's notebook. It immediately struck her as a weird mixture of frighteningly keen intelligence and barely controlled violence. At times the pen had scratched through the page. The writing itself was tense and angular. The misplaced capitals and weird spellings were an obvious sign to her that they were dealing with a highly individual mind.

Westerby had been incapable of speech when she'd got back to Cross. She had shown him the book and asked him to take her home. After what she'd seen she needed to be alone but she didn't tell him that.

First they'd gone back briefly to the flat at Cross's insistence. Westerby had waited outside by the front door, keeping a nervous watch, expecting Candlestick at any moment, while Cross made his inspection. He spent about five minutes inside and came out looking pale. Then they knocked on the door of the flat upstairs, which was eventually opened by a large slovenly woman with a nicotine moustache who said she'd never seen anyone enter or leave the basement, though sometimes in the middle of the night she thought she heard movements downstairs.

ON CLOSER inspection, Candlestick's book appeared to consist of a mixture of messianic conundrums and statistics of violence. Westerby started at the beginning and read:

> Candel stick makers and Bakers were made Generals and toilet attendants were made colnals. People who Never Had any miliTary experence or anyThing else just came ouT may it be through some form of agression, because they could diG someBody a wee bit harder.

> What your talkinG about in terms of separation of the comunities is BarBed wire, hurdles, and peace walls at tHat Time. It was like going into a room tHat has six doors in it, but all those doors are locked up and theres only one door to Go in or out, and on the other side of the door you have the fear of a posible hostile enviroment. You have half a Dozen doors and someBody Blocks off five of them. People Get frigHtened. There's only one way into a catholic or protestant area and theres only one way out. "I'm not going in there."

> THe inocent will suffer so tHe innocent shall be freed.

> *Ecce AGnus Dei*

My God, she thought, Cross had been right after all. He had made the connection. She wished he was there with her now and that she hadn't sent him away.

Out of the Depths I cry unto you O Lord! How lonG?

When tHere are two, one betrays.

Show me The man who will lead these people from BondaGe.

I have But one talent, for an exactinG crafT. Would that I could puT this craft aside, But too laTe. No one is lonelier than the samurai, except for the TiGer in the jungle, purhaps. If we are here for a purpose then what is mine if noT To acT as the insTrumenT? From tHis staTegy will come undreamed of peace.

She read the last sentence again and wondered if there was a perverse logic to the murders. Did Candlestick see them as a way of drawing attention to the senselessness of the larger project?

WhaT is to Destroy if noT To Build? In the power of Destruction lies the Beuaty of creaTtion.

If I Did not belief ThaT I haD a mission, that I am here for a reason, tHen the only choice would be to use this GifT to destroy myself.

In love is haTreD, in haTreD love.

In trust lys Betrayal. I am the poinT where the circle joins. In my terriBle Destin the larger resolution. In my Destruction my survival my survival my Destuction.

The loneliness of Betrayal.

He was here. I saw him, not expectinG ThaT. The shock of the unexpected.

Why dont they see into the shaDows, see the splits in the shaDoes. The sunsHines on freinD and fow alike.

Division (Division by aGe): Divide (by seven) but resolve,

unlike the larGer division, which offers no solution. Te smaller the diffision tHe more they musT pay attention.

My justice will Become plane to all. I douBt my vocatin I pray for the strenGth to carry out my excecution. My silence is my pain. Without silence there woulD Be know pain. Soon my voice will be heard, the dead lock broken.

The Beasts of darkness will stalk the lanD until the TruTh is out.

My loneliness Drives me. And when the slaughTer is Done will there be peace for me? Shall I at last be aBle to lay my TerriBle craft aside, lay down my sworD for the plougH. A curse on those who revealeD my Destiny to me.

I am the inTsrument, my power and my trajeDy.

The kilings will go on unTil the oTher killings stop. The killings will go on until the TruTh wich "lies" Behind evrythinG is Told. The killings will go on untill all the secreTs are revieled. The killings will enD when tHe motHers of the DeaD rise in protest.

That was his clearest statement she'd read. The murders were to be announced as a campaign against the wider violence. She wondered whether Candlestick believed this or was using it as a way of disguising his own sick fantasies from himself. She read on.

In the necessity of Brian Berrigans death the laying to rest of lies.
In the pointlessness of Mary Elams death the future hapiness of her childen.
In the swiftness of Patrick Wheens death the clarity of retribution.
In the justice of Roger Arnolds death the disappearance of oppression.
In the horror of Mary Ryans death the peace of thousands.
In the harshness of Catherine Edges death the question how long must the suffering go on.

After she had finished, Westerby called Cross and gave him a summary of the notebook, which had gone on to list incidents of domestic violence of the kind that Willcox had committed. Westerby had found this catalogue of atrocity worse than anything that had preceded it and these weren't even his crimes. Hardest to come to terms with was the fact that she could see Candlestick's point. The only way to cure an epidemic was to find a vaccine more powerful than the virus, in this case a personal and quite precise campaign of violence.

Cross was still not sure what to do. They had proof now that Candlestick was killing to a pattern. He noticed in passing that there was no mention of Warren's name and wondered about that. There was also Candlestick's flat, which needed going over. He couldn't delay his decision for much longer. But any initiative meant going through Moffat, and that he was still reluctant to do. He told Westerby to make a chronology of events, putting in anything she thought might relate.

The first instance she could recall was Molly's description of first meeting Breen in 1969 at the start of the Troubles. It seemed appropriate to begin there, given that Candlestick's apparent ambition was nothing short of an end to the conflict.

August 1969. Molly Connors meets Francis Breen (OIRA). Grows disillusioned over his racketeering. Leaves country August 1971, returns 1972 to find Breen married to her sister, Bernadette. Molly resumes affair with Breen soon after, until murder of Bernadette in 1982.

Sept 1973. Tommy Herron shot, possibly to British orders, by army deserter, Albert Francis Evans (AFE) working as a loyalist mercenary, previously intimate with Herron. Was AFE run by the security forces under the codename of Candlestick? (Source: Willcox)

May 1974. General Strike and Dublin bombings. Heatherington sting.

Info given to Provs includes identity of a member of the British-run gang involved in the Herron assassination, shot after his name was passed on to loyalist paramilitaries. (Source: Warren) The same month AFE (also a member of the above gang?) presents himself to Official IRA, after falling out with UDA, saying he wants to switch allegiance, and trailing a republican girlfriend, Becky Malone, subsequently married. According to her, AFE a peripheral figure on the student circuit. AFE's apparent source of IRA contact, Breen: origin of relationship unknown. Breen suspects AFE of being a British asset. Arranges mock execution, a test successfully passed. AFE moves to South Armagh with Becky. Married September 1974. (Sources: Becky Malone and father)

November 1974. Officials split. Breen moves over. Malone stays. Breen active in civil war that follows and 1975 foundation of INLA. AFE's activities unknown, apart from one sighting by Molly Connors, a shared drive from South Armagh to Belfast with Breen. Breen claims involvement in Airey Neave assassination (March 1979) and subsequently fears for his life, saying others involved murdered by security forces. Surmise: AFE used as gunman by loyalists 1971–73; therefore used by Breen for same purposes 1974–81. (Sources: Malone and Connors)

October 1981. Breen contacts Becky Malone's father to say that AFE is British agent after all. AFE killed by car bomb just after but never identified.

January 1982. John McKeague killed.

April 1982. Bernadette Breen and children killed. Francis Breen disappears, suffers breakdown (?)

1984. AFE meets Seamus McGinley, scares him into fleeing to the Republic, leaving behind Mary Elam.

January 25 1985. Advertisement When God has forsaken, etc, appears.

February 1 1985. Francis Breen (Brian Berrigan) found dead. Paramilitary connections: OIRA, INLA.

March 1 1985. Mary Elam killed. Paramilitary connections: UVF or UDA via Strathaven bar?

March 29 1985. Patrick Wheen killed. Paramilitary connections: none.

April 26 1985. Roger Arnold killed. British armed services.

May 27 1985. Mary Ryan found dead.

June 21 1985. Catherine Edge killed.

July 20 1985. Mrs. Eddoes.

July 22 1985. Caddy.

July 23 1985. Causley.

Westerby phoned Cross to say that she was going out to talk to Rintoul, Breen's accountant, and became flustered when Cross announced that he wanted to come too. Like her, he was keen to establish any links between Herron, Breen and Eddoes.

She talked too much on the drive and worried that Cross sensed her nervousness. Having stripped off for Rintoul, she found it hard enough to contemplate seeing him again, let alone with Cross.

"Ah, you brought a friend." Rintoul spoke drily on opening the door. Westerby felt herself blushing furiously and hoped Cross couldn't see.

Rintoul made them tea and when the three of them sat down in the tiny kitchen they could hardly do so without their knees touching. Westerby hoped that Cross was unaware of Rintoul's ironic looks.

She cleared her throat and tried to pay attention to Cross and Rintoul's conversation about the early days of the rackets.

"Francis Breen saw how things were shaping very early on," Rintoul told them, "and it was clear to him that the Troubles would be a going concern for the right people. It suited the Brits because it was more or less the last real theatre for their soldiers and their spies could come over and play. For the security forces it was one big holiday camp, with real bullets. Francis also understood that the more things got blown up the more they'd have to be rebuilt. I remember him saying, 'Mark my words, now they've got the troops over here they'll be knocking down the houses and rebuilding them with roads wide enough to drive their fucking Saracens down.' He said we should get ourselves into the contracting business. 'An expandin' contractin' business, that's what we need.'"

He broke off to share the joke with Westerby, who answered with a pained grin. Rintoul looked as though he was enjoying her discomfort. He turned back to Cross and fixed him with a lazy smile.

"Well, Franny had a friend, in Birmingham I think it was, who pointed out how easy it was to get hold of tax exemption certificates or forge them."

"How did that work?" asked Westerby, trying to sound bright.

"Let's say you're running a company of decorators and

you've got ten fellows working for you. Now, the tax you collect off them you're supposed to pass on to the Revenue at the
end of the year. Of course what happens is that your decorating
company isn't around at the end of the year, and you've pocketed the tax. It was a grand racket. Instead of paying income
tax, your worker was charged a weekly contribution to his
'patrons,' which was less than the tax he would have paid. He
would also be paid at less than the rate the sub-contractor was
charging the contractor, but as there was no record of his
employment he could easily make that up by claiming unem-
ployment benefit from the DHSS. So everyone was happy."

"And it was Breen who thought all this up?"

"You'll hear people say it was the Provos but they're either
lying or misinformed. I know for a fact it was Breen because—
and I'm not on the record here—I was the man that did the
paperwork on setting up the bogus companies."

As Rintoul continued, Cross started to appreciate the sheer
extent of the racket. In cases where a sub-contractor was
straight, Breen simply put in one of his own men as the labour
provider.

"And do you know how that one works? Any businessman
can claim tax relief on extortion monies paid to paramilitaries,
can you believe that?"

Cross thought Rintoul was joking.

"I'm serious. It may not be common knowledge but the
facility exists and Francis always made sure that anyone
straight he was dealing with knew about it."

Cross realized that he had underestimated Breen's power.
Perhaps the link that he suspected between Breen and Herron
and Eddoes was not so far fetched after all.

"That's easy," said Rintoul when Cross asked if there was
any connection between them. "There's the Loyalist Club, the
Royal Bar and the Top House Bar, the Trocadero, the Lagan
Social Club and the Manhattan."

He registered Cross's surprise.

"You mean they drank in each other's bars?"

"Not at first, but Breen was in with Tommy from the start.
They used to take business meetings in bars where they
wouldn't be recognized. At first it was to stake out their respective boundaries, then—and this was probably a key moment of
the last fifteen years that won't get into the history books—

Herron asked Franny to explain the tax certificate racket, and however many times Franny went over it poor Tommy couldn't grasp it. Tommy was cunning but he wasn't blessed with a brain. So, here's Franny: 'I tell you what, Tommy, why don't you let me do it for you?' At least that's what he says to me after and laughing fit to bust a gut. So Breen moved in on the building sites in Tommy's area and in exchange Tommy was allowed to operate his 'security firm' extortion racket in nationalist areas."

With the arrival of Eddoes after Herron's death, the process became even more smoothly run, apart from one hiccough when a member of the Official IRA was shot dead by loyalists in the city centre. According to Breen's intelligence, Eddoes himself had authorized the killing in the belief that the man was a Provisional, based on information passed on to him by the RUC.

"Of course, Francis was obliged to protest and eight of them sat down in the Royal Bar in Ann Street to thrash the matter out. Francis took 'Dimple' Vallely along with him, who wore a patch on one eye, and a couple of others, whose names I forget, that went over with him to the INLA. Well, the whole thing was an insult to the memory of the dead man. Francis, from what I heard, huffed and puffed but didn't push Eddoes, and soon it was another round of drinks and business as usual. I think it was at that meeting Eddoes said that there was a problem finding bricklayers to meet a deadline that would otherwise incur a penalty payment, so Francis offered to bus in some of his own men to finish the job in time, so long as Eddoes guaranteed their safety."

"Do you know if any Brits were involved in all of this?" Cross asked, his mind still trying to take in what Rintoul had just told him.

"Ah, one such as yourself. Why an English copper in Belfast?"

Cross answered, with more feeling than he'd meant, that he wished he knew. Rintoul looked at Cross, then at Westerby. Cross sensed something between them, an embarrassment, he thought.

"I never heard of any Brit from Francis. There were a few running around at the time, cowboys mostly after a quick buck."

Rintoul suddenly looked exhausted. He seemed to fade visibly and an expression of what Cross realized later was self-disgust passed over his face.

"You'll understand what I'm telling you is all hearsay, there's probably not a word of truth in it."

"ARE YOU all right?" Cross asked Westerby afterwards.

"Yes," she mumbled. "I was just finding it very hot in there."

To her relief, Cross didn't dwell on the point.

"Let's go and see Mr. Eddoes," he said.

"How did he manage to turn himself so respectable?"

"Once he'd made enough money illegally he went legitimate, got elected as a councillor and now rides on the moral ticket. Exactly what fingers he's still got in what dirty pies no one is sure, but he has a nice holiday home up in Antrim."

They arrived to find several security vehicles parked outside Eddoes' launderette. Cross's first thought was that Eddoes had been shot.

"Shit!" he said, jumping out and leaving Westerby to park the car.

He noticed bullet marks all over the front of the building. The big plate windows were shattered and diamonds of glass lay scattered on the pavement.

Cross announced himself to the policeman in charge, who told him that the shop had been raked with gunfire from a passing car. No one had been hurt but the staff were shaken.

"Where's the owner?"

The policeman told him that Eddoes was upstairs and they were finished with him.

Cross found Eddoes angry and distracted. He wasn't sure if Eddoes even remembered him.

"I want to talk to you about Francis Breen."

Eddoes shook his head, gave Cross a blank look and denied knowing any Breen.

"Now, if you'll excuse me, I'm busy. The glass downstairs needs replacing."

He picked up the phone. Cross was angry too and he slammed his hand down on the receiver, cutting Eddoes off.

"While you and Breen were doing your pally little deals and

covering for each other people were getting murdered in the streets on your say-so."

Cross was starting to shout. Eddoes glanced nervously towards the next room, which was screened only by a thin half-partition and glass. The door was open and Cross could see a secretary sitting at her desk pretending not to listen.

"If you don't want to talk in here we can go outside," said Cross, indicating with his head towards the fire escape.

Eddoes got up reluctantly.

Standing next to him on the exposed steps with its low handrail, Cross realized what an intimidatingly big man Eddoes was. But he was more concerned by the feeling of blind rage building up in himself.

"I'll tell you about Breen," Eddoes said eventually. "We were all in the business of fund raising, so how the hell do you suppose we were meant to find money? We could hardly register ourselves as charitable organizations. And we were all more or less afraid—of the Brits, of each other and of ourselves. No one was pointing the way or telling you the right or wrong of anything. In the end it was every man for himself. We were just ordinary fellows who had scraped along until then. Tommy Herron ran a garage. The biggest thing he'd been in charge of was a petrol pump and suddenly he had an army and money was coming in from all sides, so is it surprising he puts by a bit for himself? And what would you do if some fellow from the other side came along and offered you a deal, saying he'd make sure you didn't get shot if you did the same for him? Tell me, what would you do, under the circumstances?"

"There were innocent people getting killed while this was going on."

Eddoes gave a self-conscious worldly shrug like Marlon Brando in *The Godfather*. The film would have come out not long after the Troubles began and Cross had a chilling vision of Eddoes and Breen and all the rest of them smiling in the dark and deciding that's how they should behave, for real.

"When Breen and his pals went over to the INLA, what happened then?" asked Cross.

"It's not a question of what happened then. We looked after our own and it was easier to do that if you had a foot in the enemy camp, so yes I continued to keep in touch with Breen."

"So why is the INLA trying to kill you now?"

"Because they're a lot of unprincipled bastards," said Eddoes with a bitter laugh. "It may not look like it to you but when Breen and I ran things there were rules, things you did and didn't do. Cheating the Inland Revenue was fine and good sport, and the Housing Executive racket was state money. The security firms, well, they worked. A lot of businesses asked us for protection. I remember one publican telling me that without us helping to stop robberies and looting he would have gone bust. It breaks both ways."

"And now it's drugs."

"Hard drugs and the whole thing'll blow up for the sake of a few people getting greedy. They're looking for a quick fix, these boys, that's their trouble."

Eddoes being sanctimonious on the subject of greed was a sight Cross found hard to take. There would of course be retaliation by the loyalists who would push drugs into nationalist areas.

Eddoes was warming to his subject, hectoring Cross like a public assembly. "One big jackpot and they think they'll be able to change the course of the war because they'll be able to buy all the weapons they want. They don't understand that what's gone on for fifteen years will go on for another ten because who wants it to end?"

No one had put it like that to Cross before. He asked why not.

"Because there's too much invested in the whole thing by all sides."

Cross looked at the puffiness in Eddoes' face and sensed that his real objection was that of a man who had been superseded by men more ruthless than himself. Eddoes was no longer the hard man. He'd been softened by good suits and eating too long at the table of corruption. As Cross listened to him ramble on, he realized that Eddoes was actually proud of the fact that he and his kind had made Belfast safer than mainland cities with their muggings and rapes and riots. Northern Ireland boasted the lowest crime rate in the United Kingdom.

Exposed to the likes of Eddoes and Breen, Cross realized that he was no longer sure of his own moral compass. He felt lost in a grey zone, except it wasn't as easy as that. There were so many different greys, some almost indistinguishable. Eddoes was right. It was impossible to tell how he would have reacted under the same circumstances. He liked to think that he would have resisted corruption, but where was the line to distinguish that from canniness?

"What can you tell me about an Englishman who went around with Tommy Herron?"

"There were several."

"Fair-haired. He used the name Francis Albert."

Eddoes looked startled. "What about him?"

"He was also known as Sinatra."

"He was known as Dr. Death too," Eddoes eventually said. "He used to talk of curing a man's sickness."

Willcox had also called him that. How many names did the man have? wondered Cross.

"And if I said he killed your wife, what would you say?"

Eddoes looked shocked for a moment, then shook his head. "He got himself killed a couple of years ago."

"Was this the same man that later killed Tommy Herron?"

Eddoes looked at Cross sharply and said nothing.

"Let's talk about who killed Tommy."

"In general?"

"For a start."

"The Brits. Which Brits, I'm not sure."

"Try guessing."

"The army or military intelligence. Tommy had a lot of dirt on them and would tell anyone that'd listen. There was even a war between them for a while. And Tommy knew that the Brits had had a hand in the Dublin bombings."

Cross was confused. "But Tommy was killed in September '73 and the bombings weren't until the following May."

"There was an earlier bombing in 1972."

"What happened?"

"I think about ten fellahs got killed." He looked at Cross craftily and added, as if to test him, "Those fucking Fenians deserve everything they get."

Cross was then forced to endure a loyalist diatribe against the Republic. He saw the true fanaticism of the man as he shouted on about how the majority of deaths caused in Northern Ireland were the work of those who wanted to implement the Republic's claims on Ulster. The strategy responsible for these killings came from inside the Republic, which provided a base from which many of them were carried out and a haven for the killers afterwards.

Eddoes worked himself up into such a frenzy that he started to spit. "The hands of the Dáil are covered in the blood of Ulster! What makes them think they're exempt from retribution?"

Cross despaired of ever getting back to the point. He wondered where Westerby was. She'd been a long time parking.

"Just tell me who killed Tommy on the day," he interrupted when he could take no more.

"There was a gang, run, it was rumoured, by an Englishman attached to Military Intelligence. There was Gregory Brown, who got shot later for his part in it, a couple of Englishmen and a woman. They met in a caravan near Finaghy Road North and sometimes in a flat near Connolly station near Dublin."

Cross asked how the gang operated.

"The Brits were smart. Once they'd worked out that the various organizations were keen to claim things for themselves—such and such done in the name of the Provisional Irish Republican Army—then it was very easy to blame the Provvies for things they hadn't done. As for the business with Tommy, what I heard was they used the woman and brought in a gun, who was the man you know as Francis Albert. And the way they got to Tommy was he was seeing her and they used that to set him up."

"Who was the woman?"

"I heard she was English, that's all I know."

"If she was seeing Tommy, didn't you see her around?"

"Tommy always was a back-door man and towards the end even more. There had been other attempts on his life. Seeing her was about the only time he went without a bodyguard."

"What happened to this Francis Albert after Tommy? Breen took him on, didn't he?"

Eddoes nodded.

"And he became a gun for the INLA."

Eddoes nodded again. He looked tormented and Cross took advantage to drive home his point.

"And maybe he still is and not dead at all. You're saying it was the INLA that blew your wife's brains out and I'm saying our man did. Which may come down to one and the same thing. Maybe you still all know each other. Maybe you still all do each other's dirty work."

Eddoes took a step forward, his face a taut mask.

"I'll not have any man desecrate the memory of my wife."

"Ah, come on, man. You're up to your fucking neck in shite."

Cross recognized that edge of aggression he felt just below the surface more and more these days. He was starting to welcome it. "So what's going through your head if I say it was this same man getting into his car outside your house?"

To Cross's surprise and embarrassment, tears filled Eddoes' eyes.

"I'd think it's Dr. Death come again, and that your story about him still being an INLA gun was true after all."

Cross saw Westerby walking on the concrete apron below. She looked up and seemed surprised by the sight of them standing at the top of the fire escape. Cross motioned her up.

"What are we to make of all this?" Eddoes asked in a cracked voice and Cross thought: you old ham. He was depressed by his encounter with Eddoes. Talking to him had only succeeded in blurring the picture. It was another of those incidents that summed up so much recent history: the sharp clarity of violence followed by distraction and torpor.

Westerby joined them. She pulled a face to show her exasperation at being so long. Cross raised his eyebrows to let her see that he'd found Eddoes not much use.

"Any questions for Mr. Eddoes?" Cross asked her.

Westerby cocked her head and took her time.

"There is one. Mr. Eddoes knows our man?"

"Mr. Eddoes does," said Cross.

"Well, we all know that our man has a history of violence, so I suppose what I was wondering was had Mr. Eddoes ever witnessed any of this violence first hand?"

Westerby addressed her question to Cross. Eddoes yelped like somebody had dropped a brick on his foot.

"This is outrageous," he spluttered. "Insinuating—"

"We have a number of murders," went on Westerby calmly, ignoring the interruption, "done by your man. Your wife, for a start, and several others more brutal. Be thankful he didn't do to her what he did to wee Mary Ryan. I'd say that to find anything like what he did to her you'd have to go back a long way, to the summer of 1972. You know what I'm talking about?"

Eddoes looked nervous and reluctant. Beads of sweat shone on his forehead.

"That's when this man learned his trade," Westerby went

on. "And thirteen years later he's still killing and butchering people. He killed your wife."

Eddoes spent a long time avoiding their gaze, plucking at the seams of his carefully pressed trousers.

"I told Tommy to get rid of him, that he was a head case, though most of the time you wouldn't notice the fellow. He didn't say much, but there wasn't much he missed, and he seemed harmless enough until you put a weapon in his hand."

"Perhaps you could tell me something," said Westerby, who appeared just as impatient with Eddoes as was Cross. "Was there any question of this man working for the Brits?"

"It was said in some quarters but it never stuck."

"So what was he doing in Northern Ireland?"

"I'd say he was there for the killing."

"So, tell us about your man and the Butchers."

"I know nothing about that."

Westerby sighed with impatience. "It's your wife's killer we're talking about. How many times do we have to tell you that before it sinks in?"

Eddoes finally relented and said he knew of one occasion. Two of the Butchers had been fighting among themselves and one had dropped a beer barrel on the other, killing him stone dead, and then the man that had dropped the barrel had been shot by a friend of the first, though not a member of the gang. The shooter was arrested by the loyalists and taken to one of their social clubs and sat on the stage facing the entire Belfast command, plus all the rest of the gang which was lined up in the front row.

"Anyway, before the trial could begin," said Eddoes, "your man jumped up on stage with a gun in his hand, saying, 'This guy's a fuckin' idiot.'" Everyone thought he was going to kneecap the bastard, but he put the gun to his head and blew the fellah's brains out, all over the command. People were freaking out, picking the brains off themselves. The top fellahs were so angry they made your man clean up the whole mess. And you're saying this man killed my wife."

Cross nodded.

"Then God help us all. He's an animal."

WESTERBY looked at Cross. They were in an empty Italian restaurant five minutes' walk from her flat. After Eddoes she had spent the rest of the day going through the notebook again. She had felt soiled afterwards, and unsure. Everything in her flat had suddenly looked unfamiliar, like it was not hers, and the bath she'd had had not got rid of the grime left by the day.

She realized she was drinking too much and had barely touched her food. She caught Cross looking at her a couple of times and wondered: how do married men start affairs? Were they starting one? All the men she had been out with had been single. Even then most of them had left her feeling vaguely guilty. She reminded herself that he was her senior officer, and married.

"He's not going to stop now," she said, pushing her plate aside. "He has a taste for it."

This told him nothing new, she could see that.

"But it's more than that," she went on. "I don't think he's even begun."

"What was Mary Ryan, then, and Catherine Edge?"

Cross was angry without knowing why. Her hand came to rest lightly on his. It was the first time they had touched since the car. Cross was reminded of his first impression of her and her uncomplicated gaze. He had thought her plain then.

"It's like he's waiting to prove something. The killings so far, I think they're not the real point of the exercise, and it is an exercise."

She slipped her hand away.

"Think about it," she continued. "What have we got? A run of murders that gradually connects up."

"A pattern of religion and age. Ages forty-nine to fourteen, all divisible by the number seven."

"Exactly. Seven. I think that's what he's aiming for."

"He's already killed eight."

"No, not numbers. Age. Seven-year-old children." She paused for him to work it out and added, "You wouldn't let me say it before."

He was about to protest, then thought of his own son and felt connected to the case in a way he had not before. He knew she was right but wanted to doubt it, as he did most things.

"He's established the pattern," she said. "He won't stop there."

"Maybe he'll stick at fourteen, like he did with Catherine."

He didn't believe it, even as he said it.

"No. It's the way they go down in age. It's the children he's after. I'm sure."

Her rational assessment corresponded to what he had been feeling, messily, for some time. Until now the case had had no guts, no belly, like the killer was toying with them before revealing his real purpose. These children, he knew now instinctively, would be butchered like the animals in the barn.

"Why?" he asked helplessly.

"I can't answer that. I don't know yet."

All of a sudden he did. The words fell out of him in a rush.

"It's biblical. He's biblical. He's playing God. Or Herod ordering the massacre of the Holy Innocents." He saw the pattern and hurried on, though he had no desire to give voice to the thought. "Except they were infants, they were innocent in the way no seven-year-old is."

It was her turn to feel provoked.

"And what can a child of seven be guilty of?"

"Seven is the age of reason. When the child is thought old enough to tell right from wrong. Seven is the age we start to sin."

She tried to take in what he was saying and thought back into her own childhood and saw he was right.

"Yes," she said simply. "I remember."

AFTERWARDS they walked self-consciously back towards Westerby's flat, still talking about the case, both aware that it was a way of avoiding the unstated subject that shadowed their evening. Westerby wondered what Cross was thinking and whether he was aware of the hot itch of desire in her. She wanted to tell him but stopped instead and said, "It's odd."

"What?"

"The cold-bloodedness. There's no sexual angle. That's the usual impulse, or, rather, that's the impulse I would expect to find in a case where someone is driven to kill repeatedly. And the missing underwear in the case of both Marys suggests some sort of kink."

Westerby waited until an approaching couple had passed before going on.

"There's an angle missing. I can't see what's driving him."

"Whatever sense of mission he has," said Cross.

"Yes, but there's something more, I'm sure of it."

They walked on in silence until reaching Cross's car. He got out his keys. Staying would only make things difficult, but he did not want to go home.

"Is there anywhere we can get a coffee? I should have had one in the restaurant."

"Do you want to go back there?"

"It'll be closed. What time is it?"

"Half eleven. You're welcome to come in for a while."

"No, I ought to get home."

He made no move. What an inane conversation, he thought. He wondered how long he had spent staring at the pavement.

"Did you do that thing of not walking on the cracks when you were a kid?" he said eventually.

She didn't answer and Cross shrugged helplessly and they laughed at the absurdity of two grown people standing in the street unable to make a move. Cross took her by the hand and pulled her towards him and she slipped into his arms and immediately felt like she belonged there. There was nothing awkward about it. He lifted her face towards his and kissed her, and was surprised again by the intensity of her tongue working his.

She looked at him with a wry, breathless smile and gestured with her head towards her flat. Cross nodded and followed her inside.

They stood a long time kissing on the landing outside her flat after the automatic light had switched itself off, leaving them in the dark. They moved slowly into the sitting room, still kissing.

"Shall we go to bed?" she asked.

"I don't know. I'm too nervous."

"That doesn't matter. I am too."

She started to unbutton Cross's shirt. "We can stay in here. We don't have to hurry."

They ended up lying half-naked on the rug among their gradually discarded clothes. He wanted her but was not hard enough and was not sure how to proceed. The strain of the last weeks had left him exhausted and he was content to lie with her for the moment. He wondered if she was expecting more of him but she seemed quite relaxed.

"It's funny," said Westerby. "It feels like we've already fucked. Your body feels good. Most people's bodies feel strange at first."

"Is that what you call it, fucking?"

Westerby nodded. "What's wrong with that? What do you call it?"

"I don't know. I don't suppose I call it anything. Do you like fucking?"

"Rather more than the men I end up fucking."

Cross wasn't sure if she meant him too.

"We should try and sleep," she said and he felt again that he had disappointed her.

THE SIGHT of her unself-conscious movement around the lit bedroom, which he could see from where he lay in the living room, made him realize how much he desired her—the nape of her neck, the hollow of her throat, the rise of her breast—and from the way she moved he was sure that it was the same for her. They recognized something in each other so there was no reason to be afraid or to hold back.

The gentleness and circumspection of earlier were forgotten. Clumsiness only made them more passionate: the accidental scrape of teeth; their mismatched mouths sliding away from each other to range over each other's bodies. Compared to his exhaustion of only shortly before, Cross felt tireless. When Westerby guided him between her legs he felt her slippery heat and as he slid into her she rolled on top of him with a look of sharp exhilaration. Both of them seemed surprised at their confidence, at the familiarity of it and the lack of wrong moves until she broke off suddenly with an expression of surprise and said, "You don't mind a bit of blood, do you?" Then, seeing his bewilderment, she laughed and added, "It's all right, I'm not a virgin. My period's just come on."

Cross ran his hand over her body and said, "I'm not squeamish."

"Come here," she said, aroused almost beyond control. "Come inside me again," and when she felt him hard and secure she said, "This is how I always thought it was meant to be."

Fifty

THEY spent the night heavy-limbed and drugged with sex, reluctant to give themselves up to sleep. They dozed once or twice and took a moment on waking to realize where they were. As they drifted off again one of them would pull the other back to start over.

Intimacy gave way to a natural state of unself-conscious ease in the morning. Cross did not feel guilty, as he'd expected, and Westerby moved around the apartment with easy naked grace. Her smallest gestures fascinated him. He wondered if he wasn't falling in love.

"What are you smiling at?" Westerby asked.

"Nothing," he said, still smiling. "This room reeks of sex."

"We've not finished yet."

He took a long time leaving. There was a false start after he had dressed and they'd gone back to bed. She looked sad when he went, and confessed that she dreaded returning to the business of Candlestick.

About ten minutes later she worked out what she'd been missing, while she was sitting on the lavatory putting in a Tampax, and slapped her forehead at her stupidity.

CROSS tried to busy himself catching up on reports that he was late writing up. Hargreaves was on leave, he discovered, and he was annoyed that no one had told him. He'd also spied Moffat at the far end of a corridor and taken a sharp turn into an adjacent toilet rather than face him. He still needed time.

He found it hard to concentrate. He wondered at what point they had recognized that something was at last going to happen—in the restaurant or not until they were standing outside her flat? Occasionally he brooded on the consequences of his actions. He was being unfaithful and the affair itself was a disciplinary offence, yet he didn't care. But they would have to be careful in the light of Nesbitt's premonitory caution.

AFTER work he drove to the O'Neills' to see Fiona and Matthew and took them to a nearby park with a playground. Deidre wasn't yet back, which was a relief.

He pushed them on the swings and on the carousel and made sure Fiona didn't get bumped off the see-saw when she went up in the air.

"Hang on tight."

He couldn't say when he had last spent any significant amount of time with the children. What would they remember of him in twenty years' time: a man looking under his car in the garage?

"That's enough," he said. "Listen, where would you go if you could go anywhere in the world?"

Greenland, said Matthew. Fiona opted for Africa.

"I was thinking of a holiday," said Cross. "Somewhere nearer."

"When?" asked Matthew.

"Before the end of the summer. What about France?"

"France is boring," announced Fiona.

"I'll talk to your mum."

"Why aren't you living with us?" asked Matthew.

Cross ignored the question. Matthew was quiet on the drive back to the O'Neills', while Fiona chattered happily on.

"What's the matter?" he asked Matthew, knowing perfectly well.

"Nothing," said Matthew.

Deidre was at home. Fiona announced that they were all going on holiday. Deidre expressed her delight then followed it with a cool look at Cross.

"Whose idea is this?" she asked.

"I thought it would be good to get away."

A flicker of exasperation crossed her face.

"I'll try and come up again tomorrow," he said to the children. He ruffled Matthew's hair and the boy flicked his head aside impatiently.

* * *

THEY ate at the Italian restaurant and again were the only diners. Cross wondered how the place kept going, even with its concession to the Northern Irish taste for chips with everything, spaghetti included.

Westerby drew tramlines on the tablecloth with her fork, talking quietly about what she had worked out, pausing to look up at Cross. She seemed withdrawn and serious.

"It was staring me in the face and I didn't see it," she said. "It's been staring me in the face for days."

She went on to say that her previous assessment of the murders happening around the turn of the month was nearly right, but she had been working to the calendar month, which was wrong.

"I thought he'd broken the pattern with Catherine Edge by killing her too early, but he hadn't. It fits."

She got out a piece of paper on which she had already written out the dates. Cross glanced over them—the first five days of February and March, 29 March to 2 April, 26 to 30 April, 24 to 28 May, 21 to 25 June, 19 to 23 July.

He looked at Westerby and raised his eyebrows inquiringly.

"What do you know about the menstrual cycle?" she asked.

Cross frowned, not able to see the point. "It's monthly, but I don't—"

"Menstruation is governed by the lunar cycle—"

"How do you know he's not killing according to the moon?"

"Because it's not as simple as that."

He apologized for interrupting and told her to go on.

"It's a twenty-eight-day cycle that starts with the first day of bleeding. The bleeding lasts several days. Five is about normal."

"And you're saying these dates fit a cycle?"

Westerby nodded. "I think our man has a woman in the background. And is killing according to her cycle."

"And she knows?"

"Totally unaware, I'd say. Don't forget he's excellent at deception, but then most men are." She smiled hastily and added, "I didn't mean you."

Cross smiled back while he privately agreed. A part of him relished secrecy and duplicity, even the deception he was enjoying now at Deidre's expense. He frowned and looked at the details again.

"So each murder occurs during the woman's period?"

Westerby nodded.

"Is it that predictable?" he asked.

"If she's regular. Then these dates all fall within the first five days of a new cycle. This is what I meant yesterday when I thought there was some trigger missing. During these periods he's driven to kill."

"Why?" asked Cross.

"A lot of men—and some religions—regard women as taboo when they're menstruating. This is not putting you off, is it?" she asked cheerfully.

She put her hand under the table and ran it up his leg.

"Obviously not," she said with a smile. "Let's get the bill."

Fifty-one

CROSS called Deidre from his office to say that he was temporarily staying elsewhere as he thought the house was being watched. She didn't ask for his number. While relations between them had never been cooler, they still talked about a holiday as though everything was perfectly normal.

He asked Westerby for a short dossier providing a brief biography of their killer, a psychological profile, noting the fact that he killed according to the lunar calendar.

"Do you want me to put the exact reason?"

"No. Keep it as straight as possible, but say that we can correctly predict when the next murder will happen. Also list his aliases and a sentence or two on likely motive."

"Which is?"

"A revelation." Cross felt a chill settle on him. "He wants to show us something so monstrous that the events of the past fifteen years will pale by comparison."

"Is this for Moffat?" she asked.

"Yes. We don't have any other choice."

Moffat was untrustworthy and would sacrifice them both if it suited, Cross knew that. Moffat operated on a strictly need-to-know basis, which for Cross meant telling him next to nothing. More personally, he had systematically opposed the theory and evidence of linked killings and, in a further denial, had framed Willcox with two of the murders. But it was Cross's duty as a policeman to see the murderer caught, and the notebook was incontrovertible proof of the multiple killings. He really had no choice except to go to Moffat. Even if it meant supping with the devil.

MOFFAT was at languid ease, one Chelsea boot on his desk. Cross could not remember the last time he'd seen Chelsea boots. He flicked through Westerby's report—given to him several hours before the meeting.

"Well," he said, his drawl more pronounced than usual, "you have rather shown us up."

Cross said nothing, suspecting that Moffat's capitulation was just another tactic.

"OK, let's cut to the chase, as our American friends would say," said Moffat, swinging his foot off his desk and leaning forward, all eagerness and co-operation. "What's your assessment of this man? Is he a loner or do you think he's still being run?"

"I don't know enough yet to answer that question, but your deliberate arrest of Willcox suggests to me that our killer has connections you want kept quiet."

Moffat looked stung, but kept his temper and told Cross to go on.

"The man is killing for a reason, not just for gratification. It's important somehow, for him, that the killings weren't seen to be connected at first, but later they were, perhaps to show how stupid we are, like he's saying, 'Look, all these killings are going on under your noses and you didn't even realize, and, while we're about it, there are all these other things going on you don't know about either.' So why did you arrest Willcox?"

"Is this a conversation you want to have?" said Moffat indifferently.

Cross stared at Moffat until he turned away and eventually said, "It's not a very edifying story. Not much of what I do is."

Then he looked up and held Cross's eye. Cross, in spite of

his instinctive suspicion, felt that Moffat wanted to be frank, or was he a better actor than he gave him credit for?

"Northern Ireland actually works pretty well, and the opposing bits slot together better than you might suppose. I know that sounds cynical, but the system operates on what Reginald Maudling called an acceptable level of violence."

"You mean deals are made," said Cross, thinking of Eddoes and Breen and all the rest.

Moffat shrugged. "A French general once said that all great battles are won and lost in the interstices of staff maps. Are you a student of military history?"

Fuck off, thought Cross. "I know things go on in the interstices or whatever you want to call them. But I would stress that in this case the seriousness of the crime and the intention to kill again override any other consideration."

"Of course." Moffat nodded gravely and sighed. "Except this couldn't have come at a worse time."

"Could it have come at a better time?" Cross asked sarcastically.

"Relatively, yes. The Prots are as windy as hell at the moment. They're scared that Westminster's going to sell them out. It's happened before, of course. Churchill offered the Province to the South during the war in exchange for the Republic coming in with the Allies. Did you know that?"

"De Valera refused."

"Well, it nearly happened again in 1974 and now the Prots are on the wobble because of the new Dublin agreement that is due to be signed in November."

"What's this to do with our man?"

Moffat ignored the question. "What do you know about Stalker?"

Cross said that he knew what everyone else knew. Stalker had been invited over from England to conduct an investigation into allegations that the police had deliberately set out to murder IRA terrorists.

Moffat shrugged. "Which they did."

"And Stalker insists on saying so and publishing the results, regardless of whose toes he treads on. Which is not quite the usual whitewash job everyone was expecting."

"God preserve us from moral crusaders."

"I can see Stalker's point."

Moffat grunted. "I thought you might."

He yawned theatrically to underline his impatience at Cross's stolid defence.

"If we were officially at war with the IRA it'd be a lot easier, but we're not," he went on, "so the rules are fluid, and with so much of our work being of necessity undercover the truth is the first victim in all of this. It is necessary to lie. This is not a moral issue, it's a simple fact. Pretence, deception, stealth, without these none of the parties involved would be able to function. Were RUC officers trained by the SAS to carry out lethal ambushes, what do you think?"

"It doesn't matter what I think," said Cross. "What has this got to do with Willcox?"

Moffat, stung by Cross's bluntness, became aggressive. "I'll tell you what it has to do with Willcox. We are politically at a very delicate time and clumsy policemen stamping around in their size-twelve boots and taking the lid off things that are supposed to stay covered is not what's needed. Stalker will submit his interim report shortly and it will be highly critical of the RUC and Special Branch. What do you think'll happen? I'll tell you. It'll get sat on because the last thing anyone needs with this agreement coming up is some big political stink. Or the news that a multiple killer is running rings round us and killing for some purpose which he'll announce once he feels we've made fools enough of ourselves. Willcox was arrested as a preemptive measure."

Moffat got up before Cross could say anything and went over to the window. The view was of a rainy car park. "Fucking awful weather you get in this country. How long have you been over here?"

Cross told him thirteen years.

"I don't know how you stick it. Jolly friendly people, beautiful countryside and all that, but there's something about the place. It's like Leicester with guns."

Cross didn't laugh. He was being led off the subject.

"Why did Willcox confess?"

Moffat looked weary. "One of the things that's bloody frustrating about this job is remembering what you can and can't tell people. Need-to-know and all that. Public school, were you?"

Cross shook his head, irritated by the question, but more annoyed with himself for the feeling of inferiority it provoked.

"Smut and secrecy are no fun unless they're shared. I dare say you can see that."

Moffat sat down again and swung both feet up on the desk, and paused. For an uncomfortable moment Cross thought he was about to tell a dirty joke.

"All right, between you and me, a confidence not to be repeated. Willcox was easy-peasy, and put squarely in the frame because of Mary Ryan being killed in his lock-up. Which suggests that her killer knew Willcox. I'd go one step further and say that using the lock-up was deliberate mischief against Willcox. But I thought we could turn that to our advantage—using Willcox to trump the killer, by claiming two of his murders—and stinging him into making a slip."

"So you took the suggestion of multiple murder seriously from the start."

"Oh yes. I can't afford not to."

"In spite of what you told me."

"We needed more proof. I thought that denying your theory might drive you to prove it all the harder. Sound move, as it turned out." Moffat gave a conspiratorial grin. "Don't worry. We're both on the same side in the end."

"And you framed Willcox with the bradawl from Berrigan's farm because Mary Ryan had the same blood group as found on the bradawl."

Moffat shrugged and grinned again, and Cross saw a trace of the caught-out schoolboy quite without remorse. Cross felt a spasm of self-loathing at being so eagerly drawn into Moffat's intrigue. He asked why Willcox had agreed to confess.

"Ah, that's where it gets interesting," said Moffat, swinging his feet off the desk. "I don't know whether I'm offending your sensibilities by saying that Willcox is of as much value to anyone as used arse paper and no one would mourn his removal—least of all his wife, if you read what he did to her. Don't you find this country still pretty fucking barbaric at times?"

Cross wondered if Moffat ever considered that it was partly because of men like himself.

"The man's an animal," Moffat went on. "You'll know from his file that he was suspected of being involved in that nasty

Shankill stuff, though nothing stuck. Well, we have a super-grass who's prepared to add Willcox's name to the list of Butchers. Confronted by this and the prospect of going down for life, Willcox did a deal."

"What sort of deal is confessing to two murders? He'd be down for the same amount of time."

Moffat fiddled with a pencil and avoided looking at Cross. "The deal is that after a couple of years he'd go missing in the system and be quietly released."

Seeing the look of disgust on his face, Moffat held up a hand in apology.

"Don't worry. This is not a common occurrence. In fact, I know of only one other case of it happening. But the way I see it, any time that Willcox spends away is a bonus all round."

Cross spent the rest of the meeting in a daze. He agreed to report directly to Moffat and that Westerby should continue building a profile of the killer. In the absence of any easily accessible computers in the barracks, Moffat pointed out that it might be easier for her to continue working from home.

"I could get her clearance, but she'd be stuck somewhere very hush-hush and remote."

"What about our man calling when she's not in the office?"

"Does he call direct or through the switchboard?"

"Switchboard, I think. He calls her Jill."

"So he'd ask for Jill when nobody else would?"

Cross nodded and Moffat said, "I'll talk to the telephone people and get them to divert any calls for Jill to her home. Shouldn't be too difficult."

Moffat added that he would put a team on to following up the basement flat.

"I'd rather have known about it sooner," said Moffat. This was his only mild reproof during the meeting. "I'd prefer to have some people I know go through it, if that's all right with you."

"As long as I have access to anything found there."

"Of course. Perhaps you could put together a team to resift old leads, as well as trying to identify the source of the killer's information. What is there so far?"

"All the obvious things," replied Cross. "We thought he might have access to the central computer or market research files, credit card data. It's a question of where you start, and we're so short handed. I even wondered about TV rentals. The stuff you have to put on their forms is unbelievable."

The truth was Cross hardly knew *where* to start. Besides, if Candlestick was being leaked or fed the information in some way he'd never get to the bottom of it. But he wasn't going to tell Moffat about that.

"I'll need to talk to Willcox again."

"Fine," said Moffat airily, then more keenly, "why?"

"Willcox saw Candlestick at the time of Tommy Herron's murder—"

"What did you say?"

"At the time of Tommy Herron's—"

"You used a name."

"Candlestick."

"Yes. Where did that come from?"

"He used it to Westerby. From the old rhyme, I suppose, the butcher, the baker and the candlestick maker—"

"But it's not in the file."

"Yes, it is," said Cross.

Moffat became more animated than at any other time in the meeting. He found the relevant page, then made a note in the margin. Cross recognized the word Candlestick upside down. He watched Moffat underline it three times while he asked why he wanted to talk to Willcox.

"Mary Ryan was mutilated, so was Breen. The Butchers cut their victims too, and we know our man was around then. What I'd like to know is how he spent the summer of 1972."

Cross sent out for a bottle of Scotch, told the attending constable to leave them and reconfirmed that anything Willcox said was off the record. Willcox took a couple of large swigs of whisky, pondered Cross's request and then took him through the whole appalling story.

"There was a place on Downing Street and everybody knew that on Friday and Saturday nights the UVF killed Taigs there. And the cops knew it too—every Friday and Saturday night, and then the stiffs were dumped in the river and every Saturday morning the peelers would send a patrol to fish them out, but they never patrolled Downing Street of a Friday or Saturday night. And you can make what you like of that."

He scribbled his cigarette out in the ashtray, a proud witness of the violence he'd seen and the violence administered.

"So you're saying this was widely known at the time," said Cross slowly.

"Well enough for the cops to issue a statement saying that any Taig in his right mind shouldn't walk certain streets after dark. Milford Street. Union Street. Clifton Street. Up the Antrim Road and the Oldpark."

"And the Englishman you told me about?"

"Now there's one hard cunt."

"He was there, wasn't he?"

Willcox took a contemplative swig from his glass, nodded, lit another cigarette, and gave a harsh, appreciative laugh.

"He was doing this Fenian bastard, who would have been one of the first, and he breaks off in the middle and says, 'Get Mr. Sheehan a drink, he deserves one,' and fuck me if we don't all stand around knocking it back until he gets on with the digging again. And there was another he crucified to the wall."

"Crucified?"

"Drove a couple of knives through his hands, and all the time the Stones playing in the background. He had a little dance by then, like a shuffle he used to do."

Cross felt he was hardly guessing when he said, " 'Sympathy for the Devil.' "

"Yeah," said Willcox with a warm, cracked smile. "That's the one. *Please allow me to introduce myself, I'm a man of wealth and taste.*"

The bottle was half empty and Willcox settled, the meat of him spread comfortably in his seat, and the position of his cigarettes and ashtray familiar enough by then for him to reach both without looking.

"Brilliant," said Willcox, lost in reverie.

Cross couldn't help himself when he asked if any of them thought they were doing anything wrong.

Willcox shrugged. "Nah. There's always been hardmen in Belfast."

He pointed to the city's tradition of bare-knuckle fighting, defunct since the start of the Troubles. Cross remembered stories of local champions knocking each other stupid on bits of city wasteground, cheered on by a crowd.

"But they fought each other on equal terms," said Cross.

"The Taigs weren't fighting us on equal terms. But after we hit back they didn't go out at night without thinking twice. They respected us."

There was a long silence in which Cross tried to control his emotions. He wanted to see Willcox damaged in return for all the unthinking pain he'd caused.

The moment passed, unnoticed by Willcox, who continued to reminisce unprompted and gradually Cross, in spite of his revulsion, found himself lulled by Willcox's matter-of-fact, boozy account of events: the-then-we-did-that-and-then-he-did-that. Willcox seemed grateful for the opportunity to talk, not to unburden any guilt, but because he liked the audience.

"I wasn't there when they did the one that got them caught, and your man had moved on too by then. I don't know why that cunt didn't die. They did a really first-class job on the boy. Slit his wrists up the ways, defleshed his arms, cut his throat and reversed the car over him a couple of times. One of the fellows took his shoelaces off and ties them round the Taig's throat and uses a stick to twist them tight, like the Spanish, and someone else has this big stick with a six-inch nail and is whacking him on the head with that. Jesus, it was like a fucking cartoon. That's why they usually gave them a head job too, just to make sure: they don't talk again if you put a bullet in their ear. I don't know why nobody did that time. It would have saved them a lot of grief. I tell you it really freaked the Taigs out, hearing of these bodies that had been shot and had their throats cut. They couldn't figure that out at all!"

Willcox grinned drunkenly at Cross, who realized with a jolt that Willcox was nostalgic for this barbarism. It was the one event that invested his life with any significance. Cross hurried him on and asked about the Englishman again.

"There was him and Baker and several others, but they were the main two. Baker fucked off back to England soon after and gave himself up and tried to do a deal and name a lot of UVF fellows, but the judge saw him for the cunt he was and banged him up for life."

Talking of Baker, Willcox showed a solitary moment of self-awareness, saying that it didn't take a hardman to frighten people. Anybody could do it. You could terrorize your next-door neighbour if you had a hammer in your hand. His point—so far as Cross could grasp, because the alcohol was turning

Willcox incoherent—was that on the whole none of them was a hardman by nature. Willcox became increasingly maudlin, revealing glimpses of a softer side, a cruel sentimental streak that made his hardness all the more frightening.

"Maybe I'm going beyond the normal awareness in this situation, but there are things I picked up over the years. We didn't know what psychological warfare was, we just did it. Couldn't even spell our own names at the time, didn't even know what the terms were."

"Who taught you?"

"Well, it wasn't Baker. He'd gone broody by then, so that leaves your man."

"Who taught you to torture and murder Taigs?" Cross asked carefully.

"Fuck it, man!" Willcox banged his fist on the table, making Cross jump. "The Brits were running around shooting Protestants and they were supposed to be our friends, pretendin' they were IRA so we'd get all charged up and start our own war with the Taigs."

Overlapping images suddenly snapped into focus and Cross glimpsed how everything ultimately linked up, not in a conspiratorial sense but as a series of initiated, random connections, a sequence of undercover moves and precautionary measures whose outcome could only be guessed at. The events of the past months had taught him one thing: to look not just at the event but at the shadow of that event, and to seek out the hidden hand. In the case of the Shankill killings, Candlestick was the shadow.

He pushed Willcox on Candlestick's role but the drink had almost done for him and the gaps in his speech grew longer.

"Are you seeing the point in all of this?" Willcox finally said with a rush. "Your man was the one that started all this, taught them how. They were just a bunch of blouses before then— some of them hard enough, like Lenny Murphy—but scared shitless when it came down to it because they thought an army of big Fenian fuckers was going to walk down the Shankill Road and bugger them all to kingdom come. Then your man went out and dragged the first Taig off the street. But it was for a reason—that's what we didn't see, like it was to teach fellers like Lenny and what a headcase he turned out. Hardman numero uno. And where did he learn it from? Your man. It was your man who said to Lenny and I was there and I heard him as sure as I'm sitting here now; here's your man, all quiet and conspiratorial like: 'Why don't you slit the little fucker's throat before you shoot him, seeing how you're a master butcher?' Master butcher! Lenny worked in a fuckin' hardware store and was as fuckin' polite as they come to the old girls on the other side of the counter. And McCabe, another hardman. Who taught him? McCabe had knocked a Catholic on the head and bundled him into a black taxi and adjourned to a local pub and was drinking, and he didn't have a clue what to do until your man turns up and then they nearly come to blows when he calls McCabe a yellow bastard. So here's McCabe all of a sudden: 'Fuck it, I'm a hardman.' And he's all for cutting off this Taig's head and sticking it up on one of the fences in New Lodge. And after that it was just a question of whispering with them, like he was prompting. He said to Lenny: 'You're a fucking artist. When they start handing out prizes for this, you're top of the class.' Are you getting this? I'm saying he was the one who turned us on. Wound us up and watched us go, then fucked off to whatever he had to do next."

The hidden hand. "When did you learn he was working for the British?"

Willcox ignored the question and instead said, "And what the fuck does that tell you?"

"That the killings were in some way sanctioned."

"I said that right at the start! The whole fucking deal was about the Brits wanting us turned into some fuckin' army and I'd say with this Shankill thing someone wanted a reign of terror. I know they did because I heard Tommy Herron say it."

"Who did?"

"You're daft to even want an answer. Who tells the man who tells the man who tells the man? But I'll say one thing about your man. He was the best. Lenny and McCabe, that was just flattery telling them they were good. But your man—he made those Taigs sing like they were in an opera, and close to the end it was like him and the Taig were at one with each other. Compared to all the other shit and confusion, I don't know—it was like a fucking miracle of clarity hearing some Taig make his last confession at the hands of a master."

Willcox grinned blearily, leant his head on his hands, slumped forward on to the table and began to weep.

Fifty-two

Belfast, May 1972

"I KNOW nothing about it, for God's sake! I'm just an ordinary fellow, like the next man," squeaked Sheehan.

"Talk, you Fenian fuck," yelled a voice in the crowd.

Candlestick pummelled away at Sheehan with a mounting frenzy. This was directed less towards his hopeless victim, squealing his high-pitched squeal but trying to stay brave in the hope that Candlestick would keep his promise to spare him, than at the baying mob, watching and doing nothing. *Fuckers fuckers fuckers,* he thought, his fists seeking out the tender parts of Sheehan's body—soft unmuscled gut and genitals beneath. There were sick jokes when Candlestick kicked him in the balls, about how the Taig'd not be giving his missus one that night, to which the reply came that it was just as well because they bred like rabbits. Candlestick found the raucous banter pathetic.

He broke off for a drink. Men crowded round offering to buy it for him while Sheehan lay ignored.

"Just a glass of water from the tap," said Candlestick to the barman. The others swilled their beer while Candlestick stood silently and contemplated his work. Baker was still saying nothing, brooding, upstaged.

"Give Mr. Sheehan a drink, if he wants one," Candlestick said to the barman. "He deserves it."

Sheehan took a Guinness and held it up in salute to Candlestick, who hated the presumption of the gesture.

He took the glass after Sheehan had finished and rammed it into his head. Sheehan threw his hands up and buckled sideways, blood flowing freely. Candlestick broke away from him

and confronted the crowd. It would only work if everyone was
a party to the violence.

"Your turn," he said to a lardy youth called Willcox who
wouldn't look at him. The crowd was drawing back, reluctant
to be involved, when Candlestick spotted a young man he
knew only as Lenny and recognized the glint in his eye.
Candlestick beckoned silently. Lenny stepped forward and hit
Sheehan with an uppercut that snapped his head back. He told
Lenny to select others.

"Make them do it, even if they don't want to, starting with
that fat cunt Willcox."

They shuffled forward to take their turn while Candlestick
stopped for a drink. He allowed himself a lager. He felt the
tense and inarticulate rage inside him appeased. He noted
Willcox coming back for a second helping, grunting with pleasure as he laid into Sheehan.

THE FINE line between beating and torture was not crossed
until Sheehan, pressed to reveal information that he did not
possess, suddenly became defiant. Candlestick determined to
break him, in spirit and in body. He split matchsticks, drove
them under his fingernails, then set them alight, exalting in the
mounting terror on the man's face. Sheehan protested his innocence, clinging to the shreds of his new bravery. Candlestick
burned his flesh with cigarettes, leaving tarry scars on the soles
of his feet and hands. He did his tongue next, while Baker
yanked his mouth open and Sheehan jumped and squirmed like
a man with a thousand volts put through him. The crowd
roared approval and drummed out a deadly tattoo with its feet.
Still he did not talk. How could he, thought Candlestick, he's
got nothing to say.

The knife had an eight-inch blade and was as sharp as a
razor. Two men held Sheehan down while Candlestick cut the
fabric of Sheehan's grimy shirt and grey vest, to reveal white,
sunless flesh. He held the knife point to Sheehan's throat, to the
hollow at the base he found so desirable in women. Sheehan
held still, knowing that if he squirmed the knife would puncture him. Candlestick drew it in a delicate line down over the
man's thorax and abdomen, then across from nipple to nipple,
cuts so graceful that Sheehan hardly felt them. The cross was
almost invisible to the eye until the blood came in pearly drops.

Sheehan looked down, watching the blood start to flow freely, with a look of puzzlement. Then he started crying and began to name names, and Candlestick saw that it was because he had not hurt him in this instance that he had broken him. Had he smashed his fingers or yanked out a tooth, Sheehan might have resisted longer, but he was undone by delicacy.

He named republican families around the Antrim Road and the ones with members in the Provisionals. Candlestick knew he was making up this litany, singing for his life with no thought of the consequences. Pulling more names out of Sheehan, he was reminded of gutting an animal, the swift pull of slippery membrane as he dragged it free of its casing. As he looked into Sheehan's pain-clouded eye, he felt the first stirrings of something familiar from his childhood, the same sense of power and control he had over trapped animals, except now he could talk to the victim and make him answer and drum into him more than just dumb fear. It was the split second beyond terror that he searched for, when the void was glimpsed. He found it in Sheehan and after that they both knew that he was going to die.

This was the exact moment he had been looking for all his life. He saw that now.

Sheehan started to say the Hail Mary, unwisely, given the company. Lenny stepped forward and kicked him in the head, saying that they wanted none of his idolatry. Sheehan groaned and asked for a priest and Lenny, who had taken over now that Candlestick was done, had a raucous time extracting a last confession.

"You're not going to heaven until you tell us everything, until you've puked it all up. What about wanking, have you been doing any of that? Mr. Paddy Bogwog."

The rest of the men roared their approval, joining in with cheerful obscenities. Candlestick left them to their demented cabaret and slipped away.

He knew that after Sheehan nothing would be the same again. He had found his vocation. He looked up at the velvet sky and, remembering his mother, who had been a nurse for a while, he whispered, "I am the contagion."

Fifty-three

WESTERBY took a day to transcribe Cross's interview with Baker, which he had flown back to England for. Baker was in a low-security prison near Manchester and eager to air his grievances. But there had been a deal attached to the meeting. In exchange, Cross had to agree to write on his behalf to a politician with well-publicized anti-establishment views. There was always a deal, Cross thought ruefully on the flight home.

He went straight to Westerby's flat from the airport. "I missed you," he said simply.

His head was still reeling from Baker's pedantic verbal barrage. No question had had a straight answer, so much so that by the time he was finished Cross had forgotten the question. Baker had also found God.

Cross rolled his eyes when Westerby asked how it had gone. Later on, she listened to him on the phone trying to sort out someone to transcribe the interview.

"Would you believe it?" he said. "There's no one free until Thursday. And this has priority!"

It was then that she had offered to do it herself. In one way she didn't mind because she thought she might catch something in Baker's voice that would be missing in a transcript. But it struck her as pretty daft, given the pressure they were under, that no stenographer was available.

She had missed Cross too. She was surprised at the speed of their intimacy, by its variety and by some of the things she had said in the heat of the moment, surprised too that she was not more shocked afterwards. "Kiss me there. Do it that way." She'd never talked like that to anyone before.

It could not last, of course, but when he was there or thereabouts, she could put the hopelessness out of her mind.

Cross sensed her depression. She insisted nothing was wrong. Eventually she told him that Martin had called and wanted the computer back.

"We haven't talked about Martin," said Westerby. "Martin's my fiancé, technically."

"Does Martin know about us?" asked Cross.

"Yes and no. Yes, he knows I'm having doubts and I've met someone else. No, he doesn't know who. I've just asked for time on my own."

"What's the problem with the computer? We'll get another."

"It's a prototype. It shouldn't even be here. I don't know how seriously he needs it, but he knows I'm using it so asking for it back is a way of getting at me."

Cross laughed. "Well, we'll requisition it."

Westerby sighed. "I'm serious. This whole thing is ridiculous. We've no back-up, whatever Moffat's promised. A big murder case on the mainland would be drawing on up to two hundred and fifty officers and what have we got? The two of us now Hargreaves is on leave and we can't get a secretary to do some fucking transcript that might be the difference between a life and a death." Westerby started to weep bitter tears of frustration. "Oh, it's all so hopeless."

"No, it's not," said Cross, taking her in his arms.

"It's all so fucking hopeless. *This* and *that*."

"What's this?"

"This, us. I used to think about you so much, all the time, telling myself how stupid it was and no way was I going to get involved and all the same having these pathetic fantasies—like some schoolgirl crush—and telling myself that if I could just have a night, or two, then I'd be happy. Do you remember after Molly Connors, when we had to stay in the same room?"

Cross smiled. "How could I forget?"

Westerby picked at a loose thread in Cross's jacket, to hide her embarrassment. "I remember thinking, 'Now I've got you.' And when you came up I wasn't asleep, of course. I was lying there paralysed, praying you'd come to my bed or that I'd have the courage to get into yours."

She sniffed and looked at him, trying to smile and make light of what she'd just said. "I wish I had because I can tell you that bloody put-u-up was as hard as hell."

He took her to bed, knowing, like her, that binding themselves together was their only fragile defence against their own doubt and the hostilities of the outside world. Sometimes her fierce intensity unnerved him. He had not encountered such physical directness before and nor had anyone taken such an open interest in his body. Jealousy of past lovers not yet talked about led him to ask where she had learned such frankness and she answered, "I didn't. With you I know what to do."

AFTERWARDS they got dressed and went through the Baker tape. Baker was in effect the first supergrass. He had tried to get himself an immunity deal by offering the RUC inside knowledge of loyalist paramilitary organizations and a list of killings carried out. He had later appeared in court, a Crown witness in a case against other loyalist assassins, but his evidence was dismissed as unreliable. Unreliable was the right word for Baker, Cross thought.

"Have you noticed how he keeps trying to shift the blame?" Westerby asked.

"What do you mean?"

"Well, he admits enough—he admits to killing—but it's always somebody else's fault. Everything gets turned into a conspiracy. The RUC provide the guns to the UDA that get used for assassinations. Dah-de-dah-de-dah. Was that how he struck you?"

Cross shrugged. "At first he was just a man in grey overalls. Though, yes. When he started talking it was like he was holding all the cards, so at first you think, Christ, I've stumbled on it, here it all is. Look at what he said about Kincora."

Baker's argument linked senior RUC officers with prominent loyalist officials through shared membership of the same Masonic Orange Lodges. The history of both organizations was therefore one of tangled involvement. According to Baker, the RUC investigation into the Kincora scandal had uncovered this collusion.

Cross said, "Apparently the RUC turned up a lot of top names—loyalists and English civil servants—involved in a vice ring that used boys from the home."

"But no one's been prosecuted." She looked at Cross in surprise. "What are you doing?"

"Combining work and pleasure." He was undoing her shirt.

"The findings were sat on and the file has conveniently disappeared, according to Baker. Another conspiracy."

"But if anyone starts dishing dirt on the RUC—"

"The file'll reappear, and either there'll be another hush-up or a lot more dirty linen washed in public."

"Do you believe Baker?" asked Westerby.

"The file's gone, I checked that, and what he said may be true, but that's not the point—"

She trembled as Cross traced a line up the inside of her thigh with his nail until he reached the soft flesh at the join.

"The point is," she said, "he could only have stitched this lot together through guesswork and gossip."

"A man like Baker was a fairly low-level operative. He would not have been in possession of hard information. He didn't even really know who he was working for."

"So he needs to place himself in the centre of a large conspiracy to give some consequence to his own actions."

She squirmed into a better position, lifting one leg and draping it over Cross's shoulder, and abandoned herself to his tongue as it made its exploratory journey along the line of, and then worked its way past the elastic of—"What do you call these, knickers or panties?" he asked, and she told him knickers. "Quite. Anyway, Baker's found God, which rather colours what he says. Lots of technical remorse and a conspiracy that he's had a dozen years to sit and dream up."

"You didn't take much to our Mr. Baker, then." She moaned as Cross's mouth moved across the hard bone of her pubis and down.

"I thought he was a waste of time."

Westerby grabbed his hair with both hands, no longer able to contain herself. "Lick me," she said.

THEY stayed up too late talking. Westerby confided that she was increasingly sure Candlestick was acting alone, not killing to order. She thought so because of the overwhelming sense of isolation surrounding him.

"But that would have always been the case to some extent," said Cross.

"I think he slipped his collar."

"When he blew up the car making it look like he was in it?"

"Perhaps all those years of secrecy grew too much—always

having to pretend, always having to remember to pretend. Think of the weight of that. Wouldn't most of us buckle?"

Cross couldn't help applying her remark to them. Reluctantly he found himself wondering what the damage of their affair would be. There was no question of it being anything other than secret.

"So you think he's the only free agent in all of this, the only independent operator?"

Westerby, puzzled by his tone, said, "You sound very bitter."

"I don't mean to. It's just—I don't know—to do with kidding myself."

"About us."

"No, not about us." Yes, that too, he thought, before hurrying on. "About what I used to believe, about how things worked and how it was possible to do your job properly, and how there were still distinctions between right and wrong. Now I wonder if there isn't anyone who isn't cutting deals with the other side. Are we the only ones not in on it?"

He told her about Moffat's deal with Willcox.

"So there's this pretty little daisy chain of deals and they look at you in astonishment if you express any surprise. And somewhere in the middle is this solitary beast, waiting at the centre of the maze and pretending to be both God and the devil, and I'm frightened for the whole thing and I'm scared for us."

IN SPITE of his tiredness, Cross woke early, his mind full of the case. He watched Westerby sleeping. She lay on her front, face towards him, lips parted. Her hair looked blown about. He admired the plane of her back, the creaminess of her skin and tried to remember what had disturbed him, but lulled by the steady rhythm of her breathing he found himself drifting off again, until some half-thought jerked him back. After it had happened several times, Cross identified what it was.

Back in January during his trip to the Republic the Garda officer McCarthy had described how the Dublin bombings of 1974 had led to the collapse of an agreement between Westminster and Dublin over the North. Eleven years on, he wondered, and what had changed? They were still trying to come to another version of the same agreement.

What puzzled him was the dual role of the British. The British had been a party to the agreement but also had wrecked it with the bombings—if McCarthy's claim was to be believed. Did that mean the Brits were playing Dublin for suckers?

Cross had always assumed that the British—for all their surface rivalry—ultimately co-operated and worked towards the same end.

He frowned. But what if they didn't, just as McMahon had once told him? What if the whole thing was more complicated than anyone would admit? He remembered someone saying that the problem with the Ulster Protestants was that they'd become Irishized, which he took to mean a grand inability to sort out one's own problems; muddled, in a word. Perhaps the Brits that came over became muddled too. God knows, everything else was a mess.

Let's say, for the sake of argument, thought Cross, that the Brits are just as riven with factions and splinter groups as the republicans or loyalists. You only had to look at the RUC's often troubled alliance with the army and the security forces for evidence of that. What he had not yet done was apply that knowledge to this case.

The next question he asked required a leap of the imagination and he wasn't sure whether to feel pleased or afraid by it. *What if the secret war going on in Northern Ireland—and it was largely secret—was mirrored by another, even more secret one, involving different British factions in a struggle that went beyond accepted rivalry?*

Cross had no idea who precisely these people were. There was the army with its several intelligence networks and Special Branch, and somewhere out in the murk beyond them were MI5 and MI6, with whom Cross had had no dealings, unless Moffat was MI5.

Go back to May 1974, he told himself.

There had been an agreement between the governments of Britain and the Irish Republic in the making and it had been broken by force, and the Brits had had a hand in both. This agreement had angered Ulster Protestants and a general strike, which the British had secretly orchestrated, was the effective response.

Left hand. Right hand. Does the left hand know what the right is doing and vice versa?

So there had to be at least two British factions: one

pro-Dublin *(Left Hand)* and another pro-loyalist with paramilitary connections *(Right Hand)*.

May was also the month of the Heatherington sting. If Cross had to guess whether the pro- or anti-republican faction was behind it he would have to opt for the former *(Left Hand)*. Although the operation was designed to destabilize the Provisionals, it also, according to McMahon, softened them up for negotiation. And somewhere, at a tangent and in the margins, his own investigation shaded into that story because in the same month Candlestick made his move, at someone's bidding *(Left or Right Hand?)*, crossing the divide from the loyalist side to the republican.

Cross sighed and got up and busied himself making coffee. Outside was a clear day with a brilliant blue sky. It would be autumn soon. Perhaps it was already. Westerby's coffee pot was unfamiliar and he wasn't sure how many spoons to use and made it too strong and had to dilute it. He thought: *why have anyone defect to the Officials by 1974?* They were almost dead in the water by then. The Officials had called a ceasefire since 1972.

Cross turned his attention to the coffee. Foul. He decided to start over again. *Who benefits?* he wondered.

There was condensation on the window from the kettle and on it he wrote a quick résumé under the headings *Left* and *Right Hand*. The strike went in the second column, the 1975 ceasefire in the first.

Cross was drawn again to the coincidence and convenience of the Officials splitting, just as a ceasefire was being negotiated with the Provisionals, then being drawn into a debilitating civil war that eventually involved the Provisionals too. For most of 1975 it seemed that the republicans had nothing better to do than fight each other. *Who benefited from that?*

Before he could answer, Westerby came into the kitchen. She was wearing a thin dressing gown and hugged him for warmth. Noticing his doodlings in the condensation, she asked what he was doing. Cross buried his face in her hair. She still smelt of sleep.

"It's a game," he said. "It's all a game."

He explained what he had been doing. Westerby listened, nodding solemnly.

"If you ask who gains, the answer in some cases is quite

straightforward, at other times more difficult. Take McKeague. An embarrassment for all number of reasons to the security forces. Conveniently killed just before he's about to testify on Kincora. Who gains?"

"The Brits, of course, because they're saved any embarrassment."

"So you'd suspect them of at least a hand in it."

Westerby turned her head from side to side while she thought about it. "Yes, absolutely."

"Except McKeague was killed by the INLA. McMahon confirmed that and I've no reason not to believe him."

"Lucky Brits in that case. Is that coffee ready?"

They stayed in the kitchen. Westerby was clearly preoccupied so Cross said nothing. She suddenly put her coffee down and said in a tight voice, "What if both are true?"

"What?"

"You've taught me to look round the back of everything, so I'm asking about McKeague. What if it's true that both the Brits and the INLA killed him?"

Cross snorted. "Come on! That's the one combination that's impossible. The two are completely—what's the word?"

"Antithetical?" suggested Westerby, smiling, and he nodded. "But what if they're not? Say the Brits had a hand in his death and the INLA carried it out."

"You mean the Brits and the INLA did a deal? Bullshit!" Cross laughed in disbelief.

"Everyone else seems to do them."

"They'd never get away with it."

"Yes, but suppose they did."

Cross shook his head. "I can see the Brits dealing with anyone else. But the INLA is completely beyond the pale. Rabid. Everyone knows that."

Westerby laughed. "So are the Brits."

He watched her laughing and she watched him watching her, then, catching the look in his eye, she put her coffee down with a smile and said, "I haven't cleaned my teeth yet."

"Who cares?"

THE PARTY was a great success. Cross thought it deadly. Gub and Barbara O'Neill had invited about sixty of the Province's great and good to cocktails and, as it was a fine evening, they had drifted out on to the lawn. The security contingent of armed chauffeurs hanging round the kitchen and back door area almost matched the number of guests. These were men in cheap grey suits with watchful eyes who smoked their cigarettes cupped in the palms of their hands. As most of the guests had drivers they didn't hold back on the drink.

The topics were schools, holidays, children and gardens.

"And how many do you have?" a fearsome-looking matron asked Cross.

"Gardens?" asked Cross, nonplussed.

"Children."

"Oh, two. At the last count."

The matron soon gave up on him and Cross stood watching the guests. How comfortable, unaware and protected they looked, how at ease with their world. His own could have been a fiction or a dream for all that it touched on theirs.

Cross was aware of his father-in-law approaching. He complimented him on the party and they stood looking at the view in silence.

"Everything all right?" Gub O'Neill eventually asked.

"Since the hospital?"

"Yes, though I was thinking more of you and Deidre."

"I think you should ask Deidre that."

"I already did and she told me. Everything."

Cross stared at his empty glass. He wanted another drink.

"This isn't really the time to talk," O'Neill went on, "but I'd like to help. There hasn't been a separation or divorce in the O'Neill family. We stick together."

O'Neill caught Cross's dark look and qualified himself. "That sounds altogether too harsh. I didn't mean it like that. Perhaps it would help for you to know that for many years there was another woman in my life besides Barbara. It caused a lot of pain and upset. I suppose what I'm saying is that I understand about these things. I'm more broad-minded than you might think."

Cross tried to analyse his feelings. His father-in-law's confession had left him tongue-tied. He heard him say, "Ah, there's Deidre."

"What are you two talking about?" she asked.

"Admiring the view," said Cross.

O'Neill extricated himself, leaving them together. Deidre

gave Cross a quizzical look. Behind her he could see Matthew and Fiona running around with bowls of snacks for the guests. The evening sun caught Deidre's face, softening it. He didn't want to exchange terse pleasantries.

"I'm hunting a mass murderer at the moment."

She said nothing, but accepted the hand he laid on her arm. He wondered if he was telling her from obscure motives, trying to extract her sympathy to distract her from inquiring into other areas of his life.

"We think he started killing in 1971 for the paramilitaries, but now he's out on his own and it's going to end in a bloodbath."

"Do you have any idea who it is?"

"Yes, but he's cleverer than us."

Deidre turned to Cross, who found it hard to read her expression. "I know you think I live in my own smug, isolated little world, and don't give a damn for anything outside, like most of these people here," she said in a matter-of-fact voice. "But I do know a thing or two about the Irish. The Irish mental state is one based on siege, manipulation, victimization, destruction and self-destruction, like the Kilkenny cats. I know this and choose to avoid it, choose to try and lead an ordinary life in spite of living in a country that's ripping itself apart. That's why I never ask about your work."

"What are the Kilkenny cats?"

"When Cromwell's men put everything to the sword—the humans and then the animals—they finally came to the cats and for them they devised a game. They tied them together in pairs by their tails and slung them over a line, and watched them claw each other to death, which they did, cats being cats."

"Why are you telling me this?"

"I'm aware that the most unspeakable things go on within five miles of our front door. I know that there are many justified grievances and I can even accept with my head, though not with my heart, that violence is the only adequate voice for this. I'm just saying that I know you're more serious than I am, and that you have more of a conscience to wrestle with, and, yes, you can take the moral high ground any day. I know you think I've surrendered entirely to my parents' narrow little world, but I have a responsibility, which perhaps you don't share, which is to our children. The rest of it doesn't matter. What does is their well-being and future happiness."

To illustrate her point, Fiona fell over and Deidre hurried off to join the concerned crowd gathered around her. Cross realized he didn't know what he wanted from anything. Father and daughter had the same disconcerting knack of talking at and through you. They spoke with the entire weight of their family history behind them. Theirs was a world where nothing was acquired—even Deidre's fierce protection of her children—and everything inherited. He wondered if she ever really saw him for himself.

The party showed no signs of ending. He wandered into the house and found no one he wanted to talk to. Barbara O'Neill gave him a half-wave, a cigarette held jauntily between her fingers. She was a social smoker. The O'Neills were the sort of people who still served cigarettes at parties, laid out in silver boxes next to chunky table lighters, to the disapproval of Deidre. Cross took a cigarette and wandered back outside, away from the other guests, to where there was a bench overlooking the water. He'd not had a cigarette since hospital.

He wasn't aware of Matthew at first, standing next to him, a bowl of peanuts in offering.

Cross helped himself to a handful and said, "Come and take the weight off your feet."

Matthew sat down. Cross asked if he minded the smoke. The boy shook his head and said he liked it.

"Bad habit," Cross said. "How do you like staying here? The garden must be great."

Matthew said it was all right, which Cross took to mean that he'd prefer it if they were all together.

"You know my work is very hard at the moment. That's why it's difficult for me to be here. But I haven't forgotten about the holiday."

He had in fact but promised himself to do something about it the next day. They didn't say much after that. His conversations with Matthew usually exhausted themselves pretty quickly. He never managed to enter into the spirit of his children's world.

Cross told himself that he was content sitting in silence with his arm round the boy, watching the sunset.

HE WONDERED when he could decently leave and went and sought out Barbara to make his excuses, reckoning it would take him at least twenty minutes to work his way out of the door. Sure enough, Barbara promptly introduced him to an historian called Naylor, from Queen's University, an ancient academic who'd retained his youthful features and sticking-up boyish hair.

"And what do you do?" Naylor asked, just at the point when Cross thought he could slip away.

"I'm a policeman."

"Yes, yes, quite."

"Talking of which," said Cross, taking an exaggerated look at his watch, "back to the beat." He planned to call Westerby on the way into town.

Naylor seemed not to notice and stared off into the distance. He gave off a faintly musty smell and Cross wondered how long it was since anything of his had been to the dry cleaners.

"It's interesting how Prime Minister Thatcher has done such a U-turn on Northern Ireland," Naylor remarked apropos of nothing. "What do you think?"

The question was rhetorical, which was just as well as Cross didn't have a ready answer. Naylor went on: " 'This lady's not for turning,' and so forth. Yes, yes, quite. I think you'll find that hindsight will reveal a weak prime minister, not at all the Iron Lady she makes out. What do you think?"

"She works very hard at the Iron Lady image."

"Terrified of being seen to be feeble or feminine, except if you look at her choice of Cabinet. That's where you see her vanity. I'm told, by someone highly reliable, that she sits with her legs wide apart in meetings."

Naylor giggled and Cross saw he was very drunk for all his fluency.

"No, quite weak, quite weak, whatever her great claims to be the new Churchill. It's not him she reminds me of. It's Chamberlain—same didacticism, same absolute lack of humour. She'll be got rid of in the end."

"Really?" Cross was sceptical. "Who'll get rid of her?"

"Oh, the same ones who're pushing her into this Dublin agreement. Don't forget this was the woman who once said Ulster was as British as Finchley. Of course Edward Heath tried and failed, largely because he was ousted from office, though he managed the first stage of the process by getting rid of the Unionist government in 1972."

"Do you think the Dublin deal is a prelude to selling off the North?"

"Oh, yes. She'll dress it up in a series of fancy promises, saying it's the best guarantee the people of Northern Ireland have ever had, but that's all baloney. Anyway, it's not up to her. It's the Yanks, and what do the Yanks want?"

"A single Ireland?"

"Inside NATO, though how the Reverend Paisley takes to Mr Haughey remains to be seen. Of Haughey I once heard it said, never trust a man who wears jackets with double vents. Not altogether true, as we might see from looking around this room." He paused and giggled again. "But witheringly accurate in the case of Haughey, wouldn't you say?"

Cross realized he was enjoying the company of this dry old stick with a streak of mischievousness.

"And it really is up to the Americans?"

"Afraid so. By the end of the century they'll have the world to themselves, which gives them perhaps twenty years until the Japanese or Chinese manage to put an empire together again. Quite long enough for them to balls it up completely."

"What about the Soviet Union?"

"On its last legs. Article in the paper not so long ago about German springtime and possible reunification, within the fore-seeable future. Not impossible. Once the Soviets cease to be a threat, it's likely the conflict here will fizzle out because the North'll cease to be of strategic use and when the Americans move on there's not much point, is there?"

"It can't just be about what the Americans think."

"Can't it? The trouble with the United States is that it doesn't really understand the ins and outs of history. It only understands the broad sweep, which is why it's had to create an enemy large enough for it to understand, hence the cold war. In the thaw—and it'll come much quicker than anyone expects—there'll be an unholy mess when the Eastern European states, and the Balkans in particular, start feuding again. The Americans will not be able to get to grips with that at all."

Naylor looked up at the ceiling and abruptly shut up as though he was aware of being the party bore.

"What about Mrs. Thatcher's U-turn?" asked Cross in what he thought was a polite attempt to round off the conversation.

"Oh yes, quite. Staunch Unionist to begin with. Of course

with her Methodist background she would instinctively understand the Calvinist thrift that governs the Protestant North, and
approve. The Catholics she'd find much too swarthy and
Mediterranean—Gypsy even—and lax, not at all in the mould
of free thinking and self-sufficiency that she likes so much."

"What turned her?"

"Airey Neave's death."

Cross was suddenly alert. "Neave?"

"Oh yes, no question. Neave was in many ways her mentor.
He took a tough line towards insurrectionists and actively
sought the job of secretary of state for Northern Ireland. What
do you remember about Neave?"

Cross knew he had been a war hero whose memoirs of his
escape from Colditz had been a bestseller. He had favoured
draconian measures in Northern Ireland. These, Naylor reminded Cross, included the reintroduction of internment, a
full-scale deployment of the SAS and arrest on sight of known
republicans.

"Not policies to endear him to anyone outside hardcore
Unionists. Anyway, the point is, since Neave's death Mrs.
Thatcher has been led in quite the opposite direction. The
Americans would of course have been appalled by Neave
throwing his weight around. He would have been anathema to
them. Are you all right?"

Cross was not all right. He felt like an invisible weight was
pressing down on him. Naylor stared after him as he mumbled
his excuses and left.

CROSS had no memory of finding his car and driving away.
He saw later that he had only driven a quarter of a mile before
pulling over. It was dark and he'd not put his lights on, was his
first clear thought. He was like a man waking from a nightmare in a muck sweat with no idea of what had frightened him
so much.

It took him several goes to work out what it was. While
Naylor was talking about Neave, Cross had automatically
asked himself: who gained most from Neave's death?

According to what Naylor was saying, it was the Americans
and the pro-American British faction instrumental to carrying
out their plans. *Left Hand* or *Right Hand*? *Left Hand* in all likeli-
hood: the long-term strategists, pro-Dublin, unlike Neave. This,

then, meant the same lot that had placed Heatherington and organized Candlestick's defection—*Candlestick's defection*. That was the phrase that had detonated the explosion in his head.

Listening to Naylor he had resisted the leap his imagination had made, so violently that he'd thought for a moment he was having a heart attack.

Sitting in the car, feeling the shock subside, he started to appreciate the dreadful symmetry and the dizzy complexity of it all, a complexity that also had a deadly simplicity.

It was common knowledge that the British had cultivated Unionist paramilitaries.

But what if they'd managed to pull off the unthinkable and do the same with the other side?

What if, in the wake of Candlestick's penetration, the British had somehow managed to contrive a split in the Officials, out of which was born a maverick and unprecedented terrorist organization?

What if, in fact, the INLA was the monstrous brainchild of British intelligence?

Cross was desperate for a cigarette. He stared at the near darkness. The last of the day was reflected in a streak of light in his rear-view mirror. A couple of cars went by in slow convoy, their lights dipped. He felt in possession of knowledge that he had no desire to have.

Who gains? The INLA had helped foment a bitter feud within the republican movement, which led to a civil war that drew in the already weakened Provisionals. This was ultimately of advantage to the British. The INLA killed Airey Neave, which was also to the advantage of a British faction because it brought the new prime minister into line.

Who benefited most from the creation of the INLA?

The British.

How had the INLA managed to penetrate the House of Commons and kill one of its members within its precincts? The INLA had little operational experience, and the far more experienced Provisionals had never managed a coup like that.

Did they receive help?

And were the British ultimately behind the plan to get rid of Neave?

Cross remembered Eddoes talking about the INLA's move

into drugs, with the aim of weakening the Protestant middle-classes, and wondered again: *whose the hidden hand?*

Did a British faction still have a controlling interest in the INLA? And was this plot part of the pro-Dublin faction's attempt to destabilize the Protestant community?

Cross paused before turning on the engine, trying to shake off his thoughts by telling himself that he was succumbing to paranoid fantasy. The whole notion was ridiculous, he told himself, then straight after found himself asking: *what if Candlestick knows this too?*

Cross drove on, unable to free himself from the turmoil in his head. If Candlestick was the holder of such black secrets, Moffat could never afford to have them revealed. Candlestick alive and talking was the last thing Moffat wanted, Cross realized, and if he and Westerby got caught in the crossfire, tough.

He stopped at a garage for cigarettes. As he drove on, and the nicotine calmed him a little, his thoughts turned to Baker and his religious conversion. He'd heard that conversion and terrorism often went together, invariably after arrest and usually among loyalists. Such conversions were often designed with the judge's leniency in mind. He wondered if Candlestick had undergone a similar conversion—but for real—hence the use of religious quotations. *When God has forsaken His Mansion the Devil must do His work indeed.* Indeed, Cross thought grimly, nature abhors a vacuum.

Perhaps this conversion was Candlestick's wild card, yet to be played.

Fifty-four

CROSS had just left the following morning when the telephone rang. Westerby expected it was Martin, wanting his computer again. So far she had managed to stall him.

"Hello?" There was no answer. From his silence she knew who it was. At last.

"Hello?"

She hung on until the connection was severed. Her hand hovered over the phone, waiting for it to ring again. When nothing happened she cursed. She wanted to call Cross but did not want to risk using the line in case Candlestick called again.

The night before she'd stayed up listening to Cross after he'd got back from his party. There was a tension between them. The reminder of his life outside theirs was difficult for her and she had spent the time that he was away fretting and watching the clock. By eleven she was tired and angry. When he turned up at quarter past she didn't know if she was glad or not.

Some of her resentment was to do with his invasion of her flat. It had always been her own space, separate from her job, an eyrie to which she could retreat. Now it was just another work station and a refuge for him. What she found harder to cope with was the feeling of always being at the end of the queue. Even when they were alone, which was not often enough, it took too long to get him to herself. Candlestick was always coming between them and it was only when he'd been talked out of the way—temporarily exorcized—that they could turn to each other.

When the phone rang again she knew before she answered who it was. His flat voice touched her like a cold blade.

"What did you think of my humble abode?"

Sick, she wanted to say, sick beyond belief, but no words came into her mouth, just a terrifying blank.

Eventually she said, "It left me with a taste of ashes," not knowing what she meant by it.

There was a low chuckle at the other end. "Dust to dust."

She said a line she remembered from her father's funeral. "We brought nothing into this world and it is certain that we can carry nothing out."

"Where's that from?" he asked sharply.

"The funeral service."

"Oh, very good," he said, a flicker of appreciation detectable in his monotone. "You're quite a girl, aren't you, Jill?"

"They'll say it at my funeral and they'll say it at yours."

"Death is the only certainty. Who else is listening to us?"

"Nobody. I saw Becky the other day."

"Becky who?" he said, without missing a beat.

"Becky your wife."

There was a long silence before he said, "You and I will be as one."

Westerby felt her skin turn to gooseflesh.

"What do you want?" she said in an effort to sound businesslike. When he didn't answer she went on. "I've seen your room. I see someone suffering enormous pain and understand that person needs help."

"I want to see you." His voice came down the phone hot and salivary. Until then it had sounded as dry as iron filings.

"I don't think I can." She should not have said that, she realized. String him along, don't shut down any avenues of approach. "When?" she added quickly.

"Would you like to meet?"

"Yes, very much." *Pretend, pretend* to sympathize, she told herself. Forget about the rising nausea.

"Am I right in thinking you understand something in all of this?"

Don't be too clever with him. "You've shown me things I'm trying to understand, but you're a long way ahead."

"Don't play the cunt with me," he said sharply. Then he rang off.

She sat for a long time afterwards shaking. She felt dirty, like she was involved in some squalid seduction, pretending feelings she didn't have and swallowing her revulsion until it built up as acid in her stomach. She shivered. She felt naked. For the first time since starting her affair with Cross she felt uncomfortable with her body. She was afraid for the vulnerability of her flesh and when she got dressed she deliberately put on her thickest, ugliest jersey, a Christmas present from her mother.

MOFFAT had been impressively thorough, Cross had to admit, but had come up with nothing. The sombreness of his mood was prompted by the explosion at the flat.

"It must have been a bloody cunning device to have fooled Sparrow. Four kids without a father now."

When Moffat's team had gone back to go over the place they'd discovered the oven packed with Semtex. Only extreme precaution had prevented the whole lot going up. The building had been evacuated and the bomb squad called in. After that no one was sure what had happened. There had been a second device, perhaps, triggered by the dismantling of the first. The explosion had killed two bomb squad men and ripped through the flat. The fire started by the blast destroyed the contents before they could be rescued. All that remained was the notebook that Westerby had taken. That at least was safe.

The handwriting in the notebook had been analysed by an expert in dyslexia and did not tell them anything that Westerby hadn't guessed. Cross saw more clearly now that Candlestick's early life was one of such parental and institutional neglect that—and this he found hard to accept—even some pity was called for. What would have happened if someone had taken some care? Would he have turned out different?

Registers, credit lists and market research surveys were checked to see if any contained all the names of the victims. Here the problem was that the team assembled for the purpose was not as good as Cross would have liked. Most were reservists, and second-rate at that. They were dogged and worked to order but lacked any initiative, and with time running out both were in desperately short supply. Poor calibre apart, Cross suspected he'd not been able to tell them enough to function efficiently. There was no opportunity to display initiative even if there'd been anyone capable of it. The tight security around the Candlestick operation was strangling any opportunity for inspiration.

Moffat sympathized. He took Cross confidentially to one side. "You can't teach an old dog new tricks," he said. "The RUC just isn't equipped to cope with this kind of inquiry."

Cross looked around the room, which had the air of a class under detention. There were perhaps twenty constables working their way through different lists.

Moffat was sure that Candlestick's information came from more than one source. Catherine Edge was too young to appear on the usual adult registers, and Arnold's military background precluded him from appearing in the local civilian listings.

"How does he know?" asked Moffat. "How did he know, for example, that Mary Ryan was twenty-one?"

Cross said he knew because he'd had a long time to prepare himself. He doubted, even if they did discover his source of information, that it would lead them anywhere. Candlestick was the master of the dead end. The gutted basement flat would turn out to be another.

That indeed was the case. It had been bought in 1973 in the name of T. Worrall. A search revealed that it had been purchased cheap for cash. The previous owner was long dead and the name Worrall was yet one more alias.

CANDLESTICK left Westerby on tenterhooks for several days. She worked unthinkingly, trying to get a clearer picture of the man. A thin file—the institutional record of his childhood—was forwarded from East Anglia. In the dead of night she squeezed her eyes tight shut as she gave her cry of surrender and came. Sex with Cross became more abandoned. When she was alone she was frightened by their intensity together.

She tried explaining it to him with a lightness she didn't feel. In the past she'd always felt that there had been speed restrictions in her emotional life—driving's equivalent to a built-up area, stopping and starting—and now with no warning she was travelling at blind speed out in the open and with no reason to slow down. She felt increasingly lost in Cross's arms and gave herself up to it. For him too, she suspected, their coming together was an obliteration, a desperate attempt to counter the negative force of Candlestick's world. Everything seemed excusable under the circumstances. She was falling in love too, but that was something she would never admit to Cross and rarely to herself.

FROM the file she made a sketch of Candlestick's childhood and through phone calls to various people who'd been in charge of him as a boy she added to it. She listened to their cautious institutional voices, confirming her picture of a silent, withdrawn boy, fearsomely bright but educationally frustrated, given to outbursts of wildness and incoherent rage. He'd run away frequently. He was an only child and uncontrollable from the start. He showed up poorly at school and his dyslexia, which would have held him back, had almost certainly gone undiagnosed.

She was sure that his shadow history was one of abuse, both family and institutional. Her own background in the sex abuse unit had taught her of the frequency of abuse in any single sex institution. It always surprised her that anyone expressed astonishment at such revelations. Corral humans together, deprive them of sexual outlets, and they'll either invent their own or—if the regime were an authoritarian one—have them imposed from above.

He was the abused child in the dark and had sought out the darkness ever since.

She thought of the contrast of her own childhood, and the ease of it. They'd lived in a large, rambling house on the outskirts of the city through which she and her brothers had run free. She remembered her growing up in terms of protection and safety, only vaguely aware that not far from where they lived was a dark forest of danger like the one in the fairy stories she had liked to read so much.

The significance of seven, she wrote. The rest of the page stayed blank a long time.

CROSS was the closest to despair that she'd ever seen when he arrived that night. The hopelessness of the investigation weighed on him as a personal failure. He blamed himself for the explosion at the flat because he'd delayed unnecessarily. Westerby couldn't help wondering in passing how close she had been to opening the oven door herself.

"I should be leading by example," Cross said. "But I feel impotent most of the time." He looked at her and gave a bleak smile.

Westerby bit her lip. She knew what was coming.

It took him another half-hour to say it. When he did, she stared away, blinking back her tears.

"Where will you stay?" she asked.

"Home or go to a hotel."

"Don't go home," she said dully.

He crouched before her and took her hand. "You do see, it's not because of us."

Her sad laugh sounded like a sob. In a way, she could accept everything he had said. It wasn't as though she'd been completely blind, hadn't seen it coming. Yet, when it had, she felt like she'd been ambushed. All her rehearsed counterarguments collapsed unvoiced as panic struck her speechless. It had all unravelled so quickly. Why hadn't she dragged him to bed straight away?

"There's too much pressure. It would only—" Cross stood up again, lost for words.

She was aware of putting him too much before everything else. Thoughts of him consumed her days and ate into her concentration, affecting her work. Anything not to do with tracking Candlestick was a distraction to be put aside, she knew that, and knew the pressure they were under would soon put an intolerable burden on them, knew too that the relationship existed in a false pocket created by the intensity of the investigation. If she were being honest, the truest picture of them would be of two people in a bell jar frantically trying to distract themselves from the fact that they were running out of air.

Cross proved reluctant to leave. She could see he was torn. What he really wanted, she suspected, was her approval of his decision, when all she wanted to do was to howl with despair.

She tried not to cling when he went. She tried to sound rueful rather than pathetic when she asked: "Is this an order, sir?" She told herself that she would see him the following day as normal. He was right. Duty first.

With Cross gone she felt a terrible emptiness, in the flat and in herself. She went over their one-sided conversation. His depression about the investigation had knocked on to affect them, he'd said. He had no one else to talk to, no one he could trust, but between them they were not strong enough, and as the investigation failed they would fail each other.

Westerby shook her head, trying to disagree.

"We won't catch him. This time or the next," said Cross bitterly.

"We have to believe we will," she replied, with a lack of conviction that betrayed what she really felt. Cross's pessimism was infectious.

"Moffat'll get him first."

She saw something about him she'd not seen before and didn't like it. "You're worried about Moffat beating you to Candlestick. It's the rivalry between the two of you that this is all about."

She shouldn't have said it, not if she'd wanted him to stay. Cross had turned immediately cold and left without saying goodbye.

WHAT Westerby didn't know was that Cross had agreed to go on holiday with his family, setting aside ten days at the end of August, only a week after Candlestick was next due to strike. The arrangement had provoked the present crisis. He was mad, he told himself. However much he owed the children a holiday, he was mad. He had no time. The Candlestick investigation took priority over everything. Regardless of his doubts over his ability to bring the case to a close, it could not be delegated. He was mad even to think of going. It would not mend things between him and Deidre, only compound their differences. That process had already started in the one discussion they'd had on the phone.

"It would mean sending the children back to school late," said Deidre.

"They'd enjoy that."

"What are you playing at?"

"I'm not playing at anything. You know how little I see them."

He wanted, but lacked the guts, to say that he'd take them on his own. Deidre broke the call, saying she had a meeting. What a mess, he thought.

WESTERBY was lying in bed when the phone went. She looked at the bedside clock. It was after one. Let it ring, she thought. It rang and rang. Finally she scrambled out of bed and ran to the living room, sure that she'd be too late.

"Yes," she said.

It was Cross.

He came and this time everything was all right. As she took him into her Westerby felt certainty flood through her again. This was the answer, she told herself, his body and hers. She'd known that all along, even when he'd denied it. Their exploration of each other would somehow illuminate the larger investigation, in a way that she could not yet see, she was sure of that. The answer to Candlestick's identity lay in their coming together. The thought both frightened her and gave her courage. Somewhere in the outer limits of herself she would find him, Candlestick, the dark shadow that lurks within us all.

WHILE Cross slept she got up, not because she could not sleep but because her mind was clear and she wanted to work. The pool of light from the desk lamp, the hum of the computer, the touch of her dressing gown on her skin, all combined to create a feeling of harmony that had been absent only a short while before. She could see Cross from where she sat.

Time was banished while she worked, until she was aware of Cross asking what she was doing.

"I didn't hear you," she said. She looked round. It was daylight. "What's the time?"

"A quarter past six. You look cheerful."

She considered. "Yes, I am."

Cross peered at the screen. He was still only half-awake. "What are you doing?"

Westerby smiled. "Painting a portrait."

Cross was intrigued by her new-found confidence. She talked without hesitation, saying that in a way—though nothing had changed—she felt they had turned a corner.

"Which," she added, "is not to say we'll stop the next murder or even the one after."

"But?"

"I think I've discovered a chink. A very tiny one, but a chink nevertheless. The first sign of weakness I've been able to find."

Catching Cross's look of eagerness she laughed and said, "It doesn't amount to more than a thimbleful of hope."

"Hope nevertheless."

She nodded. Cross felt calmer after the crisis of the night before. It was the realization that he could not manage alone that had made him call her. He needed her—they needed each other—and recognizing that made any differences between them secondary.

"Where does this hope come from?"

"Let's take motive first. The ultimate motive appears to be a culling of the children."

"Culling might be putting it a bit strong," Cross said. Westerby held up her hand to override him.

"Not for a man with such a divine or diabolical sense of purpose. He talks about his terrible destiny and its connection with what he calls the larger resolution. He talks of division, division by age. *Divide (by seven),* he writes, *but resolve unlike the larger division*—the Troubles, presumably—*which offers no solution. The smaller the division, the more they must pay attention.* It seems pretty clear that his intention is the invention of a series of crimes so horrific that, as he says, the mothers of the dead will rise in protest. These killings won't stop until the other killings stop. And there's more—he says they'll go on until the truth that lies behind everything is told. He's put the word lies in inverted commas, to stress its double meaning."

"Where's the hope in all that?"

"There isn't any, yet. But the line about the mothers got me thinking. He wants them to protest. He wants them to stop what's happening. And I wondered, and you might say it's psychological mumbo-jumbo, if this isn't to do with his own mother and the concern she never showed."

Cross nodded cautiously to show that he was taking her seriously.

"These are the slenderest of clues, barely even whispers in the grass. But I think seven has an importance in his own life. It signals some crisis. Something happened to him then."

"What sort of thing?"

"Some psychological trauma. I doubt if we'll ever know with the mother so far gone, and he's probably buried it too deep to remember."

"Where's his weakness?"

"I think the nearer he gets to killing seven-year-olds, the closer he'll be to revealing himself, because he'll have to confront whatever it is he has suppressed. He'll perhaps sense that in killing the children the real target is himself. Which might, just might, give him pause for thought."

She took Cross next door and her mind ran free, the thoughts tumbling over each other as Cross's tongue and hands roamed over her body until it felt divorced from the hard pebble-like thoughts in her skull.

"Do it this way," she said when she was ready for him and he asked if he was hurting her and she didn't answer. She thought: it's easy, it's so easy. I can read you and your shameful secret, the one you run so hard from, the one you do so much to deny. Did you like what Daddy did to you? How did it start? Bad Daddy and good Daddy. Secretly you liked bad Daddy best, though afterwards you burned with shame. You wanted it to stop and not to stop. What you wanted most of all was someone to stop it for you and tell you what was right and wrong. Wanted Mummy to come in and hold your hand, but she didn't. Then you discovered she knew. Maybe she watched too, watched and knew and did nothing and said nothing afterwards, because she too was afraid of what Daddy could do to her. So she betrayed you, didn't she? Let Daddy fuck you instead of fucking her. Let you take the punishment. Unique? I used to deal with cases like this every day. People grow up normal in spite of it.

Fifty-five

WITH ten days to the start of the next cycle, Candlestick phoned again, several times in quick succession. At least Westerby presumed it was him because the phone was put down with nothing said.

Her earlier optimism had quite disappeared. Although her relationship with Cross continued to build in intensity, the rest of her life was falling apart. She knew about Cross's holiday with the children now and accepted it as a desperation measure, but that did nothing to quell her anxiety. Also Martin had taken to calling round at odd hours after his computer. She had been about to open the window, thinking it was Cross, when she saw him and darted back, hoping he hadn't seen. His phone calls were a protracted mixture of aggression and self-pity. The row wasn't really about the computer but having her back. She stalled, saying she needed time—meaning the computer but letting him think she meant herself—and told him she'd call soon.

The fifth time the phone went and nobody said anything, Westerby went on the offensive. "Why are all you men such pests?" she screamed and hung up. It rang again immediately.

"Do you still want to meet?" said the voice in its dull monotone.

In spite of herself, she let her feelings intrude. "It's not up to me, is it? I'm not calling the shots," she said tartly.

In his silence she felt him, like Martin, reaching for her. She sensed a yearning that was perhaps not there in Cross, pre-occupied as he was with all the other unresolved bits of his life.

She wanted to bring up the question of Candlestick's child-hood and didn't know where to start.

"When I was seven," she said falteringly, "I had this friend a bit like you. He had fair hair and pale eyes and we used to tell each other everything." She held her breath, hoping she had hooked him. "There were no secrets between us," she went on. "We played doctors and nurses and all the usual things kids that age do. We thought babies came from weeing together into a pot, so we did that. Did you have a friend like that?"

Again the silence.

"And we told each other everything—the kind of person we'd end up marrying, and all our secret thoughts like wishing our parents would die in a crash so everyone would have to feel extra sorry for us. But my friend had one secret he wouldn't tell me, though I'd told him all about myself and even made up stories to try and get him to say what it was. What do you think his secret was?"

She could hear the tension in his breathing. For a second, she was sure he was standing in the room right behind her.

"What's the matter?" he said.

"For a moment I thought you were here."

"Like I was close to you?"

Westerby felt her skin creep. "What do you think his secret was?"

"Perhaps he didn't have one. He just said he did."

"No, he did. I think it was to do with his mummy."

There, she'd said it. The breathing became more rapid.

"Do you think it was to do with Mummy?"

God, she sounded like a demented presenter on some toddlers' television programme. She was reminded, unwill-ingly, that the Shankill killings had also cynically been known as the Romper Room murders, a name borrowed as a sick joke from a children's item on Ulster Television.

"Maybe," he said.

"I think—" There was a noise at the other end she could not identify, a soft rustling. "I think his mummy didn't love him. I think his mummy didn't look after him when she should have done. I think she betrayed him."

The rustling continued, a noise like dry leaves in the wind.

There was a long silence, then he hung up. Later, she wondered if he hadn't been crying.

CROSS had been given clearance to consult various files on the INLA in the hope that it might take them a little further along the trail. He doubted if anything of use would turn up as Candlestick's tracks would be too well covered.

He wasn't allowed to take the files out of Moffat's office and felt uncomfortable with Moffat there. He sat with his hands over his ears like a schoolboy trying to study. So scrappy, was his first thought on looking at the documents, most of which were typed, often poorly, on foolscap paper. No doubt an intelligence handler would know how to evaluate the material. To him it barely amounted to meaningless loose ends—names of people seen going in and out of buildings, mostly.

Moffat had spent the weekend in England and seemed in a better mood than usual.

"Who do you work for?" Cross asked Moffat for the sake of mischief.

"Rather not say," said Moffat jauntily.

"And what about our man? Who did he work for?"

Moffat shook his head. "Doesn't have any bearing."

"It has some."

Moffat smirked. "His employers lost the Northern Ireland contract."

"MI6, you mean."

"Precisely."

"And what do they say about him?"

"That he was a mercenary, essentially, who sold himself to the highest bidder, and occasionally did work for them on a freelance basis."

"Not as an agent."

Moffat shook his head. "Too unreliable."

Cross felt the slipperiness return. He wondered whether Moffat was lying to him or had been lied to in turn.

They moved on to surer ground, discussing contingency plans to prevent the next murder. They knew the next victim would be a twenty-eight-year-old Protestant. The only uncertainty was the initial of his or her last name. If they were right about *Ecce Agnus Dei*, it would begin with an E. Moffat's team would draw up a list of all potential victims in the greater Belfast area.

"There can't be more than a busload's worth," said Moffat flippantly. "Send 'em all on a five-day holiday courtesy of HMG."

He seemed very cool.

As she dialled, the numbers clicked down the line softly, away into the distance. When Molly Connors answered she sounded tired, Westerby thought, as tired as her. Westerby confessed that she was at her wit's end trying to come up with some lead, however slender, on the Englishman Molly had met. She asked again if there was anything else about the drive they had shared to Belfast.

"It was God knows how many years ago," said Molly with an edge of impatience. "He sat in the back. I told your inspector this."

Westerby apologized and said that she wasn't wasting time. It was urgent, perhaps even a matter of life and death. She heard Molly sigh.

As it turned out there was little wrong with Molly's memory. She remembered the journey very well, starting with the disagreement she'd had with Breen over the state of the car's tyres.

"What did Breen talk about?" Westerby asked.

"Everything and nothing," said Molly. "He thought Becky looked peaky and needed feeding up. Francis rambled on in the way Francis rambled on. If he was in the mood he could keep up a running commentary on anything."

"Do you remember anything in particular?"

Westerby listened to her silence and imagined Molly shaking her head.

"Did the Englishman say anything?"

"Not to speak of," said Molly. She apologized for not being able to remember more. She had been nervous, she said, because she was due to see Bernadette more or less straight after Breen and hadn't been able to cancel.

"Did you feel uncomfortable seeing her?" asked Westerby.

"No, but Francis was in an odd mood, now I come to think of it."

Breen had been increasingly preoccupied the closer they got

to Belfast and had tried to get Molly to break her date with
Bernadette and meet him instead later. He badgered her until
she had almost given in, but had refused because she did not
want to be seen to be weak in front of the silent Englishman.

They agreed Breen would drop her at the Royal Victoria
Hospital, where Bernadette was a nurse. Having lost the argument, he ignored her and started telling one of his stories,
addressing himself to the Englishman. The story she remembered was about the hospital and concerned someone known to
both men. Breen told it as an example of the sometimes mind-
boggling inefficiency of the security system. An activist of his
acquaintance had found work in the medical records department of the hospital, which gave him access to the addresses of
thousands of people, including those in the security forces.

She remembered Breen laughing his booming laugh and
saying, "Would you fucking believe it? The fellow's known to
the army and RUC. They even bloody interned him. Then they
let him walk into a job like that." I remember the story very
well because he was so busy telling it that he drove straight
past the hospital and dropped me at the bus station instead, and
we had a row about that."

"Thank you," said Westerby. "You've been very helpful."

Her heart was beating hard as she hung up. She told herself
not to get excited, it was probably nothing. After looking up the
number of the Royal Victoria, she picked up the phone again
and asked for personnel.

The head of personnel passed her on to a clerk and Westerby
gave her the information she needed and said she would wait
however long it took.

The woman came back empty-handed. There was no one
listed in staff records under the names Evans, Francis or Albert.
Perhaps he had used another name. She checked with the head
of the department, who'd been there a dozen years. No fair-
haired Englishman had worked there during his time.

She hung up, disappointed.

Five minutes later she was back on the telephone to the hospital, again to the records department. The same clerk sounded
less patient this time and took a lot longer. There were no
medical records at the hospital for any of Candlestick's victims. Westerby had the wrong hospital.

She tried the City Hospital, and when the personnel department did not answer she got the switchboard to put her directly through to records.

Panic struck, and she rang off as soon as she heard the voice. Her immediate thought was: *He's there. It's him.*

She doubted herself straight away. Had the man that answered the telephone had that same flat English accent or was it her imagination?

She wasted the most frustrating twenty-five minutes of her life trying to get hold of Cross. He sounded abrupt when she finally reached him in Moffat's office. After she had finished, he said, "I see," like he was dealing with some low-level bit of information and told her to wait there.

It took him half an hour. He wanted Candlestick alive. This had meant not telling Moffat, who would no doubt bring in one of the tactical squads which would lure Candlestick into a field of fire, exactly as Moffat wanted. Cross proposed to her that they go immediately to the hospital. Seeing her hesitation, Cross asked if she was certain that it was Candlestick. She said she was sure and not sure. He said they should at least reconnoitre, even if they did not have the chance to arrest him without calling in help.

They drove to the hospital in tense silence. Westerby was not convinced that she and Cross and an old service revolver were adequate opposition.

THEY went straight to the records department. Westerby asked the first clerk she saw if there was an Englishman working there, while Cross tried to look inconspicuous.

"Fair-haired," she added, looking around hopefully.

The clerk nodded and said that she wasn't sure if he was in. "He only does a couple of days."

Westerby had to avoid looking at Cross in case she betrayed her excitement.

The clerk went off to look and came back with the news that he was probably in the staff canteen.

The canteen was crowded with lunchtime diners. Cross and Westerby tried to look as natural as possible as they joined the long queue waiting to be served. There were about a hundred and fifty people in the room and no immediate sign of Candlestick. Westerby scanned the heads of the diners.

"I can't see him," she said to Cross.

"There are more tables round the corner."

The canteen was L-shaped and part of it ran away behind the food counter. They wouldn't be able to see round the corner until they got to the head of the queue. Westerby spotted some toilets on the far side of the room and told Cross to wait.

She walked towards them, feeling unreal and exposed, frantically searching around while trying not to look obvious. The tables down the side of the food counter were behind her and she wouldn't see them until her return. She wondered if he was eating alone.

In the toilet she splashed her face with cold water, avoided looking at herself in the mirror, took a deep breath and walked back out.

HE WAS sitting at the back of the room staring out of the window. She didn't spot him at first and couldn't see his face properly until she got closer. Then she saw it was him. She was sure it was. Yet he looked so normal in his brown tweed jacket, a little scruffy even, which she hadn't expected. But that wasn't what made her nearly miss him. He'd grown his hair. The semi-crew cut she'd been expecting was gone. His hair was long, almost biblical.

Now that she'd seen him she felt calmer. He didn't look up and continued to gaze out of the window. He was sitting alone at a table for four. Westerby made a mental note of the area around him. It was slightly emptier than the main dining space. A group of four sat immediately across the gangway from him. The tables and chairs were fixed, she noted, making getting in and out awkward, which could be to their advantage. It meant he couldn't push back his seat. Here's the plan, she thought to herself.

He glanced up briefly and seemed to look straight through her, then went back to staring out of the window.

She joined Cross at the head of the queue, next but one to the cashier. His tray had been loaded unthinkingly. Westerby calmly took it and told him to pay.

She spoke softly and urgently, her head close to his, making sure no one else could hear. Cross nodded and gripped the gun. His raincoat was the kind with a pouch pocket. It meant he could slip his hand through the opening and hold the gun unencumbered.

Westerby said, "He doesn't suspect anything. He's looking out of the window. He's grown his hair, by the way."

Cross went over the plan in his head, checking for any fault. Westerby sitting herself down next to Candlestick should be enough distraction for him to get into place. They would have no more than five seconds of surprise, she'd said. Cross decided he would fire under the table without warning, if necessary. He looked forward to the prospect, even relished it.

Westerby led the way. Over her shoulder Cross saw Candlestick come into view and thought, like her, how ordinary. Someone brushed past, making him suddenly think that he must look horribly conspicuous in a raincoat. Everyone else was either in hospital uniform or indoor clothes. Something felt wrong and he glanced down and froze. The gun was exposed, sticking out of his coat like some ridiculous metal tool, there for anyone to see. He hastily flicked it back under cover and told himself to concentrate. They had about fifteen feet to go.

Westerby focused only on the diminishing distance between her and her target. She was so sure of herself that she could see the handcuffs snapping on the wrists that lay resting on the table, waiting.

Six feet away Candlestick jerked his head as if stung. He swung round and his eyes locked on Westerby's. They blazed with uncontrolled fury. She had never seen anything like it. Something's warned him, she thought. He's seen something.

For a frozen moment they stared at each other. Westerby saw a sneer of recognition. He knows me, she thought. His hatred was of such intensity that she could almost feel it burning her flesh.

She reacted instinctively as soon as Candlestick started to scuttle sideways out of his seat. She hurled her tray as hard as she could, then dropped to the floor to give Cross a clear aim.

She heard rather than saw the tray hit its target, followed by the crash of falling china, and looked up to see Candlestick scream in rage as scalding tea splattered down him.

Cross lost vital seconds dragging the gun free of his pocket. The front sight snagged in the material, delaying him further. As he cleared it Candlestick was grabbing hold of the nearest diner, yanking her up by the hair, so hard that she screamed. Cross levelled the gun a fraction too late. Candlestick already had the woman against him and a canteen knife at her exposed throat. There wasn't any way Cross could risk firing.

He watched helplessly as Candlestick dragged the woman backwards towards a set of double doors behind him. He took a step forward and Candlestick jerked the knife against her throat. The woman screamed again. Cross could hear a hum of consternation building in the background. Westerby shouted that they were police and everyone was to stay where they were. Cross was surprised at how much he took in—the young woman with dyed black hair and a white face, and the fact that she wore a canary-coloured cardigan—but the detail that impressed itself upon him most of all was Candlestick's look of sheer malevolence.

He was gone in the blink of an eye.

THEY searched for ten minutes and found nothing, their dashed hopes turning to frustration and anger. They'd been *that* close, said Westerby holding up her forefinger and thumb. "Two more seconds and I could have touched him."

"What alerted him?" asked Cross.

"He saw something," she said without being able to say what. She thought back to the look of recognition she'd seen in him. It wasn't for her, she realized. It was Cross. He knew what Cross looked like. The thought hit her like a truck. It was in the notebook. He'd known all along. He'd been referring to Cross in the hospital when he'd written: *He was here. I saw him, not expecting that. The shock of the unexpected.*

But even before then he'd seen something. Recognizing Cross came afterwards.

A minute or so later they ran into Moffat in one of the hospital's endless corridors. He was with a small posse of plain-clothes officers all armed and looking urgent.

"What the fuck is going on?" said Moffat. He was beside himself with anger. "Where is he?"

"You tell me," said Cross.

"Jesus fucking H Christ!" said Moffat, jabbing a finger at Cross. "You. Come with me."

Westerby watched them march away down the corridor. The arrival of Moffat and his men was what must have alerted

Candlestick, she realized. He would have seen them piling out of their cars.

She looked at the men left with her.

"Thanks for fucking it up, boys," she said and wondered queasily how they'd known.

Fifty-six

THEY made Cross wait a couple of hours, keeping him isolated in a conference room.

After the hospital Moffat, still incandescent with rage, had told Westerby to go with him. This left Cross to drive back to the barracks alone. He wondered how Moffat had known they were at the hospital. Then it hit him. They must be bugging Westerby's apartment. There was no other way Moffat could have known. The realization left Cross clammy. In that case they would be privy to everything. It had not occurred to him until then that Moffat mistrusted him in return.

Immediately on his arrival at the barracks Cross had been summoned to Nesbitt's office and, after being made to wait in his lobby for an hour, Nesbitt had come out and told him to go to the conference room.

Compared to the time they'd made him wait, the meeting was insolently brief. Moffat was there, looking supercilious. Cross asked to speak to Nesbitt alone. He had decided that a full statement, including criticism of Moffat's role, was his best hope.

Nesbitt told Cross to shut up. "Would you say that WPC Westerby is a good officer?"

"Yes."

"One of the best you've had?" Cross caught Moffat smirking.

"Yes."

"There's increasing pressure to promote women in the

force, as you know. Would you say that Westerby is future DI material?"

"Yes, sir."

Nesbitt sighed. "So would I. I don't have to warn you what the punishment is for a married officer involved in a relationship with a policewoman."

Cross asked Nesbitt on whose authorization had Westerby's apartment been bugged. Nesbitt declared that the information was not germane to the discussion.

Cross's voice rose in anger. "Excuse me, sir, but if someone is eavesdropping on the private life of one of my constables that information is invalid and confidential." He turned to Moffat. "No wonder I didn't trust you—"

"And jeopardized a whole investigation."

Cross addressed Nesbitt again. "It's my belief that Mr. Moffat, for reasons quite outside our investigation, wants the man we are seeking dead."

Nesbitt held up his hand. "Are we talking about a shoot-to-kill policy?"

"You know we are."

"There is no such policy."

Cross snorted in disbelief. Moffat interrupted smoothly, saying that as far as he was concerned he and Cross had been working jointly. "Until I became aware of the extent of DI Cross's paranoia, that is."

When the blow came it came from an unexpected quarter. Nesbitt drew Cross by reminding him of the investigation he had been under at the beginning of the year, for sexual harassment.

"What would you say," said Nesbitt, "if WPC Westerby brought a similar charge against you?"

Cross could not believe what he was hearing.

"If she did then I'd resign," he said with as much dignity as he could muster. "Is WPC Westerby bringing such a charge?"

"That depends," said Moffat.

"On what?" asked Cross.

"On you."

If Westerby brought the charge then it was obvious he would be forced to resign. If she refused both of them would be punished or shunted so far sideways that they would resign out of boredom. Or he could do the decent thing for her sake and resign anyway.

Cross saw they were playing on his loyalty to her. He sighed and congratulated them on their cleverness, and added that if Moffat had applied even a quarter of the ingenuity he had just shown to catching their killer they would have had him arrested weeks ago.

"Am I suspended?" he asked.

"We'll let you know," said Nesbitt.

THAT was it, then, he kept thinking, on the way back to his office. Moffat had won. He remembered Westerby pointing out the rivalry between them. Perhaps that's all it was, a tussle of vanity to see who was the cleverer. He felt sick.

He sat for a long time, ignoring the frequent ringing of the phone. When he left he took his messages and drove to Westerby's. The light was on but she did not answer.

He sat in the car, hoping she would come out. There was jazz on the radio, nervous be-bop that agitated his mood. He'd have to go to a hotel, he decided. He sifted through his messages. There was one from the boy Vinnie, with a Dublin number. So the lad had gone away after all. The news cheered him up briefly.

He glanced at the other messages. There were several from Sally, the children's minder, asking him to phone her at the O'Neills'. The last said it was urgent.

He remembered the holiday. He'd forgotten about that again. All the time in the world now for holidays, he thought grimly as he started the car.

He found a phone box that worked and called the O'Neills'. Barbara answered.

"Oh, there you are. Where have you been?"

"What's the matter?"

"Matthew's got himself lost."

"Lost?" echoed Cross, feeling a stab of panic.

"I'm sure it's nothing to worry about," she went on blithely.

Cross drove there in a hurry. What a day, he thought grimly. He kept telling himself that Barbara O'Neill was right and there was nothing to worry about.

She was at the house with Fiona. What had happened was that Sally and the children and some of their friends had gone off to the woods to play hide and seek. When it had come to Matthew's turn they'd not been able to find him. She thought he might have fallen and hurt himself but no one was panicking. Yet, thought Cross. A couple of local constables were out searching.

Cross asked where Deidre was.

"She wasn't in the office. She's usually back by now."

He sighed. He phoned the tourist office but the switchboard had closed for the night.

HE FOUND them a mile or so from the house, down a side road that was not much more than a track. Gub O'Neill, immaculately clad in stout brogues, long socks and waterproofs, had clearly taken charge. He told Cross that they'd swept the woods where the children had been playing but with so few of them they'd not got far.

"It's easy to get lost in there if you don't have your bearings. He'll have picked up a path, probably, and gone wandering round in circles."

O'Neill sounded optimistic. He'd asked one of the policemen to radio for more help, he said, and rolled his eyes to indicate his opinion of the man's calibre.

"We've got to find him before dark and these are big woods. Matthew could be anything up to three miles away by now. Temperature's going to drop a bit tonight. Wouldn't want him out then."

Cross excused himself and went over to Sally, who was standing alone looking distraught.

"I told him not to go too far. I don't understand. He's never done anything like this before."

She explained how Matthew had been bored because he had been the eldest and had found the game too easy. When it had been his turn to hide, Fiona had been distracted by one of the others grazing a knee, so they had not started searching straight away. Sally choked back a sob and wrung her hands.

"I was annoyed at first. Matthew's old enough to know that the others were too young to go far. I didn't start to worry until we started calling. We called and called."

Her voice was alive with panic. Cross could see how hard it must have been for her to prevent her anxiety spreading to the children. Once Matthew was not immediately to be found she had driven them back to the O'Neills'. Cross told her she had done the right thing.

"Don't worry. We'll find him."

"I knew I shouldn't have brought them here. I even had a feeling something like this would happen."

Cross reassured her that he did not hold her in any way responsible.

"Did you reach Mrs. Cross?"

Sally shook her head. "They said she was in Cushendall but when I telephoned the hotel she was visiting they didn't know about her being there, so I expect there was a muddle."

Six more policemen arrived, making ten altogether in the search party. Cross tried to put out of his mind the question of Deidre's whereabouts.

They formed a line and set off, taking it in turns to call out Matthew's name. For half an hour they swept in a wide arc, then back towards the rendezvous. As darkness fell a couple of hours later torches were switched on, their beams dimmed by a rising mist. A helicopter joined them, hovering low, using its searchlight to scan the tracery of forest paths. It made darting runs, sometimes moving forward until its sound was almost gone, then sweeping back again, the beam of its light catching them as it passed over, turning their faces ghostly blue.

When they returned to the vehicles Deidre was waiting. She wanted to join the search, but Cross persuaded her to stay at the house and prepare something warm for when Matthew got back.

"We'll make another sweep," he said. "Don't worry. He's a sensible kid."

"What if someone's taken him?"

"Nobody's taken him. He's just got lost." He hoped, for her sake, that he sounded convincing. *Please God,* he prayed, *it's too soon for seven.*

Cross searched, unaware of the others. Panic at the thought of not finding his son fuelled the greater panic that he had fallen into Candlestick's hands. A fine rain began to fall. Cross sensed the search party losing heart. *Please God,* he prayed again, *it's too soon for seven.*

Fifty-seven

THE BOY was in the boot, just like he had once been himself almost exactly twelve years before, except the boy was tied up. The thought made him snicker because he and the boy had nothing in common, apart from their travelling in the boot of a car.

He grinned at the driving mirror. Things couldn't have turned out better, after all.

He drove fast, dwelling on the good memories he had of where they were going. One fine winter morning earlier in the year he had walked down the hill, aware of the dew on his boots and the give of soft earth beneath his heel, amused at the fact that he was there to kill Breen before the booze did. Breen, now hidden away as Berrigan. He'd seen him from his camp on the hill on the few occasions Breen had ventured out. At first he hadn't realized that the distant tottering figure was Breen. Not yet fifty and as stooped and shuffling as a man of eighty.

It did not prepare him for the shock of Breen close to. In the four years since he'd seen him he'd aged terribly, and bore no resemblance to the man he'd once been. He found a pathetic broken wreck sitting at the kitchen table in a puddled stupor at eight in the morning.

"Is it really you?" Breen had asked, blinking at the sight of him, backlit by the open door. His eyes rolled around, searching for a focus. Candlestick laughed at Breen, trying to work out whether he was a ghost or not.

"So you didn't get blown up after all," he finally said as Candlestick shut the door.

"I can't say you're looking well, Francis."

Breen wheezed, which set off a hacking cough. "How did you know where to find me?"

Candlestick tapped his nose conspiratorially.

Breen poured himself another drink. "Breakfast," he said grimly. "Breakfast, lunch and dinner. And yourself?"

Candlestick let Breen pour him a glass which he didn't touch.

"Sit down, sit down," Breen said and when he saw that Candlestick would not, his eyes took on a puzzled look, tinged with apprehension.

"Why're you here?"

"I've come for your debriefing, Francis, and this time I'll drag the whole sorry story out of you."

HIS THOUGHTS were "lepping" around as he drove. "Stop lepping around and hold still," is what his father used to say as he took the strap to him. He'd been stung by the sight of the policeman and his bitch in the canteen. Victim number ten had been very lucky, he thought, as a result of this acceleration in his plans, and victims number eleven and twelve. He'd go back and kill them later, for the neatness of it and to honour his obligation. He'd not expected to get his hands on the boy so soon after the copper and his cunt in the canteen. They'd been that close they could have touched him.

He'd followed the wife sometimes on the days he wasn't working, not that she was on his list, but being the copper's wife made her a curiosity. He'd seen her at the tourist board and even knew by the once or twice he'd driven behind her that she'd taken the kids and was living out near the lough.

After the shock of the canteen, his first thought was to kick back, to show he wasn't to be monkeyed with, and maybe doorstep the wife or the blue rinse—the mother, presumably— that lived in the fancy house where the wife and kiddies were staying. Hit back hard. He'd even thought about going into the house and taking a pop at the lot of them. That'd give the copper something to think about.

From high in a tree overlooking the house, he had realized, as he basked in the afternoon sunlight, that nothing gave him more pleasure than watching a place whose people didn't know he was there. That was when the feeling of holding lives in the palm of his hand was strongest.

Fifty-eight

IN HIS wildest moments of hope Cross was sure Matthew would be waiting at home, having maybe found a taxi. He knew the address and number because Cross had taught him them.

When he had told Deidre he was going home to check, she had given him a look that said his responsibility was to the search. He could have sent someone else, but by then he was sure the search was a waste of time. Matthew was gone.

He thought he heard the phone ringing deep inside the house as he pulled into the garage, then lost it in the noise of the metal door swinging automatically shut behind him. He decided it was his imagination, then he heard it again, barely penetrating the heavy silence. He ran, praying that his prayers had been answered.

It rang off as he reached it. He screamed obscenities at the lump of plastic.

Minutes later it went again. Cross snatched up the receiver. "Matthew?"

It was Westerby. Cross felt a burst of irritation and said he couldn't talk. He presumed she wanted to conduct a post-mortem on the events of that afternoon.

"Wait, sir. It's about him."

She sounded cold and professional. She told him Candle-stick had called her demanding to talk to Cross.

"What about?" Fear clutched at his heart.

"He wouldn't say. He asked for numbers where you might be. I didn't know what to do."

"You gave them?"

"Yes." Westerby sounded cowed, like she was expecting a reprimand.

Cross hung up abruptly. He allowed himself the small hope

that Candlestick trying to make contact was a sign Matthew was alive. His palms were slick with sweat.

THE CALL came half an hour later. The voice was dull, matter of fact. "You know why I'm calling."

"Is he safe? Let me talk to him," said Cross.

Candlestick said the boy's life depended on him. "I want you to issue a public statement. Then you get the boy back."

"What statement?"

Candlestick told him that a copy of it had been put through his letter box. He was to read it and expect another call.

It lay in an unmarked brown envelope on top of the pile of unsorted mail on the mat. Cross read:

I am the Psalm Killer. I am the candel Stick of TRrue liGht. To the peple of Northern Ireland, I say: put a way your wepons. I have killed 9 (nine) people so far that all of you migt live in peace. I will kill many more untill you learn to live with eacH otHer. I WILL KILL Youre CHILDREN. The deaths of Francis Berrigan-Breen Mary Elam Patrick Wheen Roger Arnold Mary Ryan Catherine Edge MarGaret Eddoes Brian Caddy & Charles Causley were all the secreT work of Myself & I anounce them noW i) because your securiTy forces will not let you see tHem as the work of ONEman, ii) to say to you that these killings are But a start.

They will cese when the other killinGs stop. They will cease when tHe British goverment announces to the people of Northern Ireland the folowing. That in 1972 it used aGents to create a Riegn of Terror against Roman CatHolics. That tHese same aGents instiggated the shanKILL murders on the instructoNs of the British in the same way that iT Had useD Agents to shoot Protestants by way of insitement. That in 1974 it, or a faction of its government, gave aid to bomb-ings carryed out in the Republic of Ireland. That in 1974, it or a facTion thereofF, conSpireD to bring about the creation of a terrorist organisation, the INLA, with whom it colabor-rated. That with the help of the INLA, the british Gover-Ment, or a faction thereof, conspired to bring about the death of the British politican Airey Neave. That they also com-bined to murder John McKeague, a longTerm aSSet of the Security forCes.

The people of Nothern Ireland have lived in hell for SIX-TEEN (16) years. To tHem I say, Deliverence lies in your hands. & I am the instrument of that deliverance. Your proTest will end the kiLLings. Recognice that the bRitish have never broght a solution to Ireland. The solution is Yours. Listen and you shal be SaveD. Ignore my voise and I will MaSSacre your children until the DefneSS falls from your ears.

Cross's first thought was that Moffat would not buy it. "Fuck him," he could hear Moffat saying behind his back. "Stay silent and what does he do? Murder a few of their children, but where does that get him if no one will let him voice his demands? He's cut off and still operating within an acceptable level. He's misplayed his hand. Cover-up is the one thing we do better than anyone."

For a moment, Cross thought of leaking the information himself, but where? The usual outlets would refer it for security clearance. He thought swiftly, trying at least to come up with a semblance of a plan.

WHEN Candlestick called back, Cross said that he had no problems with the terms but time was needed to authorize clearance. Candlestick said he had an hour.

Panic overtook Cross again. He didn't dare trust Matthew's safety to Moffat and his gang. Beyond that he had no idea other than to stall. The egomaniacal vanity of Candlestick's design and his hunger for recognition meant there might at least be some grounds for negotiation.

When the phone went again he had to let it ring while he brought himself under control. His heart was thumping like a bass drum.

"I'm told it will take twelve hours to get the necessary clearance," he said. Candlestick said nothing, calling his bluff. Cross ploughed on. "They're talking about putting it on the news some time tomorrow."

"Ulster or national?"

"I don't know. It's all being referred through London. There are points you've made which are disputed."

Again there was silence at the end of the line. Cross prayed that his picture of furious activity was convincing.

"They're taking issue with some of your points," he repeated. "You can imagine the panic this is causing."

"What points?"

"The INLA stuff. I believe you, but we're dealing with people who don't know half the time what their other hand is doing."

"These terms are not negotiable."

"I told them. The disagreement is not with you. They need time to agree among themselves."

He felt like a man building a bridge without supports over a canyon. He wondered who else was listening in on their conversation.

The silence went on longer than the others, undermining him. The first rule of negotiation was to make the other party talk and he was failing.

"Daddy?"

Matthew's scared and tiny voice cut into his heart.

"Matthew, are you all right?" He couldn't think of anything less silly to say. The boy choked back a sob.

"Listen. Everything will be all right," Cross said. "Do as the man says. He's looking after you until I come. I'm arranging everything so I can get there soon."

"What does he want?"

"He wants me to do something then you'll come home."

"I don't want to live at Grandpa's any more."

"You won't. We're going on holiday, remember, and we'll all be together."

There was another silence. Cross could hear movement. The boy whimpered, then there was the sound of a door closing and he heard the flat voice again, urgent in the receiver.

"He's a nice boy, not any trouble, unlike some cunts I could name. Twelve hours. Every hour after that I cut off one of his fingers, and then I start on his toes. Are we clear about this?"

Blood pounded in Cross's head. He sought desperately to stamp out the idea of his son's mutilation.

"I want to hear you say you're clear about this."

"Yes," he said and put down the receiver.

He tried to bring his stampeding thoughts under control. He had until noon next day and told himself not to think what might happen after that. Six hours to try and find Matthew, then he would have to call in Moffat.

He drove to Westerby's. Her flat was in darkness. He rang the bell. Eventually her window opened. Cross motioned her to come down and she held up her hand to say she needed time to dress.

He waited in the car and when she joined him they didn't touch. She looked done in. It felt like weeks rather than hours since the débâcle in the canteen. He'd suffered enough upheaval since to last a lifetime. Nothing to what Matthew must be going through.

He told her what had happened and they drove in silence until Westerby said, "Try the lock-up."

They parked a couple of streets away and walked to the alley, which was unlit and deserted. Westerby was wearing soft shoes and whispered to Cross to wait.

She came back shaking her head. "It's padlocked from the outside."

"We haven't a hope in hell," said Cross, on the brink of collapse. "I've failed the boy and I'm failing him now."

"We have to go on. There's no one except us." She spoke with a surprising harshness. "This is no time to start feeling guilty."

He looked at her and saw for the first time the strain she had been under since that afternoon, and the pressure of seeing each other again.

"Tell me everything," she said.

He went back over the evening and showed her Candlestick's statement. Westerby read it and said, "It's consistent. But he's under great stress."

"How do you know?"

"The writing and spelling are much more erratic. With luck he's getting careless."

Westerby shut her eyes and for a moment Cross thought she was falling asleep.

"He's becoming blurred," she said, her eyes still closed. "Why's he suddenly gone off at an angle?"

"Because he saw how close we were to him today?"

"And he wants to punish you for it."

He heard her sudden sharp intake of breath.

"How old is Matthew?" she asked with great reluctance.

Cross tried but couldn't bring himself to say.

"Oh, fuck," she said, seeing his distress. "He's skipping three. He's broken the pattern."

She was silent for a long time.

"I can't stand this," she said. "I can't stand any of it."

Sickly fluorescent light splashed over them as they drove down empty streets. Westerby took a deep breath and dragged her thoughts together.

"He knows where you live. He knows where the children were staying. He went after Matthew because of what we did to him this afternoon. So it's personal. Personal enough to break the pattern. Also he now wants to talk to you."

Until then, she explained, he had been content to talk to her, but now it was Cross he wanted.

"Why?"

"Because he has your son, obviously, but it's more complicated. You're the one who knows more about him than anyone else. Only you can appreciate the extent of his achievement."

Cross permitted himself a moment of wryness. "Not a position I appreciate."

"He needs you," Westerby said. "You realize that."

"Needs me? What? To negotiate on his part?"

"Think where he started."

Cross did not get her drift. "In the back streets of Belfast."

"Started killing."

"In bars in the Shankill."

"With?"

Cross slowly realized. "An audience."

"He wants you there."

He slowed for a red light, which changed as he drew up. He accelerated aggressively and said bitterly, "Then why doesn't he say where he is?"

"You have to earn the right to be there."

Cross could see that. It was up to him.

"He wants the confrontation. He wants you as a witness." Her voice spooked him. It was like an incantation.

"Witness to what?"

"To his loneliness."

"He needs an audience," Cross repeated.

He remembered the first murder site he had attended, remembered the terrible sense of isolation hanging over the scene, over the discarded body and over the deed itself. The ultimate unwitnessed deed, the last private act. Cross could see how it would be sharper for being watched.

"He'll be somewhere you know," she said.

He suddenly knew where. He'd known for some time, though had not admitted it. The place still haunted him.

"Are you sure?" asked Westerby when he told her.

Cross nodded. He turned the car round and headed west out of the city.

Fifty-nine

THEY stopped off on the road and Cross spoke to a sleepy-sounding Donnelly from a call box. Ten miles further on Cross called back.

"He says he heard a car arrive some hours ago," said Donnelly. "What's this about?"

"I'll call you later," said Cross, thanking him hurriedly.

They had driven most of the way in tense silence. Neither referred to what had gone on since Moffat's intervention in the hospital.

Ballybofey was a ghost town. After that Cross lost the way in the forest tracks until he saw the burnt car.

"We'd better walk the last part," he said. "The sound of an engine will carry out here."

He asked if she was all right. She nodded.

They left the car half way up the last hill, closing the doors quietly. The hill was steeper than it looked and by the time they reached the gate they were breathing hard. "We've no jurisdiction here," Cross said.

"I know."

He told her she didn't have to come any further.

"I know," she said and took his arm as they set off. The moon came out, bathing the valley in cold light. The farmhouse gleamed malevolently, a sight so arresting that they stopped. There were no lights on. Away to the left the valley lay in dark shadow. Cross felt Westerby's grip tighten, then slip free. When they set off she walked apart from him.

They approached cautiously. Cross took out the gun and peered through several windows, front and back. The place showed no sign of occupation. The front door was unlocked as before. He lifted the phone. The line still worked.

They moved carefully through the forlorn rooms, the gloom relieved occasionally by splashes of moonlight. In the last room Cross recognized the mattress. Nothing had been touched.

He looked at Westerby. Her face was pinched with tension and she looked small and frail.

He checked the safety catch on the gun, saying, "They'll be in the barn. Phone Moffat—"

"Moffat?"

Cross handed her the gun. "Take this. He'll search me anyway."

"I'll come with you."

Cross shook his head. "I'll offer myself as hostage instead of the boy. Tell Moffat where we are. It's up to him whether he tells the Gardai or comes in alone."

Moffat would fly in the SAS. "Stick to him like glue. I want us out alive, not caught in some crossfire because he's told them to get trigger happy."

He looked at her. His face was lined with sadness. "I'm sorry for everything," he said. He kissed her quickly on the mouth and was gone.

HOW LONG she stood there she didn't know. The weight of the gun in her hand brought her out of her trance and she set off cautiously down the staircase, stirred by childhood fears of the dark, and felt her way to the phone. An owl hooted, startling her. The house was suddenly darker. She heard the first splashes of rain, then a steady downpour.

She picked up the receiver, paused, trying to think, then gently replaced it. She imagined the helicopter, the search-lights, the demands shouted over a loud hailer. Moffat would come in announced. He wouldn't leave it to stealth and if Cross and the boy were sacrificed then that was a price he'd pay for the prize of Candlestick. Either way they'd lose, because in any sort of showdown Candlestick would kill Cross and the boy first. Of that she was sure.

There was only her left. She had a small element of surprise on her side, Cross's gun and nothing else.

She let herself out of the house and into the rain.

Sixty

CROSS made no effort to disguise his entrance. He came in slowly, shutting the door after him, expecting to be greeted by the barrel of a gun and the frightened face of his son. He had been sure Matthew would be there. Seeing him unharmed was his first and in a way only goal. Everything after that he'd pushed from his mind.

His first surprise was how neat and weirdly cosy the barn was. After the tension and discomfort of making his way there through the rain, the dry interior was almost welcoming. It bore no signs of its previous carnage. A storm lamp cast a soft glow and there was a camp bed and a folding chair, a primus stove and even a radio cassette with tapes. The camp area had been swept. It was also deserted.

He called out Matthew's name softly. There was no answer. Then, trying to sound matter of fact, he said, "If anyone's watching, I'm crossing to the chair."

He was being watched, he was sure. He added, "I'm not armed," and held his coat open.

He walked cautiously to the chair, careful to make no sudden move. He was shivering, from fear and his soaking in the rain.

Candlestick slipped quietly into Cross's life.

* * *

CROSS heard nothing, only the feel of the gun's muzzle against the back of his head. He raised his hands slowly.

Candlestick frisked him from behind, making no move to face him, which disoriented Cross.

"They'll not agree to your terms," Cross said. "You know that, so there's no point in harming the boy. Let him go and I'll stay in his place."

"We'll be gone before they arrive."

Cross tried to calculate the distance of the voice.

"Before who arrives?"

"Whatever back-up you have in mind."

"There isn't any."

"Har-de-har. We'll be gone anyway. So they hung you out to dry?"

"Who?"

"Whoever holds your strings. You wouldn't be here otherwise."

"Unless they're waiting outside."

"You said they weren't."

A burning pain shot through Cross's head. He realized he was being yanked by the hair. He tumbled backwards and hit the ground with the brief impression of Candlestick above him. He saw the cold steadiness of the eyes, then a blur of an arm as the pistol smashed his cheek.

When he came to, the side of his face felt on fire. Candlestick swam in and out of focus. He was sitting on the camp chair, leaning forward, the gun dangling provocatively between his knees, studying him. Cross saw the man's expression change—the whole face was bizarrely transformed, like it was being pulled by wires. Cross realized the man was grinning.

"Welcome to my world."

The eyes glittered, diamond hard in the mirthless mask. Cross felt a trickle of sweat down his spine. *Start somewhere,* he thought. *Start anywhere, just get him talking. Bounce him around. He needs to talk.*

"Show me the boy. I want to see him safe."

Candlestick shook his head.

A stab of panic—what if Candlestick had already killed him? But Candlestick read his mind and said the boy was unharmed.

Breen was the spine, Cross remembered thinking once. Find

out what happened to Breen. Draw Candlestick on Breen and it might just distract him enough.

"When you killed Bernadette Breen and her children," he began, putting each word together like a clumsy child with building bricks, "you meant to kill Breen."

"No. It was Bernadette and the children I meant to kill."

"Why? What had they done?"

"Nothing. Regrettable, but there it is."

"Why kill them?"

"Because of what it did to Francis."

"It broke him."

"Quite."

"Was it because he once nearly had you shot?"

Candlestick gave a sharp look in Cross's direction.

"Well," he said, "you have done your homework."

"If Breen was your godfather, why kill him?"

"Francis was not what he seemed, it was as simple as that."

Cross had the impression of two indistinct overlapping images about to snap into focus. He told Candlestick about the Heatherington sting and afterwards Candlestick said he hadn't known about it.

"But it fits," he said laconically.

"At the same time the Brits got you over to the Officials. And by the end of the year they had their ceasefire with the Provos *and* had split the Officials."

Candlestick shrugged. "Divide and rule. That's how it goes."

"But—" said Cross. Candlestick watched with sardonic amusement. "It wasn't because of *you* the Officials split. You were an instrument, not the agent, a trigger."

Cross had it. The two pictures slid together. *Look for the shadow,* he'd told himself. Now he could see the figure that had cast the shadow.

"Breen," he said. "Francis was the keeper of the secrets. When you finally came for him, what did he tell you, as you nailed him down and pulled his teeth out one by one? Did he sing like those other Taigs?"

"They all sing in the end."

Cross had been puzzled by two things in the events of May 1974: Breen's antagonism to Candlestick's defection, and some missing connection between his defection and the split in the Officials.

"Breen knew you were a British asset, didn't he? But, to find out how reliable you were, you had to be tested. Pushed to the limit to see if you sang. But you didn't."

Candlestick stared at Cross impassively.

"When did you realize Breen was a British agent too?"

Candlestick shrugged. "Much later."

In Cross's estimation Breen must have been working for the British from very early on. He would have been able to report on growing dissent in the ranks of the Belfast Officials and the increasing disagreements with the Dublin leadership. Then, in the wake of the split, which was ideological, slip in the shadow of the gun. Breen, under British instruction, was the agitator of violence, the conduit.

"And you," he said to Candlestick, "were slipped in as protection, to be sacrificed for Breen if necessary, isn't that right?"

Candlestick nodded slowly. "I was a Brit so I was always kept to one side by Francis, but his protection meant no one went sticking their finger in my face, and I did the jobs I was asked to and was good at it. But then my handler said the INLA was panicking they'd been penetrated, and my name was on the list. So I decided to become a dead man, went up to Belfast, found a fellow that looked enough like me and blew him up."

He smirked at his cleverness.

"And so, after years of being kept in the dark"—Cross remembered Westerby's phrase—"and being a small player in someone else's game, you decided to invent one of your own. One that would make them all sit up and take notice."

Candlestick cocked his head and looked pleased. "I hadn't thought of it like that before."

The vanity of having an audience, thought Cross.

"When I was a lad," said Candlestick, "you could see clear all the way to the horizon. A tree was a tree and a ditch was a ditch. And then I got into this business and, well, they tell you something's one thing and it turns out to be another."

Cross took a deep breath. "You can't beat them. This whole struggle will take its own time. They'll silence you and they'll silence me if they think we know too much. Why do you think they arrested Willcox?"

Candlestick shrugged. Cross told him that Willcox had confessed to two murders as part of a deal. He saw he'd caught Candlestick off guard and tried to push the advantage. "If you hadn't led us to Willcox in the first place—"

"He was a wanker," said Candlestick defensively.

"Get out while you can. You're already in the South. No one can touch you here."

"No one can touch me anyway. Get up."

He levelled the gun at Cross.

"Now kneel down."

Cross felt the cold point of the gun in his ear. He slowly raised his hands in surrender and remembered the priests of his childhood, arms aloft in benediction.

"Twelve years ago I killed Tommy Herron. That was the best. I thought it would always be like that. But everything winds down, gets dull with repetition. Even killing gets to feel like old elastic. The tension goes, the edge, the feeling that once kept you buzzing for days and makes you different from all the other cunts. At first it's the best thing you ever did and in the end it means no more than sneezing. You walk in a room, you trigger someone, you leave. It's over so fast and the way these things are planned you're in and out in less time than it takes to piss."

Candlestick grabbed Cross by the hair again and twisted his face round.

"But look at me now and know that in a month or three months *you* were going to kill *me*. Know that I was living only on your say-so. Think of the power and the control. That's what gives the swelling to a killing. Pumps it up so you're pistol hard for the cunt that's waiting."

The noise of Candlestick cocking the gun sounded deafening to Cross. He screwed up his face, waiting.

A wail from the back of the barn saved him.

"STAY there," Candlestick hissed.

Cross knelt, trembling, his breath whistling like old bellows. He looked up as Matthew entered, pushed out of the shadows.

His mouth gaped at the sight of the boy—he had no head. Cross went completely numb. Then he saw. The boy's head was covered by a black hood. Matthew walked with his arms outstretched like a blind boy feeling his way. As he got closer, Cross could see the material sucking at his gasping mouth each time he drew breath. Anger at seeing Matthew hooded drove away his fear.

"Let me see his face," said Cross.

Candlestick stayed the boy with his hand. He then reached behind him and there was a blur as something shiny cartwheeled through the air and landed at Cross's feet.

It was a knife with a sculpted handle, broad bladed and around a foot long.

"Pick it up," said Candlestick. "Feel the blade."

One side of the blade was serrated. Cross felt the clean edge with his thumb and winced. There was a razor thin line of blood where he'd touched it.

"That knife has done good work," said Candlestick in a weird high-pitched voice. Cross looked at it with a mixture of fascination and revulsion.

"God said to Abraham, kill me a son." Candlestick gave a queer giggle.

The boy turned his head, trying to understand what was going on. Candlestick pressed down on the boy's head and put his mouth to his ear.

"Whoo-whoo-whoo!"

He laughed. Cross wondered whether it was Benzedrine kicking into his system that was making him so charged up. Candlestick looked at him with a terrible bonhomie.

"Go on, admit it, you're flattered."

"Flattered?"

"Because you believe everything will be revealed, that I— flattered by your persistence—will yield my secrets."

"I'm here for my son."

"How touching." Candlestick sneered and raised the gun straight-armed at Cross's head. "Put down the knife now. Drive it into the ground and take three steps forward."

Cross hesitated and Candlestick screamed at him to do it. The boy jumped with fright and whimpered. Cross leaned forward and stuck the knife into the earth. Candlestick moved behind him and he felt the gun at his head again and the guttural whisper of the man's breath hot in his ear.

"I'm *on*! And I'm going to do your cunt in. Do you know what, Tommy? Afterwards I'll fuck the boy. All the while thinking of you, Tommy, only the best thoughts."

"I'm not Tommy," said Cross uncertainly.

Tommy Herron, he presumed. Cross suppressed a shudder, trying not to imagine what had gone on there, and prayed that he could draw some slim hope from Candlestick's crazed distraction.

"You're all the same to me," Candlestick said with strange tenderness. "Tommy, Mary, Francis, young Matthew there."

A chill settled over Cross at the mention of his son. He looked at Matthew, who appeared calmer now.

"Do you know what this is?"

Candlestick held out a piece of folded paper over Cross's shoulder. He told him to take it and open it.

Cross saw some sort of painting, torn from a book. In the gloom of the barn it was hard to make out the detail. It showed two figures surprised in some act of—"Abraham and Isaac," said the voice in his ear—sacrifice. Cross remembered. As a test of faith, God had instructed Abraham to kill his son, only to reveal the order to be a cruel hoax. Cross realized that there would be no last-minute reprieve for them.

"What are your feelings contemplating this scene?"

Cross said nothing.

"Do you think there is a God to intervene? Try praying now and see what happens."

Cross shut his eyes and tried to quell the tide of rising panic.

"Or is it the devil's turn now? Poor wee Mary Ryan gabbling the Hail Mary over and over. So many of them do. That rather than the Lord's Prayer. *Now and at the hour of our death*. It is, Mary, it is. The hour is here. She would have done better with the Lord's Prayer. *But deliver us from evil, amen*. What are your feelings looking at this picture? You never said."

Cross clenched his teeth. He'd not give him the satisfaction.

"Aww," cajoled Candlestick, like Cross was a child spoiling his game. "I think your feelings are not pity for the boy, or even respect for the father's awe in the presence of God, but a very exact curiosity at the surge of power you feel with the knife in your hand. You *know* the dead. You tidy up after them. The dead are your business. You must wonder how it feels to *do it*—*lead us not into temptation*—just as the priest in confession wonders what this fucking business is all about."

Cross shook his head vehemently, trying to block out the words, before they could reach the part of him that knew it was true.

He was aware of the knife being pressed into his hand. *This is another of his games,* he told himself.

"Move," the voice said.

Cross was nudged forward by the barrel of the gun. Inch by inch they moved in a slow procession towards the boy, who gazed around in sightless fear.

Cross tried to find the split second that would allow him to turn the knife on Candlestick. He imagined sliding the blade in, slipping it between his ribs, up into the aortic chamber, lifting him on the knife's handle until his feet dangled free of the ground and his eyes popped in bloody surprise. He truly wanted to see the blood run from his nose and his mouth and ears and eyes. If it didn't he'd cut the cunt until it did.

His mind snapped back. He tried telling himself that time wasn't quite used up. Candlestick would not deny himself the satisfaction of killing the boy, however much he might make it look like he wanted Cross to play the executioner. Candlestick was too driven to let anyone else do his killing. Cross prayed that he could use the knowledge to his advantage.

Candlestick halted Cross in front of Matthew.

"He's the sacrifice. Do it and the other killings stop. Refuse and they go on."

"You couldn't stop if you tried. Go ahead and kill the others," said Cross. "You must be able to see that their deaths mean nothing to me compared to his."

"I'll kill him anyway, and the others too. You've five minutes to decide."

WESTERBY was drenched and her reserves ebbing. It had taken much longer than she had expected to cover the ground between farm and barn. The physical effort of her slow, wet scramble across the rutted fields had at least distracted her from what was waiting. Several times she'd lost her bearings before she at last saw the barn through the driving rain. She was lucky not to have missed it—it was away to her left, not straight ahead as she had thought. She wasted time negotiating her way round the back, looking for a second entrance that was not there.

Peering through the crack in the main door, she could see Cross's back. She willed him to stop blocking her view.

The first thing she heard was Candlestick's voice saying,

"Well?" and Cross, a long while after, replying, "Give me the knife."

She watched Cross stoop to pick up the knife that was thrown in front of him and move slowly forwards. He still blocked her view.

She would have to go in blind, she thought grimly, gripping the gun and levering the safety catch off. She could not understand why Cross had been given the knife.

She saw the boy then, in his hood, and Candlestick dragging him by the sleeve and making him kneel. She had to force herself not to cry out.

She gradually understood what she was seeing. "Please God," she said and threw her weight against the door, hoping that surprise would give her enough of an advantage.

She got off one shot, knowing as she pulled the trigger that she'd missed. She then lost sight of Candlestick behind Cross and when he re-emerged he had Matthew and was grinning with bared teeth, his gun held to the boy's throat.

Westerby had no choice but to drop her gun. She kicked it away as she was told. Candlestick then ordered Cross to throw down the knife and move back.

She was puzzled by the glint in Candlestick's eye—a mixture of wild glee at her failure, but also of fear, no more than a tiny nugget but enough to give her hope. Her arrival was an element he'd not foreseen.

Words were her only weapon now. She felt surprisingly calm, compared to outside. The burning spasms in her stomach had subsided. She was aware of the dull throb of a headache above the bridge of the nose which she used to concentrate all her attention on Candlestick.

When Matthew tried to squirm free, Candlestick told him to hold still, otherwise he would make him watch while he killed his daddy. The boy froze and Westerby imagined his eyes searching the darkness of his hood for some sign that the nightmare would end.

"He won't kill you, Matthew," she said.

Candlestick jabbed with the gun at his head. Westerby flinched, knowing he was only a fraction away from pulling the trigger. The gun then swung towards her. She glimpsed its black snout and saw the spit of flame. The gun was back at Matthew's head before she realized that he'd deliberately fired wide. The singing noise she had heard had been the bullet passing by.

"You'll not kill him," she repeated.

"Watch me."

"You won't." Westerby shook her head. "Because the time isn't right."

Was it her imagination or had she startled him? She tried to picture the tiny casket deep inside him where desire and fear fought for control.

"I am the sacrifice," she said.

He regarded her curiously as she spelled it out for him—she was the next proper victim. Her age made her that. Eddoes, forty-nine, Caddy, forty-two and Causley, thirty-five. The next had to be twenty-eight. It had been her own birthday just the day before she and Cross had first made love.

"And I'm bleeding," she said.

Westerby saw his confusion, muddled with eagerness.

"That's important, isn't it?" she went on.

She took a step forward, seeing his inquisitiveness. She prayed that Cross understood what she was trying to do.

"I know all about the bleeding," she said. "And why the deaths only happened then."

She took another step forward, losing sight of Cross. She reached up to undo her jacket. Again Candlestick made no move.

"If I'm bleeding, you can get it up? Isn't that how it goes?"

"Shut up, cunt."

She was getting to him. She reached up and undid a button of her shirt.

"You don't really want to kill Matthew. Not in your heart of hearts. He's only seven. Something happened when you were seven. Something that made you wish you were dead."

Candlestick sneered.

He's bluffing, she told herself. *I've hit a nerve.*

"Why's the bleeding so important?" she went on. Again there was the glimmer in his eye, the focus shift away from the boy. "Has it something to do with your secret as a little boy?"

The tug of his curiosity pulled her forward. She risked undoing another button on her shirt. She was no longer aware of the boy or Cross—this was a battle of naked wills between the two of them.

Each step a thought, like walking a tightrope. One false move and we all fall.

She was aware of the cool night air on her skin where her shirt was open and of Candlestick looking at the shadow between her breasts. She was wearing nothing under the shirt.

Would she have thought of this without the strange incident with Rintoul? she wondered. And how old had she been when she had undressed for the two boys that long-ago summer? Seven, perhaps. She remembered the surge of power it had given her, showing herself off. It was the first time she had been aware of that feeling and it far outstripped any fear of getting caught. She looked at Candlestick and told herself to forget about his gun and bullets, treat them as toys. This was just another childhood game they were playing. He was nine feet away, maybe ten. The boy was still now, as inert as a rag doll. As for Cross, she just had to trust that he was using her diversion as she hoped.

"Tell me about the bleeding," she said, undoing another button and parting the front of her shirt to show him the swell of her breasts. Ten more paces and two or three more buttons.

She suddenly faltered. She had a flash of him raising the gun and blowing her brains out. The confidence drained out of her. The boy seemed to sense this and cried out, "Daddy!"

Candlestick poked the gun at Matthew's temple.

"Stop it!" he yelled, his voice edgy. Seeing him so rattled, Westerby risked another step.

"You kill when she bleeds. The bleeding controls you, doesn't it?"

She saw that she had hit home.

"Who is she? Another innocent like Becky? Some doormat you wipe yourself on?" She pressed on before he could answer. "I got it wrong at first. I thought you killed when she bled because you couldn't have her then. Because her bleeding made her taboo. But it's not that, is it?"

She undid the button by her navel. Seven paces.

You want to touch me. You must touch me. You need to.

She said these things to him in her mind, willing him to submit.

"You kill with the bleeding because when she bleeds is the only time it works for you. She bleeds. You kill and afterwards you can fuck. Is that what you do? Fuck after?"

Candlestick gave a roar of anguish and swung the gun up. *If he doesn't fire at once,* she thought. She stared down the barrel again, praying for the tremor that wasn't there.

"What happened when you were seven? Shall I tell you?"

Her hand strayed to the last button.

"Shall I whisper in your ear?"

HE WANTED desperately to touch her, to rest his head against the warmth of her breast. She was parting her shirt now, letting him see. He lowered the pistol. He'd wait until she was close enough, until he could smell her bleeding, then he'd kill the copper and the boy and have her. That much was clear. He was mystified by her, confused by her understanding. She was the only one to show compassion, and in her compassion lay betrayal, he knew. He could see her riding him in a frenzy after he'd done the copper and the boy. Their blood mixed with her own bleeding would stir her lust until it boiled and he imagined the hot jolt of putting himself into her. Bitch! he thought. She'd sooner give him over to the copper than give herself to him. He shoved the boy aside and reached out with his hand to touch the white of her skin. So soft, so smooth. He looked into her eyes. They were the same faraway blue as Becky's. He placed the gun against her pelvis—he'd shoot the other two any second now—and felt himself harden. "Show me," he said, and she pulled aside her shirt. He smelt the warmth of her skin, a soft, milky smell that made him want to lay his head there and sleep.

WESTERBY cupped her breasts. Candlestick was fixated, then, sensing her control, he tore his gaze away.

"I know your secret," she whispered. "Rest a while and I'll tell you. Come and sit down over there."

She gestured with her head towards the camp chair, and felt herself being nudged with the pistol in its direction.

As they turned, she saw Cross out of the corner of her eye and her anger at him mounted. She wasn't sure that he'd moved at all. The distance between him and the gun was hopeless. The strength drained from her. She sensed Candlestick noting her hesitation.

In whose compassion lies betrayal, he thought. *So lonely baby,* he whispered.

He said something she didn't catch. If she could get him to sit, they might just have a chance, but that depended on Cross.

They reached the chair and he sat. She opened her shirt and took his free hand, put it to her tongue, licked his fingers and placed them on her nipple.

She saw his eyelids grow heavy with desire and close—not for long enough.

At the root of her disgust she felt something, which, to her shame, she realized was arousal. The power she felt had made her moist.

"Tell me my secret," Candlestick said in an urgent whisper.

"Your secret is—" Her feeling of a moment earlier gave way to a wave of loathing. She felt the keen edge of Cross's jealousy like a stab.

"Tell me," he repeated.

"Do you really want to know?" she asked.

"Yes."

"When you were a little boy—"

She felt the gun dug hard into her pubic bone. "Tell only me," he said.

She leaned forward until his head was inside the open tent of her shirt and grazed her breast. The gun stayed where it was, but the rest of him relaxed.

"What happened," she whispered, "is when your mummy was bleeding"—she sensed his body stiffen—"your daddy"—a strange clicking noise came from the back of his throat—"your daddy used to come to you, didn't he? When Mummy was bleeding."

She heard the start of a choking sound and felt what she thought were tears on her skin. Still the gun did not budge. She took a deep breath and said, "And Mummy let him, didn't she? When you were seven."

He was nodding and shaking his head at the same time, sniffing at her, moving down until his head was burrowing between her legs. She had to suppress a quiver of revulsion. Then he suddenly broke away and stared up at her, puzzled.

"You're not bleeding," he said.

The gun dropped for just long enough. She shoved with all her strength, toppling him and the chair over, then threw herself to her left.

Two shots sounded in quick succession. As Westerby fell

she glimpsed the panicked child running around in circles, screaming, his arms stuck out in front of him. She couldn't tell where the shots had gone. Candlestick was scuttling on all fours trying to dodge Cross's aim. But Cross could not get a clear shot because of the boy.

"Matthew, no!" she heard him shout.

The warning was too late. The screaming boy ran straight into the arms of Candlestick, who snatched the knife from the ground.

Candlestick sank back on to his knees, swaying as though in the grip of possession. He held the boy in front of him like he was a talisman. His stare was glassy, but Cross couldn't tell if he'd been hit.

"Ecce Agnus Dei!" he shouted hoarsely.

The serrated edge of the knife was at Matthew's throat ready, yet the hand that held it stayed, Cross saw. Had Westerby's guess been right?

Candlestick's face contorted with pain and with a despairing cry he shoved the boy aside, revealing for the first time his bloody front. He pitched forward like an animal and, baring his teeth, stared evilly at Cross. His face was greased with sweat, his breathing laboured. His eyes started to dart in all directions, like he was watching an invisible swarm.

Westerby crawled to where Matthew lay whimpering and took hold of him. She removed the hood and cradled the tremulous child in her arms.

"Let go of him!" Cross shouted.

She saw from his look of disgust that he regarded her as contaminated by Candlestick. But she held on, burying Matthew's head against her to prevent him from seeing, telling him over and over that he was safe.

Cross aimed his gun at the point between Candlestick's eyes, and, like Candlestick, found himself hesitating. Candlestick gave a harsh bark and blood flowed from his mouth. Pain clouded his features and he made a strange hepping sound. Cross took aim again, telling himself that it was no worse than putting an animal out of its misery.

Candlestick sneered. "Do it, cunt. Go on, you yellow cunt. Pull the fucking trigger."

Cross couldn't. Couldn't in spite of the black anger he felt. He had been shaken to the core and the humiliation of impotent watching had nearly overridden his concern for Matthew's safety.

Candlestick made the strange hep-hep sound again and his body twisted sideways in another spasm of pain. A thread of bloody saliva drooled from his mouth.

Cross decided. Candlestick should live to suffer, even if he hadn't got much longer. Killing was what Candlestick did to others. Not killing him now was his punishment.

Candlestick tried to push himself up. He worked himself on to his knees, lost his balance and sat back heavily, his legs bent awkwardly. He stared down at himself in blank astonishment, and prodded the entry to his wound with his little finger, slipping it into the hole until he winced. His hand was still holding the knife and he seemed surprised to be reminded of it.

With a screech that summoned the last of his strength he lurched to his feet, moving with a force and speed that startled Cross. The hand that held the knife moved equally fast, reaching up and slashing once across, then back.

Cross saw the lateral tear appear in Candlestick's throat—a jagged grin. Candlestick lifted the knife again, this time using the serrated edge to saw at his throat. The rasp of steel cutting through gristle was drowned by a harsh gurgling, like some terrible final emptying. Then the blood came. Gouts, bright splashes, spilling down his front, then jets of it as the overworked heart beat harder in response to the adrenaline flooding his system.

The knife fell from his twitching hand. Soon the whole body began to convulse like it was in electric shock. As it shuddered and jerked, the power of his gaze grew more concentrated. Cross found himself unable to tear his eyes away. The look was beady and unknowable. Cross felt himself the inheritor of that last, dark stare—he would be the bearer of its terrible secrets. Candlestick reached out to touch him and Cross, appalled at being cheated by death, threw himself at the man.

They toppled to the ground. Cross was distantly aware of hammering Candlestick with the butt of his pistol and hearing the satisfaction of bone break. He was aware too—only just— of someone grabbing him and being astonished by his own strength in shaking himself free. He returned his attention to the thrashing limbs. The collarbone close to the slit throat, he smashed that, and the wrists too, hammering like he was driving nails in. Then the nose, with its sharp sound of hard bone splintering. He could hear his own rasping breathing, mixed with the other man's screams and then what sounded like the start of his last rattle. Cross raised the gun again to bring it down on the teeth and checked. The mouth was grinning up at him, a sardonic smile of triumph. He saw the eyes glittering and undefeated.

In his hesitation Cross saw himself for what he was—no better than the man beneath him when he had slaughtered the animals on the same killing ground.

Candlestick raised his head and spat at Cross's face. As Cross recoiled Candlestick grabbed his ears and he found himself dragged down by a vicelike grip. The strength of the man was terrifying. Cross felt like he was being pulled over the edge of a precipice. Again he saw the shiny, concentrated air of victory, and closed his eyes tight in a useless effort to avoid his own sense of defeat.

The grip subsided. The body gave a final convulsion and when Cross next looked the eyes had gone milky. He was about to extricate himself when they came briefly alive again. He saw a distant calm in them, then Candlestick gave a long-drawn-out sigh that sounded like faraway sea.

Cross stood, like a man climbing out of the grave. He could not see Westerby or the boy. Was it she who had attacked him, trying to prevent his frenzied assault?

He looked down at Candlestick, shrunk in death. He bent down and picked up the gun and, putting it behind Candlestick's ear, pulled the trigger. The body jumped from the impact and Cross felt the satisfying jolt of the recoil as it travelled up his arm, and savoured the sharp smell of cordite that cut through the visceral stenches of Candlestick's last struggle.

Westerby and the boy were outside. He decided to send them to the house while he buried the body in one of the soft peat ditches. If anyone wanted to claim it later they could.

Cross looked around. It was a beautiful dawn, a good omen for the future, though in his heart he knew that the blackness of that night would always be part of him.

The boy wouldn't let him touch him.

Sixty-one

November 15, 1985

CROSS watched events as though through the wrong end of a telescope. Everything looked sharp but remote. It was suddenly winter—a clear late autumn had given way to raw, overcast days. The cold he had caught on the night of Candlestick's death refused to go away.

Most of the time he felt curiously untouched. He told himself that he was all right. Then with no warning, sitting at traffic lights or in a meeting, his eyes would begin to prick. When with others he had to hurriedly excuse himself before he started to weep uncontrollably.

The loose ends of his life retied themselves, not to his satisfaction. He was too distant to take much of an active part in their resolution. A half-forgotten term from his boyhood religion—sins of omission—came back to haunt him.

It was a day of damp asphalt. Watery sunlight tried to penetrate the morning fog. Cross shivered inside his coat. Doody and the rest of the scene-of-crime squad moved about their business. There was none of the usual wisecracking within his hearing. Hargreaves pointed to the body dumped on the steep grass verge under a hedge.

"Head job," he said.

Business as usual, thought Cross.

The body lay on its front, dressed in thin jeans and a denim jacket. The black hood covering the head took Cross back to the barn, and he made fists of his hands in his pockets until he blanched the memory.

The body was barefoot, a sign, along with the hood, that the killing was sectarian, the victim an informer. He supervised the removal of the hood. The entry wound was behind the right ear. After the photographer and medical examiner were done, the body was turned over. Cross stared at the lad's face for a long time, then turned to Hargreaves and said, "You'd better tell Blair."

He walked back to his car. The last time he had seen the boy was when he'd called round and given him the money to go to Dublin. *Why had he come back?* He remembered their strange drive together when he had talked about the state of his marriage and Vinnie had said that he was feeding false information to Special Branch. Cross examined his conscience, wondering if there wasn't more he should have done.

It would have been the homesickness that had brought him back. Cross had seen it before with lads who had got themselves into trouble and gone away, only to discover their new lives insufficient, and had returned home dazed. With the boy's death Cross learned a hard lesson about himself. He probably didn't have the strength to leave either, and if he did it would only be to return.

THAT night on television Vinnie's death rated a small item on the local news. He had been shot by the Provisionals, the newsreader said in her carefully neutral tones, for being a police informer. Most of the news was taken up with that day's signing of the Anglo–Irish Agreement at Hillsborough Castle. Cross wondered briefly about all the invisible cogs, and how they ultimately fitted together, and at what point the strange submerged careers of Breen and Candlestick overlapped with the political machinations that had brought about this treaty, and how much the woman signing it knew of all that. He put the thought aside, telling himself that it was just another television news story. He had seen over the edge of the chasm and he had no wish to do so again. His responsibility was to his work and his family, clear duties that would allow the days to take care of themselves.

There had been a strange postscript to Vinnie's death. As Cross was leaving a car had drawn up. It was Stevens the journalist looking scrubbed and fresher than when Cross had last seen him. They had spoken briefly about the shooting and as they had parted Cross suggested that they meet. Stevens had shaken his head.

"I'm still interested in what we were talking about," said Cross.

Stevens feigned ignorance. Cross noted the expensive suit and new brogues and wondered if he was safely in Moffat's pocket now, passing on whatever he was told.

DURING the night a helicopter flew low over the house, waking Cross and Deidre. Deidre mumbled sleepily and settled again. Cross worried that it had woken the children. He got up to check. They were both asleep. Matthew stirred when Cross smoothed away the frown from his brow, and mumbled, "Sush-sush."

For a long time after the barn Matthew had said nothing apart from that same strange noise: "Sush-sush-sush."

Cross realized what it was later. "Helicopter," he had said to Matthew in the hospital, where he was being kept under observation. Matthew had blinked in acknowledgement. It was the beating of the helicopters that had come to take them away. Matthew hadn't responded when Cross had kissed him goodbye except to give another ghostly "sush-sush."

Westerby had telephoned from the farm and two helicopters had come. Cross had watched the disposal team hurriedly bag up Candlestick's corpse and swing it into the second helicopter. He had meant to bury the body. But an overwhelming lassitude had prevented him and he had sat alone for a long time before walking back to the farm where the three of them had waited in huddled silence. Matthew sucked his thumb, in a state of shock. Cross and Westerby were drained of all communication. Then Moffat arrived and urged everyone on. They were there illegally and he wanted them out in five minutes. Moffat, in spite of his air of disapproval, was clearly gleeful at Candlestick's untidy end, which was the tidiest ending for him. Cross was aware of Moffat looking at him strangely, with a mixture of fear and respect.

"What went on in there? The body was in a hell of a state."

"All your dirty little secrets are safe," Cross had said as they got into the helicopter.

HE HADN'T seen Westerby since. She'd taken immediate leave and then been away on a nine-week course. He wondered if their relationship had been permanently damaged by what had happened in the barn, or even before. With the satisfactory resolution of the Candlestick case, the matter of her charge of sexual harassment was quietly forgotten. "It was a conversation that did not take place," said Nesbitt, who overlooked the fact their affair was a disciplinary offence. On the contrary, he even hinted that he should make the most of it until Westerby's promotion came through.

For Matthew's sake, he and Deidre agreed to bury their differences. They were aware that this was just another holding measure. "We should mend the child before mending ourselves," she'd said, then added, "Though perhaps it's only by mending ourselves that we'll mend the child."

He didn't know. Perhaps some things never got solved. Or mended.

AT WORK he wrote up the case for Moffat. All the murders had been committed by the same man, in addition to the countless killings he had undertaken as an assassin for the loyalists and the republicans, but none of this was reflected in Cross's report. It stated that Francis Breen and the wife of Billy Eddoes had been killed by the same man, who was now dead by his own hand. He left it to Moffat to decide whether Willcox would still go down for the murders of Mary Elam and Mary Ryan. As for the others, they were filed among the statistics of unsolved sectarian murders for that year. There was no mention of conspiracy, no mention of secret work for the security forces, no mention of the INLA. He wondered briefly about Eddoes' story about the INLA moving drugs into respectable Protestant areas. It was difficult now not to see the hidden hand at work in everything. If a British faction wanted a united Ireland and anticipated a Protestant reaction, what better way to undermine them than by peddling drugs to their children? He remembered the note he'd found among the papers of the dead journalist Warren, noting how the Nazis had flooded the Polish market with pornography prior to invasion. Perhaps the same principle was still at work.

What would have happened, Cross wondered, if the scale of Candlestick's plan had been revealed? Would he have panicked everyone into seeing sense? Would the Brits have owned up? He doubted it. They'd been getting away with not owning up for centuries. As for the Irish, perhaps Deidre was right with her story about the Kilkenny cats. It would take a lot more than a massacre of the innocents to make them bury their differences. Like his marriage, an uneasy truce was the best that could be hoped for, with the certain knowledge that hostilities would be resumed sooner or later.

He finished his report for Moffat with the sentence: "WPC Westerby acted with the utmost courage and devotion to duty throughout. Without her efforts this case would not have been brought to a close."

That part of the report was true at least. But what of their affair? he thought. Had it been turned into just another secret to be buried along with all the others?

HIS DISGUST had flared only once and predictably it was in his last meeting with Moffat, a supposed celebration of a successful conclusion. His anger was directed at the smugness of the man's cover-up, to which he was a party. He thought of poor Mary Ryan, lying eyeless in the wasteland. Didn't her death deserve explanation? Didn't her parents at least have the right to know that she was murdered for a reason?

"What if I don't keep my mouth shut?" he asked. His voice was quiet and reasonable.

Moffat saw he was serious and said, "Ah, well, yes. I wondered if it would come to this." He fiddled with his pen. "Honest coppers can come to grief. Stalker wants to get his hands on a surveillance tape that'll prove the RUC deliberately shot up some Paddy against the rules. If he persists, then—" Moffat shrugged.

"Then what?"

"He'll find himself on some trumped-up disciplinary charge. Perhaps one of his social contacts will turn out to be not quite seemly. If it's not in the greater interest to have him dig up the dirt, then he'll be stopped, just as you will."

Cross stood up to leave.

Moffat said, "Wait a minute."

He produced a file from a drawer and flicked through the pages, then spoke quietly in matter-of-fact terms for a couple of minutes before telling Cross that he could go. They didn't shake hands.

Back in his office, Cross laughed in disbelief at the immaculateness of the stitch-work. His connection to McMahon had been noted, and the fact that he had used these meetings to pass on information to the Provisional IRA. Through one of Special Branch's informers it was known that the RUC had been penetrated at a high level and a senior officer had been turned. It took Cross a while to recognize this story as the one Vinnie had told him in the car: the Provisionals had instructed him to leak to Blair the false story of a senior informant in their ranks.

And now that man was him.

Cross shook his head at the devilish cunning of it all. These people made Candlestick look almost naive. The deal was clear: Cross's silence in exchange for theirs. Even if he did leak anything it would be immediately discredited as he would be arrested and charged with collusion to murder.

"Murder?" said Cross when Moffat had mentioned it. He wondered for a moment if Moffat was going to try and pin Candlestick's death on him.

"This tout who was shot the other day, Vincent O'Connor," said Moffat. "You had dealings with him, I understand."

Cross nodded slowly.

"Well, old son, here's the speculative thought for the day. Said Vincent's as dead as doornails and I'll be bound that this RUC man who was fingered by young Vinnie was the one who fingered him in return to the Provos. Collusion to murder. The tabloid newspapers would turn that man into a monster."

FOR TWO days Cross had found himself walking the city. Instead of going to work he walked, looping through Catholic and Protestant areas without regard and without knowing why. Only once was he stopped, by a youth in Protestant Ballymacarrett who asked abruptly where he thought he was going. Cross brushed him aside and went on unchecked. His mind felt drained. At the end of the first day he'd gone home as though everything was normal and read to the children and watched television with Deidre. The following day she'd looked at him oddly when he said, "I think I'll get the bus into work."

He'd walked instead and this time found himself roaming the city centre. He heard the noise first of all without being able to identify it, then saw as he emerged from a side street a great river of people flowing towards the centre. Cross was stunned by the crowd's size. The whole of the centre of the city had been taken over. There were thousands of them. For a moment he wondered if the spontaneous protest dreamed of by Candlestick would have turned into something like this. Except then it would have been Protestant and Catholic alike, where these were just Protestants marching against the Anglo–Irish Agreement. What if he were to gatecrash the speakers' platform, he thought, and say, "I am an officer of the RUC and I have a statement to read that proves beyond doubt—"? To see Moffat's face at that moment would be worth it.

Cross stood, letting the crowd move round him. He looked at the sky and thought of Matthew and Mary Ryan and all the rest. He imagined the ghost of Matthew's innocence, riding untouched with the others in the clouds. He saw Mary Elam reunited with her children and safe from her troubles, saw Maureen McMahon laughing and speeding with the boy Vinnie reckless at her side, and he saw all the others, secure from the likes of Candlestick and Breen, safe once and for all. Several streets away the crowd grew noisy. Cross pulled up his collar and walked on. It was coming on to rain.

Sixty-two

HE KNEW what he had to do. Perhaps God had forsaken His mansion, but that did not mean he had to do it Candlestick's way. Perhaps he and Candlestick were the point where the circle joined, where good came of bad.

It took him a week to organize. Then one clear morning he checked carefully under the car as usual before opening the garage door and reversing out. The package was on the seat beside him, twenty foolscap sheets that he had laboriously typed himself. He remembered his briefcase was still in the house and left the car idling on the forecourt while he ran back in for it. Deidre was in the kitchen with the children and called out, asking what he was doing. He told her and hurried across the hall to say goodbye again, sticking his head round the door, saying that he would not be back late. Matthew and Fiona were involved in some game of their own and ignored him. He was glad to see that the boy was less withdrawn. Fiona, being the sturdier, had been quite unscathed by the events of the last weeks and it was her practical sense of play that had helped Matthew back to normality, far more than the efforts of Deidre or himself.

He drove away, experiencing a moment's doubt about whether he was doing the right thing. Thinking about the meeting he was going to, he wondered if there was an ulterior motive that he wasn't admitting to himself. No, he decided. His reasons were straightforward.

Westerby was due back from her course that day. It would be difficult seeing her and he had no doubt he would handle it badly by being standoffish and awkward. He berated himself. After everything they had been through—good and bad—it would be sad and ridiculous if they ended up being remote and aloof.

He looked at his watch. He was in good time as he crossed the Lagan and headed south through Ballynafeigh. He switched the radio on and while he fiddled with the dial trying to find some decent music he remembered an old song— *wonder wonder wonder who who who wrote the book of love*—and tried to think where he had heard it before.

Sixty-three

WESTERBY spent the day at work waiting to bump into Cross. She was nervous of seeing him. Her leave had been spent lying alone on a beach in the Canaries trying to sort herself out. To her surprise it was not only the events of the barn that had preyed on her mind but her affair with Cross. She wanted it to continue while fully realizing the hopelessness of its chances after what had happened to Matthew. His long recovery would make any relationship between them impossible. Besides, there was the whole business of Moffat and Nesbitt knowing. The mean little trap which they had confronted her with—shop Cross or we'll destroy the pair of you—had been forgotten in the aftermath of Candlestick's death. Moffat had said as much in the helicopter on the way back to Belfast while Cross and the boy had slept, exhausted.

Westerby had come back from her holiday with a tan, looking different and wanting to see Cross, only to discover that she had been posted on a course which took her away for another couple of months.

During that first day back at work she changed her mind endlessly. She avoided the canteen in case he was there, then regretted it. She had no idea what his attitude would be. Finally, unable to stand any more, she decided to see him in his office. As she walked down the corridor she rehearsed what to say. Regardless of what he thought, she wanted to tell him that she bore him no hard feelings for what had happened between them. It was something she had entered into with open eyes and wanted. She had loved him and still did, even though she understood that their affair could not continue. She stopped half way down the corridor, telling herself there was no way she could bring herself to come out with any of this. Just say it, she told herself.

Cross's door was shut. Westerby knocked. There was no answer. She opened the door. The room was empty and the desk neat, like it hadn't been used that day.

She was walking back down the corridor when two constables ran past in a hurry. There seemed to be some kind of flap on. When she got back there the main office was in turmoil. She saw Hargreaves looking pale and asked what was going on.

"It's DI Cross. He's been shot."

She knew as soon as he spoke that he didn't mean wounded.

THE WORD was that he had shot himself.

His car had been found down a narrow lovers' lane south of the city. No one had any idea why he had driven there unless it was to kill himself. The gun was still in his hand and there was a single bullet wound to his temple.

It had taken Westerby several days to assemble this information because Cross's death was subject to a cover-up, an irony that she thought he would have appreciated. The semi-official version given out was that Cross had been murdered in the line of duty. A statement had been issued by the Provisional IRA stating as much, and then retracted. The suggestion that it was McMahon's men avenging their leader's death was the rumour that held strongest in the barracks. It gave everyone an obvious focus. But as the days passed, that was eroded by a counter-rumour which suggested that Cross had shot himself in a fit of depression.

As she listened to these stories in the office and the canteen, she saw that Cross had been much more of an outsider than she had realized, too remote to have been popular, too thoughtful to have joined in. In a strange way there had come about an almost tangible feeling of relief with his going, an acknowledgement that he had never really been one of them. This was the undercurrent. On the surface everyone expressed shock and dismay.

Westerby did her grieving in private. At night she missed him more than she could have believed, but found herself incapable of crying for him. Her tearless mourning left her brittle and abrasive.

The funeral orations painted a picture of a man she didn't recognize. The burial service was a full uniformed affair with more top brass than she'd ever seen in one go. She shut her eyes and ears to most of it, trying not to look at the casket and think of him inside. She glimpsed Deidre and Matthew and his sister and wondered if she had the courage to give her condolences afterwards.

Why his left hand? she kept thinking.

Cross had been right-handed.

She had phoned the doctor who had examined his body at the scene of the death, without really knowing why beyond trying to allay the turmoil she felt. Her deepest fear was that Cross might have shot himself after all. If he had, she wanted to understand why. But try as she might to reconstruct those final moments she could not see him doing it, even imagine him contemplating it.

The doctor had told her that Cross had been found in the driver's seat with a bullet through his left temple. The gun was in his hand and there was nothing to suggest that anyone else had been involved. The position of the body and the head wound were consistent with a self-inflicted act. Westerby then spoke to Doody, who had been at the scene of the crime. Doody had been suspicious of her questions at first, but his dislike of Cross got the better of him and he talked freely, confirming what the doctor had said. Doody's unstated verdict was that Cross didn't have what it took to be a policeman and the suicide had not surprised him. He added that there had been no additional fingerprints in the car.

"What state was the ground?"

"Bone hard," said Doody. "You're wasting your time."

She'd sat in her own car and tried to imagine what might have been going through Cross's head. It was then that she had first asked herself, *Why the left hand?*

She'd made a gun of her own left hand and pointed it at her temple, then did it with her right. She would use the right, definitely, and either put the gun against her temple or, to be even more certain, shoot herself through the mouth.

CROSS was buried among generations of O'Neills. Westerby noticed the largest wreath was dedicated to Beloved Husband and Father. During the service she felt herself ever more adrift. Nothing squared with her version of events. The dignity, the politeness, the stoic suffering and the fiction of the personal testimonies left her wanting to scream. She was tempted to stand up and say that Cross was a man who had lived among the dead and tidied up after them with a solitary dedication that set him apart from all the careerists come to pay their so-called respects. She wanted to tell them about the pain of the barn and his troubled conscience and how they had both delved deep into the muck of their country's secrets. She wondered if Moffat was there.

As the funeral ended and the congregation was breaking up Westerby caught sight of a striking, enigmatic woman standing alone, smoking. To her surprise the woman nodded coolly and made her way over. She introduced herself as Miranda Ramsay and said she had something for her from Cross in her car. She used Cross's first name, Westerby noticed.

They made their way through the crowd and walked in

silence the quarter of a mile or so to the car. Westerby was bursting to ask who she was.

"We met because of Niall Warren," Miranda finally announced without being asked.

She unlocked her car and took out a buff envelope.

"This is for you. He sent it to me for safekeeping."

Westerby glanced at the envelope. It was sealed and there was no name on it.

Miranda told her that it had come in a larger envelope with a note saying she should pass it on to Westerby if anything happened to him.

"You're like he described."

Westerby frowned, wondering what else Cross had told her. She weighed the envelope in her hands.

"What is it?"

"I don't know. I only read the part addressed to me."

"Did he give any indication that he might kill himself?" Westerby asked carefully.

Miranda looked shocked and shook her head, frowning.

"Did he strike you as a man capable of that?"

What Westerby was really wondering was why Cross was using this woman as an intermediary. As far as she remembered, he had never mentioned her. She didn't like Miranda Ramsay because she could imagine the way she made Cross look at her.

"I didn't know him well enough to say."

It was said with such regret that Westerby realized there was a troubled sadness to her not apparent before. They stood in awkward silence, uncertain how to part. Westerby was aware of being inspected.

"So you were the copper's ride?"

Westerby was jolted by the sudden crudeness of the remark, and the reduction of their affair to something crass and dirty.

"Did he tell you he had me too? In the Europa Hotel."

Westerby's shock turned to anger at the idea of Cross and her.

"So," Miranda went on, apparently oblivious to Westerby's upset, "we have something in common. I was sorry not to have known him better."

She leaned forward impulsively and brushed her lips against Westerby's cheek, and said, "Sad days."

* * *

SHE LEFT the funeral without talking to anyone else or going to the wake. Instead she went home and changed, turned on the fire and settled down to read Cross's document. Glancing through the pages, she thought what a painful struggle it must have been for him to have typed. Each page was littered with little spots of white correction fluid. The sight of these pathetic blobs was too much for her. For some reason she also remembered that Shel Silverstein had not written "Total Eclipse of the Heart" as she had once told Cross. It was Jim Steinman and now she had no way of telling him, and she broke down for the first time since the barn, bawling out her rage and loss, and fear and confusion. Then, when she thought she was drained of any further feeling, she shocked herself by masturbating hard and angrily at his not being there, concentrating all her attention on the gritty core of desire inside her. The shock of her coming jolted her backwards and even as she came she continued to work at herself, kneading herself uncontrollably with the heel of her hand until she fell back gasping and exhausted, wondering what had possessed her.

She felt bad, not about what she had done but for the discovery in herself of such fierce and concentrated emotion. After the barn she had believed there was nothing left to know about herself, that she had seen and survived the worst.

She read Cross's document in a sober and chastened mood. It filled in all the missing bits for her, particularly Breen's role as a British agent. She noted too the blank in Candlestick's life between faking his death and his re-emergence to kill Breen. "I don't suppose we'll ever know," concluded Cross at the end of that section.

It was clear that Cross wanted this information to receive a wider hearing. In that he and Candlestick were, ironically, in agreement. Westerby was less certain. She doubted in the end if the story would surface. Too much was in place to stop it. Also she wasn't sure if she wanted to sabotage her own career. She was no crusader.

SHE WAS drawn back into the case in spite of herself. All it took was the question she was bound to ask eventually: if Cross didn't kill himself, then who did?

The obvious answer was the Provisionals, except why did they deny it after the initial claim? The IRA was always keen to publicize its killings for propaganda—another crown copper dead. Because of what Cross knew about the INLA it was possible it had got rid of him, but that organization too would have announced the shooting.

If he had been killed by the security forces—because it was known what he knew and known that he intended to take it further—Westerby wondered shakily where that left her. Was she a target too? The feeling grew, feeding her incipient paranoia. What made it worse now Cross was gone was that she had no one to talk to. She realized she was quite friendless. Cross's favouritism had isolated her from her colleagues, who now gossiped behind her back about their affair. As for a life outside of the force, that had long gone, with the irregular hours and the overtime.

People and events slithered past her and Westerby was aware of the tight grip of anxiety on the back of her neck, and wondered if she was next. She thought she might be suffering delayed post-traumatic stress, but didn't do anything about it because in the macho world of the RUC any sign of weakness, especially in a woman, was taken as a sign that you were not up to the job.

This had happened to her once already, when she had asked to be relieved from the sex abuse unit. At some point, the parade of scarred women and buggered children had got under her skin—the memory of them still worked away inside her like larvae. Worse, she had been in danger of becoming inured and immune. And worst of all, she sometimes found herself actively hating the whiny voices, the pathetic excuses, and the flinches of the victims. Not the kids, just the women, but how long would it have been before her indifference extended to the children?

Sometimes everything felt so weird that she wondered if she wasn't part of Cross's dying dream. *But the nightmare is over,* she kept telling herself. *It should have ended in the barn. So why does it feel like it's still going on?*

There was something she was missing, she kept telling herself, something she had noticed but overlooked. Some message from the dead.

She read over Cross's pages until she had memorized whole chunks of them, and read back over Candlestick's notebook, trying to work out what it was he was withholding. She got out the files on each of the murders and reluctantly studied the scene-of-crime photographs. *Some message from the dead,* she kept telling herself. Breen lying headless in the road told her nothing. Nor the photograph of Mary Elam with her half-shut eyes slid away to one side, like she was slyly looking at something out of the picture. Wheen's death showed a crumpled figure folded into his own boot and Arnold's photographs were still with Special Branch. She hadn't been there for Mary Ryan's death and her scene-of-crime pictures, which she hadn't seen before, shocked her more than the others: the stark frenzy of the mutilation and the discarded body with its legs so obscenely parted.

She put the photographs aside. These were things she thought she would never have to think about consciously again. She pinched the bridge of her nose, trying to free the images from her mind.

"Oh, my God," she said aloud.

She picked up the main photograph of Mary Ryan again. It had been taken from above and showed the whole body. The head lolled, its features partly burned out by the glare of the flash. The arms lay away from her side at an angle of forty-five degrees. The knees were bent and spread to reveal the dark shadow of her pubic area.

The first conclusion anyone would jump to was that the positioning was deliberate and sexually provocative, the work of a pervert. Yet there was nothing else in the case to suggest that.

"Oh fuck," said Westerby. "Of course."

It was obvious looking at the photograph again.

"There were two of them."

It had taken two people to carry Mary Ryan's body.

One had taken hold of her arms and the other had held her under the knees, and the way the body had been left was the way it had been carried.

Candlestick had had an accomplice.

Sixty-four

SHE HAD resurfaced in 1981, this time as his handler, travelling up from Dublin. "Well, blow me down," she said, wondering if he'd pick up the echo of Tommy Herron in her words. Later he asked if she still thought she owed him one. She took him outside and made him do it standing up in an alley behind the hotel.

She made it clear she used men and drifted between them, sometimes for three weeks, sometimes three months. It was a cause of friction between them. She had caressed his face and told him he was different.

"I've got plans for you."

"What plans?"

She'd laughed. "We're going to fuck everyone."

She told him she had never seen such a dead country, with its pathetic men, and so dominated by its cult of death which was to be seen everywhere, in the disproportionate length of its deaths columns, with their sentimental and elaborate obituaries and anniversary commemorations and invocations. She saw their work as the logical extension of this cult. It was their mission to expose its folly and to reveal its secrets. If the British were past masters at the art of secrecy, the Irish were not far behind with their men-only societies. Why, she asked, were Irish women so fatigued? It was a country of laughing men and knackered women. She had never seen so many chemists: the country was awash with pharmaceutical prescriptions. She taught him the underlying assumptions of Irish culture—that a wife and children were a man's property, a tradition reinforced by laws of Church and State. She mocked the whole brothers-in-arms sham and showed him the sordid reality behind it—a level of family violence that had reached epidemic proportions. For the larger violence to end, the domestic violence at its root must end, and what was the death of so many children if it brought a people to its senses?

She honed his messianic zeal, gave him a purpose, led him to believe he was in control, and used him later, when the killings began, to satisfy the impulse that had been triggered in her the day they had killed Tommy Herron, that arching sense of ecstasy she knew would never be reached again unless it was prefaced by death. She'd watched while he'd broken Breen's spirit and body, torn between prolonging her pleasure at the expense of his drawn-out pain and seeing him finished off so that she could satisfy her desire's aching need.

In a world of secrets theirs were the most forbidden of all. The daring of her strategy was also her licence. In control she discovered what lay beyond: a voluptuous abandonment that man alone could not satisfy. Men usually failed her. Too often she saw the child in them. (He fucked best when she was bleeding, as she had been with Tommy Herron, and she started to make sure her visits coincided with her periods.)

"There are very few Christians in Northern Ireland. Its people hate each other in the name of Jesus Christ." That was Bernadette McAliskey née Devlin, she told him. The trouble began in childhood, she went on, particularly for the boys who grew up in a world they saw only as black and white, where the only adults who appeared to control their destiny, and act as if their actions made sense, were paramilitaries: they filled the children's need for strong, protective parents.

She remembered a Brazilian woman saying: "Of course women do all the work here. Of course nothing ever changes unless women change it." The same applied there, leading a woman Official to observe: "When we stand shoulder to shoulder with our guns we're equal, but when the shooting is over, the men go off to the pub to talk of strategy and the women go off to the kitchen to cook their supper."

When the business of Breen came up she had gone to him and said, "We're on our own from now on." It was time for him to get out, she explained, and told him she needed him for her work. She called him "My little Candlestick," to annoy him. He had no humour.

When he understood that he'd been put into the Officials as insurance for Breen he wanted to kill Breen without delay. She persuaded him to wait. She drove him to Breen's home and showed him his wife and children, and smiled and said nothing until he worked it out for himself.

"It'll take time," she said.

After their deaths she went to Breen saying she was from London and under instructions to get him out. He was easy, so groggy with grief and guilt and sentiment that he followed like a lamb. She organized the farm across the border, checking on him from time to time to make sure his deterioration was going to plan. Within three months he was broken, punched out by drink.

When they drove his body to the dumping ground, they fucked in the van in among the trees, with Breen like Tommy Herron behind. After placing the body in the road, he wanted to go but she made him wait, standing hidden in the trees close by, waiting for its discovery. The sight and sound of his head being run over—the final, delicious full stop to his life—nearly made her swoon with pleasure. She walked back to the van on unsteady legs, while he urged her to hurry, and while he drove she fell sated into the deepest sleep of the justified.

She wondered what broke him. He was not the same towards the end, troubled, even. Perhaps it was the children he recoiled from. She couldn't see why. He'd never shown any conscience before. Children had always struck her as particularly unpleasant, fine in theory, *in imagination,* but who in their right mind would want them?

Wee Mary Ryan had been the best since Tommy. Dead Mary watching her hunched down on his splayed body.

The eyes were her idea. She'd read in a story—she read a lot—of a woman at a bullfight taking the eye of the bull, which had been ejected by the force of the death thrust, and inserting it inside herself. He'd done that willingly enough, handed her Mary's on a plate. They'd been in the garage where they had once collected the car which they'd used to kill Tommy Herron.

Sixty-five

THE MORE Westerby tried to imagine this woman the more she grew sure that the killings—for all their apparent sense of purpose—were after all sexually driven and had a sexual trigger. The observation *He needs an audience* came back to haunt her, and she grew to believe that the woman in Candlestick's life was not passive but active, perhaps even the architect of their plan. Candlestick had written of himself that he was only the instrument. The killing and the fucking went hand in hand, she was sure, but could not say why.

Westerby felt this sexual itch herself, an almost uncontrollable desire that ambushed her when she least expected it. What demons, she wondered, had been unleashed in her. She began to pray for the first time since childhood, for Cross at first, then for herself. *But deliver us from evil for Thine is the kingdom, the power and the glory, for ever and ever, amen.*

After immersing herself so much in Candlestick's life, she felt sometimes that he was not dead—just as she was sometimes certain that Cross was waiting on the other side of the door and would enter any minute—and still communicating with her.

She understood him so well now that she knew which moves to make. She went to Willcox and forced herself to look into his abuser's eyes. She had not met him before. His stolid air of violence frightened her and brought back all the memories she had tried to reject of battered women and small children with swollen vaginas and torn rectums.

She asked the only question left—"Was he with anyone on the day he came to kill Tommy Herron?"—and came away with the answer, and a name. Maggie. And a description. Of someone she knew, not knew but had met.

She dreamed of a house. She couldn't work out if this house was her own in the future or where Candlestick had lived with the woman, with its children's room and no children and a little sign on the door, painted in twee lettering, saying *Romper Room. Hush, hush, whisper who dares, Christopher Robin is saying his prayers*. A lullaby voice drifted down the stairs, a woman crooning: *Bye baby bunting, Daddy's gone ahunting*.

She was sick in the morning and knew what she had suspected for some time. That she was carrying Cross's child.

Epilogue

MAGGIE picked up the phone, dialled and said, "This is Miranda Ramsay."

Westerby wrote down the address. How shall I prepare myself, she thought, for what I have to do? How shall I arm myself? *Had she kissed Cross as she put the gun to his head?*

The house looked a bit like the house in her dream, bright in November sunshine. It was small and on the edge of the city, within sight of fields, standing by itself, but was different in little ways that allayed her sense of premonition. She shook the thought from her mind, telling herself that this was the time for cold reason, and smiled brightly as Miranda opened the door.

Westerby stepped inside, into the cool dark hall, and the door shut after her.

In the time left to you, Maggie thought, as she closed the door behind them, *you will come to see that there are layers of evil, like the levels in any building. Come into my cellar, then come into my bedroom and I will show you that there are mirrors for evil too. After the letting of blood, the slaking of lust.*

Outside in the far distance a siren howled and Westerby was reminded of a line from a song.

Heard the little girl dropped something on her way back home from school.

I was once that girl, she thought. *What happened to her?*

So young and bold, fourteen years old.

She was twenty-eight. She knew that with this woman there would be no jumping out of sequence.

Numbers add up to nothing.

Twenty-eight divided by seven equals—

So lonely baby.

Acknowledgements

The following books proved useful, and sometimes essential, guides to the complex labyrinth of Northern Ireland. *The Psalm Killer* is a work of fiction, though I have on occasion used real people and drawn on factual incidents described by others.

Anderson, Don, *14 May Days: The Inside Story of the Loyalist Strike of 1974* (Gill & Macmillan, Dublin, 1994)

Anon, *Northern Ireland: Reappraising Republican Violence; A Special Report* (Research Institute for the Study of Conflict and Terrorism, London, 1991)

Armstrong, Gary, *From the Palace to Prison* (New Wine Press, Chichester, 1991)

Asher, Michael, *Shoot to Kill: A Soldier's Journey through Violence* (Viking, London, 1990)

Bailey, Anthony, *Acts of Union: Reports on Ireland, 1973–79* (Faber and Faber, London, 1980)

Barzily, David, *The British Army in Ulster,* vols. 1 and 3 (David Barzily, Belfast, 1973 and 1978)

Beattie, Geoffrey, *We Are the People: Journeys through the Heart of Protestant Ulster* (Heinemann, London, 1992)

Belfrage, Sally, *The Crack: A Belfast Year* (Deutsch, London, 1987) As well as being a first-rate reporter of Belfast life, Belfrage has an excellent ear, so good that it was impossible sometimes not to borrow. While most fictional characters in *The Psalm Killer* are the product of imagination, the O'Neills owe an enormous debt, and some of their dialogue, to her chapter "True Blue."

Bishop, Patrick, and Eamonn Mallie, *The Provisional IRA* (Heinemann, London, 1987)

Bowyer Bell, J., *IRA Tactics & Targets* (Poolbeg, Dublin, 1990)

Bradley, Anthony J., *Requiem for a Spy: The Killing of Robert Nairac* (Mercier Press, Dublin, 1993) Contains material on Baker.

Brewer, John D., with Kathleen Magee. *Inside the RUC, Routine Policing in a Divided Society* (Clarendon Press, Oxford, 1991) Provides details of daily police work, and deviancy within the system, plus material on the role of women in the RUC, attitudes towards them and on the operations of the sex abuse unit.

Bruce, Steve, *The Red Hand: Protestant Paramilitaries in Northern Ireland* (OUP, Oxford, 1992) Includes accounts of the forming of paramilitary organizations, the Shankill murders, the career of Tommy Herron, racketeering and collusion between enemies. The tax dodge on page 321 is a paraphrase of one described by Bruce.

————, *Northern Ireland: Reappraising Loyalist Violence* (Research Institute for the Study of Conflict and Terrorism, London, 1992)

Clarke, A.F.N., *Contact* (Secker & Warburg, London, 1983)

Clutterbuck, Richard, *Protest and the Urban Guerilla* (Cassell, London, 1973)

Coogan, Tim Pat, *The IRA;* revised edn. (Fontana, London, 1987)

Costello, Mary, *Titanic Town: Memoirs of a Belfast Girlhood* (Methuen, London, 1992)

De Paor, Liam, *Divided Ulster* (Penguin, London, 1970)

Dillon, Martin, *The Dirty War* (Hutchinson, London, 1988) Covers a wide range of covert activities, including particular operations by the security forces, among them those involving Baker and Heatherington. The most complete version of Baker's flight and religious conversion can be found in Dillon. The description of Candlestick's murder of a waiter is based on Baker's shooting of Philip Anthony Fay in August 1972, described by Dillon, who was also the main source for the murder described on page 111. Actions attributed to Baker by Dillon have been appropriated by me and given to Candlestick, which is not to say that Candlestick was in any way inspired by the actions of Baker or that Candlestick is anything other than a fictional character. The death of Councillor Healey is based on Dillon's account of a similar abduction and murder. The case of Heatherington is a simplified version of one found in Dillon and elsewhere. The meeting between the IRA and the UDA in the Royal Bar on page 322 is reported by Dillon. There is also a rare reference to a speech by Unionist MP Enoch Powell, claiming that Airey Neave's death was the result of conspiracy by factions in the British and U.S. governments. However, the deduction that British intelligence had some hand in the creation of the INLA is entirely my fiction.

————, *The Shankill Butchers: A Case Study of Mass Murder* (Hutchinson, London, 1989)

————, *Stone Cold* (Hutchinson, London, 1992) Material on McKeague, the Kincora scandal, Baker and assassinations carried out on the orders of Tommy Herron.

Dillon, Martin, and Denis Lehane, *Political Murder in Northern Ireland* (Penguin, London, 1973)

Dorril, Stephen, *The Silent Conspiracy: Inside the Intelligence Services in the 1990s* (Heinemann, London, 1993)

Dorril, Stephen, and Robin Ramsay, *Smear! Wilson and the Secret State* (Fourth Estate, London, 1991)

Feldman, Allen, *Formations of Violence: The Narrative of the Body and Political Terror in Northern Ireland* (University of Chicago Press,

Chicago, 1991) Contains taped interviews with witnesses of sectarian violence, including the Shankill killings, plus useful material on the language of violence. Breen on different forms of sectarian assassination (page 244) is taken from a transcribed anonymous interview quoted by Feldman. The candlestick maker quote on page 309 is from a Feldman interview, as is the one after. The name Doctor Death, used by Willcox and Eddoes, is real and is mentioned in interview, as is Eddoes' story on page 328. Willcox's account of the sectarian murder on pages 342–3 is drawn from interviews quoted by Feldman.

Fields, Rona M., *Northern Ireland: Society Under Siege* (Transaction Books, New Brunswick, N.J., 1980) I have taken first-hand descriptions from the chapter "Psychological Genocide"—Cross's dream in Chapter 1 features some of them—and am grateful to Fields for her account of the story of the Kilkenny cats.

Fisk, Robert, *The Point of No Return: The Strike Which Broke the British in Ulster* (Deutsch, London, 1975)

Foot, Paul, *Who Framed Colin Wallace?* (Macmillan, London, 1989) Includes a chapter on Kincora plus much information on black propaganda operations mounted by the security forces.

Forde, Ben, with Chris Spencer, *Hope in "Bomb City"* (Marshall, Morgan & Scott, Basingstoke, 1979)

Fraser, Morris, *Children in Conflict: Growing Up in Northern Ireland* (Basic Books, New York, 1977)

Gearty, Conor, *Terror* (Faber and Faber, London, 1991)

Gebler, Carl, *The Glass Curtain: Inside an Ulster Community* (Hamish Hamilton, London, 1991)

Hamill, Desmond, *Pig in the Middle: The Army in Northern Ireland, 1969–1984* (Methuen, London, 1985)

Hansford Johnson, Pamela, *On Iniquity* (Macmillan, London, 1967) The quotation about the Nazis and pornography, found by Cross among Warren's notes, is taken from her opening chapter.

Holland, Jack, "The Profits of War" (*Spectator*, 26 February, 1994)

Holland, Jack, and Henry McDonald, *INLA: Deadly Divisions* (Torc, Dublin, 1994) Detailed account of the emergence of the INLA, the initial split in the ranks of the Official IRA, the resulting civil war, and later operations, including drug dealing. The shooting of Ronnie Bunting (page 250f.) is a fictionalized version of the facts presented by Holland and McDonald, including the widow's assertion that her husband was killed by men with English accents.

Holmes, Ronald M., and James De Burger, *Serial Murder* (Sage Publications, Newbury Park, Ca., 1988) See page 89.

Jenkins, Richard, *Lads, Citizens and Ordinary Kids: Working-class Youth Life-styles in Belfast* (Routledge & Kegan Paul, London, 1983)

Jones, Richard Glyn, *Couples Who Kill* (True Crime, London, 1993)

Kelley, Kevin, *The Longest War: Northern Ireland and the IRA* (Zed Press, London, 1982) Contains vivid descriptions of early rioting and the impact of the army upon the civilian population. Much of the detail of Molly's memories of the riots of 1969 draws on Kelley.

McGivern, Johnny, "It Was One Damn Good Car: The Diary of a Belfast Joyrider," (*Independent on Sunday*, 4 April, 1993) This brief, vivid memoir of a kneecapped joyrider, later killed in a high-speed chase with the police, was the inspiration for Vinnie's story.

McWilliams, Monica, and Joan McKiernan, *Bringing It Out in the Open: Domestic Violence in Northern Ireland* (HMSO, Belfast, 1993) Includes transcripts of case histories of physical abuse, used by me in Chapter 28.

Morgan, Robin, *The Demon Lover: On the Sexuality of Terrorism* (Methuen, London, 1989) Quotes Paul Theroux's *The Kingdom by the Sea*, on a "cult of death" in Northern Ireland; also refers to an epidemic of domestic violence, linking it to the wider violence.

Morrison, John, *The Ulster Cover-Up* (Ulster Society, Lurgan, Co. Armagh, 1993) Some of the academic's views in Chapter 53 owe their origins to Chapters 9 and 10.

Murray, Raymond, *The SAS in Ireland* (Mercier Press, Dublin, 1990) Information on the Baker operation and Herron's death, plus details on Herron's internecine rivalry with the British army.

Norris, Joel, *Serial Killers: The Growing Menace* (Arrow, London, 1990)

Parker, Tony, *May the Lord in His Mercy Be Kind to Belfast* (Cape, London, 1993)

Robertson, Geoff, *Reluctant Judas: The Life and Death of a Special Branch Informer* (Temple Smith, London, 1976)

Rusbridger, James, *The Intelligence Game: The Illusions and Delusions of International Espionage* (I.B. Tauris, London, 1989; revised 1991)

Ryder, Chris, *The RUC: A Force Under Fire* (Methuen, London, 1989)

Shannon, Elizabeth, *I Am of Ireland: Women of the North Speak Out* (Little Brown, Boston, 1989)

Taylor, Kevin, with Keith Mumby, *The Poisoned Tree* (Sidgwick & Jackson, London, 1990)

Toibin, Colm, *Walking Along the Border* (Queen Anne Press, London, 1987)

Urban, Mark, *Big Boys' Rules: The SAS and the Secret Struggle Against the IRA* (Faber and Faber, London, 1992)

White, Jon Manchip, *The Robinson Factor* (Panther, London, 1976)

Wilkinson, Paul (ed.), *British Perspectives on Terrorism* (George Allen & Unwin, London, 1981)

My thanks are due to the following, who can be named, for their help during the various stages of writing this book: Neil Belton, Ros Franey, Lord Gowrie, Liz Jobey, Glyn Middleton, Jan Needle, Niall O'Connor, Murray Petit, Andrew Rosthorne, Ruscombe Smyth-Pigott, Iain Sinclair, Lucretia Stewart; to Ian Chapman at Macmillan and Maria Rejt for her editorial improvements; and especially to Emma Matthews, and to my agent, Gillon Aitken, for encouraging the project in the first place and for his enthusiasm and patience in seeing it through.

Glossary

Anglo–Irish Agreement Signed November 1985, the Agreement gave the government of the Republic of Ireland some say for the first time in the affairs of the North. Previous attempts at such an agreement had been thwarted by Unionist Protestants, particularly in 1974.

Baker, Albert Walker British soldier who became a bodyguard for Protestant paramilitary leaders, later imprisoned.

Bunting, Ronald INLA leader with a Protestant loyalist background, his father an officer who had served in the British army. Assassinated 1980.

DHSS Department of Health and Social Security. Government department.

Divis Flats A high-rise modern estate and Catholic stronghold in Belfast's Lower Falls, and headquarters of the Irish Republican Socialist Party.

Dublin bombings In May 1974 three car bombs exploded in the Dublin rush hour, and another in the border town of Monaghan, killing twenty-eight people. No one was ever arrested.

Fenian Loosely and derogatorily, a loyalist term for a Catholic.

Fianna Youth section of the IRA.

Garda (pl. Gardai) The police force of the Republic of Ireland.

Head job (slang) Assassination.

Heatherington, Vincent British agent. Assassinated 1976.

Herron, Tommy Protestant paramilitary leader. Assassinated 1973.

Homer (slang) Freelance job, usually armed robbery, carried out by para-militaries for themselves rather than party funds.

INLA Irish National Liberation Army. Paramilitary organization founded 1975, following the split in the Official IRA. Military wing of the IRSP. Known for its ruthlessness. Assassinated Airey Neave, 1979.

IRSP Irish Republican Socialist Party, also known as the Erps. Their HQ in the Divis Flats was known as the Planet of the Erps after the film of similar name. Founded 1974 as a non-military party after a split in the Official IRA.

Kincora Homosexual scandal named after the Kincora Boys' Home that broke in the early 1980s, involving loyalist paramilitaries. Suggestions of blackmail and the involvement of politicians and the security forces led to rumours of a conspiracy and hush-up.

Kneecapping Punishment given, usually by the Provisional IRA, often to petty criminals.

Left-footer (slang) Roman Catholic.

Loyalist One who favours retaining Ulster's British links *(OED)*. Usually extremist.

McKeague, John Protestant paramilitary extremist, founder of the Red Hand Commandos, a minor but notorious faction. Linked with British intelligence. Assassinated 1982.

M15 British government department responsible for internal security. Ran agents in Northern Ireland.

M16 British government department responsible for security interests outside the United Kingdom. Ran agents in Northern Ireland.

MRF Mobile Reconnaissance Force, a.k.a. Mobile Reaction Force. Covert military unit run by the British Army in the early 1970s. Undertook assassinations.

Nationalists Those in favour of a united Ireland.

Neave, Airey British conservative politician, strongly anti-IRA, known to be in favour of draconian measures. Assassinated 1979 as he was about to take up political office in Northern Ireland.

Northern Ireland A unit of the United Kingdom comprising the six counties of NE Ireland *(OED)*.

ODC Ordinary Decent Criminal. One without paramilitary allegiance.

Official IRA The rump of the party that did not defect when the Provisional IRA broke away in 1970. Ceased active operations against the British in 1972.

Orange Order Sectarian Protestant organization, founded 1795. Named after King William of Orange, who defeated the Roman Catholic King James II of England at the Battle of the Boyne in 1690 and was his successor to the British throne.

Orangie (slang) Sectarian Protestant.

PLA People's Liberation Army. Militant paramilitary organization, precursor to the INLA. Surfaced briefly after the 1974 split in the Official IRA.

Peeler (slang) Police.

Prod, Proddy or Prot (slang) Protestant.

Protestant The majority of the population in Northern Ireland, overwhelmingly in favour of remaining in the United Kingdom. Mostly descendants of the Scots, who settled from the sixteenth century on.

Provisional IRA Largest Republican paramilitary organization. Carried out assassinations.

Provo or Provie (slang) Member of the Provisional IRA.

Rah (slang) Provisional IRA.

RHC Red Hand Commando. Breakaway Protestant paramilitary organization, founded 1972 by John McKeague, which occasionally overlapped with the UVF and carried out assassinations.

Republicans Militant Nationalists in favour of breaking the North's links with the United Kingdom to form a united Ireland.

Roman Catholic   The minority of the population in Northern Ireland, with strong cultural and religious ties to the Republic of Ireland.

Romper Room   Space set aside for torture and killing by loyalist paramilitaries. *See* **Shankill Butchers**. Named after an Ulster Television children's programme.

Romperings   Interrogation and torture with specific reference to a series of killings carried out by loyalist paramilitaries. *See above.*

RUC   Royal Ulster Constabulary. Northern Ireland's police force. Almost entirely Protestant.

Shankill   Protestant area of Belfast with strong paramilitary connections.

Shankill Butchers   Killings undertaken by loyalist paramilitaries in the early 1970s involving the abduction and torture of Roman Catholics in front of an audience. *See* **Romper Room**.

Shoot to kill   Policy of assassination carried out by the SAS and later the RUC. Subject of the Stalker Inquiry.

SAS   Special Air Services. British army regiment employed as a covert military strike force. Officially not in Northern Ireland until the mid-1970s.

SB   Special Branch. Part of the British police force. Ran agents in Northern Ireland.

Squaddie (slang)   A soldier.

Stalker, John   Head of 1984 inquiry into allegations that the RUC had pursued a policy of "shoot to kill" against the IRA.

Sticky, Stickies or the Sticks (colloquial)   Official IRA members, named after their sticky paper fund-raising lapel badges that replaced ones with a pin.

Stoley (slang)   Stolen vehicle.

Stormont   Seat of government in Northern Ireland until 1972, when it was abolished and replaced by direct rule from London.

Taig   Derogatory Protestant term for a Roman Catholic.

Tout (slang)   Informer.

The Twelfth   The twelfth of July, the annual holiday fortnight, noted for its marchings and parades, particularly by Protestants celebrating the anniversary of the Battle of the Boyne.

Ulster   Loosely, Northern Ireland. For Roman Catholics and Republicans the word has Protestant connotations and the North of Ireland is preferred.

UDA   Ulster Defence Association. The largest Protestant paramilitary organization.

UDR   Ulster Defence Regiment. Part of the British Army, dependent on local Protestant recruitment.

UVF   Ulster Volunteer Force. Initially founded in 1912 as a force against the movement for Irish independence, later incorporated into the British army. Also an illegal, except briefly, Protestant paramilitary force that carried out assassinations.

Unionist   One who favours retaining union with the United Kingdom.

Whitehall   Seat of British government in London.